He stepped closer
couldn't take a deep br
touching the wide white
brain fizzed and popped. Her skin screamed at his nearness.

It hurt. And it was the kind of pain she remembered, back when she felt things. Like poisonous heady desire. The kind of pain that felt good, like a summer night so hot it melted your reason down to instinct.

A deer in headlights, she didn't even see his hand come up, couldn't brace for it. His touch against the corner of her mouth was electricity and her skin, every inch of her body, was water. The heat of his flesh, the calluses on the tips of his fingers, pulsed through her. Pooled in her stomach.

She gasped. Flinched. Her carefully constructed life cracked and hunger flooded in.

"Chocolate," he breathed and then licked his thumb.

Lust was an avalanche through her body, eradicating villages and people. Little skiers minding their business.

She stepped away, breaking the contact, and her mind jerked out of pause right into fast forward.

A million years ago, men and the way they could make her feel were her favorite candy. The best kind of sweetness. But no longer. That woman was gone. Never to be seen again. She was stronger than desire. Tougher than want. She wouldn't be brought down by a man again.

Never. Again.

Molly O'Keefe

BANTAM BOOKS
NEW YORK

Can't Buy Me Love is a work of fiction. Names, characters, places, and incidents are the products of the author's imagination or are used fictitiously. Any resemblance to actual events, locales, or persons, living or dead, is entirely coincidental.

A Bantam Books Mass Market Original

Published in the United States by Bantam Books, an imprint of The Random House Publishing Group, a division of Random House, Inc., New York.

BANTAM BOOKS and the rooster colophon are registered trademarks of Random House, Inc.

ISBN 978-0-440-42307-2
eBook ISBN 978-0-345-52560-4

This book contains an excerpt from the forthcoming book *Can't Hurry Love* by Molly O'Keefe. This excerpt has been set for this edition only and may not reflect the final content of the forthcoming edition.

Cover design: Lynn Andreozzi
Cover photograph: George Kerrigan

Printed in the United States of America

www.bantamdell.com

9 8 7 6 5 4 3 2 1

Bantam Books mass market edition: July 2012

To Maureen, Sinead, Stephanie, and Eileen.
While I might be able to do this without you,
it wouldn't be nearly as much fun.

chapter 1

This was not how Tara Jean Sweet imagined her engagement. Perched on the edge of her eighty-nine-year-old fiancé's wheelchair wearing a skirt so short there was a good chance the photographer was getting a shot of her uterus.

But at the top of the very long list of what was wrong with this picture were the cows.

There were ten of the hulking, stinky animals, handpicked by Lyle Baker himself to be as much a part of her engagement photo as his ten-gallon hat and the big blue sky backdrop of Crooked Creek Ranch.

Look at me! the cows said—metaphorically of course. *Look at me, I'm so damn rich.*

As a young girl, planning her dream engagement, there hadn't been many cows. None, really.

She tugged on her pink leather skirt, but Lyle lifted his trembling hand to stop her.

"Leave it," he gasped, refusing to wear the oxygen for the photos, a decision that was probably pinching precious minutes off his very short remaining life span.

But he was the boss so she didn't nag about the oxygen, tried to ignore the cow lowing in her ear, and left the skirt alone.

Sighing, she curled her upper body around Lyle as best she could without bumping into the various monitors and wires that ran off him as if he were a supercomputer.

"Smile, baby," his voice an agonized whisper.

A flash popped and she turned up the wattage of her smile, getting as much teeth and as little brain behind it as she could. She knew the drill. Had been living it for four years.

From the fur lining on his wheelchair, Lyle pulled a cigar the size of her forearm. She plucked it away from him.

"You've got to be kidding."

"Give it back." The words wheezed past his cracked lips.

"As your bride," her smile was sharp, letting him know the game worked both ways, "I must insist."

The photographer laughed and Lyle's scowl faded away, replaced by a calculating smile.

"You think this is gonna work?" She laid a hand on the old man's papery cheek. He was so smooth; age and disease had turned him into a river stone.

How did we get here? she wondered, sadness a dark lining to her victory.

Lyle turned toward her with obvious effort and she saw his runny eyes glittering. Nothing like a devious plan to get the old man's heart pumping.

"Watch 'em come running."

Luc Baker stepped out of the team doctor's office into a viper's nest of reporters.

Camera flashes exploded in his face.

"Holy shit." Beside him, his teammate, Billy Wilkins, who had waited for Luc after his physio appointment, winced at the blinding lights on the video cameras.

Luc didn't even blink.

Twenty years in the NHL, the last seven in Toronto;

vipers were part of the job. And right now the viper's nest was well and truly stirred.

"Ice Man!" the reporters yelled, using Luc's nickname.

"Is it true you're having extensive brain surgery?"

"Is it true you have brain damage?"

"Are the Cavaliers going to buy out your contract?"

Luc smiled and lifted his hands, calming the seething knot of parasites in front of him, like a priest before a congregation.

"Luc?" Jim Muggs, from the *Toronto Star,* cut through the chatter. "What did the doctor say?"

Scar tissue on your frontal lobe. Possible brain-eating protein. Increased chances of lasting cognitive damage.

For a second, Luc's vision went red and his instinct was to grab Billy's crutch and clear a path of cracked skulls and broken camera equipment, just to avoid answering that question.

"Dr. Matthews says I'm good to go next year," he lied, forcing his lips to curl into a smile. "I'm ready to work hard in the off-season and bring the cup back to Toronto."

"Brain damage?" Billy swiveled around on his crutches, stepping slightly in front of Luc. "I swear to God, you guys are worse gossips than my grandma's church group—"

"Dr. Matthews also said," Luc interrupted with a smile and he felt the sharp focus of every lens, "that I needed to hurry up and get my personal guard back on the ice."

He clapped a hand on Billy's shoulder, and everyone laughed.

Gilcot never would have gotten close to Luc if Billy hadn't blown out his knee in game three of the finals.

"Gilcot's been suspended for the first three games of

next season. Do you think that's reasonable?" Muggs asked.

"Gilcot rang my bell." Luc shrugged, downplaying the injury. "It's not like we're having a tea party out there."

But the truth was, hits like Gilcot's and concussions like Luc's were at a crisis point in the NHL.

A couple of the reporters laughed and the atmosphere in the viper pit changed. He had them right where he wanted them. This interview crap wasn't any different from controlling the tempo of a game.

And no one controlled tempo like Luc Baker.

"Dr. Matthews is leading a study on the effects of repeated head trauma on professional athletes. Will you be a part of it?" Muggs asked.

Luc nearly jerked, the question a razor blade against his belly. Him and a bunch of drooling, early-onset Alzheimer linebackers from the NFL?

No thanks.

Matthews had asked, but Luc had rejected the idea. Just as he'd rejected everything Matthews said during the extensive exam.

Retire. Get out while you're ahead.

"No," he said. "Dr. Matthews's work is important for the future of athletes in professional sports, but it has nothing to do with me right now."

"Luc takes one bad hit and you guys are ready to make him a head case just to get a headline," Billy said. "It's sick."

Luc squeezed Billy's shoulder, appreciating his loyalty, but Billy didn't know the whole story.

"But it wasn't just one bad hit, was it?" a woman's voice piped up and Luc's control buckled slightly. The rarely seen beast of his temper shook itself awake.

Adelaide Eggers, of course. She was the worst of the bunch, like a bulldog, from years of having to prove herself in the Junior A locker rooms all across the Northwest Territories.

A guy couldn't hide from Addie Eggers. Couldn't bluff her with a joke and a juicy quote. "As a kid you participated in peewee Rodeo in Texas. You sustained multiple blackout concussions, am I right? They called you the Knockout Kid."

"Adelaide." He smiled into the flashes, absorbing them like he would a controlled slide into the boards. "You need to get a life outside of Google."

The reporters laughed and he saw a lot of bent heads. The Knockout Kid would make the top-ten list of terrible athlete nicknames tomorrow morning on TSN.

Billy glanced sideways at him. "*Rodeo?*"

Great. Now he knew the whole story.

"It was a long time ago," he said to everyone. "I'm fine. My head is fine." Except for the brain-eating protein. "We're ready to put this season behind us."

Again, he rested his hand on Billy's shoulder, and just like that the pack was thrown off the scent of his concussion and onto Billy and his knee.

"Billy, how is physio going?" Adelaide asked. "Is it true you'll be out most of next year?"

"Hell no." Billy got a little reckless with one of his crutches, about to use it as a bat against the ankles of the nearest ESPN cameraman. "Six months' recovery. Tops. I'll be back before the second half next year."

"Six months' recovery for a man half your age." Addie raised a killing eyebrow.

"Why don't you guys go back to giving him a hard time?" Billy jerked a thumb back at Luc.

"Don't bring me into this."

"You are the oldest man in the league," Addie said to Luc. "Thirty-seven is—"

"I know how old I am."

"You don't think about retiring?"

"Not without winning the cup for Toronto first."

Luc got knocked out at the end of the third quarter of game seven in the finals. The Bull Dogs were able to tie it up and The Cavaliers lost in a shootout. They'd been close. So damn close. If he and Billy hadn't been laid up, he'd be drinking out of the cup right now, instead of answering questions no one should be asking him.

"What do you think of your chances next year?" Addie asked.

"Well, if we can keep everyone healthy, I think our chances are great."

"And after that?" Addie asked, a sly grin on her face.

Matthews couldn't give him any concrete proof that he had this Tav protein, or even would have it. So he had a buildup of scar tissue on his frontal lobe? There wasn't a pro athlete who didn't, except for maybe the baseball players. But the increased chances of future concussions was going to be a problem when his contract was up.

Post-concussion syndrome wasn't something anyone wanted to have. And he had it. And it was documented.

The league was getting twitchy about head injuries. Lindros and his glass jaw had changed the game. And that was before Sidney Crosby's concussion made global headlines. No one wanted to take a chance on a guy who couldn't take a hit without getting knocked cold.

All that aside, if Luc wasn't thirty-seven years old, standing at the edge of his contract, the word "retire" wouldn't have even passed Matthews's lips.

He'd accused Matthews of that, but the old man had disagreed. Said he'd seen too many athletes burn themselves out, damage themselves beyond repair in pursuit of the dream.

The damage a second concussion would do to your brain will end your career. You'd better pray you don't get another concussion and you'd better pray you don't get traded. Without Billy Wilkins chasing guys down, it's open season on you. This is your last year in the league.

This next year was the year he was born to play, on the team he'd helped create. He was going to make history. Oldest man in the NHL, bringing the cup back to a city that hadn't seen it in over fifty years.

No one, not even his old man, could look at that and call it nothing.

"Ice Man?" Adelaide said when he didn't answer her question. "Your contract is up after next year, are you planning on going free agent?"

"After that, I'm done."

His heart burned as he said it, but that was the agreement: rest, recoup, finish the contract and get out.

Reporters hummed at the news, practically vibrating at the unsolicited retirement announcement.

"Come on," Billy scoffed. "Any team will want you for a few more years. Look at Gary Roberts. Ray Bourque. There's always room on a team for experience. Hell, someone should hire you just to teach Lashenko how to play the damn game."

All the reporters laughed. Billy and Lashenko had a blood feud that had started in the Olympics three years ago.

Acid burned in Luc's dry stomach. He wished he could agree. He wished he had two, three more years in him. He wished he could ride out his career for as long as he could—hell, he'd even go to Europe, play there until his body gave out.

But his body—not even his body, his brain of all things—*was* giving out on him.

"We're done here," he said, holding on to his anger, hiding it like a weakness that would eat him from the inside out.

The reporters fired more questions at him, but he held up his hand and cut through the crowd like a knife.

His life would be over in a year.

An hour later, Luc slid the key into the lock of his penthouse apartment and suddenly remembered that his home was not his own, and peace and quiet were probably not going to happen here.

But before he could take the key out and go over to Billy's house, or find some dark bar on Front Street, the door swung open, revealing his sister, Victoria Schulman, looking about as tense and thin as a piano wire.

"Hey," he said, accepting his fate and stepping inside. He loved his sister, adored her and her son Jacob, but trying to ignore the panic that she was so hopeless at hiding was exhausting.

Vicks, he thought, not for the first time, *just let me help you.*

It was only money after all, and he had plenty of it.

"Where's Jacob?" He looked over Victoria's thin shoulder for his seven-year-old nephew. Luc had been carrying a whoopee cushion in his coat pocket for about a week and he kept forgetting to give it to him.

"Danny's," she said, her fingers nearly crushing a white envelope.

He shrugged out of his coat and dumped it onto the chair he kept by the door for just that reason. But she made that little coughing sound in her throat and with a sigh, he picked it back up.

She opened the closet door and handed him a hanger, as if she were the hostess of a party he'd been invited to attend. In his own house.

She did that sort of stuff all the time; announced dinner menus as though foreign dignitaries were about to sit down and eat chili with them. There were even flowers in his house. Everywhere. Pink ones in vases he'd never seen before.

Being the Queen of Manhattan Society hadn't prepared her to be a penniless guest in her brother's home. Her husband, Joel the Jackass, had ripped away the only life the woman was capable of living with any comfort.

Made him want to beat the guy to a pulp for putting his sister in this position.

But Joel had handled that himself a year ago . . . with a bullet to his brain.

Luc took the hanger from her. "You don't need to do this stuff," he told her, trying to keep his patience.

"I'm just trying to help—" She caught herself and smiled, holding up her hands. "Okay."

"So," he said, hanging up his coat and closing the closet door. Her stress was like smoke in the air and he wanted to clear it. "Everything okay?"

"We need to talk." She stuck out the crushed envelope.

"What is it?"

She shook the envelope at him. "Just . . . look at it."

Swallowing his sigh, he slid two pieces of paper out, one big, the other smaller. He flipped over the smaller one.

"You've got to be kidding," he muttered, staring at the picture of his eighty-nine-year-old father, surrounded by the Angus cattle he adored so damn much, with a blonde wearing pink leather, and not much of it, draped across his wheelchair.

"She looks like a blow-up sex doll," he said, and Victoria laughed.

"That's what I thought." For a second the tension dissipated, but then it surged back like a high tide. "Read the other one."

He flipped over the big piece of paper and it took him

a second to realize he was staring at a wedding invitation.

His father was marrying the sex doll, whose name was Tara Jean Sweet. Who the hell had a name like that? Porn stars, that's who. Strippers.

The blessed event was happening next month at Crooked Creek Ranch. Pig roast to follow.

Time slowed for Luc, the way it did when he was in that sweet spot behind the net, the ice open in front of him. He could see every move in every player's head and outsmart them all.

The bastard was getting married.

Funny, he had never seen that coming.

"It's a joke, right?" Victoria asked. "It has to be."

He shoved the invitation and that ridiculous picture back in the envelope. *Tara Jean Sweet. Please.*

"Who cares?" He tossed the envelope on the hutch in the foyer. It slid right off, landing on the floor, and he didn't bother to pick it up.

But Victoria scrambled to grab it.

"Who cares?" Victoria followed him when he took off down the hallway toward the living room. "*I* care, Luc."

"You shouldn't." He pulled loose his tie, then tossed his coat across the white couch some designer had picked out for him. No doubt Vicks was going nuts at the negligence, but he didn't care. "Didn't he disown you?"

"No. I mean . . . I don't think so. He just kicked me out."

Christ, his head hurt.

"That money." Her voice was climbing the rafters; the neighbor's dogs were going to go berserk in a second. "I need—"

The sigh—weary and impatient—slipped from his mouth before he could stop it and she closed her mouth, pinching her lips together.

The gray day outside the wall of floor-to-ceiling windows suited him. The traffic jam on Yonge Street matched his frustrated mood.

He just could not catch a break.

"You don't need anything from him." He tried to sound like a never-ending well of patience, a beacon of gentle understanding, but it was a total lie and Vicks knew it.

"We have nothing." Her voice creaked like an old floor tired of all the weight. "Jacob and I—"

"I can take care of you and Jacob. I've told you that."

"I don't want your charity."

"But you'll take that bastard's? You'll take money from him?"

"I earned that money." She lifted her chin. "We both did. Being that man's child was a job. Those summers—"

"I want nothing from Lyle." End of that discussion. He stepped into the cream and black kitchen—again some designer's sense of masculine—and pulled open the stainless-steel fridge to get a beer.

He felt her eyes on him as he paced and drank, trapped in sophisticated clothes and an ugly kitchen. "You could get a job," he offered. "Hell, I'd pay you to redecorate this condo."

"A job?" she asked as if he'd suggested she become a hit man. He didn't understand this attitude of hers, as if work were something totally out of reach. She had jobs before. Not great ones but, she'd worked. "I have no qualifications or experience."

"I'm not sure my designer did, either."

"This isn't funny!"

"I'm not laughing. I'm trying to get rid of this stupid idea I can see in your head."

"I need the money."

"Vicks, maybe if you hadn't given it all to the lawyers—"

"I couldn't keep that money." Funny how strong her voice was now, how resolute. "Joel stole from those people. Bankrupted some of them—"

"I know, I get it. I do. But, Christ, you're stubborn."

She smiled slightly. "I learned it from my big brother."

He sighed, bracing his hands against the counter. She was going to go down to Texas and take on their father—her intentions were a neon billboard all over her pale face. "We should at least find out if it's really true."

"You're going to call Dad?"

He laughed and pulled out his cell phone. "Better," he said. "I'm going to call his keeper." He hit speed dial before holding the phone up to his ear.

"Maman," he said with a smile.

A year ago, Victoria had had her pride shoved down her throat by her husband and as humiliating and awful as that experience had been, as soul-crushing and horrifying, it freed her from pride. From hubris. From everything in her life except Jacob.

In return, it gave her clarity. A worldview that was based on survival.

She'd earned her inheritance. She needed it. And there was simply no way a woman named Tara Jean Sweet was going to take it away from her.

Victoria carefully pushed herself into one of the terribly uncomfortable bar stools that lined the kitchen counter. Luc was on the phone with Celeste, his mother and Lyle's ex-wife, who paid lawyers a lot of money to stay on top of the old man and make his life miserable. If anyone could find out if this was joke, it was Celeste.

Luc ran a hand through his dark hair, rubbing a spot on his forehead as if something under the skin was bothering him. He'd been doing that a lot lately, and she'd started to wonder if that hit he took in the last game had done some serious damage.

"*Non. Non.*" His laugh was a revelation and it made her smile. French wasn't a language they shared. Because her own mother, Lyle's mistress, had been a bored New Yorker with an appetite for self-destruction and Celeste had been an elegant and snobby French-Canadian model.

In those long and bleak summers she and Luc had shared in Texas, learning to hate their father, the "half" part of their relationship had become irrelevant. They were born eighteen months apart and they might as well have been twins.

Luc's conversation grew terse. His hands were white-knuckled around the phone and the neck of his beer, and Victoria's stomach sank with a sick gurgle into the soles of her feet.

Not a joke.

Luc hung up, and Victoria felt herself begin to fray and snap. She smoothed the hem of her gray wool skirt with shaking fingers—as if that would help. As if all that stood between her and a life of security was a wrinkled hem. "It's true, isn't it?" she asked, not quite able to look her brother in the eye.

She wished she were a different woman. Better able to care for herself and her son. But she wasn't. She was Victoria Schulman and right now, she needed her father's inheritance.

"It's true," he said. "Maman was notified by her lawyer that Dad changed his will two weeks ago. If he marries that . . . woman, she inherits everything."

His eyes were so pitying and she couldn't pretend not to see it.

"And I'll lose everything."

"I'm not going back there, Vicks," he said through clenched teeth. His shoulders curled and bunched as if he wanted to hurl the beer bottle across the room. "I haven't been back there in twenty years and I don't give a shit who he marries, or if he's dying. I'm not going back."

"I'm not asking you to." But she was. Oh, she was. And he knew it; her act didn't convince anyone, least of all her brother. "You've done enough. I'll go alone."

"Right," he scoffed. "You down there with him . . . by yourself? Someone will get killed."

"It might be Bimbo Barbie," she said with a smile.

Luc laughed through his nose and it took a few minutes, but she saw his mind change, just like she'd known it would. If there was one thing she could count on in this world, it was her brother.

"And that I gotta see," he said.

Relief that she didn't have to be strong fizzed through her body like cheap, too-sweet champagne.

Luc picked up his phone. "But first we need to find out everything we can about this Tara Jean woman. You still have the number for that private investigator?"

The purpose in Luc filled her, too, and she shoved off the stool to go find her purse and Gary Thiele's card. When the lawsuits started rolling in after Joel's suicide, she'd hired a P.I. to weed out the fraudulent ones.

She handed the worn card to her brother, who grabbed her cold fingers in his warm palm.

His dark eyes, so like their father's, were warm with affection and pity, a combination she hated but had grown used to. "We'll get you your inheritance, Vicks. I promise."

Thank God.

chapter 2

Tara Jean Sweet was driven by a demon. A white-trash demon standing in twelve-dollar stilettos.

Shorter! the demon screamed, and Tara flipped her pencil and erased the hem on the sketch, redrawing it a few millimeters higher.

More pink. Pinker.

And fringe! Lots of fringe.

Oh, the demon cooed, sucking on a Virginia Slim . . . *bedazzle it.*

"Come on, really?" Tara muttered, staring down at the sketch of the last skirt for Baker Leather's fall line. It was short, pink, and fringed. What's more—

I said bedazzle it!

"Fine," she muttered, amending the sketch and making notes in the corresponding notebook.

The demon, for all her faults, knew what the leather-wearing woman wanted, down to a very uncomfortable line of thongs.

As muses went, the demon was a bitch. But she was never wrong.

Tara spread out the sketches, the short skirts, the tight pants, the bustiers and feminine biker jackets. Boots and shoes. Belts and earrings. Purses. Bags. Fifty new products for the five hundred Baker Leather stores in Texas and Oklahoma.

They looked good. The demon earned her spot in Tara Jean's head.

She took a handful of Mike and Ikes, picking out the yellows because yellow washed her out and she'd been taking the yellows out for over twenty years. One by one, she popped the rest in her mouth.

From the bottom drawer of her two-drawer filing cabinet, she pulled out three thick files and sorted through the sketches from the last three years, deciding which ones would be brought back for the fall line. She decided on the black duster with the red feather trim. Popular on Halloween. She also kept the suede mittens with the fur lining and matching hat—a perennial favorite. The blouse with the pretty heart cutouts on the collar. She imagined librarians who thought themselves edgy bought that one.

Her demon nodded in agreement.

The last sketch was an old one, three years according to the date stamp on the back. The paper was faded, the brown rim of an old coffee-cup stain on the top corner. Her first design. The one that had turned her life and Baker Leather all the way around.

The pink calfskin cowboy boot with the tooled leather, one-and-a-half-inch heel, and delicate metal toe.

She shook out the box of Mike and Ikes but there was nothing but yellow. So ugly, she thought, but she ate them anyway.

In three months, at the end of July, she had a meeting with the Region Four Nordstrom buyer about possibly getting her boots in Nordstrom all across the southeastern United States.

It would be . . . Tara blinked, trying to find a word for it. She hadn't grown up with dreams of designing. She was utterly unmoved by pink cowboy boots.

But the money . . . that she had dreamed of. Growing up in a trailer on the far side of Nowhere, Arkansas, she'd dreamed of money like it was Prince Charming coming to save her from the cigarette stink and beer-stained filth she'd been born in.

It was simple. The Nordstrom deal meant freedom. She'd sold her soul to cement it; now she just had to deliver.

Ya welcome, the demon cackled.

"Thanks, Momma," Tara whispered. The demon was a mixed blessing, here to help after a lifetime of neglecting Tara when she needed her mother the most.

She chose to ignore the deeply psychotic nature of it all.

Tara sighed and stretched, rolling her neck, staring up through the glass panels of the renovated greenhouse that she used as an office and studio. The bone-white moon was high and full in the cloudless sky. The small pool of light from the desk lamp threw deep shadows in the glass house and the moonlight made it all somehow spookier.

She was here way later than she liked to be. Night on the ranch was creepy. All that sky. The empty space. It wasn't natural. It seemed as though all her secrets and ghosts waited for her under that moon.

Lyle insisted that she work from the ranch—it's how it had always been. Since the turn of the century, when Lyle's great-grandfather started making chaps and boots and selling them from the stables to every cowboy and rustler within a hundred miles.

Lyle's granddaddy had bought Crooked Creek and since then, the land and the leather had gone hand in hand.

By the time Lyle's daddy died, Baker stores were all over the Southwest. Their leather was being worn by teenagers, homemakers, even a few state politicians.

But when it fell into Lyle's negligent hands, the stores and the brand started to nose-dive. He cared more about raising registered Angus cattle than he did about selling their pink-dyed hides. But when Baker Leather was about to go bankrupt, he woke up to what he'd done to the family legacy.

Five years ago, hat in hand, Lyle went to his son, the successful hockey player, and asked him to get his photo taken while wearing a pair of Baker boots. Luc had refused. And while there was no medical proof, Tara believed that was the beginning of the end for Lyle's health. A year later, he was admitted to the hospital after a series of strokes.

Lucky for all of them that she stumbled into his hospital room when she did.

Tara filed the drawings and locked the beat-up metal cabinet. Tomorrow would be an early day—Edna and Joyce were showing up at dawn to start making samples of the designs.

The demon loved that.

Uppity bitches, the demon scowled, running pink fingernails through the black roots of her long blond hair. Edna disapproved of how short the skirts were.

Tara clicked off the light and the black-and-white topography of her office threw her off, damaged her depth perception. The headless tailor dummies seemed to shift in the shadows, as if they were coming for her, and she felt her heart beat hard in the back of her throat.

It's not him, she told herself, earning herself some credit in the freak-out department.

But someday she knew he would find her. And he would come for his pound of flesh.

Until then, however, it was just the moon, a couple of tailor dummies, and her own imagination.

She pulled on the tight purple suede boots with the black heel that went with the matching knee-length purple skirt she wore. The more demure of last year's line.

You look like a librarian, the demon whispered.

A beloved two inches taller, she hustled out of the office, locking the door behind her. Which was more than stupid considering the glass walls, but old habits died hard. The gravel of the path from the greenhouse to the parking area crunched beneath her feet and she hummed under her breath to fill the roaring silence.

So many animals out there. So many miles of nothing. Funny how nothing but flat land and a big starry sky could feel so damn suffocating.

She walked around the yellow blocks of light thrown through the kitchen windows of the big house, keeping to the dark shadows, hoping Ruby or, worse, Eli wouldn't see her. She just wanted to go home tonight. Sleep in her own bed, drink her own coffee in preparation for her long day tomorrow. Was that too much to ask?

She dug through her deep purple hobo bag for her keys, feeling the guilty thrill that she might just make it off the compound without being noticed.

In the bottom of the bag she found ten pencils, an empty pack of gum. Two fuzzy Swedish fish.

"There you are," she murmured, pulling out the necklace with the pretty key charm and the broken clasp she thought she'd lost.

Stupid big purses, it was too easy to lose everything.

Including her keys. Every damn day.

Ah ha! She wrestled them from the small pocket in front and glanced up.

Only to see a man waiting in the shadows by her car. Her heart thundered in her chest, trying to break free from her ribs.

It's him.

Fear paralyzed her.

"It's only me, Tara," a thick, deep voice said, and Eli stepped into the light, his face still hidden by the brim of his ever-present hat.

"Christ, Eli," she panted, relief making her woozy. "You scared the shit outta me."

"That's what happens when you try to sneak off."

"Come on, Eli, we both know they're not coming."

"We don't know that—"

"It's been nine days and we haven't heard anything!"

Eli tipped up his hat and rested his long, lean frame against the car. "You agreed, Tara Jean," he said, his voice a low, slow lick. What he meant, of course, was "he bought you, Tara," but Eli was a gentleman and wouldn't say such a thing.

Guilt shimmied in her stomach.

"Fine." She threw her keys back into her bag. "But you get off on this jailer thing. I know you do, Eli."

His chuckle warmed the night.

They turned and walked up the gravel path to the stone steps of the big house. Built from oak and stone, the heart of the big house was the same one that Great-Granddaddy Baker had bought with money from making all those chaps. But the generations had added to the home, until it was seven thousand square feet of "holy hell."

A wraparound verandah, a sleeping porch, turrets, two two-story wings, a glass portico; it was like an architectural death match, and both architects had died.

The demon loved it.

So classy, she sighed.

"He's going to die all by himself, isn't he?"

Eli, who over the last few years had become the totally secretive, silent ninja cowboy brother she never knew she wanted, just shrugged. Like it didn't matter.

But she hated that. Lyle Baker was a son of a bitch in every sense of the word and probably a few that she wasn't entirely aware of, but death wasn't something anyone should meet by himself.

"He's got us," Eli said. Tara Jean's smile hurt with bitterness. Eli might just be a saint, for all she knew about the man. But she was a lying con-artist thief of wholly questionable roots who had sold herself and her vacant smiles to Lyle Baker in exchange for financial freedom.

Surely he deserved better than that.

"Do you know his kids?" she asked. "The ex-wife?"

All she knew was that in the four years she'd been in Lyle's life, his family had never visited. Never written or called. Except for that disastrous meeting with Luc in Dallas that she'd only heard about from Ruby, the live-in housekeeper and gossip, there hadn't even been a clue they existed.

He nodded, his square jaw rigid. Eli's father had been foreman before him and Eli grew up on Crooked Creek.

She sighed and stopped on the top step. "Eli, do we really have to go through the process of me dragging your opinion out of you, or can you just tell me what you think?"

"Celeste is beautiful and I think she might have loved Lyle, but he took care of that."

Tara nodded. Five minutes in the old man's company and it was easy to see what he might do to someone who loved him. "The kids?" she asked, fearing the worst.

Eli opened the door, lamplight spilling across his hard face.

"Eli?"

"Mean," he said.

"That's it? Mean?"

"And spoiled."

"Spoiled, like how? Like me?"

"No one is spoiled like you." His lip twisted and it might have been a smile. Or gas. Hard to say with Eli.

"Eli—"

He blinked, something dark and different in his eyes, but then it passed. Vanished.

And he kept his mouth shut. Which was just the sort of thing that Eli did. All the time.

"That doesn't bode well for them showing up here," she said, feeling bad for Lyle, for all of them wrapped up in this crazy scheme.

He shrugged. "There's a lot of money at stake and people will do just about anything for money."

She felt his eyes on her and she forced herself to meet them, daring him to ask her, or better, to tell her what he knew about her. And not just the engagement—hell, that was a legitimate business deal compared to Tara's past.

Say it, something in her cried, raged actually. A deep well of fury that just got bigger and bigger, right there in the middle of who she was between her sugar tooth and naturally perky boobs. *Just say it.*

But as always, Eli was silent.

Tara brushed past him into the big house with its marble-eyed hunting trophies and cowhide rugs. It was like a Western-theme bar had barfed all over the place.

"I'll see you in the morning," Tara said, resigned to her fate and the too-soft bed of her guest room. Eli nodded, and silently left, all but disappearing into the still and soft Texas darkness.

Ninja, she thought, longing for the skill, *totally ninja.*

"Tara?" A soft voice, and a not-so-soft poke, startled Tara out of a deep sleep and she lifted her head from its nest of pillows.

"Ruby?" she asked, glancing toward the still dark window. She couldn't have been asleep for more than a few hours. "What's wrong?" She snapped upright, pushing her hair out of her face. "Lyle?"

"He's fine."

"Is it his oxygen?" she asked, tossing aside the blankets. "I told him the doctors—"

Ruby Fernandez put a hand on her shoulder and Tara realized the housekeeper was standing over her bed wearing a black silk robe that fell from her shoulders like a cape and a sleep mask she'd pushed up onto her forehead, displacing graying brown hair up around her head.

Tara didn't have that much experience with housekeepers, but she was pretty sure they didn't usually look like a Hispanic female version of Batman.

"They're here," Ruby said. "I put them in the den, I didn't know—"

Tara blinked, the tumbler inside her brain clicking around, searching for home, realization dawning. *Them.* They'd come after all.

"That's good, Ruby. Perfect."

"I didn't think they'd come."

"None of us did."

"They wanted to see him, but I told them no."

"Good."

"Imagine showing up the middle of the night, demanding to see a dying man. No shame." Ruby swore in Spanish, and Tara tended to agree with most of her assessment of the sorts of people who would do such a thing.

"Go on back to bed. I'll . . . ah . . . I'll handle them."

Ruby left, her black robe sweeping out behind her. She left the door ajar and a slice of light fell over Tara's bed, across her hands.

Whose hands are these? she thought, not quite recognizing them, the bones and veins, the long nails with French tips. But then she clenched them into ivory fists, and those she recognized.

It's just one more fight, Tara Jean, she told herself.

Here we go.

She pulled herself out of bed and unbuttoned the one button that still clung to the old flannel shirt she slept in. Since phase one of the engagement plan had gone into effect, she'd moved some things into the dresser in the guest room. She yanked open the first cabinet and three small piles of silk and lace stared up at her. Red, white, and black, the royal colors of seduction. Of wickedness.

She thought of what Eli had said about the kids—Luc and the girl. What was her name, Nicki? Mean and spoiled.

Ten years since the girl had been home or talked to her father. Five since Luc had broken his father's heart and sent him into the hospital with a stroke, twenty years since he'd been back to the ranch.

Ten years. Five years. The math of an old man's heartbreak.

She chose the red.

This was going to be fun.

Luc wanted to tear his skin off. He wanted to rip out his gritty, tired eyes, change his day-old clothes, and pretend that he wasn't here. In this place. Again.

His father's goddamned den.

Like he was a ten-year-old guilty of some minor crime, waiting, hands shaking, stomach in knots, for his old man to show up to dole out the punishment.

He wrapped calm around himself as best he could, hiding the chinks in his armor that the anger revealed.

It's just a room, he told himself.

But it didn't work. He hated who he was here. Hated what he became surrounded by these walls.

His father's son.

"Take Jacob into one of the guest rooms," Luc said to Victoria.

"He's fine." Over his shoulder he saw her sitting on

one of the deep wood and black leather couches, with the antlers carved out of the armrests and the serape thrown over the back.

Jacob's head was cradled in her lap, his face flushed with sleep.

The sight, the flash of her pale fingers in Jacob's dark curls, filled him with a killing anger. That his father's games, his schemes would drag them here. His sister so close to a nervous breakdown he could see the cracks. His nephew . . .

"Well, hello y'all," a voice purred from the door and his vision went red. And redder still when he turned to look at her. Tara Jean Sweet stood there, posed in the doorway. One hand on the door frame, the other on her hip, like she'd made just such an entrance a thousand times.

"You've got to be kidding me," Victoria muttered, but he barely heard her.

Bimbo Barbie wore red silk that ran, slick and smooth like a crimson oil spill, over a whole host of impressive curves and valleys. There was a big pile of blond hair on top of her head, with long curls sweeping her cheeks and the tops of her shoulders.

He gritted his teeth, anger popping in his head like popcorn.

He knew this woman. Never met her, but knew exactly who she was, down to her bare feet. She might lie about her name, change it a thousand times, but she couldn't change who she was.

A glorified puck bunny.

The kind of woman who hung out at the arenas, throwing herself at the guys just so she could say she'd screwed a professional hockey player.

A mercenary. A whore. That's all she was.

Preparing for a fight, he shrugged out of his spring

jacket, tossing it over the club chair so hard he nearly knocked it over.

"I'm Tara Jean," the woman said, stepping into the room like she already owned it all. But her name, according to Gary Thiele, the private investigator, was actually plain old Jane Simmons. Born poor in Arkansas and looking to change that.

There were no reporters here. No game at stake. With an internal sigh of delight, Luc slipped the leash off his anger and felt it course through his body.

"Where the hell is my father?" he barked.

The blonde blinked empty blue headlight eyes at him as if she didn't quite get it, but then she smiled, soft full lips slowly exposing white teeth. The move was so practiced he practically heard the orchestra music.

"Well, now." Her fingers petted a curl that dangled over her breast. "Lyle's a bit tuckered out."

"Don't be disgusting," Victoria hissed from the couch. Tara Jean turned slightly and the negligee slid over her breasts and hips, and something dark and wicked twisted inside of him.

He used to screw those puck bunnies. Once upon a time he'd used them the way they wanted to be used.

"Well, hi there," Tara said, and then her eyes went wide with surprise. "Who is that?" She pointed at Jacob as if he were a raccoon who'd put on pants and walked indoors.

"Where the hell is my father?" Luc nearly shouted, not wanting that woman to even look at Jacob.

It took a second, but Bimbo Barbie pulled her limited focus from Jacob.

"It's two o'clock in the morning," Tara said, her Southern drawl as thick as Spanish moss. "I must admit you've caught us a bit unaware. Clearly, we did not receive your travel plans." Her tone was sharp, and he realized she was scolding him. *Scolding him.*

Bull. Shit.

He strode out of the room, leaving her breasts and protests in the den. He did not for one second give himself the chance to recognize the hallways and the pictures. The rooms, the smell of countless hickory fires in the big fireplace in the living room. The fear that crawled up his neck, as if he were a small boy about to be beaten for some minor crime. He banked on the fact that the old man was still in the master suite, and he made quick work of the double staircase that split the big old foyer in two. He turned left at the top of the steps and headed back into the east wing.

"Luc." She was behind him, running to keep up. "It's the middle of the night. He's sleeping—"

He stopped in front of the master suite doors and the blonde caught up with him. She was flushed, her breasts heaving under the red silk and lace of that ridiculous negligee.

She was sex—up for grabs, and he suddenly wanted to be the one grabbing.

Yep, those puck bunnies had been fun.

"Don't," she said. "Truly, Luc—"

He looked right into her baby blues and pushed open the door. The smell of sickness—sour and chemical—wafted from the room, accompanied by the occasional beep and the rhythmic suction of medical machinery. He stepped into the room, around the door, and felt again that Gilcot hit. The world falling away beneath his feet.

A man slept slightly reclined in an elevated hospital bed. But that . . . skeleton in the bed wasn't Lyle Baker. Not even close. The big man with the barrel chest and the hazel eyes that could see a boy's crimes before he even committed them—was gone. Wasted.

A corpse lay in his place. His thick black hair had fallen out and his coloring matched the white sheets beneath his head. A breathing mask led to a respirator. A heart rate monitor attached by unseen wires beeped beside him.

The old man twitched in his sleep, his fingers scratching against the sheets as if pushing away nightmares.

Luc wanted to be glad, delighted even, that karma had come back to kick the old man's ass, but he was shell-shocked. Gutted.

"Satisfied?" the blonde asked, like some kind of watchdog.

Luc stepped back, the door blocking the sight of the ghost on the bed. He took a quick breath, getting his head back in the game.

Apparently, Bimbo Barbie had a secret steel edge to her, because her eyes were sharp, stabbing him right in the chest.

Good, the competitor in him snarled. *Let her test that edge against me and see where it gets her.*

"My nephew is tired," he said. "Find him a room."

She blinked, no doubt pissed off by his tone. No one liked being treated as though they were a servant, especially women who skated the edges of that role. But she lifted her chin, throwing back all that blond hair.

"The west wing is ready for you. I'm sure you remember—"

"My old room. Of course."

Rattled, Luc left the woman standing there, racing away as fast as he could, from all that sickness and all that beauty.

chapter 3

"You don't have to do this right now," Tara said the next morning as she helped Lyle shrug into his thick navy robe so he could greet his family in something other than his pajamas. He leaned forward, his meager trembling weight against her arm as she pulled the sleeves up to his shoulders, wishing the velour were armor.

"Course I do." Despite his frailty, his voice was stronger than it had been in days. She knew it was temporary—the excitement of having his children here—but when that excitement wore off, he'd be wasted with fatigue.

They're going to kill him, she thought. *He's so excited, and they're going to walk in here and just destroy him.*

She patted his thin chest. She couldn't feel the bones of his ribs under the velour of the robe, but they were there, morbid mile markers to the end.

"They're angry, Lyle. Luc—"

"His God-given name is Wayne. His middle name is Luc."

"Not to him, honey. And he and Victoria are coming in loaded for bear."

His eyes focused on her and she saw the fever under his skin. "They got a right." His thin lips lifted in a smile. "But they're here, ain't they? Here to fight. My plan worked."

"You're so weak," she whispered.

"I'm dying, Tara Jean. Now stop being a damn wet nurse and bring me my children."

There was no arguing with him, considering the amount of energy he'd put into orchestrating this very moment.

She stood up from the thin slice of bed she'd been sitting on and walked over to the mirror. Big hair, lots of makeup, a grass-green silk shirt unbuttoned just enough to reveal the girls' best sides. She leaned over slightly and arranged things to optimum advantage, her fingers cold on her skin. Impersonal. Considering how disconnected she felt from her body, she might as well be arranging fruit. But her jeans were tight and her heels were high.

As man-eater costumes went, it was flawless.

And the man she wanted to eat was Luc, just so she could spit out his bones.

She walked down the dark quiet hallways to the den where she'd told Ruby to situate them. It gave her a huge amount of glee to think of Luc Baker being managed, led around, and patrolled. The memory of his eyes on her last night, as if he knew every terrible thing about her, was an uncomfortable one. And no doubt today would only be worse.

She paused in the doorway to the den, watching her opponent pace in front of the big desk, all that anger and suppressed energy simmering just under what she had to admit was a gorgeous surface.

His black hair was thick and had a surprising curl to it, softening the sharp planes of his face—the high cheekbones and strong chin. She knew he was a hockey player, but you'd never guess by his face. It was perfect. Elegant.

Luc Baker was a big man, tall and thick through the shoulders and chest but lean through the waist. He fit his thousand-dollar, gray pin-striped suit with sublime perfection. His fuchsia tie was a bright and stylish pop of color. Not knowing any hockey players, she'd expected jeans and a beer-stained T-shirt.

Interesting that he dressed to see his father as if he were going to a lawyer. Or a funeral.

He moved with grace. Power. Precision. Nothing wasted. Nothing superfluous. He was like a blade, sharp and lethal.

Anger spiked her right through the chest. She wasn't about to be threatened or bullied by a man who was only here for money. He could glower and threaten all he wanted.

There was nothing he could try that hadn't been tried before.

"Well, now," she said, stepping into the den where Luc paced like a caged panther, all dark hair and darker countenance. He exuded menace and when he turned to face her, she felt his anger like a punch in the stomach. "I trust y'all slept all right?" she asked, turning it on with the force of a locomotive. "Enjoyed your breakfast? I swear, Ruby makes about the best—"

"Where is my father?" Tara hadn't seen Victoria by the window. Tall and thin as fishing line, she blended into the dark drapes. Victoria's face—china white, as if she'd never seen a ray of sun in her life or just had the private number of the best dermatologist in New York City—was pinched. The arms she held across her chest were clutched tight as if she were just barely holding herself together.

Unwanted empathy twisted through Tara, who knew all too well what it felt like to have only yourself to protect you from the forces that wanted to tear you apart.

Empathy. What garbage.

Tara reminded herself she had no allegiance to that woman—and her demons were her own. Perhaps if Victoria hadn't walked away from Lyle ten years ago, never to speak to him again, she wouldn't be so damn wretched right now.

Tara still couldn't believe the woman had a son. When the news hit about Victoria's husband, Lyle had been in the hospital and Tara had read him the newspaper. When the first story about the Ponzi scheme broke, Lyle had laughed himself right into cardiac arrest.

After that, she'd stayed away from the news about Victoria and her husband and instead read Lyle the obituaries and crossword puzzle. Just as he liked.

If he'd known he had a grandson, Lyle would have moved heaven and earth to bring the boy here and would probably have killed himself in the process.

The memory of the kid sleeping in his mother's lap last night, his dark curls damp against his forehead, knocked her sideways, but she took a deep breath and wrangled herself back to center.

"Well, now you'll have to excuse sweet Lyle, but he doesn't get around much anymore. He'd love to see you, but it will be in his quarters."

"Fine," snapped Luc and she could feel his gaze, those deep hazel eyes, rake over her body, reaching under her clothes to the skin and the blood and bone beneath.

Her body shook at the sensation, like a trailer in a tornado.

For years now, she'd been numb. Frozen deep. Unmoved.

But now, in the face of this man's hate, she . . . quivered? Unbelievable. Shocking, even.

He stepped toward the door, as if ready to charge back down the hallway the way he had last night. But she stayed where she was, reaching one arm up to place a hand on the frame. His eyes sparked, his lips tightened, and he stopped a few inches away from her.

Lightning bolts flashed between them, and all the fine hair on her body trembled and lifted.

You can't bully me, she thought, planting her heels all the way through the earth. Her eyes locked on his and she smiled, just enough so that his eyes dropped to her red, red lips.

Sinner's lips, Grant Wasinsky, the worst of Momma's boyfriends, used to say, before Momma got wise to his intentions and kicked him out. Too late, as it happened. But points for trying.

And the heat in Luc's gaze proved he wasn't as immune or disgusted by her as he wanted to be.

"Behave yourself," she whispered, and waited long enough for his dark eyes to crawl back to hers. Desire and disgust mingled in his expression. "I belong to your daddy."

"Ignore her," Victoria breathed as they followed Tara Jean's perfect, denim-covered ass down the hallways. Tara Jean was blathering on about the house, as if they didn't know a thing about it. As if they hadn't run these hallways in their pajamas, their bare feet, their boots—searching for a place to hide from the old man's belt.

"She's baiting you," Victoria added through pinched lips. "And you're falling for it."

Vicks was right and he knew it, which made him angrier. Tara Jean was nothing. Less than nothing.

They stopped in front of the bedroom door. Tara Jean paused as if she were about to say something, but he didn't give her the chance. Whatever was about to happen, as bad as it might get—it was all between Luc and his sister. Just like it always had been.

"It's bad," he said to Victoria, taking her hand in his. He felt every bone, the pounding of her blood. "We don't have to do this."

She nodded once and squeezed his fingers. "Let's go."

He reached past Tara Jean, who'd been watching him

and Victoria with unreadable eyes, and opened the door, pushing it wide to reveal the bed, the machines, and the man served by all of it.

Victoria gasped.

"Well now," said the skeleton on the bed. "Ain't this something."

Animated, the skeleton looked a lot more like the father Luc remembered. The bright eyes, the smile. The arrogance.

The king was dying, but he wasn't dead yet.

"Why don't y'all have a seat." Tara stepped past them, toward the two chairs pulled up beside the bed. Luc held out his hand, stopping her. He didn't touch her, but he could feel the heat from her ridiculous body. The silk of her shirt fluttered against his palm and a shot of electricity sizzled through him.

Behave yourself, he seethed.

"You can go," he said.

She smiled and leaned toward him slightly, pressing the silk of her shirt, and then the taut skin of her belly, into his hand. He went flush from the heat.

"Not on your life."

She swept past him and walked around Lyle's bed. She hitched a curvy hip onto it and curled her body around the old man's. A vine suffocating the life it climbed all over, except Lyle smiled at her, running a frail hand over her thigh and leaving it there.

Luc's fingers twitched.

"Wayne—" Lyle said.

"It's Luc, Dad. Has been for years."

"That's not what it says on your birth certificate."

"Well, it's what it says on my checks."

Luc managed to smile, rubbing it in, pleased that he was managing to stay calm. Delighted to see the bright spots of anger on the old man's cheeks.

"How are you doing, Daddy?" Victoria asked, taking

a tentative step toward the bed. Lyle's dark eyes swung to her and she stopped, as if repelled by a force field.

Luc stepped forward to protect his sister from the menace in the old man's eyes.

"Where you been the last ten years?" Lyle asked as if Luc wasn't even there. Victoria stiffened.

"You kicked me out, Dad," she said, putting her hands at her side.

"Not for ten years I didn't."

"I can't read your mind," she said. "You told me if I married—"

"I know what I said." A feral grin split his face. "And I was right, wasn't I?"

Victoria flinched as if he'd punched her, and Luc reached for her hand. But she shook him off and stepped closer to the bed.

After this thing with Joel, she'd left amateur whipping-post status behind and gone pro. Every stranger on the street that recognized her name or her face from the news had something to say to her, and she just laid herself bare for their hatred and bile.

Luc couldn't stop her. Couldn't even figure out how.

"You were right," Victoria said. "Joel was a crook. He . . ." She took a deep breath. "He left us with nothing."

"And that's why you're crawling back here—"

"Stop it, Dad," Luc intervened. "She's been punished enough."

Lyle's eyes—sunken in his skull—blazed. "Not by me, she hasn't. Your mother ruined you," he snapped at Victoria. "You haven't done a day's work in your life—"

"We didn't come down here to be abused by you, Dad," he said.

"Still fighting your sister's fights?" Lyle sneered.

"Daddy," Victoria whispered.

"Stop hiding behind your brother, you coward!"

"This is ridiculous." Luc grabbed his sister's hand even though she resisted. "We're leaving. We never should have come."

"She has a son," Tara whispered, running a long-fingered hand over the old man's cheek. "A little boy."

Lyle blinked. Blinked again, and Luc realized that the old man didn't know about Jacob. Luc didn't know whether to laugh or to grab Jacob and run back to Canada.

Victoria looked over her shoulder at him and Luc shrugged.

"How old?" Lyle barked. His pale hands shook against the sheets.

"Seven," Victoria answered. "His name is Jacob."

"A grandson?" A monitor next to Lyle beeped and beeped again. A red light flashed.

Tara turned, suddenly efficient, to check the computer's readout.

"Sweetie," she said, "you need to calm down."

A nurse rushed in wearing a pair of pink scrubs with bunnies on them that seemed so ridiculous, so incongruous, Luc couldn't look anywhere else. The bunnies wore sunglasses.

This wasn't what he wanted. As much as he hated his father, he didn't want to watch him die.

"Is he here?" Lyle asked, and Victoria, her eyes wide, just nodded and the monitors went berserk again.

"Dad," Luc said. "You need to calm—"

Tara Jean's eyes narrowed with a fury so palpable he could taste smoke and fire in the back of his throat.

"You need to leave." All that Southern peach was gone. She stood, her arms wide, corralling them from the room.

"Is he okay?" Victoria asked.

"Mr. Baker," the nurse said as she lowered the mattress. "Can you hear me?"

"Oh my God," Victoria breathed.

"Get. Out," Tara said, and Luc reluctantly realized she was right. They were in the way, and Lyle's wild eyes kept seeking out Victoria.

He put his arm around his sister, leading her out of the room. Once they stood on the navy-blue runner in the hallway, the bedroom door slammed shut behind them.

The hallway buzzed with silence, all the sounds from the bedroom eaten by the thick wooden door.

"This is a nightmare," Victoria whispered.

The thin white lines of strain around her mouth tore at him. "Vicks," he whispered. "You don't need this man's money. We can—"

"I do." Her midnight eyes were bright, feverish. "I know you don't understand that. But I need his money."

"That stuff he said—"

"He's said it all before. I've never understood why he was even with Mom when he hated her so much."

"He didn't know about Jacob?"

"He kicked me out, Luc. It's not like I was sending him Christmas cards." The sarcasm was a nice change, and he stroked her arm.

"But with all the press last year?"

"I kept Jacob out of it as much as I could." She wrapped her arms around herself. "He probably wasn't following all that closely, just enough to know he was right and the rest of the world, especially me, was wrong."

"He's been keeping tabs on me for twenty years."

"ESPN practically does that for him." Her smile was the saddest thing he'd ever seen. "And it's no secret he likes you better."

There was nothing he could say, so he didn't even bother.

She glanced back at the door. "I had no idea he didn't know." After a long moment she shook her head, as if getting rid of her maudlin thoughts. "I'm going to go find Jacob; I'm sure he's bored out of his head. What are you going to do?"

"Wait," he said, thinking of Tara Jean Sweet and the buried steel beneath all that blond bimbo. "I'm gonna wait."

Victoria found Ruby and Jacob on the front porch. He was showing the housekeeper his Transformers and Ruby, wearing a rhinestone Minnie Mouse T-shirt, one size too small, was pretending to be interested.

Victoria had one of those out-of-body experiences looking down at her son. Just a few months ago—the worst night of her life, worse than the night Joel told her what he'd done, worse than the night he'd killed himself—she stared down at him in his hospital bed, so small, so tender and vulnerable, lost among the sheets.

The doctors had told her to prepare herself for the worst, that the H1N1 virus was too strong, and his lungs, already compromised by his asthma, were just too weak.

So she'd lain in bed with him and told him about the morning he was born and how he used to curl up in her arms and play with her hair. She read him all his favorite stories and she held him as close as she could, feeling every young bone beneath his thin skin.

And she wished she could die too.

But she woke up the next morning and stared into his open eyes. "I'm thirsty," he'd said, and she'd wept buckets of tears.

The doctors warned that he wasn't out of the woods yet, but every morning he woke up and she knew, despite the way her life had been stripped down to the bone, that she was blessed.

But now, she looked at Jacob and she was tired. Tired

of worrying. Of doubt. Of fear. Of being inadequate to every task.

He was her blessing, and she wasn't sure how to take care of him.

Her mother would say she needed a man. Someone to replace Joel as a payer of bills, a provider of security. That had been her mother's solution to every problem.

"Thank you," she said, and Ruby stood, wincing when her knees creaked, pulling the hem of her shirt down past her tummy. "I know this isn't your job."

"You're right." Victoria gaped at the woman; honestly, she wasn't like any housekeeper Victoria had ever known—and she'd known her share. It was amazing the woman had a job.

"But it's nice to have a child here." Her round face creased with a wide smile and Victoria relaxed. "He's a good boy."

"Yes, he is," she whispered, feeling fragile against the glare of the sun, the slight cool breeze. Her father's words, while not unexpected, had stripped her raw. Left her sore.

"Hey, Mom," Jacob said, barely looking up from his small army of Autobots.

"Heya, bud, how you feeling?"

Jacob just rolled his eyes, no doubt tired of the question.

"He needed his inhaler," Ruby said. "Twice."

"I always need my inhaler," Jacob said, his voice too old. Too over it all. "It wasn't bad."

"And . . ." Ruby pulled a pink rubber pancake out from the back pocket of her jeans. "This. Boy about gave me a heart attack."

The whoopee cushion. She was going to kill Luc for giving that to Jacob.

Jacob laughed and Victoria arched a silencing eyebrow.

"Sorry," she muttered, taking the toy. "My . . . father seemed to have had some kind of . . . attack," she added, thinking Ruby should know, since she seemed to know everything that happened on the ranch.

"Is he okay?" Ruby's panicked sadness stunned Victoria. Silenced her. How in the world did that man inspire such warmth in other people, in *servants*, rude ones at that, when his children were left shivering in the cold?

"I . . . I don't know."

Just like that, Ruby disappeared back into the house.

"Grandpa okay?"

Grandpa. That word out of her little boy's mouth made her teeth itch. Her heart burn.

"I think so," she hedged. "What do you say we take our stuff out of the truck—"

"I thought we weren't staying long."

They'd taken only their overnight bags into the ranch house last night, but their suitcases—for their worst-case scenario—were still in the car. "Well, we're going to be here awhile, pardner. So help me out."

Luc's giant SUV rental crouched in the parking area like a big black monster. Same kind of car Joel would have driven—the kind of car that made every other person on the planet seem small. Insignificant. Something to be rolled over.

Luc liked it because he was a big man, with big shoulders and long legs.

Joel liked it because he was a small man.

With a tiny penis.

"You need some help?" a rough voice like steel wool asked over her shoulder. She spun, startled to find a man, tall and thin, standing far too close. He wore a dusty denim shirt, unbuttoned at the neck to reveal collarbones and damp skin.

He smelled like sunshine and horse.

"Excuse me," she said, her voice sharp, and the man

shifted back. He wore a big cowboy hat and the sun behind him made it impossible to see his face.

"Sorry." She didn't know if he was smiling, but something in his voice sounded like he was mocking her.

She tried to see beneath the hat, but he shifted away, reaching past her for the bag. His arm was inches from her face, and she could smell the sweat of him. Earthy and masculine.

"What . . . what are you doing?" She sounded affronted, which wasn't entirely what she intended. She was just so off balance.

"Getting your bag." Now, when he turned she could see under his hat.

Green eyes stared holes through her. A thick, full mouth smiled, but again, the emotion behind it didn't seem kind.

"You don't recognize me?"

She blinked, feeling somehow suspended by his gaze. Removed from the hard-packed earth, the sun-baked metal of the car at her back.

"Should I?"

She felt his hot breath against her cheek; his eyes touched every part of her face. "I guess not." He pulled the luggage down and set it on the ground, popping the handle up. He turned slightly and tugged his hat at Jacob, who stood slack-jawed with delight.

"Y'all have a good day," the man said, and then he was gone and she crashed back into her physical reality.

"Who was that?" Jacob asked as if they'd just been visited by Superman.

"I have no idea."

chapter 4

The door to Lyle's room opened a sliver and a very different Tara Jean slipped into the hallway. She was limp, exhaustion like a blanket over her shoulders, dimming her impressive wattage.

Luc's heart spiked hard and he stood up from the chair he'd been waiting in.

"Is he okay?" She jerked at the sound of his voice, her hand covering her throat in surprise.

"You spooked me." Her hand stayed at her chest, covering the bare skin at her neck as if she were suddenly too naked. It was a nice act, as far as suddenly demure tramps went.

He didn't apologize and they stood there in a simmering silence. Two feet and a thousand miles of differences between them.

The sun from the window at the far end of the hallway highlighted both her beauty—the perfect skin and the lush lips—and her flaws. The small lines around her eyes and mouth. The spray of freckles across her nose. She looked almost normal—well, as normal as a woman that beautiful could look.

"Is he okay?" he repeated, and she nodded.

"Good." He pushed past her for the door. But she got her tiny body right in the way.

"He's resting," she said, each word enunciated

through her teeth. A guard dog with a push-up bra. Honestly, he was nearly charmed.

"I'll wake him."

"I don't think you understand what's happening here," she said. "He's dying. And it's not a matter of months. You go in there and it might not even be days."

He smiled, leaning close. "We can't have that, can we? Not until after the wedding, right?"

It looked like she was chewing her tongue, but then her smile spread across her face, as bright and empty as a pickle jar.

"That's right, sugar," she said. "Try not to kill him before I get my hands on all that money."

"You're a piece of work," he said, disgust slipping over him.

"And you're going to kill him if you go in there worked up like you are. Cool your heels and try again later."

Her eyes raked him, stripping off his clothes and a few dozen pounds, and then she left as if trusting her good sense to have swayed him, or maybe she just didn't care all that much.

Either way, it was a mistake for her to leave, because when she turned the corner he slipped into the room.

The skeleton was unconscious on the bed, so still it was as if his body were held in suspended animation.

Is he dead? Luc's ribs were an empty net.

Then he noticed that Lyle's chest rose and fell in time with the gasping machine beside the bed. The mask over his mouth fogged and then cleared with every breath.

Not dead. Yet.

Luc stepped closer. Closer again. Close enough to see the old man's big hands hidden among the hills and valleys of the blue blanket thrown over him.

He stopped. It was an old ingrained habit: staying

close enough to see his hands, but just out of reach in case the old man got it in his head to take a swing.

Seemed unlikely at the moment, but Luc wouldn't count Lyle out until they had six feet of dirt over his coffin.

Luc's heart pounded hard in his neck and he tilted his chin, stretched his throat, trying to make the pounding go away. Years ago he'd dealt with this crap. His fucking daddy issues. They were gone. Sliced to ribbons under a hundred pairs of skates.

He was known for his cool on the ice. He played without emotion, with total control. A machine.

Ice Man.

But here he was with one eye on the old man's hands, his other on the door, as if he were ten years old. And scared.

Growing up, Luc had been small for his age. Something that used to infuriate Lyle, as if Luc were refusing to grow just to spite him. Those beatings . . . it had been as though he was trying to force Luc's bones to comply to his will.

But when Luc turned fifteen, everything changed. In four months he'd gained fifteen pounds and five inches.

He remembered, because for the first time he'd been excited to go down to Texas and show Lyle that he couldn't be pushed around anymore. That he wasn't puny. Or chicken shit. An embarrassment.

That winter, awake at night with growing pains, Luc had nursed dreams, elaborate and extensive visions of kicking the ever-loving shit out of his father.

But his mom must have caught wind, because he didn't go to Texas that summer. Instead, Celeste had signed him up for hockey camps and touring leagues. And then hockey took over his life. His love for the game, his natural affinity, the home he found among the guys—it became the fire that fueled him.

Visits to the ranch became fewer and farther between. He stopped going down during the summers. Never went at all during the winter. March break had been about it.

On the bed, Lyle coughed and then wheezed, his head shifting against the pillow. The oxygen mask slipped, revealing thin, pale lips, and Lyle gasped. Gasped again.

Luc watched, waiting to be moved. Waiting to care.

Your father is dying. Right now. In front of your eyes.

But it didn't happen. The dying or the giving a shit about it.

Part of Luc's shit-kicking fantasy had involved a little speech he'd give Lyle while the old man was lying in the dirt, his nose broken and his lip bloodied.

It was a good speech, changed and tweaked some throughout the years. And it was a shame Lyle had never heard it.

Luc had given that speech once to a woman, the night the Canadian Juniors won the World's. That night he'd watched teammate after teammate get hugged by fathers with tears in their eyes. Teammate after teammate invited their dads to come celebrate, and so he spent the whole night surrounded by so much fatherly pride it ruined the victory. Turned the whole night sour.

So, he'd picked up one of those puck bunnies who'd been waiting for a shot to add his sweater number to her list of conquests. Surly and poisonous, he'd gotten drunk and laid.

And when the girl asked what he was so angry about, he gave her the speech.

Weaving at the foot of the bed, wearing his boxers and clutching an empty bottle of vodka—a champion with nothing but a bright future to look forward to—he told Lyle Baker what a shit father he had been. How every single good thing Luc managed to accomplish had nothing to do with being a Baker. That in the end, Lyle would die. Alone. Unloved.

The words of that speech were burned into his brain. Unforgotten. After all these years. After Olympic Gold. Stanley Cup Finals. He was an elite athlete. Paid a fortune. Respected by the world.

And he couldn't let go of those words.

His body twitched with adrenaline, and he couldn't outrun it or even slow it down.

He stepped closer to the bed, where Lyle's gasps were fast and shallow, the plastic edge of that oxygen mask cutting into his chin.

Get up! he wanted to shout. *Wake up, you coward!*

Let me tell you what a shitty father you were. Let me tell you how much I hate what you're putting my sister through. Let me tell you how much it sickens me to even think of you even looking at Jacob.

He told himself that he was just here to protect his sister, but part of him was here for another shot at his dad. Another crack at the speech. The split lip. All of it.

But, looking at the gasping dying skeleton, he realized it wasn't going to happen.

He was never going to get satisfaction from Lyle. Even if the old man were healthy and whole, he wouldn't care what Luc thought of him.

Why the realization always came as a surprise, he couldn't say.

You're better than this, he told himself, the way he had year after year. Disappointment after disappointment.

You don't need this man in any way. You never did.

Brick by brick he rebuilt the wall he kept in front of the red-eyed temper he'd inherited from his father. Brick by brick he made it stronger. Thicker. Impenetrable.

His control had to be complete if he was going to take

care of his family. Get rid of the bimbo and get back to his life on the ice.

The adrenaline deflated and the cold air that filled him every other day of his life returned, pushing the anger back into the corners and crawl spaces, where it had lived for the last twenty years.

He was Luc Baker, leader of the Cavaliers, and he had nothing to do with the corpse on the bed.

At long last, Luc lifted his hand and shifted the oxygen mask back over his father's mouth and nose, allowing him to breathe.

Tara Jean pushed another yellow Mike and Ike through the barbed-wire fence. Right into the sloppy mouth of one of the cows.

Please, she thought, wiping off the cow slobber on her jeans. *Please let me have done the right thing.*

Telling Luc not to go into his father's room seemed like the most surefire way to insure he would go into the room, like waving a red cape in front of a bull.

And granted the plan had all the sophistication of a Hallmark Special, but she had to hope that once he was in the room Luc would take a good look at what his father had become and if there was a working heart inside that big ol' chest of his, it might be moved.

She had to pray that Luc would see his father for the lonely, pained man he was. So desperate to see his family he'd concocted this ridiculous scheme.

Lyle was dying. Only an animal would look at his flesh and blood and not care. Right?

All the shit her mother had done to her and Tara still managed to sob like a child in the hospital when her mother died. And Lyle may have been a doozy of a parent, but he had nothing on Rayanne.

Excuse me, the demon muttered. *I'm right here.*

"What do you think, cow?" She looked into the beautiful bovine eyes of the candy addict she'd created. "Did I do the right thing?"

The cow lowed softly and blew a raspberry past big elastic lips.

"Yeah," she whispered, her heart a clump of dirt in her chest, "probably not."

Her skin broke out in goose bumps seconds before she heard someone coming up behind her. There was only one person on this ranch—hell, maybe in the world—that could give her skin a reason to wake up.

"I imagine you went in?" she asked when the footsteps stopped behind her. She knew, to the inch, how far away he was, her body doing the finite math between her flesh and his.

"Of course I went in." His voice cool and filled to the brim with mocking superiority.

With Luc's arrival, the cow shook her head, making her ears flop. The bovine equivalent of a hair toss.

Tara Jean rolled her eyes. Honestly, some women couldn't get past a set of shoulders.

"So?" She turned on her heel. The sun was behind him, set against that blue eye-shadow sky. Judging by the scowl on his face there had been no deathbed revelation. His hate was rooted all the way down.

Plan Deathbed Reconciliation had not worked. Which was not surprising. It was a pretty crappy plan.

"Is he still breathing?" She cracked the hard shell of a red candy with her teeth.

His smile was the meanest thing she'd ever seen. And she'd been on the receiving end of some maliciousness in her life.

"Oh, stop," she said, tired already of the theatrics. "You can't scare me."

Luc took another step closer, his beautiful calf-skin loafers covered in fine Texas dust, and all of her warning signals and alarm bells clamored for her to step away. Out of reach. But she stood her ground.

"I'm only going to say this once." Luc took off his sunglasses, revealing his daddy's deep hazel eyes. Good God, the man was cold! She needed a sweater just to be this close to him. "You're not going to marry my father."

"Really?" she asked, playing her part without much conviction. "And why's that?"

"Because I will make your life hell."

"A will is a will. And you can argue he wasn't in his right mind and all that stuff." She waved her hand around as if she just couldn't be bothered with the legalities of it all. "But there's not a judge in this part of the world that will see it your way. And you know it."

His narrowed eyes delighted her, sent her inner self soaring. Those sticks she poked at him had found their target.

"I don't care about his money." She snorted. People might say they didn't care about money, but those people were liars. "I'm talking about your life. *Jane.*"

Her skin shrank. Her bravado cracked like that candy shell between her teeth.

Jane.

"How—"

"You think I'm stupid? As stupid as my father? I hired a private investigator—and you hid your tracks well, you really did. Tara Jean Sweet doesn't exist. Not really. No phone. No address. My dad must pay you in cash, right? A couple hundreds on the bedside table?"

She clenched her fists, refusing to rise to his lame bait.

"But four years ago a woman named Jane Simmons was in the hospital at the same time as my father. A woman fitting your description."

She knew she should have dyed her hair. If she were a

brunette, they probably wouldn't be having this discussion.

"Changing my name isn't against the law."

"No. But my investigator isn't finished yet. And the reporters haven't even gotten started."

Chewing her tongue, she forced herself to stay where she was. To stand her ground, because the only man in the world who believed in her had paid her to stand here and take Luc Baker's shit.

"The reporters, particularly the Sports guys—they're relentless. And they're the ones who would be on you, because if you marry Lyle you're stepping into my world, honey. You know what those parasites would do to a woman like you?" he asked. "They'll dig up all your little secrets. Every inch of dirt and filth you keep hidden behind that smile."

She swallowed. There was so much filth behind her smile, he had no idea.

"And I suppose you've got all that power?" she asked.

"One word," he purred, managing to be both evil and seductive. "One press conference. One photo. I can ruin your life."

Right. One photo. Anger settled in along her spine. Righteous fury on behalf of the man dying inside that ranch.

"Mr. Big Shot," she cooed, inching closer even though it made her skin hurt. "All that power and you'd waste it on me?"

He started to smirk but she kept talking, using far less sugar and much more poison. "When you couldn't be bothered five years ago to save your father's company?"

That he looked confused ignited her own back-alley temper. "You don't remember?" she asked.

"Remember what?"

"Your father meeting you in Houston, asking you to

wear his boots. Have your photo taken. One photo. As a favor."

"You have no idea what you're even talking about. We hadn't spoken in years and he shows up at my hotel asking for favors. After the way that man treated my sister and me, he had no right to think I would wear his crappy boots."

"He was desperate," she said, through gritted teeth. "And you are his son."

Immediately she knew she'd crossed some line.

But she had so many lines in her rearview mirror that another one wouldn't change a thing.

"He had his first stroke after that meeting," she told him, sharpening the sticks she'd carried for four long years on Lyle's behalf. "The first of three that put him in the hospital a year later. In intensive care."

She had the powerful feeling of being assessed. Measured. And she knew clear as day that she'd come up wanting in his eyes.

"If you're trying to make me feel guilty, it's not going to work."

He stood there, immoveable. A glacier of cold, hard purpose. It was rather familiar; she had, in fact, been trying to manipulate and placate a similar glacier for the last four years. But Lyle had a living, scheming heart under all that ice and enough fire to keep him alive long after doctors' predictions. Luc seemed like he was ice to the core.

"You're a lot like your daddy."

She expected him to get angry. Braced herself for it. But he laughed. "You have no idea what I'm like." He looked down at his watch. "I'm going to take my sister and nephew back home where they belong and I'm going to give you a week to pack up your lipstick and high heels and get the hell away from this family—"

"Or?" She looked down at the chipped paint on her

thumbnail. Honestly, was there a bigger lie in the world than "chip proof"?

He stepped closer, his suit jacket pressing against her hands, and she dropped them to her sides. Suddenly, she wished she hadn't baited him. For a woman who was trying to just do her part and stay out of the way, she'd managed to position herself right out in front of the cannons.

"Listen," he sneered. "You trash-eating—"

"Trash-eating?"

He blinked, stunned slightly off course, which had been the point.

"That's a new one," she said. "Truly. I had you pegged as a traditionalist. I expected 'gold digger' or even just 'whore,' but trash-eating? Really, if your opinion mattered even the slightest bit, that one might sting."

"Marry him," he said, breathing sparks and lightning bolts that burned through her bluster and scorched her throat, her skin, "and there won't be a rock you can hide under."

"Is there a problem here?" Eli, the ninja, appeared behind Luc, breaking the charged atmosphere. And Tara took a much needed step back, searching for clear air and distance, quickly gathering the ragged ends of her composure.

Trouble, she thought, *this man is pure trouble for me.*

"No," Luc answered, his eyes raking and then dismissing her. He glanced sideways at Eli and then did a double take. "Eli. I didn't realize you were still on the ranch."

"Where else would I be?" Eli asked, making it somehow seem like an insult, and she wanted to hug him. Buy them some team jerseys.

"I suppose you're right." Luc looked at Eli with warmth that was not only surprising, but slightly disarming. Even Eli's ninja-ness seemed to wilt. "But it's good to see you. How's your dad?"

Tara didn't have the capacity for small talk, not after being threatened so effectively, so she turned back to the barbed-wire fence and took a few steps away from the two men.

The sugar-addict cow followed, and Tara opened her palm. The candy had melted into sticky red goo and she held out her hand for the cow to clean it.

Jane Simmons. She hadn't heard that name in four years. Hadn't thought of that girl since she buried her.

She heard Luc leave and her spine relaxed.

"You know these cows are on highly restricted and carefully monitored diets, don't you?" Eli asked over her shoulder.

"This girl has a sweet tooth," she said with a shrug. "What can you do?"

Eli touched her shoulder and she flinched, feeling brittle and sun-scorched.

"You okay?" he asked.

No, she thought. She'd sold her soul one too many times. And it was getting a little threadbare.

"Right as rain," she said, smiling brightly. She turned, making sure not to look Eli in the eye. "I better get to work, it's a busy day. Sample sewing and all."

"You're not fooling anyone," Eli said.

She wanted to laugh.

I'm fooling everyone, she thought.

chapter 5

Luc couldn't find anyone. Not his sister. Not Jacob. Even Ruby was missing. Or maybe he just wasn't looking in the right places. A whole new wing of the house had sprung up since he'd been here last and every time he thought he knew where he was going, he kept walking into the empty kitchen.

It was, no doubt, Bimbo Barbie's work. Every one of Lyle's mistresses and wives had put their mark on this house in some way. And it only made sense that Tara Jean's contribution would turn it into a maze.

On his third trip through the kitchen, he opened the refrigerator door and found the big mustard-colored Tupperware pitcher, which in his youth always had sweet tea in it. Right now, choking on his frustration and the fine Texas dust, nothing sounded better.

The phone tucked into his front pocket buzzed and he pulled it out to see the display. Beckett Jones, his agent.

"Hey, Beckett," he said, picking up the call.

"You watching ESPN?" Beckett asked.

"No. Should I be?" Fucking ESPN. Half the guys traded last year found out by watching ESPN.

"No," Beckett said quickly. A little too quickly. "It's just rumors right now, and you know how ESPN loves rumors."

"What's the rumor?" Luc asked.

"Three Cavaliers for Ivan Lashenko," Beckett said.

"Lashenko?" He collapsed back against the counter and wiped off the cold, clammy sweat that had suddenly formed on his forehead with the sleeve of his expensive jacket.

Lashenko was the Russian phenom with the slap shot and the attitude. He was also the top-gun right wing for the Dallas Mavericks, the only standout on a dismal team. The Mavericks hadn't even made the playoffs this year and without some serious changes, they wouldn't make it next year either. Lashenko was the only currency they had, and he'd be a free agent in two years.

He and Lashenko were both right wings known for their finesse, stick handling, and slap shots. While Luc led the league in assists, Lashenko was the high point scorer, and more important, fifteen years younger.

Pray you don't get traded—those were Matthews's words.

And now, the Cavaliers were going to trade Luc.

Without Billy.

They were taking him away from the dream team he'd helped create and the year he was meant to play.

He'd finish his career on a third-rate team, watching in some bar while his Cavaliers won the cup.

It was like being plunged into ice-cold blackness. He was lost. And hurt.

"I've got calls in to Dunbar," Beckett said. Dunbar being the GM of the Cavaliers and keeper of all trade secrets. "I should know for sure soon. But I don't think they're going to trade you."

"Because every team needs two star right wings?"

"When one is getting older, yeah," Beckett said, pulling no punches. "You know, you haven't told me what the doctor said after the Gilcot hit."

"He said don't get traded to Dallas!" Luc answered. And then, because he could see the end of his career from the kitchen in his father's house, he flipped the phone shut.

But the volcano of his anger was exploding with nowhere to go. The headache that pulsed behind his eyes splintered and fractured, slicing through his whole body.

Control it, he demanded, asking something superhuman of himself. But in the end he failed. Just as he always did in his father's house.

Boiling over, he turned, found the pitcher of tea, and hurled it against the wall.

Fifteen minutes and two tea-soaked towels later, Luc was fielding calls from half his teammates.

"I haven't heard anything," he tried to assure Gates, who was taking these trade rumors as if it were news of his parents' divorce. "And rumors are just rumors."

"But you're in Texas—"

"It's family stuff, Gates. Honestly. I swear I'm not going anywhere."

He managed to get off the phone for a second before Billy called.

"Holy hell, man," Billy said by way of greeting. "This is nuts—the team is acting like you died."

Luc sighed and stepped out of the kitchen and down one of the hallways, hoping it led to his room. "Just try to spread the news that I'm not going anywhere."

"You know that for sure?"

"Of course not," he snapped, "but there's no point in everyone losing their minds right now. Gates was about to start crying."

"I'll cry if they bring Lashenko here. I swear, Luc, I might just kill that asshole."

"Oh for God's sake, Billy. Control yourself."

He realized he was heading down the hallway toward his father's room and he almost turned around. Then he heard Jacob's muffled voice, and his protective instincts roared to life.

"I'll talk to you later, Billy. Just try to keep the guys from making any kind of statement to the vipers."

"Yes, Grandpa," Billy said, using the team's nickname for Luc. He hated that nickname and Billy knew it, so Luc hung up without saying goodbye.

The closer he walked down the hallway toward Lyle's room, the louder Jacob's voice got, and concern for his nephew momentarily outpaced his concern for his career.

He pushed open Lyle's bedroom door in time to see Lyle lift the oxygen mask off his face.

"What . . . you . . . got . . . there?" Like a hand coming out of a grave in some B-movie, his trembling, bony fingers pointed at the Optimus Prime Jacob carried.

Jacob lifted it and stepped closer. "He's an Autobot. He transforms between a robot and a truck."

"Show . . . me . . . ," Lyle whispered and Jacob started to flip apart the robot, but it was hard without a place to put it. "Here . . ." Lyle said, patting the side of the bed.

Jacob took two more steps and put the toy on the bed.

Too close! Too damn close!

From the corner of Luc's eyes he caught movement—Victoria lifting her hands to her mouth, her eyes dry and calculating. No doubt wondering how much this reunion might pay her.

Disgust for his sister washed over him, quickly souring into anger.

This was what she'd come to. How far she'd fallen.

"What the hell is going on in here?" Luc barked, bursting in through the open door. Victoria jumped and so did Jacob, as if caught doing something wrong. But Lyle, his eyes glued to Luc, reached over and grabbed

Jacob's arm. Jacob pulled away, but the old man was stronger than he looked.

"Get your hands off the boy," Luc said through clenched teeth.

Lyle smiled, his white lips pulling away from gray teeth, revealing blood-red gums.

Jacob whimpered and twisted his arm free. He got away, running toward his mom.

"Go," Luc said to Victoria, who for a moment seemed about to resurrect some backbone. In the end though, she just led Jacob from the room.

"He's my flesh and blood, Luc," Lyle said. "Just like you. You can deny it all you want, but that's the God's truth. You're mine."

Luc leaned forward, the cloying scent of illness and death filling his nose. "You don't own me. You can't control me."

"Watch," his father gasped, "me."

Seconds later, Luc slammed the door shut on the small study his sister had hustled Jacob into.

"This is a joke, right?" Luc blinked away the image of the old man's hand on his nephew's arm. That macabre smile.

The old man was up to something and Luc didn't want to know what. He didn't care.

All he cared about was getting back to Toronto and repairing his career.

"Jacob wanted to meet him," Victoria said, standing in front of a window that was draped in yellow curtains. The sun filtered through, surrounding her in an eerie glow. She looked radioactive.

"I don't want to meet him anymore." Jacob held his robot in front of him like a shield. Luc looked pointedly at his sister, still unable to believe that she'd taken her son to that man's bedside.

"Jacob," Victoria whispered, crouching down to look in his eyes. "I think maybe you should go rest for a while—"

"Rest?" he protested, and Luc fought his instincts to intervene.

"Or go see what Ruby has in the kitchen?"

You mean besides a mess of sweet tea? He'd cleaned up some, but it was still a sight.

"I saw some cookies in the drawer," he told Jacob.

"You guys can't just get rid of me whenever you want."

"Jacob," Victoria sighed, pinching the bridge of her nose. "Please. Ten minutes."

Jacob scowled at both of them and left the room.

"What the hell are you doing, Victoria?" Luc demanded when the door was shut behind the boy.

"He wanted to meet his grandfather." She stuck to her lie, and Luc gaped at her.

"Bullshit."

She jerked as if he'd hit her, and his shoulders twitched with the need to do something. Push something. Hit something. His job on the ice was so clear. The expectations were simple. Puck in net. Manipulate the forces against him. Stay three steps ahead of everyone.

Out here—in the real world—things were too damn messy.

"Dad is dying. I don't think he's about to go into one of his rages."

"He had his hand on him!" he cried. "Jacob was scared. Don't you remember what that was like? How you would cry—"

"I remember."

"And you're so desperate for money, you just stood there?"

Victoria smoothed her clothes, running her hands over the straight edges and buttons, her tell. Her perpetual effort to keep up the façade at the moment it was hardest.

"It was fine before you showed up," she said lamely.

"You're introducing your son to our abusive asshole of a father to ensure your inheritance. That's not you, Vicks."

It was the ranch that was making her act this way. This place ripped away everyone's decency, leaving behind the rocks and bones of selfishness and survival.

"Judge me all you want. But you have options. You've always had options. I have none."

"Christ, how many times do I have to tell you—"

"Get a job? Like it's that easy. I have no skills, Luc. I have nothing to offer anyone. I am exactly what Daddy always called me—totally worthless."

"This is your chance to change that! You don't have to be useless your whole damn life."

The air in the room went cold and she shrank even further into her skin, her bones. Away from him.

"I didn't mean that," he said quickly, as softly as possible, but she still flinched.

"Yes, you did," she whispered, her voice thick, and he hated that he'd made his sister cry. His sister who'd been so tough while her life and her pride were ripped away from her over this past year.

"The only thing I managed to do right was get Joel to marry me. *Me*. The bastard daughter of a bastard daughter. I caught his eye. I was the one he pursued. He could have married anyone he wanted and he chose me, the hostess at his goddamned golf club. And he made me a queen, Luc. I was untouchable. A force to be reckoned with. Me."

She was killing him. Destroying him. The girl who'd

been ridiculed by her father, the very man who should have loved her, had found a way out of the dark, only to have the light ripped away. It broke his heart.

"And then everyone forgot where I came from. For the first time in my life, I actually got to be who I wanted to be, instead of who I was born to be. And now . . . it's all gone. And I can go back to being a hostess and let everyone laugh and point, or I can go find myself another husband to take care of Jacob and me. Or, I can get as much as I can from my father, because he didn't give me shit growing up but bruises and nightmares."

Luc knew this was the truth, that these were the options Victoria saw, but she was blind to all she could be.

"Tell me, Luc. Tell me what I should do."

"Let's just leave this place," he said, wanting to take her somewhere she could heal, because this place wasn't it.

But she shook her head.

"Jesus Christ, Vicks, I can't stay here." He couldn't. Not when his life was falling apart a thousand miles away. And frankly, he was tired of being the only witness to his sister's self-flagellation.

"I'm not asking you to. In fact . . . it would be easier if you left."

"You want me to go?" That was a first and it didn't sit well. Not at all.

She nodded, and his hurt temper flared.

"Fine." He pulled out his cell phone. "One more day. And then I'm gone. I'll get a driver to take me to the airport so that I can leave you the car."

She nodded, her lips pressed tightly together. It was a shit act. He could still see her fear and worry.

But for her sake, and maybe because he was so damn tired of trying to protect a woman who wouldn't take the steps to protect herself, he pretended to buy it.

* * *

Tara Jean hung up the last of the nearly complete samples—the pink leather skirt with the fringe and the studs.

The demon purred with pleasure.

Tara looked at the rack of samples, finished but for the rough open seams down the back. They looked odd, so perfect in front but totally ragged in back, as if they'd been hurt, somehow. Victims of violent leather crimes.

But they'd stay unfinished until the final fitting in two weeks.

"Honestly, Tara Jean." Edna looked sideways at her as she packed up her leather-working kit. "No one is going to buy a skirt that short."

"I don't know," Tara said, mostly just to egg Edna on. "It's pretty hot."

"Hot," Edna scoffed, tucking away the leather awls and skives. Edna wasn't all that much older than Tara Jean, but with a name like Edna, the woman had been born old. Having twins didn't seem to help. Edna constantly had foul-smelling crusty fluid on her shoulder from one of the babies leaking on her. And then there was the breast milk issue. She pumped. Like a cow. And wanted to talk about it.

It was like spending ten hours a day with a biology experiment.

And then there was the perm. Edna was the last woman under sixty sporting a chemical wave. Honestly, the eighties were over and no one had bothered to inform Edna.

But perm and leaking breasts aside, the woman was a magician with a swivel knife.

Edna and her husband ran a successful leather repair business outside of Fort Worth, and Tara Jean paid the woman a small fortune for her disapproval and incredibly delicate leather needlework. She made the seams look like cross-stitch.

"Thanks for the hard work," Tara said. She'd pushed Edna and Joyce hard, choosing to hide out in the greenhouse rather than deal with the drama on the ranch.

But there was no more hiding.

She'd heard that Luc was leaving early tomorrow morning on the first flight out of Dallas. Victoria and the boy were staying, and Tara needed to see how Lyle was doing with those developments.

Because from where she stood, his elaborate plan to reunite his family under one loving roof was going up in flames.

"You know it would be so much easier if you'd have let me bring in the babies—"

Tara shook her head, her stomach twisting into a knot. "Hard to work with screaming babies."

"I told you, they don't scream. They're very sweet. A little playpen in the corner—"

"Anyway," Tara interrupted, ignoring Edna's disapproving gaze. She tore Edna's check out of the book and handed it over with a bright smile. Putting a whole lot of "no more chitchat" behind it.

"Thanks again."

Edna took the check and smiled as she counted the extra zero.

"Until next time." Edna folded up the check and tucked it into the front pocket of her hideous mom jeans.

See, Tara Jean thought, *money can buy anything—even Edna's approval.*

She cleaned up the last of the mess, sweeping up the leather scraps, putting away the mats and French knives. And when all was right in her kingdom, she locked up and headed into the ranch house to see what she'd missed.

In the kitchen, Ruby was putting together a dinner tray for Lyle.

"Applesauce and tomato soup?" Tara winced.

"Don't forget the pudding." Ruby lifted a little snack cup.

"Who could?"

"He keeps asking for a steak." Ruby folded a napkin and put it under the spoon she would use to feed him. "I'm tempted to give it to him," she whispered. "Just to see him happy."

"A steak would probably kill him." Tara took the tray from Ruby's hands. "I'll give him dinner. You have a rest."

Ruby smiled. "I promised Jacob I would watch *Iron Man* with him. I think he's a little scared, and I love me some Robert Downey Jr."

Tara put the tray down on the table so hard the dishes rattled. "You do enough around here, Ruby. You don't need to babysit that kid on top of it!" She shook her head. "I can't believe the nerve of those two. Asking you—"

"Please, honey." Ruby put a hand on her ample hip. "When have you ever known me to do something I don't want to do?"

"Still—"

"Stop." Ruby patted Tara's hand and Tara looked down at Ruby's dark fingers, her blunt nails. She barely felt it. It was as if her skin was dead and had been for years. She heard fire victims were like that. They couldn't feel anything through the scar tissue.

Her past had built up enough scar tissue to keep every sensation at bay.

Except for Luc. She felt him. Which was disturbing.

She was glad he was leaving. Her skin could go back to sleep and she could resume the numbness that helped her wade through life.

"I like the kid." Ruby's soft tones hid an iron core,

forged from years of working for Lyle. "He's very bright, and he's been ill for so long."

"Ill?" she asked before she could stop herself.

"Very," Ruby whispered, channeling the dramatic Mexican soap operas she lived for. "In the hospital and everything."

Tara picked up the tray, reminding herself that she did not give a shit. At all. "Either way, you don't have to babysit."

"What do you think I do all day?" A wicked twinkle gleamed in her eye. "Lyle is nothing but a big toddler."

"I won't argue with that." Tara headed up the back steps through the dark hallway toward the master bedroom.

The door was cracked, and she knocked softly before pushing it open with her shoulder.

"Dinner is served." She tried to sound upbeat and not heartbroken by the sight of the big man laid so very low. *How much longer,* she thought, *can he last?* Even in the two days she'd been hiding in the greenhouse, it looked as if he'd lost weight. His skin hung like crepe paper after a Fourth of July party.

Lyle turned toward her, the oxygen mask absent from his face.

"You're looking better," she lied, sliding the tray onto his bed.

"Where have you been?" he panted.

"Making the samples. Getting ready for the winter line."

"Good?"

"Very. And to celebrate, we've got something special tonight."

"Porterhouse?"

"Better. Pudding."

Lyle's gasping laughter brought sharp, hot tears to

Tara's eyes. She blinked them away as fast as she could and made a big show of stirring the applesauce.

"Let's start with an appetizer, shall we? The chef has prepared a surprise." She turned to Lyle only to find his eyes, clear and focused, right on her.

"You're beautiful," he said, and she smiled.

"Flattery will not get you a steak."

"Tara." Trembling, his hand hovered over the covers, reaching for her. She put down the sauce and curled her hand over his.

Please, she thought, *please don't go. Not yet. I'm not ready for you to be gone from this earth.*

"You're more beautiful . . . than you know."

"I don't know about that." She straightened the edge of his blankets with her free hand, looking everywhere but at Lyle. "I'm pretty aware of my charms."

He squeezed her hand and she caught his crooked smile. "I'm so lucky you stumbled into my hospital room when you did."

"I'm the lucky one," she whispered. "You saved my life. Dennis—" The name stuck in her throat. Four years since she'd said that name, but not a minute had gone by without her wondering when he'd find her.

"He's behind you. All of that is behind you."

No wonder I can't stop looking over my shoulder.

"You saved the business. Those boots . . ."

"That makes us even?" she asked, knowing it was so far from the truth it could only be a joke.

"More than even. You brought my kids here. My grandson—"

"You paid me, Lyle," she whispered, the shame of it, the necessity of it making her sick to her stomach.

"Doesn't matter. It worked. They're here." Joy changed him, lifted the pallor of death and made him luminous.

That's what children do, she thought, glad at least that

they brought Lyle some pleasure, that they illuminated the dark places.

"Did you see my boy?" Lyle asked, as if Luc were ten instead of three years shy of forty.

Oh, I saw him. But she just nodded, not wanting to tinge Lyle's fantasy with reality.

"He hates me," Lyle said. Apparently, reality didn't bother him. "Proud and stubborn."

"And that's good?"

"He's . . ." he tapped his chest with a hand covered in liver spots, "just like me."

She shook her head, unable to agree. "Maybe on the outside. But on the inside he's a different kind of animal. He doesn't have your heart."

Any heart, really.

"Oh, don't be fooled. He's always been a crybaby. Gets it from his mom."

"What about your daughter?"

He shrugged, and the face he made said so much about how little his daughter was worth in his eyes that Tara felt bad for the woman. She truly did. That kind of damage handed out by your daddy could cripple you for life.

"She brought my grandson," he said, as if she were a chauffeur rather than his only daughter. His heart monitor beeped, and Tara glanced at the readout before stroking his hand, trying to calm him down.

He would never forgive Victoria for keeping his grandson from him. Tara didn't know much, but she knew that.

"What was the point of all this?" she asked, hurting for the people he'd hurt. "Nothing's changed. Luc still hates you. Victoria hates you so much she hid her son from you."

"Getting them back here was the point." For a moment he seemed drained; the light, the fire, all that was

Lyle Baker dimmed and she clutched his hand, her eyes on the monitor. "I'm dying, Tara."

"Don't—"

He rolled his eyes at her. "And they may hate me, but they're mine. My children. Flesh of my flesh."

It was an ugly sentiment, proving what she knew too well to be true—that Lyle was far from perfect. "This ranch, the Angus, Baker Leather, Victoria and Luc. They belong together."

"I don't think they agree with you."

"I was too hard on them when they were kids. Too clumsy. I know that . . . I see . . ." He stopped, his eyes bone dry, but wretched nonetheless.

"Luc is leaving tomorrow," she said, smoothing a hand down his cheek. "You can't make him stay."

"He'll stay."

"Lyle—"

"For his sister he'll stay. For his sister he'll do anything. And she'll stay for the money."

She patted his chest. "All this conniving cannot be good for you."

"You know what would be good for me?"

"You can't have a cigar. Or a steak."

"Scotch."

"You can't have that either."

He lifted her hand and pressed dry, feathery lips to her palm. "Then let's live dangerously and start with the pudding."

Luc sat up, the dark night swallowing every detail of the room. A headache pounded hard behind his eyes.

Christ, where—

The pounding wasn't in his head. It was coming from the door.

He was in Texas. His old bedroom. And it was the

middle of the night. The digital clock on the bedside table said four in the morning.

The knocking continued, growing sharper and harder.

"I'm coming," he snapped, flipping the blankets off his body. He slipped into a pair of jeans, zipping them as he walked across the thick carpet.

"What?" He yanked open the door.

Tara Jean stood there. Diamond-bright eyes set in a face ravaged by tears.

"He's dead."

"What?" He blinked.

"Your father is dead."

chapter 6

When Pauly Soutka, Luc's Junior A coach, died, Luc had cried. He'd cried during the service, while carrying Pauly's coffin out of the church with the rest of his teammates; he'd cried while they lowered the old man into the ground.

Like a child lost at a mall, he'd cried. And half his team cried right along with him.

His grief had been so deep, so consuming, he couldn't pretend that his heart wasn't breaking. There was nothing he could do to stop the tears and he didn't care. Pauly was dead. And his world suffered for it.

His dad had seen the footage on ESPN and he'd made a special phone call just to tell Luc he was a crybaby. A disgrace to the Baker name, blubbering all over national TV like a girl.

It had been a real special father-and-son kind of moment.

Now, standing beside his father's grave, his sister's warm hand tucked into his elbow, he couldn't care less. If he tried, and he wasn't about to expend the energy, he doubted he could muster up the slightest bit of grief. A scrap of regret or sadness.

Maybe he shouldn't have started the day with that whiskey.

He definitely shouldn't have had the second one.

But Lyle Baker was only going to be buried once. A toast to the dawn seemed in order.

But now he was numb to the hundred people who were here to pay their respects and was instead totally preoccupied with Bimbo Barbie. Or rather her very conspicuous absence.

"Where's Tara Jean?" he whispered into his sister's ear while a white-haired minister kept calling Lyle a "complicated man of strong belief."

That must be minister talk for "total asshole."

Vicks shrugged, her pale face and thin body so perfectly suited to bereavement black, it hurt a little to look at her. To see all that his sister was, swallowed up.

"I haven't seen her in three days," he said, "not since she told me about Dad."

"She probably left, since he died before they could get married."

"Yeah, you're—"

Beside him, his mother, Celeste, pinched him through the sleeve of his black jacket.

He glanced over, only to receive her steely blue-eyed censure. Victoria tensed and snapped her eyes forward, too quickly to absorb any of Celeste's displeasure. And he stood between them, sweating in a thousand-dollar suit in the late-May Texas sun.

I should have made that last drink a double.

The minister droned on and Luc, without being too obvious, tried to find Bimbo Barbie in the crowd. Why he cared, he wasn't sure; maybe he just wanted to rub her face in all she'd lost, or watch her try to scramble off her back, having had her world turned upside down.

Or maybe he just wanted another look at that body as she walked away.

The sun steadily rose in the east, changing from a milky egg yolk behind clouds to a blazing ball over the poplars that shaded the family plot. Cows dotted the hills to the south. The house, in all its mismatched glory, was just north. The sun caught the glass panes of the old greenhouse.

They were surrounded by Lyle's neighbors and business associates, all their eyes shrouded by sunglasses. He wondered how many of them would really miss Lyle. And how many of them were beaming behind those shades.

Lord knows he was.

But nowhere was Tara Jean Sweet.

His pocket vibrated, and he dropped his sister's hand to fish his phone out. It was a text, but before he could see who it was from, Celeste snatched it out of his hand and dropped it in her gray bag, without once looking at him.

It was probably Beckett. And undoubtedly important.

His mother tucked her hand into his, squeezing his fingers.

"He's your father," she whispered. "Be better than he was."

Good Christ, he couldn't fight that.

He took a deep breath and replayed, minute by minute, last season's playoff win over the Quebecois.

An hour later the farce was over and Luc led Victoria, Jacob, and his mother into their wing of bedrooms. He beelined to the liquor cabinet in Celeste's suite and poured himself whiskey. A lot of it.

"It's a little early, isn't it?" Celeste asked, unclipping her hammered-silver earrings and sitting down on the bed.

"And inappropriate," Luc agreed and drank half the glass.

"I raised you better than that."

"You did." He pulled another tumbler from the cabinet. "Would you like one?"

"A double."

"Can I have my phone back?" he asked, handing her the glass. His mother lifted her eyebrows. "Please," he sighed, and she slipped the phone into his palm.

He turned away while Victoria busied herself with Jacob, undoing the suit jacket the boy had complained about all morning.

His mother watched Victoria and Jacob, her eyes hungry. It was no secret she wanted some grandkids to spoil.

It was too bad he was the only child Celeste had. Because grandkids weren't springing from his loins anytime soon.

He shrugged out of his own coat and threw it over Celeste's bed.

The text was from Beckett:

They are interested in Lashenko. No other word, yet.

He finished his drink in one long swallow.

"Is there something wrong with your head?" Celeste asked, her soft voice made fluid by her French accent.

He realized he was rubbing that spot on his forehead, where it felt like a cattle prod was impaled above his left eye.

His mother's hand curved over his shoulder, and her touch was like a web over the worst of his instincts and emotions, giving him fragile control over the seething, terrible mess that bubbled just under the surface of his skin.

He could tell her, she was his mother after all, and she'd made worse things better by sheer force of will, a perfectly raised eyebrow, and a kiss.

But what could she do? Fix his head? Turn back time?

If only.

Telling her would only cause her grief.

"You look beautiful," he said, making her smile and distracting her from her concern. "Like a dove."

She ran a hand down the front of her cool gray suit. "You're drunk," she accused without any heat.

"You're right. But you're still the most beautiful woman I know."

"It kills me that you're wasting all this charm on your mother."

"He's only charming when he's drunk," Victoria chimed in. She smiled, swift and careful, and affection cooled his anger. Beat back his uglier emotions.

"She's right," he said with a wink.

His mother still watched him, her blue eyes piercing beneath her dramatic silver hair. The bone structure he'd inherited, the sleek nose, sharp cheekbones, and high forehead, made her look aristocratic. As if she were only a few steps down the bloodline from royalty.

She was sixty-two and he couldn't look at her without thinking about her being twenty-four when she had him, married to a man almost double her age, stranded down here on this ranch. They'd divorced months after he was born, so he never knew his parents married. Couldn't imagine what that was like.

"Why'd you marry him?" he asked.

She blinked in surprise and then quickly hid it under all her still waters. "I was pregnant. And he was . . . persuasive."

"Did he hurt you? Is that how he persuaded you?"

Luc understood the beauty people saw when they looked at his mother. He recognized it. But when he looked at her, all he ever saw was the woman who made him a dog costume for Halloween when he was five and a cat costume for herself, and let him chase her through their ritzy Montreal neighborhood.

Four years in a row.

It was hard for her to be at his every game, but when she said she was going to be there, he'd look up from center ice and see her in her spot, three rows up from the visitor's net.

She slapped another kid's mother once. He wasn't sure why; she'd never told him the story. But in front of all the other parents, Celeste Baker had backhanded some hockey mom.

This woman was his champion. And it killed him that she had ever suffered under Lyle Baker's "love."

"He never . . . treated me that way. It seems he saved all of that for you children when I wasn't here to stop him." Her eyes flickered over his shoulder to Victoria and Jacob.

"Did you love him?" he asked, unable to see it. Nothing in Lyle Baker inspired love. Respect, maybe, if you didn't spend too much time with him. But not love.

Not from a woman like Celeste.

"That's so hard to believe?"

He laughed and stared at the bottom of his cut-glass tumbler, wishing he had some ice. All this warm booze was drying him out.

"He was a hard man, but for a while . . . it was good. When I found out how you were treated . . ."

The glass caught the light, sending prisms across his legs. They'd never talked about this. And twenty years later it still seemed like a secret he should keep from her. "That's why you sent me to hockey camp that summer? You found out?"

"I heard you at night, talking in your bed. I knew what you wanted to do to him and . . . well, it wasn't hard to put it together. Why didn't you tell me? All those years?"

He shrugged. Pride, maybe. Crying to his mom seemed like it would only make things worse.

"It's a million years ago now."

"*Luc.*" She touched his hand where he rubbed his forehead. "What aren't you telling me?"

"I'm fine," he said, desperate to change the subject. "Ready to be gone and at the beck and call of all your charitable whims." The long level look she gave him indicated she wasn't fooled. But wouldn't push the issue. Now.

"You've been blessed, Luc. The least you can do is donate some signed hockey pucks to a few worthy causes."

"So I'm told," he said. "Thank you for keeping my karma in working order."

Her laugh was deep, that startling bark so at odds with her elegance. "It takes more than a few silent auction donations to do that, my son. In fact, I have joined the board for Sick Kids Hospital—"

Victoria's head snapped up. That charity had been a favorite of hers and she'd been on the board until they asked her to leave.

"I'm sensing there will be more than signed hockey pucks in my future."

"We'll talk about it once we're done with this current mess," Celeste said.

"They're reading the will this afternoon," Victoria said, pressing back Jacob's wild dark curls that were springing up in the humidity.

Luc tucked his phone back in his pocket. The old man was dead; his career was hanging by a thread. It was time to go home.

"Fine," he said. "But after that I'm leaving."

Victoria nodded, not looking at him.

"Can we go with you?" Jacob asked, and Luc felt bad for the kid. He really did.

But Victoria shook her head. "We're going to stay a little longer."

"Why?" Celeste asked, and Luc inwardly cringed. His

gracious mother turned into Godzilla around Victoria. Their mutual tension fed off each other, like that of rabid cats, making both of them act like idiots. It had been going on for so long that neither of them knew how to break the pattern.

Victoria braced herself and looked Celeste in the eye—a show of maturity it had taken her years to accomplish. "We have nowhere else to go," she said.

"Nonsense," Celeste said. "You're staying with Luc."

"That's not our home."

Celeste's eyebrows rose. "And this is?"

"Mom," he whispered. "It's Vicks's choice."

She opened her mouth, but Luc stared at her hard and finally she nodded. "Of course," she said, gracious at last, but far too late.

He'd spent most of his life trying to convince his sister that Celeste didn't hate her. It never seemed to work.

All of Celeste's cool and imperial efforts to befriend Vicks came off as disapproval and only made things worse. He caught Celeste's eye, and she seemed to be asking him to help smooth the rocky road between her and her husband's mistress's child.

But some things were beyond even the Ice Man's ability to control. He grabbed his whiskey.

"I'll see you in the den for the will reading," he said, then went back to his room to make some calls.

An hour later, without his suit coat and tie, Luc walked into the den, and judging by the looks his mother and sister gave him, he was late.

Celeste and Victoria sat on the deep couch with the carved antelope armrests. His mother looked ridiculous sitting next to the serape thrown over the back of the couch, like serving champagne with beans.

A tall, thin man who looked vaguely familiar stood in the front of the room, by Lyle's big desk.

"I'm Randy Jenkins," the man said, holding out his hand. "Your father's lawyer."

"Great," Luc said, shaking the man's hand. He had a good buzz going, and this whole scene felt fuzzy. In a very pleasant way. If you were going to the reading of your father's will, might as well do it drunk.

"You don't remember me, do you?" Jenkins asked, a sly smile on his thin lips.

"Should I?"

"I competed against you in the peewee circuit when we were kids."

Oh God. Randy Jenkins. Honestly, this day could not get worse.

"Of course, good to see you, Randy."

Randy had not just competed against Luc in those peewee rodeo competitions, he'd slaughtered him. Not that it was hard. Kids in wheelchairs outwrangled him.

"A pleasure to see you," Randy said. "I've been an avid fan of yours since you played for the Hurricanes."

"Never would have pegged you as a hockey fan," Luc said.

Randy shrugged. "We've all got our surprises. And I have to say, these rumors about Toronto trading some folks to Dallas for Lashenko are pretty interesting. Particularly if it's you. We could use your experience on the team. Your leadership." His gray eyes twinkled behind his glasses, and Luc had the sinking feeling that the whole damn hockey world was thinking the same thing. This trade made sense. Farm out the old guy, bring in the hotshot. The math was pretty fucking simple. "I had hoped you might be willing to substantiate those rumors."

"I'm not going anywhere," Luc practically barked. Jenkins pushed his thin glasses up higher on his nose.

"Then who do you think they'll trade? Billy Wilkins?"

"Billy's hurt. He's out the first half of the season no matter where he goes."

The never-pleasant early-afternoon hangover began to burn through his buzz. To say nothing of his manners.

Normally, he could talk hockey all day, but somehow doing it with Randy Jenkins seemed wrong.

"Look, Luc, I don't suppose I could have an autograph for my son. He's a young player with some skill—"

Luc looked over at his mother and sister, sitting so straight their backs were miles from the sofa. Eli Turnbull stood in the back, totally unreadable. "I don't think this is the time."

"Right." Randy waved a hand between them. "Of course, my apologies."

"But later," Luc said, a small peace offering. "No problem."

Randy nodded and sat down behind the desk, then started flipping through papers.

Luc headed over to the bar in the corner next to Eli.

"Have a drink, Eli." He checked the ice bucket, hoping for the best, only to be disappointed. "Is there no ice in Texas?"

"It's one in the afternoon, Luc."

"The ice only comes out at night?"

Eli's lip twitched, which Luc understood to be a clear indication the man was ready to drink. "Whiskey?" he asked, smiling at the cowboy. It was a stretch to say they'd grown up together, but there had been that one March break when they'd taken one of his dad's bottles of Wild Turkey behind the barn and gotten drunker than any two kids should. He'd woken up with a black eye, no shoes, and a hangover like the fist of God squeezing his brain. "Like the old days?"

"We didn't have old days." Eli was back to being stone-faced. Luc always knew that guy was no fun.

"Yeah, you're right." Luc poured himself two fingers of whiskey and then, because it was a long walk to the empty club chairs, he added a third. And then he poured an equal amount in another tumbler and left it for Eli.

Just in case.

"Now that Luc is here, we just need Tara Jean," Jenkins said.

Luc paused before sitting in one of the club chairs. "Why?"

"She's named in the will."

"Oh Lyle, you son of a bitch," Celeste muttered.

"I don't think she's still here," Luc said.

"She's in the greenhouse," Eli said. His voice sounded like it had been dragged down a long gravel road.

"She wasn't at the funeral," Victoria said. "Or the wake."

Eli shrugged. "She's been in the greenhouse."

Luc sighed and stood. His motor revved at the thought of going toe-to-toe with Tara Jean again.

"I'll go get her."

He stepped to the door, but Eli got there before him and stood in his way.

Luc blinked. The cowboy moved fast.

"She's grieving," Eli said, his green eyes sizing Luc up. Luc couldn't help it, he snorted. The loss of her fortune, maybe. Eli shook his head. "She is, and you make things worse for her and we'll have words."

Words. That was cowboy for *I'll put my fist in your face.*

"Don't worry." Luc clapped a hand on the smaller man's shoulders. "She'll survive."

Luc brushed past Eli and through the sliding glass door at the back of the room. The top of the greenhouse was visible over the lilacs that were going brown in the sun.

What the hell was she doing in the greenhouse?

She didn't seem the amateur horticulturist type.

He took another sip of his drink and rounded the corner. Through the glass walls he caught sight of a couple of people standing around.

A party?

He had to laugh. That girl had brass balls the size of watermelons.

The arched wooden door to the greenhouse was warped and stood slightly cracked. It didn't take much to push it open.

There were no plants. And the people were actually headless dummies. All of them wearing leather. Weird.

A long table marched down the center of the room, T-ed by a rack of clothes. Leather clothes. At the other end of the table was a desk.

"Sorry," he said to the woman sitting there, hunched over paperwork. "But I'm looking—"

The woman looked up. Her face was red and splotchy, as though she was in the middle of an allergic reaction. Her eyes were obliterated by puffiness. A ponytail made a valiant effort to keep stringy blond hair in place, but most of it fell into the woman's face.

She wore an old flannel shirt, held together by one button. Under that, there was a man's white tank top, covered in brown and black spots.

It took a second, because he was drunk and because never, ever in his life did he expect a professional gold digger to be seen in public looking so terrible, but when the penny dropped, he laughed.

And couldn't stop.

"Tara Jean Sweet," he said, "you look like shit."

chapter 7

Her grief was worse than she'd thought it would be. She'd prepared for something bittersweet. But this pain was hard and sharp—glass she couldn't swallow.

"Crying over all your lost millions?" Luc looked disreputable, with his hair mussed and his tie pulled loose, like a dangerous man in a cologne ad.

"Don't forget the cows."

"Of course," he agreed magnanimously. He looked around at the studio like it was a curiosity, a freak show at a circus, and not a very good one.

And she wanted to be cool about it. Untouched. As controlled as he was. But she couldn't.

"Get the hell out of here, Luc," she snapped, unable to muster up anything more cutting to say.

"Should I call you Tara Jean or Jane? I mean, frankly, you're not like any Jane I've ever met."

"Out."

"Tara Jean it is."

"I'm not kidding, Luc. Leave. Now."

"Wish I could, Tara Jean." He stepped farther into her workshop. "But I have been sent to fetch you."

Get up, she told herself, trying to rally. *This man is invading your kingdom. Tell him where to go. Show him how tough you are.*

But she couldn't even be bothered to clean up the candy wrappers that littered her desk.

"What is this place?" he asked, walking along the big table toward the rack of clothes.

"None of your business."

"Honey, if you want to fight, you're going to have to try harder than that."

See? she told herself. *Even the heartless bastard is telling you to pull on your big-girl panties and get on with it.*

He reached out to touch the fringed pink skirt, and the demon shook in anger.

"Don't touch that!" She found herself on her feet, her hands clenched into fists at her side.

"That's better." His smile was loose, suspicious.

She narrowed her eyes. "Are you drunk?"

He drained the last of the liquor in his glass. "I am."

"That's disgusting. Your daddy was buried—"

"Yes, he was. And I was there." He walked down the long aisle toward her desk. And maybe it was because she was dehydrated and sick to her stomach from grief and candy, but the look in his eyes made her feel painfully unsafe.

It was her lack of armor. Christ, she didn't even have on a push-up bra. Or lipstick. How could a girl feel tough without lipstick?

"The question is," he stopped in front of her old metal desk, "where were *you*?"

Hiding, mostly. But he didn't need to know that.

It was perfectly clear what she'd been doing. Crying and binge eating. Grief took her to some ugly places. So she didn't say anything and a slow, lazy smile split his generous lips, revealing those white, white teeth.

If she was any other woman, she might have been turned on.

"Do you have anything to drink around here?" He held up his empty glass.

"No."

"No?"

She stared at him.

"Funny, you seem like the kind of girl who likes a wine cooler in the morning."

A few years and another lifetime ago, he wouldn't have been wrong. Jane Simmons had been a drinker. Among other things.

"What is that?" he asked, pointing to her desk, where the sketch of the pink boot that Nordstrom was considering was covered in candy wrappers.

"A boot."

He shuddered dramatically. "Good thing I didn't agree to Dad's marketing scheme. I never would have lived down wearing pink boots."

"These aren't the boots he wanted you to wear, you idiot." The insult tasted good on her lips—salty and strong—and she got a boost from it. "These are my boots. And this is my workshop and I would appreciate it if you would leave. Now."

He blinked up at her, and it would be so much more comfortable for her if she could just tell herself that he was stupid. A dumb hockey player. A shitty son. A nobody.

But his eyes blazed with intelligence and her skin woke up under his gaze like it was the touch of a lover. The warmth spread over her body, stirring parts of her that hadn't felt warmth in years.

It stung. Hurt. And she hated it. Hated him for making her feel it.

"You design for Baker Leather?"

See? she told herself. *Not dumb at all.*

She swallowed and nodded, feeling stupidly as if him knowing this piece of her story left her a little more naked, more vulnerable.

His grin was wolfish. Mean. He hooked a thumb at the cream bustier behind him. "This the prostitute line?"

She didn't even bother to defend herself, to cry protestations. She'd learned long ago that no one listened.

"Go away."

"If I leave, I have to take you with me," he said, turning away. "You don't look like you're eager to hear the lawyers. And I'm in no hurry."

She sat back down and helped herself to a Riesen, even though her teeth hurt from all the sugar.

"You're in no hurry to see what your daddy left you?" She talked while she chewed. The caramel centers in these damn things just about pulled out her fillings. But that was why she liked them; they punished her while she ate them.

He appeared to be in deep contemplation of the tailor dummy in the maligned cream leather bustier. "Can't say that I am."

"I don't believe you."

"I've got a lot of money," he said. "More than him, probably. I don't need any more."

"Then why'd you come rushing down here when it all got threatened?" She smiled, sitting back in her ratty shirt as if it were silk and lace. He might feign indifference, but he was a man like any other. And men liked her. "Or was it that picture we sent?"

His fingertip touched the thin leather strap of the bustier, tracing along the top, and it looked so damn big. Masculine.

Her skin shook. Too much sugar, she told herself, pushing the bag of candy back into the desk.

"I think a better question is why you're in here crying instead of in the house trying to get what would have been yours if Lyle hadn't died so soon."

"So soon? Are you kidding? That man hung on longer than anyone expected, just so he could get a look at you and your sister again."

His deep hazel eyes watched her and she tilted her chin, unbowed.

"I wish you were wrong," he murmured.

She sat back, stunned by his lack of armor. The humanity he'd revealed behind the mask. It wasn't grief, but it wasn't cold anger, and that was surprising.

She had no inclination to appease his grief or guilt or whatever it was that was making him drink on the day of his father's funeral, but she wanted to defend Lyle.

His scheming, for all the pain it caused, had been hatched from a pure place.

"Your daddy loved you," she whispered.

His smile was so bitter it was as if he'd bitten into a rotten nut.

"He had a shit way of showing it. On my end it felt like anger and hate most of the time. The rest of the time it just felt like ownership."

The air conditioner clicked on, a gunshot in the silence. It was redeeming, somehow, that he not only understood his father, but was saddened by it all.

That he wasn't a glacier all the way through wasn't anything she wanted to know about him. She didn't want to understand him, or feel empathy for his complicated pain.

"Is that why you're drinking your way through the day?" She tucked her feet up under her legs. "You're all choked by regret? Wishing you could go back and do it all differently?"

"Hell no," he said. "I'm drinking because it's a damn party."

He looked down at his empty tumbler and up at the thin, fragile glass of her greenhouse as if he could already see the arc. The smash and rain of glass all over her work.

Danger crackled. His muscles, thick and heavy—

masculine in the extreme—bunched under his fine white shirt.

She held her breath, held hostage by the moment—the grief and anger had a knife to both their throats.

But then, he closed his eyes, and his shoulders relaxed. As if he'd put out the fuse, the moment was gone. Controlled.

She sucked in a deep breath. Ice Man, indeed.

"We should go," he said, turning away. "They're waiting on us."

"Go on." She kicked her legs off her chair and pulled herself up to her desk as if she were about to apply her nose to the grindstone, when really she was going to Hoover as much sugar and comfort as she could the second he was gone. "I'm working."

"You're worried about Maman?"

Perceptive bastard.

She ran her tongue over her fuzzy teeth, felt the puffy skin on her face without having to touch it. She was a bona-fide mess and those women in there—the regal Celeste and the heartbroken Victoria—would turn their noses so high up in the air, they'd get dizzy.

You've been judged by better than them, she reminded herself.

"No."

"You should be," he said with a wolfish, messy smile. "She's gonna eat you alive."

Lord, the man was pushing her buttons.

"Then let's go." She stood, jamming her feet into her ragged bunny slippers.

She stepped out from behind the desk and suffered Luc's slow perusal.

He stepped closer. Closer again. Until she couldn't take a deep breath without her breasts touching the wide white plains of his chest. Her brain fizzed and popped. Her skin screamed at his nearness.

It hurt. And it was the kind of pain she remembered, back when she felt things. Like poisonous heady desire. The kind of pain that felt good, like a summer night so hot it melted your reason down to instinct.

A deer in the headlights, she didn't even see his hand come up, couldn't brace for it. His touch against the corner of her mouth was electricity and her skin, every inch of her body, was water. The heat of his flesh, the calluses on the tips of his fingers, pulsed through her. Pooled in her stomach.

She gasped. Flinched. Her carefully constructed life cracked and hunger flooded in.

"Chocolate," he breathed and then licked his thumb.

Lust was an avalanche through her body, eradicating villages and people. Little skiers minding their business.

She stepped away, breaking the contact, and her mind jerked out of pause right into fast forward.

A million years ago, men and the way they could make her feel were her favorite candy. The best kind of sweetness. But no longer. That woman was gone. Never to be seen again.

She was stronger than desire. Tougher than want. She wouldn't be brought down by a man again.

Never. Again.

"I keep wondering who the hell you are. Jane Simmons? Tara Jean Sweet? I never get any closer to an answer."

"I could ask you the same thing. Wayne." She pulled herself up by her spine. By her muscle and sinew.

His smile was feral and calculating. A predator sizing up his prey. "Depending on how things go in the den, I might be your worst nightmare."

That was better. She was safer with anger. More comfortable with hate.

"Then let's go."

chapter 8

Victoria traced her fingers around Jacob's palm, over and over again. When he was sick in the hospital and she had to wear a hazmat suit just to sit by his side, this was what she'd do. She'd draw hearts and smiley faces. Numbers and letters. She'd spell her name on his skin, a map to bring him back to her.

The tension in the den was sickening, and if it weren't for Jacob telling Celeste scene for scene about the *Iron Man* movie he'd watched against Victoria's better judgment, it would be intolerable.

A powder keg.

As it was, Victoria had to stomach Queen Celeste smiling down at Jacob as if he were just another part of her kingdom.

He's mine, she wanted to hiss and yank him away. But Jacob liked Celeste. And Celeste was kind to Jacob in her own way. As if he were a dog, but her favorite dog.

And Victoria was so nervous she could throw up, so having Jacob distracted worked in her favor.

How much do I need? she kept wondering. It wasn't as though she needed to live the way she had lived with Joel. That kind of money had been a false security of the worst kind. But she needed to take care of Jacob. School. College. Medical bills. A modest home.

The door to the den opened and Luc walked in, smiling as if he'd just heard the best joke. Victoria might have written that off to Luc being a jolly drunk, but at his heels was Tara Jean.

Looking like death warmed over.

Laughter, surprised and unchecked, bubbled out of her throat and she clapped a hand over her mouth. Celeste glanced sideways at Victoria with a wicked little smile on her million-dollar mouth.

For a second, all those differences between them—that Victoria was the daughter of Lyle's mistress, that Celeste hated her, that she hated Celeste—all of them were gone. Two women, in a glance, sharing a joke at another women's expense—it was a female language born thousands of years ago.

But Tara Jean lifted her chin and sailed past them to go stand next to Eli Turnbull, and the moment popped.

Eli lifted an arm over Tara Jean's shoulders and pulled her to his side. Tara Jean curled up there. Safe. Protected.

Victoria's heart coiled, shrinking from the pain. Not that she cared one way or another about Eli, but that Tara Jean, Bimbo Barbie, had a strong shoulder where she could rest her head during all this pissed Victoria off.

I did everything right, she thought for the millionth time, the vile acid of her anger as biting as it had been that first long night her life had begun to unravel.

Ponzi scheme.

Thinking the words made her skin cringe.

"We can get started," Mr. Jenkins said.

"Mom," Jacob whispered, "you're hurting my hand."

Victoria unclenched her fists and kissed an apology on her son's palms while Mr. Jenkins made his way through the necessary legalese.

"Mr. Baker made some changes to his will before he died," the lawyer said after droning on for what seemed like hours, and Victoria tuned back in.

In her lap, Victoria's fingers twisted into knots.

"Tara Jean, as agreed, will get forty percent of Baker Leather." Jenkins glanced over the top of his glasses toward Tara Jean. "In deferment to your wishes, he has left you no money. And I . . . I need the . . ."

Tara Jean stepped forward, wiggling the giant five-carat sapphire off her knuckle. It landed on the desk with a thunk.

"As agreed?" Luc asked from the club chair where he was sprawled. He turned twinkling eyes over to Tara Jean, who visibly bristled. "What did you do, I wonder, to earn such a thing?"

"Don't be disgusting," Tara Jean hissed, which was all very ironic considering the way she'd acted when Victoria and her brother arrived at the ranch.

If she wasn't chock full of nerves, Victoria might be interested.

How much did she need? she wondered. A million, easy. If she wanted to stay in Toronto. New York was an impossibility. Too many people associated her face with Joel's crimes.

"Eli Turnbull, in recognition of your hard work and the years of hard work dedicated by your father, you are given control of the Angus herd and fifty percent of the profits upon sale."

Victoria had no idea what that meant, and Eli's face didn't indicate whether that was a good thing or a bad thing.

"In addition," Jenkins continued to read, "the two hundred acres that were your father's before he sold them to Crooked Creek Ranch is available to you for purchase, at cost and interest free."

In the ensuing silence, the page Jenkins turned was loud.

"That's it? The two hundred acres Dad sold twenty years ago? At cost?" Eli was red-faced, his lips barely moving. Now she realized he was angry. How surprising to see him with an emotion. "What about the rest of the land that belonged to my family?"

"The will doesn't mention any other land."

The room was held hostage until finally, white-lipped and controlled, Eli nodded once and everyone took in a breath of relief.

Good God, Victoria thought, giddy with nerves, *we're off to a rocky start.*

"For Celeste." Jenkins cleared his throat and opened a safe-deposit box at his elbow. He took out a dozen velvet jewelry boxes of various sizes and slid them toward the front of the desk.

Victoria could feel Celeste's hard-wired stillness. The woman practically rattled in her seat.

"You gonna get that stuff?" Jacob asked in a whisper.

"Why don't you go get it for me," Celeste said with a smile that hummed with sorrow.

Victoria closed her eyes for a moment. The restrained and repressed emotions in the room were threatening to cut off all air supply. They'd all just asphyxiate in silence.

Jacob came back with the velvet boxes stacked to his chin.

"There's a note. From Lyle," Jenkins said, his eyes darting up to Celeste's and then back down to his paper. "These are yours," Jenkins read. "They always were. They always will be. Divorce changed nothing. Not for me."

With trembling hands, Celeste took the boxes from Jacob and set them on her lap. She didn't open them. Her eyes, full of tears that dared not fall, stared straight ahead.

Diamonds, Victoria thought, her desperation turning her into an ugly, grasping mercenary. *Lots of diamonds.*

Victoria could live off one of those boxes for a year, she had no doubt.

Jenkins turned another page and Victoria held her breath, waiting for her name.

Half a million. She'd sell the last of her jewelry. She could live frugally. Plant a garden. Get rid of the car.

"Wayne Luc Baker, you are the sole inheritor of the twenty-five hundred remaining acres of Crooked Creek Ranch, including all mineral and water rights and all other assets, which includes a fifty percent interest in the Angus herd and sixty percent control of Baker Leather."

The words detonated like a bomb. *All of it? Luc got all of it?*

"You've got to be kidding me," Luc said, staring slack-jawed at Jenkins.

"Yeah," Tara Jean piped up from the back of the room. "This is a mistake."

Jenkins shook his head. "It's all Wayn—Luc's."

What about me? Victoria thought.

"Good Christ." Luc ran a hand down his face. "This is a nightmare."

Yes! It is!

"I'll sell it," Luc said, his face growing stormy. "Fuck him. I'll sell it."

"I'll buy it." Eli sounded hard and sure and confident.

"Great." Luc nodded. "Name your price—"

"It's not that simple," Jenkins said.

"It is," Luc insisted. "For me it's that simple."

"What about us?" Victoria asked, her voice the weak, pathetic cry of a weak, pathetic woman.

Luc turned, and she refused to look at his face. She knew he didn't understand her and she knew she disappointed him, but she couldn't be like him. She couldn't not care.

"Jacob and me?" she asked. "There's nothing in there about us?"

"May I continue?" Jenkins asked, staring at Luc as if he were a child behaving badly.

Luc nodded, his control regained.

"Victoria Schulman and her son will receive a trust of one million dollars."

She collapsed back against the seat, her body boneless, her mind empty with relief.

"On the condition—"

Her body curled upright. "What condition?" she asked. How like him, how very like her bastard father! Even after he was dead he wanted her to crawl.

"That Wayne—"

"My name is Luc," Luc said through his teeth.

"That Mr. Baker acts as CEO of Baker Leather and stays at the ranch without selling it for the duration of his off-season. Five months at minimum."

chapter 9

Shock emptied Tara Jean's body and she was just a crumpled paper sack in dirty sweat pants.

Luc was her boss.

Why didn't she see this coming?

She'd thought, when she bothered to think about it at all, that Lyle would split the rest of the company shares with his family, but as the 40-percent owner, she'd be in control. And she would be her own boss.

Or even if Lyle gave one of his children control of Baker Leather, that person would be an absentee owner. Collecting checks and leaving her to run the business no one seemed to care about.

But now, Luc was her boss and he was here.

Lyle, what did you do to us?

Luc had bolted the moment his death sentence had been delivered.

Celeste had left after him.

Victoria remained on the couch, a black puddle of despair.

Tara Jean had a relationship with despair. She knew the pit well, but Victoria would have to find her own way out. Tara Jean didn't have a rope to throw her.

Not that Victoria would have taken it.

Numb, Tara Jean signed the last of the paperwork that had been drawn up three months ago. The day after the doctors told Lyle he didn't have much longer to live.

The day he'd concocted this whole plan.

Her services had been paid for with a 40-percent share in Baker Leathers. Lyle got the whole gold-digging fiancée act and she got security.

For the first time in her life she got security.

Amazing, how he'd managed to save her and screw her all at the same time.

Thank you, Lyle, you son of a bitch. She sent the prayer heavenward and stepped out of the way so Eli could sign.

She wanted to say something to Eli. To ease some of the hurt and disappointment he must be feeling. But he just walked out of the den, shoulders back, eyes straight, never giving the impression he'd just been fucked by Lyle Baker.

Tara Jean was tired. Heartsore and desperate to be back in her own home, and she practically ran out of the ranch house to her studio.

This was a new chapter and she needed to come back here on Monday with a tactic, a plan for managing Luc. She pushed open the greenhouse door and headed over to her desk to get her purse and keys, and some much needed distance between her and the house that betrayal had built.

Honestly, Lyle, she thought, *when you play God, you go all out.*

She took off her slippers and slid her feet into the only shoes she had here. Three-inch black stilettos.

Overkill with sweats cut off at the knee, but that was where she was at.

"Did you know he was going to do this?" a voice asked from behind her and she jumped, smashing her hands and hip against the metal edge of her desk. She swore and tried to shake out the sparks.

"Answer the question!"

She spun to face Luc, dark and looming in the doorway.

For a second her heart sputtered in fear. He was a man pushed to the wall. And men pushed to the wall were dangerous animals.

"No," she said, pulling her bag out of the drawer and swinging it over her shoulder.

"Bullshit." The word exploded out of his mouth and she realized he was here to take his anger out on her.

"Think what you want." She stepped toward the door. But, predictably, Luc didn't move and she lost it. Whatever scrap of control or cool that might have survived the firebombing of the last few days just gave up the fight.

"You think I wanted this? You? As my boss? He's playing around with my life too."

His eyes didn't budge from hers and she felt as if her skin might start smoking at any moment. They were bound in this. Stuck together, and as much as she might want to fight and claw her way out, she couldn't.

Play nice, the demon whispered.

"He said you'd stay for your sister," she said after the silence started slapping her around a little.

"Well, he sure rigged it that way, didn't he?" He rubbed a hand through his hair, looking every minute of his age and occupation.

After that absent touch earlier today, she'd told herself she wouldn't be moved by this man. But here she stood, in the same damn place just a few hours later and she felt bad for him. Bad. For him?

Which was honestly ridiculous.

The man was her freaking boss.

"You gonna do it?" she asked.

"Stick around?" He braced himself against the door frame. His muscles pulled against his shirt, and all that desire that had woken up a few hours ago was running around her body like a toddler on a sugar rush.

She nodded, trying to slap that toddler into a harness. "And run the company."

His smile was sharp, lethal. "Worried about your boss?"

"This company matters to me, Luc. And yes, I'm worried that you're going to run it into the ground out of spite."

"I'm not . . . I don't care enough to run it into the ground. I'm a fucking hockey player! I don't belong here."

"So," she said as if he might not understand English. "Are you going to leave?"

He stared off at the horizon, shaking his head, as if the decision hadn't been made yet. Her mouth fell open, stunned that he was considering kicking in his sister's teeth like that.

But if there was one thing she knew, it was that people were really only loyal to themselves.

Luc was no different.

The web Lyle had constructed had Luc well and truly stuck. If she weren't a victim of the old man's machinations herself, she'd be impressed.

"If the inquisition is over," she said, rattling her keys for emphasis, "I'd like to go home."

"Home?" His dark eyebrows knit together over his eyes. "You don't live here?"

"Your private investigator didn't tell you that?"

He breathed hard through his nose and after a moment shook his head. "After I found out you'd changed your name, I figured the rest of it didn't matter and I called him off."

"You had me pegged, huh?" She couldn't resist the sarcasm. "Figured the worst and left it at that?"

"Don't be sanctimonious, Tara. He paid you forty

percent of a leather company to pretend to be his fiancée, didn't he? It was all an act, wasn't it?"

What to do when this whole charade was over hadn't even crossed her mind. Of course she'd thought when it was all said and done, Luc and his sister would pick up their millions and head back to the land of the spoiled.

She'd never imagined coming clean. Or having to explain herself.

"Yes," she said, her voice loud and bright in the dim of the greenhouse. The sun was heading down behind the other side of the house, bringing premature night to her kingdom. "He knew you'd try to stop the wedding and all he wanted was to get you down here."

His laughter was rocky, covered in dirt. "Well he sure knew us, didn't he. And he used the right kind of bait."

She bristled, her feelings injured despite herself. "Your father was good to me."

"I'm sure he was," he said, insinuating and nasty.

"He never touched me. Never."

His eyes skated over her body, carved figure eights around her chest. It was ugly and juvenile and she knew he barely meant it. He was a playground bully, and all he wanted was to see someone else bleed.

"Screw yourself, Luc. I'm leaving." She stepped past him, into the heat of the afternoon.

He laughed, low and dry but without rancor, without the bitter edge that kept her on her toes, and the sound was so unexpected it was like finding diamonds in her breakfast cereal.

Their eyes caught for a moment. And then another. His body tensed, leaned slightly toward her, and she could feel the kiss in the air between them. She could see it in his dark, shuttered eyes, in the heavy set of his shoulders.

In another life, she might have let him kiss her. They were both grieving in their own way. He wasn't quite the devil she'd first thought he was, though she wasn't sure he wasn't a different kind of devil altogether. He was beautiful and she was weak.

But this was now. Now after Lyle died, giving her this security, and she didn't have to kiss men to feel better. Even if she wanted to.

"I'll see you on Monday." She slid her aviator sunglasses down low over her eyes.

"I can't wait." His voice managed the high-wire act between threatening and inviting.

The pea gravel crunched and slid under the thin soles of her shoes, every stone a small pain, a reminder, until she couldn't take it anymore and she stopped.

Tara turned to face him only to find him watching her.

Don't do this, she told herself, *you don't care. Not really. And these people don't care about you. If you were on fire, Victoria would drink the water rather than use it to put you out.*

But there had been so much grief lately, she didn't want to witness any more.

"Your sister," she said, and paused, not exactly sure what she wanted to say. Don't break her heart? Don't hurt her any more than she's been hurt? Is one good shove away from losing it?

"You don't need to worry about my sister," he said, circling the wagons. Right then, she knew he wouldn't leave. She was going to have to live with him for five months.

As her boss.

He stood there, just outside the doorway to her world, to everything she had fought and bled for. He was a creature of privilege. His sister, too. And boo-hoo, their daddy didn't love them like they wanted to be loved. They'd survived. More than survived.

He had money. Safety.

Christ, Victoria had a son.

The two were on a totally different planet from the one where she lived. And while betrayal and pain and long, lonely nights might seem universal, it all depended on who was experiencing it.

"You're right," she said and left.

Luc couldn't look at his sister without wanting to start tearing the ranch down brick by brick, so he went to the one place he was sure she wouldn't be.

Celeste's room.

Maman was propped up against the headboard, looking a mess. Well, as much of a mess as Celeste ever looked. Her jacket and shoes were gone. Her hair, rumpled on the pillows. Her lipstick smeared all over the glass of amber liquid in her hand.

Around her, like blue velvet islands rising from the white sea of the duvet, were the jewelry boxes.

They were all still closed.

"You all right?" she asked, looking at him over the rim of her glass as she finished her drink.

He nodded and grabbed the Scotch from the liquor cabinet, poured her another, and then put it back.

"You're not joining me?" she asked, and he shook his head.

He was reaching an uncomfortable place, where frenzy and anger fed off each other until he didn't have control. And he needed control.

He'd almost kissed Tara Jean. If that wasn't an indicator that he needed to get his shit together, he didn't know what was.

The woman was like that candy she was always eating. Sweet, but bad for him.

"What's in the boxes?" he asked. He sat at her feet and his weight pulled the smallest of the blue boxes toward him.

"Go ahead," she said, her negligence a thin veneer over an unexpected grief.

The box creaked open in his hands.

Heavy-duty bling. In ring form.

"My engagement ring," she said, and she used her leg to sweep the rest of them toward him. "Open the others."

There was a gold and diamond necklace that looked like something a queen might wear.

"When I caught him cheating. The first time."

A thick diamond bracelet set with emeralds as big as his eyeballs.

"The day you were born. His heir. He was so excited."

Pearls.

"His grandmother's. I wore them at our wedding."

Dangly opal and diamond earrings.

"When Victoria was born. An apology. In very poor taste."

A dozen boxes. All with a story to tell.

"The guy was a bastard," he sighed.

"Not always. And not at first. He was, a long time ago, kind in his own way. I think . . . perhaps when I left, things got very bad."

"It's not your fault he hurt us, Maman."

"I'm sorry, son, but I don't quite believe you." Her smile was cracked and broken, full of a lifetime of sadness. He put his hand over hers and she clutched his fingers.

He waited for her to say more, but she was silent and it felt good to sit there beside his mother, bathed in the familiar scent of Chanel N°5.

"I'm glad you're here," he said.

"I imagine you'll be sticking around," she said, and he stood back up. The frenzy, the hot dance of his nerve endings needed to be cooled off.

"It would be the right thing, wouldn't it?"

"Are you thinking of doing the wrong thing?"

"Is it so hard to believe that it might be good for Victoria?" he asked. "That if she was forced to stand on her own two feet maybe she'd stop looking to other people to solve her problems?"

"You want to be the one to make sure she does it?" She took a sip, her cagey eyes missing nothing. "She'll hate you, and it will probably be forever."

It was the truth. He knew it, but knowing it didn't make it sit better.

"And what about Jacob?" she asked, turning the screws.

"I know about Jacob," he said. "I get it. I understand. All right."

His words echoed into a silence that pounded at his head.

He had to get out of here, he had to burn off this anger or he'd lose it. He pulled his shirt out of his pants.

"Where are you going?" Maman asked.

"Running." Dr. Matthews's orders had been explicit. He needed to rest. No working out. No ice time, no physical exertion, for at least six weeks.

But he couldn't just sit here and do nothing.

"Luc," his mother whispered, and he paused to look at her before walking out the door. A gorgeous, ageless woman surrounded by all that was left of love.

Diamonds and regret.

"You can't undo it," she whispered. "Your decision right now, what you do with your sister, you can't change it once it's done. You . . . you can't go back."

Her pain ran headlong against his anger, doing nothing to cool it. Nothing to calm him. He nodded once and left. Buttons flew off his shirt as he yanked it free.

Goddamnit. Had he even packed his running shoes?

"Luc?"

His sister's voice was a dagger between his shoulder

blades. He took two deep breaths before turning to face her.

So pale and resolute, she stood in the hallway, so thin and fragile a good wind would knock her over.

The men in her life had kicked her. Used her and betrayed her. Both of them. Father. Husband.

He couldn't join their ranks.

"I'm staying."

"You . . . you don't have to do that."

That she tried made him love her more.

"Yes, I do," he said, and then, because everything in his life was falling apart and he couldn't be trusted not to scream his rage into the face of his sister, he left.

To battle the demon of his anger on his own.

chapter 10

At five o'clock on Monday morning, Tara Jean was ready to start her new life. She'd hibernated for twenty-four straight hours and woken up with a plan.

She simply wouldn't deal with Luc. Not unless she absolutely had to.

Also, she decided, it was time to get rid of the crutch. The monkey on her back. She'd quit smoking two years ago, drinking four years ago, sleeping with inappropriate men six years ago—surely she could kick the candy habit.

Considering that this truly was the first day of the rest of her life, she wore the kind of leather that made the demon happy: short and tight.

A red skirt from her first design season that wasn't much bigger than a Band-Aid, with an oversized white button-up shirt, which she didn't bother buttoning much of. The black peep-toe heels and big chunky necklace classed her up a bit.

She'd make the Bakers forget they'd ever seen her bunny slippers.

The dawn was pearly and damp, the color of pigeons after a rain. But the moment she stepped outside, all of the hair on the back of her neck stood in terrified attention.

You're being watched.

She ducked back into the vestibule of her building,

pulling the safety door shut, unable to breathe until she heard the big lock catch. Her panicked breath bloomed against the cross-hatched glass as she peered out into the small parking lot, waiting for movement. But the cars didn't even twitch.

She looked to the right and left of the door as best she could through the glass, and she was patient, but she didn't see a thing move. Not for many long minutes.

You're being paranoid, she told herself. Her hand cupped the heavy pounding of her heart, holding panic in her palm. She'd changed her name. Used disposable cell phones, didn't have a credit card. The apartment was leased under Lyle's name, utilities paid for by the company.

But Dennis was out of jail by now. And he'd be looking for her.

She crushed her hair against the glass, resting her head on the door. Adrenaline made her stomach churn and her head fuzzy.

"Stop it," she whispered. "Just stop it."

What you should do is get in your car and drive away, the demon said, sucking on a Virginia Slim.

"What the hell do you know?" she muttered.

She didn't want to run. Not anymore. She had a new life, and this was the first damn day of it.

Taking herself in hand, she pushed open the door and held her head high as she walked to her car. She wasn't going to cower. Not for the likes of Dennis Murphy.

The morning was already hot by the time she got to the ranch and the sun hadn't even been up very long, which did not bode well for the rest of the day and its relationship to her hair.

Her body, against her express demands, tightened in expectation.

Luc.

As if to defy her body and those expectations, she

didn't look around as she got out of the car. She didn't glance over her shoulder, seeking him out.

Nope. She opened the greenhouse and the first order of business was taking every stash of candy—from the gummi bears in the supply cabinet to the Riesen in the bottom drawer of her desk, the Mike and Ikes in her purse, all of it—and dumping it in the garbage can.

It hurt, she couldn't lie, but it was a new day.

After that bit of housekeeping, she unpacked the sleek laptop Lyle had bought her. She'd had wireless installed in the whole ranch last year, so it took only moments for her to access her emails.

Her business phone rang, distracting her from an email from a Nigerian prince who so desperately wanted to give her his money.

"Baker Leather," she said, deleting the email.

"Hi, Tara Jean, it's Randy Jenkins."

She felt actual affection for Randy, who, during the process of her taking over operations for Baker Leather, never treated her with anything but respect.

"What can I do for you, Randy?"

"Well, I'm looking for Luc."

"Luc?" She spun in her chair. "Why'd you call me?"

"Because he's not answering my calls. And I know you're still at the ranch. Is he?"

"Far as I know," she said, though she had no real proof. A sense. That expectation low in her belly. Her skin buzzing with dim electricity.

"Well, I think you better hunt him down. I need him to come in and sign papers so the Crooked Creek and Baker Leather can actually do business."

"I'm doing plenty of business."

"Well, not for much longer if he doesn't come in here and relinquish signing authority. You can't sign a check for over five thousand dollars, Tara Jean. Not without a letter from me signed by Luc."

"What are you talking about?" she asked. "I own forty percent of the business!"

"That doesn't change things. Not unless Luc cooperates."

She slouched back in her chair, staring up through the glass ceiling at the birds flying through the blue sky.

One thing she was sure of: there was no way, absolutely no way she was going to get tangled with Luc on the first day of her new life.

"We paid all the big bills before Lyle died," she said. "I can handle things until next month."

"And then . . . ?"

"And then, I figure you'll have taken care of this little problem."

There was a long silence that gave Tara Jean the impression that real business owners didn't act this way. Fine. She was learning.

"Well, if you see him, tell him to get his ass into Dallas, first thing."

"Absolutely," she said, scanning her emails. If she had any intention of seeing him, she'd tell him.

Around lunch she headed toward the big house, looking for a sandwich.

She found Eli on the porch, sweating and drinking sweet tea. He was staring off down the driveway, toward the gravel road that led to Springfield.

Eli was a staring-off-into-the-distance kind of guy, and she didn't think anything of it until she stepped onto the verandah and he gestured with his glass over Tara's shoulder.

"You talked to him?"

"Luc?" she asked. Now that Lyle was gone, there could only be one *him*.

Eli nodded and Tara turned to see Luc, in shorts and a T-shirt, his head bowed on his neck like a boxer stepping into the ring, running through the midday June heat.

Deep in her body, as if kindling had been set, ready for a match, a fire ignited.

The gray shirt he wore was nearly black across his shoulders and down his spine. His legs . . . good lord, the man had nice legs.

"What . . . what's he doing?" she asked, trying not to sound slightly out of breath.

"Running. Every day. Twice a day."

"You talked to him?" She treaded lightly, sensing a whole lot of pissed-off beneath his ninja calm.

"Can't get him to slow down long enough to say three words."

She thought about that call from Randy. And how Eli had been screwed in the will, how he was probably dying to turn this place on its ass and couldn't do it without Luc signing those papers.

I am not getting near that man today, she told herself. *Not if I can help it.*

"You got anything sweet?" she asked, watching Luc's body get smaller and smaller as he chased dust and sunlight across his own dry, flat land. "Candy? Gum?"

"Cough drop." He held out a Halls in a crumpled white wrapper.

"Gross."

But she took it anyway.

Tuesday morning, Luc was all over the radio on her drive to the ranch. Apparently, Melanie in the Morning had a GIANT crush on the hockey star and she was all aflutter with the idea that Luc Baker might actually get traded to the Dallas Mavericks, which Tara could only assume was a hockey team.

Melanie in the Morning further theorized that being

in Texas for his father's funeral was probably just a cover—that Luc was really here to talk to management and work out with the team.

Melanie probably didn't realize how stupid she sounded. She never seemed to.

Tara Jean flipped the radio off in disgust.

But a day that started bad only got worse when she got to the ranch.

"What do you mean, you're pregnant?" she asked Jennifer Hodges, who, when she wasn't knocked up, was Tara's small-sized sample model.

The final measurement for the samples was scheduled for two weeks away, the beginning of July, the second-to-last step before Tara Jean hand-delivered them to the factory where they were cut and sewn in bulk. Most of the fashion world used factories in Taiwan and Bangladesh to keep costs down, but Lyle had liked to brag that they made clothes for Americans, by Americans. Using the hides of American cows.

Cost him a freaking bundle, but it was something to be proud of.

But the final measurements were going to be a problem since Jennifer hadn't kept her legs together.

"I'm sorry," Jennifer said. "I'm seventeen weeks and I've already gained ten pounds and my boobs are huge—"

"Great, fine." Tara pinched the bridge of her nose and eyed all that sweet, sweet candy that was still in the garbage can. "Don't worry, Jennifer, and . . . congratulations."

Christ. What was with all the breeding going on around here?

Now she needed a small model. For next week. She'd give it a shot herself, but her C-cups hadn't fit into a small since she was in seventh grade.

Today, when she went in for lunch it was Ruby standing on the porch, watching Luc run down the driveway through the shadows from the tall poplars.

"I can't say I like the man," Ruby whispered, as if Luc might hear her from a hundred yards away, "but I love watching him run away."

"You dirty bird," Tara laughed, and Ruby smiled.

"I'm old, not dead. Here." She handed Tara the mail. Tara flipped through it, and opened up the envelopes from Jones Tannery and All-American Shipping.

Both overdue bills.

What in the world was going on here? Lyle had signed those checks, hadn't he?

She made sure of things like that, usually taking the books and the bills into Lyle's bedroom and helping him put his shaking, indecipherable signature on the right line.

She'd begged him to give her the authority to sign bigger checks before he died, but he'd been so wrapped up in getting his children down here, he'd pushed it off.

Or maybe he never intended to do it.

The betrayal bit deep.

"Ruby, have you cleaned out Lyle's room?"

"Not yet." The smile and gleam slowly leaked from her eyes. "Today, maybe."

"Well, I'm just gonna check and see if I left something there."

Ruby nodded and since Luc had run out of sight and the show was over, she headed back into the house in front of Tara.

Lyle's room was quiet. Abnormally hushed and dark, like a church or a bar bathed in daylight. The pieces of medical equipment sat blank-faced and unneeded, their cords curled uselessly around their necks.

His sheets had been stripped. A naked pillow sat alone on his state-of-the-art hospital bed.

The table by the chair where she usually sat was still

filled with the various pills and creams that made Lyle comfortable. The books she and Ruby had read to him were still splayed open, their spines bent forever to the page where they'd stopped reading, like a clock stopped just when he'd died.

Oddly enough, she wasn't sad. It was as if the weekend had dried her out and looking at these things, the flotsam of a man's last days, she only felt glad that she'd known him.

She lifted the *New York Times* crossword puzzle that Ruby had been doing with him and found the invoices she was looking for.

Unpaid.

Great. The last hope she'd had that this was a mistake died.

Now she was going to have to get the checks signed by Luc. Unless she could call the bank and sweet-talk someone into seeing things her way.

It was stupid, but she wanted to hold onto this little fantasy that the company was hers. That she didn't need anyone, much less a man, to make her plans come to fruition. She'd had enough of leaning hard on a man's strong shoulder her whole damn life; she wanted to do this on her own.

"Did you know my grandpa?" a small voice asked and she jumped, her heart a startled bird heading for the trees.

"Christ, kid," she muttered, turning to face Victoria's little boy, Jacob. Who'd been sick.

The boy clutched an inhaler in one hand, a giant robot in the other, and in this room, with its big furniture and the very adult nature of the equipment, he looked so terribly, terribly small.

"You were going to marry him, right?" he asked, shaking a long dark curl out of his eyes. The kid had beautiful hair. Black and curly. Shiny, like the coat of Eli's horse.

"No," she said honestly. "It was just pretend."

"My mom and uncle call you Bimbo Barbie."

She snorted before she could help it. "That's . . . ah . . ."

"It's not nice." The expression on his face, that tilt to his chin and the unflinching look in his eyes—it was a little pup version of one she saw on his grandfather.

And his uncle.

Something tight and hot clenched in her chest. Was this kid defending her? He didn't even know her.

"Yeah, well, it's not the worst I've heard." She looked around for Victoria. "Where's your mom?"

"She's signing me up for dance classes."

"Dance classes?"

"I don't want to go. But she's not listening to me."

He shrugged. And she knew that shrug, remembered the weight of it on her own shoulders—the tension, the way it hurt sometimes like her bones were breaking to pretend she didn't care.

And she wouldn't care now. Not about his pain.

She tapped the bills against the edge of the table and sighed. "Well, you should probably get out of here," she said.

For a second, the boy's blue eyes searched hers and she could see in the kid's face—plain as day—that he missed his mom. Could feel her absence even though she was close.

That he was bored. And a little scared.

"See you around," she said, and walked away, forcing herself not to look at him any more than she had to.

Tara called their account manager at the bank and tried to sweet-talk him into letting her have signing rights over those damn checks, but Matthew Pierce was impervious to sweet talk.

"I need a letter from the power of attorney, signed by Luc Baker," he said. "That's it."

"You sure?" she asked, trying to project as much nudity into her voice as possible.

"Absolutely."

She hung up before she started calling him names.

Because she was weak, she checked the garbage can in the greenhouse, but Ruby had already taken out the trash, and her candy supply with it.

The world ain't fooled by all your airs, Tara Jean, the demon said. *You and me, we never get nothing in this life without asking for it, usually on our knees.*

She was going to have to talk to Luc.

Today. The second day of her new life.

Being around him, it was as if she had fresh skin, raw and sensitive. Brand new.

Which was ludicrous. There was nothing brand new about Tara Jean.

She'd been putting this off for too long. She checked her look in the mirror behind her desk. A black leather vest with nothing under it revealed toned arms and shoulders that truly were a gift from God, because it wasn't as if she lifted anything heavier than a Tootsie Pop. On the bottom she wore a pair of wide-legged, white linen pants and red shoes that did incredible things for her ass.

A small silver chain with her mother's delicate cross nestled between her breasts. An ironic statement, mostly.

She imagined Luc's eyes there, on her body, the pale soft skin of her chest, and her body flushed, hot and prickly.

She rearranged the girls, fluffed her hair, put on some lipstick, and, praise Jesus, found a yellow Mike and Ike in the bottom of her purse.

As Lyle would say, she was ready to bring down some big game.

chapter 11

Luc pitied the next person who asked him for something.

He really did.

Vicks was in some kind of fit, signing Jacob up for lessons and clubs and classes that the poor kid had little to no interest in. And worse, she was trying to schedule Luc for chauffeur duty. Maman had already started talking about getting his team to the annual Sick Kids Children's Hospital Christmas Gala. Eli was hanging out on the perimeters—sitting on the porch when Luc went for a run, lurking in the shadows when he got back.

Please, Luc had thought more than once as he walked by the silent cowboy, *ask me for something. Anything.*

Because then we'll have some words.

Which, in this case, was hockey player for *I will take you out.*

But Eli was cagey and he kept his mouth shut.

Luc tugged the gloves up higher over his wrists and wrapped his fingers around the twine of the next bale of hay. He lifted, walked thirty feet, and heaved the hay into the far corner of the horse arena.

He should email Dominick, the Cavaliers' trainer, and let him know about the hay bale workout. Because this shit was no joke. The muscles of his shoulders, back, and arms screamed with the effort.

It reminded him he needed to call Gates and tell him to lay off the strippers. He was becoming ESPN's favorite Athlete Behaving Badly.

After he moved all of this hay, he'd call the guys and check in.

His shirt stuck to his skin, cold and clammy, and he took it off, tucking it into the back waistband of his running shorts.

Once the arena was cleared of the hay bales and the bags of feed that sat by the door leading out toward the paddock and the Angus fields beyond, he was going to bring in some workout equipment. Running wasn't enough, and he was starting to lose weight. And the headaches were getting out of control. He woke up every morning feeling like there was an ice pick buried in the middle of his forehead.

No wonder Matthews wanted him to rest.

He would never admit this to anyone, but there were mornings when he wanted to stay in bed. Pretend, for a few hours, that he wasn't Luc Baker and that one workout might really change things.

But then he thought of his team and the Stanley Cup. He thought of having a drink out of the championship cup by his father's graveside.

That would be almost as good as the speech.

And he thought of spending days locked inside this ranch with his memories and somehow, every morning, he'd find his way into his workout gear and out onto that road where the miles seemed longer than usual.

A barn cat hissed and ran past him for the open doors leading to the short covered walkway that connected to the barn, a good fifty feet away on the other side of the building. Dust motes sparkled in the air between the dirt floor and the vaulted ceilings. Barn swallows darted down from their nests in the rafters, buzzing his head in warning. *Try it,* he thought to the birds, his mood so poisonous he was ready to take on wildlife.

"Uh-oh," said a smooth, sexy voice, and his pulse leapt with sudden dark excitement. He turned to see Tara, looking like a cross between a biker babe and a . . . well, porn star. Even in loose white pants, she looked like sex. "Eli's not going to like you messing with his arena."

"Well," Luc said, heaving another bale of hay onto the pile. "It's not his arena anymore, now is it?"

She pursed her shiny pink lips and his core temperature spiked. Lust and anger coiled through him, a dangerous and unpredictable mixture.

"What are you doing?"

"I'm going to make a gym in here," he said. "Bring in some workout equipment."

"You're supposed to be training, aren't you? That's what all the running is about?"

"Why, Ms. Sweet, have you been watching me, too?"

Her breasts pressed against her black leather vest, not straining the tiny black buttons, but giving them a good workout, and something about the barely harnessed nature of her outfit turned him on harder and faster than he'd been turned on in a long time.

All he wanted was to press on one of those tiny black buttons with his dirty, sweaty fingers, ease it from its hole, and give them all a little relief.

"Not as much as Ruby," she said, her perfect full lips kicking up into a naughty smile. "You're her new hobby. She's given up crocheting."

He wanted to lick her from the curve of that naughty smile to her toes. And back again.

"You know, you were all over the radio this morning." When she stepped farther into the arena, he could see the tips of her bright pink toenails in her shoes, another tease, another glimpse at the ordinary that on this woman seemed painfully, erotically extraordinary. "Melanie in the Morning has been following the trade rumors very diligently. She has quite a crush on you. I'd worry about a stalker if you do end up down here."

"I'm not playing down here."

"Melanie will be heartbroken."

"I'm so glad you find this funny." The bale of hay he threw flew past the pile, exploding against the wall. "But this is my life. And the fact is, I need to be on some ice!" She blinked at him, all empty headlight eyes.

"So go get on some ice. What's the big deal?"

"The big deal?" There was a tide rising in him, lifting boats of anger and resentment, a whole fleet of frustration. "I'm a hockey player, one of the best, in case you've been living in a cave for the last ten years. And my doctor has told me to rest for the next few months, but right now there are thirty other men, fifteen years younger than me, all working their asses off to take my place. I've got one year left, and I am stuck—here!" He heaved the hay over his shoulder, feeling every muscle and sinew burn with the effort. "I can't sneeze near an ice rink around here without every sports journalist in the world up my ass asking questions about a trade, or the Cup, or my goddamned head!"

He'd said too much and he forced himself to breathe. To center himself in the cool confines of his control.

He turned and found her leaning against a hay bale, wiping a smudge of dirt off her white pants.

She glanced up, as if she was just now noticing his silence. Her eyes opened wide, playing dumb better than any blonde he'd ever seen. Or maybe she just *was* dumb. Yet conniving.

All he really knew about her was that he wanted to get naked and sink as deep as he could into her.

"That sucks," she said.

"Perfect assessment." He marched another bale of

hay across the arena. Sun flooded in the open doors, palpable heat stretching across the dirt floor.

Sweat ran down his back, past the waistband of his shorts. And he could feel her eyes on him, moving across his shoulders and over his legs. His ass.

His body was a product of his game, chiseled and honed by rivers of sweat and blood, and he fully appreciated that women liked how he looked. Wasn't, at times, above using what his looks brought him. The women who fell into his bed like overripe fruit.

But there was something in the way this woman looked at him. Surreptitiously. While his back was turned. As if she wasn't just hiding her interest from him, but from herself as well. It was in direct contrast with her sex goddess looks, and the contradiction made him crazy.

It made him want to flex his muscles, throw her over his shoulder, and show her what he could do with this body.

There was not a single part of him that didn't want to touch her. But some modicum of sense in him knew it wouldn't be a good idea.

He wanted to wipe the floor with his good sense.

"How about you?" he asked. "Prostitutes R Us doing a booming business?"

"I will have you know Baker Leather cleared 1.5 million last year. And the Texas First Lady is one of our most loyal customers."

"Five years ago Dad told me Baker Leather was going bankrupt," he said. "That's why he needed me to wear those boots. You're telling me that's changed in five years?"

"Five years ago, your father didn't have me."

"So, you're responsible for turning it around?"

"Li'l old me," she said, somehow managing to be both sarcastic and proud.

"Well, now, go figure." His sarcasm was a slap shot right back at her righteous defense of herself.

Her eyes narrowed. "Don't be an ass."

The fact that he was taking his evil mood out on her wasn't missed by either of them. "Sorry." But not very. "Did you have something to say, or did you just come in here to stare?"

"I'm not staring."

"Don't be a liar," he said, mocking her.

"Fine." She stood in front of the bales of hay still to be moved, a delectable, five-foot-three roadblock. "I came in here to talk."

She crossed her arms, and her breasts crowded her chest as if searching for high ground. They were natural, those breasts. Perfect and round. They'd be soft to the touch, womanly and full. Her skin would give, her nipples would harden against his lips, firming in his mouth.

His dick got harder. And he grit his teeth against the pleasure.

"About what?" She was a magnet, and he stepped closer so that he could smell her—lip gloss and sugar.

"I . . . ah . . ." She swallowed, and he grinned at her. But Tara only lifted her chin, not ready to stop pretending.

Fine, he thought. But if she wanted to play like there wasn't any heat between them, he didn't have to play along.

Somehow the idea of getting her to admit to her desire turned him on even more. It suddenly became a goal.

And he liked goals. Part of his job description.

She was silent, panting slightly when he didn't move.

Slowly, like a cowboy in every bad late-night skin flick he'd ever seen, he reached past her and picked up another bale of hay and walked through the sunlight to toss it onto the pile.

She cleared her throat, and he smiled.

"I need you to take a ride with me. To Dallas, to see Randy Jenkins."

Iron suffused his muscles and his anger. The smile turned into a smirk.

"Really?" That it was her, asking him for something, gave him an evil delight. A sick glee.

"You need to sign some papers so I can do my job."

"Well, as you can see, I'm busy."

"I understand moving hay is pressing business, but if you don't sign those papers, my hands are tied. And so are Eli's."

He stepped toward her like he was going to grab another bale of hay but stopped right in front of her instead. All those little black buttons on her vest screamed and begged to be released.

Something wicked and hot brewed in the space between them, taking up oxygen, filling his head with treacherous ideas about running his hands over that tiny leather-restrained waist, palming the perfect round globes of her ass. She would feel so good in his hands, against his body; those curves were meant to be touched, palmed, and kissed.

Bitten.

Sucked.

God, he wanted her.

"Frankly, I'm pretty sick of everyone needing something from me."

Her blue eyes darkened and he knew it wasn't sympathy, not from Tara Jean. So he braced himself for her anger. Looked forward to it, even.

"Yeah, poor you," she spat and his body sizzled, his fingers burned. "I didn't write that will, Luc. None of us did, so stop punishing us for what your father did."

"You know, that would be a very noble thing to do."

"And you're not noble."

"Not in the slightest."

"Okay, fine, what do you want?"

Restlessness and anger cheered. Lust sharpened itself into a knife buried in his gut.

"What do I want?" he murmured, his eyes on her shiny pink lips.

Her skin broke out in goose bumps and her shoulders went back. Her nipples were hard points against the black leather. "I'm not for sale." Her voice was a hot, hard whisper of anger. "Not anymore."

"We're all for sale, Tara Jean Sweet." His eyes traveled down her body, taking breaks at her hips, her breasts, the long length of her legs.

Watching that naughty little tongue of hers, he realized what he wanted from her. More than he wanted to slip that vest off her beautiful skin. More than he wanted to fill his hands with her breasts.

He wanted a kiss.

Her lips, perfect and pouting against his. A little tongue. Perhaps a lot of tongue.

And he wanted her to admit that she might not like him, but she wanted him.

That would make him feel less like taking an axe to everything on the ranch.

"And if you want me to sign those papers, I'm going to need a kiss."

He took off his gloves and tossed them on the ground, all the while watching her wrestle with her pride. The right thing to do, he was well aware, was to let this go. To tell her he'd go to Dallas and sign those papers and she didn't have to do anything. But he was sick to death of doing the right thing. Choking on self-sacrifice.

"Just a kiss. That's it." Her hands twitched into fists, and he wondered if she knew what she revealed in that unconscious gesture.

Oh, Tara Jean, what have you had to sell to get here?

He nodded, hating himself a little, but far too turned on and curious to stop.

"Fine." She tossed back her hair, her eyes hard and flat like blue mirrors, giving away nothing, and since he wasn't totally fond of his reflection at this low moment, he looked away. "But I'm warning you, neither one of us is going to enjoy this."

"You gonna bite me?" He tried not to sound excited by the idea. "Because that would pretty much nullify the agreement."

"I'm not going to bite you. But I'm cold, sweetheart—frozen, all the way through. It'll be like kissing an icicle."

"Is that supposed to dissuade me?"

"Nope, just making it clear that enjoyment isn't part of the deal."

He laughed; he couldn't help it. "I don't think enjoyment will be a problem."

A bead of sweat slid out from behind her thick blond curls and traveled across the smooth skin of her neck, over the ridge of her collarbone to the inward slope of her breast, where it gained speed and vanished beneath the black leather.

"Cold?" he murmured. "I don't think so."

"You don't know me," she said, her voice as frozen as her body was hot.

No, he didn't, but that didn't matter.

Right now, all that mattered was getting his mouth on her. Her body against his.

His fingers grazed her shoulder, his thumb sliding under the thick, creamy seam of the leather vest. Goose bumps rippled over her skin and her breath escaped in a long, slow sigh.

"You feel that?"

She didn't say anything, her eyes over his shoulder as though this was something she had to endure.

Endure, he thought, shame creeping up alongside his lust. She wasn't something to punish. The skin, soft and damp between her arm and the leather, was the most perfect skin he'd ever touched.

And he might have bullied his way into this kiss, but he wasn't going to punish her.

Her eyes flicked to his, big and round, blue as the sky outside the arena doors. It was, for a moment, as if he were seeing her for the first time. Her beauty punched him in the gut, left him reeling. He couldn't do this; he wasn't this man. He lifted his hand from her shoulder, stepped back. "You really are beautiful—"

"Oh, for Christ's sake," she muttered and leaned into him, pressing her lips to his with all the finesse of his first girlfriend in eighth grade.

His finger hooked into the leather of the vest and his other hand cupped her face, the silk of her hair tangling in his fingers. The bones of her chin, the curve of her ear, were like glass under his fingers.

She waited, every muscle tensed, like a bird in the palm of his hand. He pressed soft kisses against the corner of her lips, the velvet skin of her cheek. He breathed a kiss against her ear and felt her curl against herself, like ribbon on a present. Her heartbeat began to pound against his palm.

But she didn't step away.

He tasted the strong feminine tendons of her neck and found them delicious. She even tasted like candy.

"If you don't want this, step away," he breathed across her skin and heard her swallowed moan.

"Walk away, Tara," he said. "Right now, or—"

"Or what?" Her challenge was heady, the heat in her eyes—all of it called to the wicked and base parts of himself.

She wasn't walking away, so he kissed her. Really kissed her. Her lips, soft and pouty, were firmer than he'd thought, and he carefully licked the corner seam. When she didn't jerk away, he ran his tongue along the closed crease, a beggar at her door.

Her full bottom lip was too much to resist and he used his teeth, sucking it into his mouth, and she gasped and flinched against him, pressing her breasts against the bare skin of his chest.

Oh, dear God, yes, he thought. Between the sweat and the leather, the hard points of her nipples and the sweet curse of that cross between her breasts, he was a goner.

His hands clenched in her hair and her head tipped back, her mouth opening, and any resistance he'd felt in her body was gone. So he took what was offered. His tongue slid inside the delicious wet heat of Tara Jean's mouth.

She moaned, soft and deep in her throat, and her tongue pressed back and soon there was no distance between them. His erection found a home against the taut, flat belly beneath her white linen pants, and her arms curled around his neck, her nails a sweet pain against his skin.

A man could die like this, he realized, sucking on Tara Jean's lips, her tongue. His hips arched hard against her and she pressed back, making him see stars. Her teeth bit into his tongue, and whatever control he might have had snapped. Rough now, his hands slid down her back, cupping the sweet curves of her hips. She was perfect, and he was momentarily distracted by the apparent absence of underwear.

His arms lifted her slightly, balancing her weight like she was nothing, to set her up on one of the bales of hay.

Her fingers dipped under the edge of his shorts, the T-shirt he'd tucked there falling down his legs to the floor. From the top of his ass, her fingers slid up his back, over the thick ridges of muscle along his spine. His teeth closed down on her tongue and her nails bit deep into his skin.

"Yes," he muttered, leaving her lips, finding that sweet candy skin of her neck. Her breath hitched and burned against his cheek. The siren song of the leather vest reached a crescendo and he dropped his hand between them, cupping her breast, finding the hard bead of her nipple beneath the leather. She jumped, electrocuted, and it was so real, so pure and hot, he brought his other hand down to cup her other breast, the leather slick under his fingers, her nipple a hard point.

He didn't realize she was pushing him away until he heard her say, "Stop."

He might be an asshole, but he wasn't that kind of asshole, so he immediately stepped away. She wobbled slightly and he put an arm on her elbow, the shock of the electricity between them running from her skin to his.

What the hell just happened, he wondered, staring at her down-turned face as she climbed off the stack of hay.

Perhaps it was all the blood in his crotch instead of his brain, but he honestly had no context for the power of that kiss. It wasn't supposed to be like that. No kiss in his life had ever been like that.

Cold? he thought. *An icicle? Was she insane?*

She tilted her face up, perfect and collected. The shock of her composure made him feel like a boy who'd come in his underwear.

"Get cleaned up," she said in a voice a shade too rough. A shade too deep. Those lips of hers told the tale—they were swollen, the pink lip gloss kissed right off, revealing the pinker shade of her lips. "We'll leave in a half-hour."

He dropped her elbow, balking at being a dog on a leash for her. "Tomorrow," he said. "I want to finish this."

She looked at the hay and then up at him. "Randy Jenkins's son plays hockey, a lot of it if Randy's incessant talking about it is any indication," she said. "I bet Randy could get you access to a rink without anyone knowing."

He blinked at her, stunned.

Watching her walk away, mesmerized by the swing of her hair and ass, he realized that of all the people in his life right now, she was the only one interested in helping him.

chapter 12

Tara Jean's mom, Rayanne, loved big men. When Tara Jean was growing up, the river of men that flowed through their trailers and crappy apartments all had necks the size of Rayanne's waist.

She'd said once that they made her feel small and safe.

Until, of course, they got mad at her. And then all that brute strength came to bear on Rayanne and spilled over onto Tara Jean.

Which was why, as a rule, Tara Jean stuck to thin guys. Some of her boyfriends might have even weighed even less than she did. And she was okay with that, because the theory was that she could hold her own in a fight with a skinny guy.

Of course, that proved to be just as much bullshit as the rest of her theories.

But the point was, back when she was attracted to men and felt anything other than numb, she didn't like big guys. Men like Luc, with their big arms, strong chests and all those sweat-slicked muscles, did nothing for her.

She stood in front of the window unit in her studio, the cold air blowing right down the front of her vest, turning her nipples to ice but doing nothing to calm the fire under her skin, and wondered when that had changed.

Because she liked Luc's body. She really, really liked it.

The second she'd walked into that arena, her body had started humming in pleasure, a motor tuned just right. And she was having a very hard time turning the damn motor off.

Why hadn't she walked away when he gave her the chance?

That kiss was powerful. And sweet. Better than every piece of candy she'd thrown away.

Through the wavy glass beside the wall unit she saw Luc step out of the house and down the porch. He wore another one of those suits, black this time, with a red tie. His hair was dark and slicked back off his high forehead, making his nose and chin sharp. Sunglasses hid his eyes and he looked menacing. Dangerous.

But her body cooed with sweet delight at the memory of his tenderness at the beginning of that kiss—so at odds with the asshole he was trying hard to be. He'd looked into her eyes and the façade had just crumbled.

You're so beautiful, you really are.

She'd been called beautiful plenty of times, but not quite like that. Like she was something new. Something he'd never seen before. And his restraint, when she'd told him to stop. The way he'd stepped back without any hesitation, even with his erection making a mess of his shorts, had been about the most chivalrous thing she'd ever seen.

Which was a sad statement on the men she usually slept with.

Imagine that control, the demon whispered. *Imagine all that power and restraint under your hands. Beneath your lips. Imagine the places he could take you.*

She cranked off the air and grabbed her glasses and purse off her desk. A hundred miles to Dallas.

A hundred miles.

That would be a good lesson in control.

She stepped out into the sunshine and jangled the keys to her Honda.

"You're kidding," he drawled, his face smooth and shiny from a recent shave. He'd cut himself just above the collar of his white shirt: it was so human and real against the canvas of all that perfection.

Her fingers twitched, flush with an evil desire to touch him, to dig through his clothes and ruffle his hair to find the other signs of his messy humanity.

"We'll take my car," he said.

She shrugged, relieved. Her tank was barely half full and she didn't have any cash. Her salary from Baker Leather was laughable. Truly a joke. And she put almost all of it into savings. A contingency plan, or an escape route, depending on if her past came back to haunt her or, in the end, she wasn't as good at this job as the demon led her to believe.

Getting herself up into the black SUV almost required a pulley system and a harness, but she climbed in and Luc started the mighty engine, which purred against her feet and reverberated through her body, hitting extra notes low in her belly.

He backed out of the parking area, his hand braced on her seat.

So close. Too close. She tried not to stare at the fine hair on his hands, the size of his palms. Tried not to remember the way he'd lifted her as though she weighed nothing.

The skinny boyfriends couldn't ever do that.

Needing a distraction, she pulled a pack of strawberry gum out of her bag and held out a piece to him. He took it without comment, sliding it into his mouth, and then he grimaced, spitting it back on the wrapper and wadding it up.

She chewed on her own and grinned. "You don't like it?"

"Tastes like strawberry plastic."

"My favorite kind."

"All I ever see you eat is candy."

"You a dentist?"

His laugh was a little huff out of his nose and then he was quiet, tucking the gum and wrapper into the ashtray. She looked out the window at the bluebells in bloom, a sea of them on the low hills, nodding their heads in the wind as if in approval. As if to say, it's okay. Don't worry. Everything will be all right.

"Why'd you change your name?"

"Do I look like the Jane type?"

His eyes ran over her and her body responded with a deep purr.

"Frankly, Tara," he said, looking her right in the eye for a moment, sounding baffled, "I don't know what type you are."

"Why'd you change *your* name?" she shot back, and his eyebrow lifted.

"I never much cared for the name Wayne." His voice was as dry as the desert.

"I never much cared for the name Jane." It wasn't the truth, of course. But she didn't need to tell him that she was running from her past. The past he'd threatened to expose.

He glanced over at her and she braced herself for a stripper comment, but in the end he just nodded. "Fair enough.

"How'd you meet my dad?" He shifted his hands around on the wheel, pretending to be nonchalant, and she wondered what was agitating him. Talking about his father? Or talking about his father with her?

"Your private investigator already told you, remember? The hospital."

"He didn't tell me why you were there."

"I was a candy stripper."

His laugh surprised both of them.

"I didn't expect you to be funny."

"It's one of my lesser charms." She pretended to puff up her hair, and his half-grin sliced right through her stomach.

"Tara, you were right the other day. I saw that picture of you and I heard your name and I had you pegged. And now that I'm here—"

"Stuck here."

"Right. Stuck here. I realize I don't have you pegged at all. I keep thinking I have you figured out and then you do something to change everything and . . . I've misjudged you a thousand times and I don't want to do it anymore."

A pinprick of panic punctured her heart. Despite her efforts he was seeing through the Bimbo Barbie act, and she didn't know, couldn't even begin to guess, what he saw beneath the show.

"And you don't have to answer my questions. We can just sit here for an hour—"

"I had been in a car accident."

"A bad one?" His glance was concerned and she was touched, truly, but she was lying to him and his concern made her queasy.

"Bad enough. Lyle and I were on the same floor. I used to go into his room and read to him."

"Read? To Lyle?"

"The Sports page," she said, wondering why she was telling him this; blurring the lines between fiction and reality was a surefire way to get caught up in some lie. Some half-truth. And this man was too perceptive already. "He had a son, you know, a big-shot hockey player."

That shut him up, and in the silence she plucked an emery board from the front pocket of her bag and went to work on her right thumbnail.

"Is that something you do a lot? Read to old guys in hospitals?" She had to give him points for trying so hard not to sound disbelieving.

"I did." She took care of the ragged edge on her pinky. "Hospitals and nursing homes."

"Only the rich men?" He was trying to joke, but it was far too close to the truth to be funny.

"The good-looking ones." She winked at him, but he was wound tight and he sat there emanating the kind of pained stress that spoke right to her heart. She lived with that stress, stretched taut between wishing she felt nothing and feeling all too much.

"Only the lonely ones," she revealed, because in the end that was the truth. "The ones who had no visitors. No family. No one to read the Sports page to them. They were grateful to have someone do something nice for them."

Very grateful. She pressed the rough edge of the emery board hard against her cuticle until blood welled up. Payment—late, and not nearly enough—for all that gratitude.

"It was like giving them back a little piece of themselves. A cup of tea in their favorite mug. Warm socks. A blanket their wife made. Their favorite book, outside with the sun shining on their faces. But mostly they wanted someone to read them the crossword puzzle and the obituaries. One man," she laughed suddenly at the memory that sprang out of nowhere, "Mr. Beanfang, he liked me to read the newspaper to him while he was in the bathroom. I used to shout it through the closed door."

She didn't have to look at him to see his shock—she could feel it, cold and hard against her face, which burned with embarrassment.

What was the point of telling him that, Tara? she wondered.

But when the silence stretched on she glanced up at him, saw him staring at the road. The bluebells were gone, replaced by hardscrabble sage and dirt.

"And Dad just took a liking to how you read the Sports page? Offered to bring you to his home so you could do it full time?"

She gaped at him slightly, realizing he was angry with his father on her behalf. Amazing! That was a first for her and she didn't quite know how to respond.

"There was nothing sordid about it, Luc. He was lonely. And dying. He was worried about what would happen to Baker Leather once he was gone. I didn't have any other job prospects, so when he offered me a chance to come out and learn the business, I took it."

"You have a lot of experience designing leather skirts?"

"I told him I did." He shot her a wicked look and she rolled her eyes. Honestly, he was years too late with the sarcasm. "He knew I was lying. Believe what you want, he was kind to me."

"Kind." Luc shook his head as if the word didn't make any sense. She waited for some other vicious comment or look from him, ready to defend Lyle against his son's hate, but he stared out the window as if the scrub brush were a threat that needed to be watched.

From the bag at her feet, she pulled out a tissue and pressed it to the bead of blood on her pinky, the red seeping across the white like a poison. She watched and wondered if she was the poison or the thing being poisoned, which was a ridiculous thing to wonder, so she crumpled up the tissue and threw it into her bag.

"Hey Luc," she said. "If . . . if you have questions about me, just ask. No need for private investigators."

She stared at him, as earnest and naked as she'd been in years. She already had Dennis to worry about. She didn't want to worry about some P.I. digging through her secrets and carrying them back to Luc.

"I don't intend to have him do any more digging."

"Thank you."

The silence stretched, cracks formed, the past lurked, and Tara had no desire to slip into those horrible places.

"So, Luc, what do you do besides hockey?"

"You're joking."

"No, surely you've got some kind of charity. Isn't that what you rich people do? Give your money away so you don't feel so guilty?"

He laughed a little as if they were sharing some inside joke. The sun came out from behind a cloud and he put his shades back on, and she felt as if he were hiding. "My mother takes care of my karma."

"Okay. But you have to have a hobby. You breed dogs? Knit? Play bridge?"

"Does trying to keep my star center out of jail count?"

"No. Well, maybe. Is he often in jail?"

"Often enough."

"All right, that's half a hobby. What else?"

"That's it, Tara. I play hockey, work out, and try to keep Gates out of jail."

"And I thought my life was boring." She laughed, she couldn't help it; honestly, what a cliché.

"Why is that funny?" he asked, the smile gone. "I love what I do. I don't want to think about anything else. I don't need anything else."

The ferocity surprised her; the hair on her arms stood on end in a sudden prickly awareness. She should let it go, like a scab that wasn't quite ready to come off.

But she couldn't help herself.

"No wife? No little Lucs carrying hockey sticks and wearing miniature suits?"

"No wife," he said. "No family."

"Friends?"

"I have my team, Tara. They're all I need."

"Fair enough," she said, slightly chagrined by his honesty. And at the same time a little sad for him. If he'd been a footnote in his father's life, he was doing the same to everything in his own life that didn't involve being on the ice.

"What about you?" he asked.

"No wife for me either," she said, backing up and away from the thin intimacy they'd built, the fragile bridge between them.

"Where are your friends?"

"He just died."

The easiness between them scattered like crows after a gunshot.

His mouth shut so hard she heard his back teeth click, and she wished she'd never started this conversation. Wished she'd never gotten in this car. They should have driven separately. Or, better yet, Luc should have acted like a reasonable adult rather than a jerk and just taken care of his inheritance when he was supposed to.

"The private investigator told me you grew up in Arkansas."

She twisted her body toward the window, giving him every signal to shut the hell up.

"Where?"

"Does it matter?"

He glanced at her. Her distorted body reflected back at her in his slick sunglasses. "I'm not passing judgment."

"A trailer." She stared out her window. "In the middle of nowhere."

Her cell phone beeped and she fumbled in her bag for it. Another email from her Nigerian prince, but Luc didn't need to know that.

"Excuse me, but I need to do a little work."

"Tara Jean," he said after a long moment. "If you're angry about what happened in the arena—"

"I don't care about what happened in the arena." She didn't bother looking up from her cell phone.

She could feel his gaze on her, as if it were his large, hot hands. And she wanted to scream because she was smarter than this. Savvy to the wayward temptation of a handsome man's grin. What she was a sucker for, though, was his quiet and startling interest in *her.* If kissing him was a mistake, then liking him was a disaster.

The rest of the drive passed without a word between them until Luc asked for directions to the lawyer's office.

Once Tara had hand delivered Luc to a very pleased Randy Jenkins, she headed out into Uptown and got herself an iced coffee and, because that drive was harder than she'd thought it would be, a donut.

With sprinkles.

Because sometimes a girl needed her crutch.

She sat on a bench off McKinley, outside the lawyer's office, and watched the world stroll by.

"Well, well, well," a voice purred over her shoulder. Her heart collapsed in her chest and she choked on her breath, drowning in panic.

Run! the Demon screamed.

Desperate, her eyes searched the faces of the men walking past, praying one of them would see the danger she was in.

"If it isn't sweet Jane Simmons . . . oh, wait, that's not you anymore, is it? It took me a while to track you down, Tara Jean. I have to say, I don't much like the new name. Makes you sound like a stripper."

"How the hell did you find me here?" Her voice cracked to pieces in panic.

"I've been watching that ranch for about a week. You don't leave the place, except to go home. And your apartment has got all those locks, Jane, honestly. Someone would think you were scared of something." His smile showed every tooth. "This is the first chance I've had to catch you alone."

He sat beside her, a thin man, handsome to her once, terribly handsome, with his aging high-school-football-star looks. Brown hair with a hint of gold, bright white teeth, a dimpled smile. Those eyelashes that stretched for miles. It was all a façade hiding ugliness so profound it had destroyed her life.

The donut she'd eaten began to crawl up her throat. *Get up!* The Demon screamed. *Get up right now!*

Every muscle tensed to stand.

"Hey now, honey." Dennis put a hand over hers and she yanked it free, repulsed by his touch.

"Don't touch me," she said through her teeth.

"Fine." He dropped the act, but slid in closer. "But don't go running off. We have some things to talk about."

She would have vomited on him if her body weren't frozen.

"You've been busy since I've been gone." He stretched his arm across the bench, as if they were just two people chatting. "Luc Baker, that's a hell of a mark."

"Luc is not a mark," she said, finding her voice and a new source of fear. Luc getting swirled into these waters was not something she wanted to consider. Ever.

"His sister, then?" Dennis asked, and ice rolled down her spine. "The stick lady, what's her name? Victoria?"

While Dennis had been watching her, he'd been watching the whole Baker family. And of course he'd assume the worst.

Suddenly, she felt her strength return like a cold wind coming down from the mountains. This man was a worm and he was dangerous, but he couldn't hurt her in front of all these people. And she wasn't timid Jane Simmons anymore. She wasn't this man's doormat. Not anymore. Not ever again.

"Go away." Her voice was metal and steel and it rang out in the sunshine. "Honestly, move on, Dennis. You and I are done."

"Come on, now, baby. Do you think I'm just going to let you go? We made real money—"

"No." She shook her head, resolute in this of all things. "I'm not doing that anymore."

"Right," he drawled, clearly not believing her. "Fine. But you owe me some money. From that last geezer."

"There is no money, Dennis. I gave it back." She smiled slightly, pleased to have thwarted him, to have taken something he wanted and tossed it away where he could never get it.

"Now, Jane." His fingers reached for her cheek and she jerked from his touch. "Last time you told me that line, you got hurt."

"You beat the shit out of me, Dennis," she snapped. "Put me in the hospital. I'd say we're even."

"Even? That was ten grand—"

"Look at me, Dennis, I'm not doing that anymore. It's over. There's no money."

She forced herself to meet his gaze and not back down. *You don't scare me,* she thought, *not anymore.* He couldn't hurt her on this crowded street, not really, and she wasn't about to let him back into her life. It was as if her own strength had sealed up the cracks where he'd always found entrance.

He was so little, sitting there in his second-hand clothes.

"You've gone clean." He nodded his head, as if he was in total approval, but she knew better. He'd taught her better. "That's admirable."

"Stay away from me, Dennis," she said. "I've got a new life."

He lurched toward her, his hands clenching her wrist so hard the bones rubbed, and she gasped at the sudden pain. "You got shit, Jane. A woman like you wants to believe you can do better. But you can't. You're good for one thing, and it's best when it's dirty."

She didn't realize she was on her feet, blinking in shock, until he switched his grip on her hand, as if they were shaking hands. No one watching would think it was a manacle holding her to the past, keeping her in the filth.

"Tara Jean?"

She stiffened in panic. Luc. It was Luc behind her.

Dennis stood, smiling like a salesman, and she wondered if Luc saw that or if he only saw the charm.

So many people only saw the charm until it was too late.

But Luc was frowning down at Dennis from his professional-athlete height. Worry in his eyes. She didn't need Luc curious, or worried, or involved in her situation with Dennis in any way.

So she put on a big, bright happy smile. "Luc, this is an old friend of mine. Dennis. Dennis Murphy."

"Luc Baker," Dennis said, holding out his hand. "I'm a huge fan."

Luc's giant paw swallowed the smaller man's hand and Luc glanced over to Tara. She smiled, hoping—praying actually—that it was convincing.

"Nice to meet you," he said, and Tara took a deep breath.

"Well, Dennis, it was good to catch up," she said. "Best of luck to you."

He opened his mouth as if to say something, turn some screw, slide some blade between her ribs, but she pulled Luc close, putting her arm through his, insinuating that this big, giant professional athlete at her side would squash Dennis like a bug if she wanted. If she just said the word.

Dennis closed his mouth.

Giddy and light-headed, she leaned on Luc's arm as they walked back to the car, feeling as if she'd just fought the devil.

And won.

chapter 13

Tara was good, Luc would grant her that. She was calm and cool sitting in the passenger seat of the SUV. She didn't fidget, she didn't *seem* in anyway disturbed.

But she was one unsettled woman.

Maybe it was the total stillness of her, the way she didn't play with her hair or cross her legs over and over again, the way she had on the drive to Dallas. A girly, strawberry-scented tornado in the front seat determined to distract him from the road.

Now, she just stared out the front window, her face blank.

Eerily blank.

"Who was that guy?" Luc asked.

"Dennis?" Her smile was a work of art, nostalgic as if the name were attached to fond memories.

But he didn't believe her. Not for a moment.

He nodded, watching her and the road in equal measure.

"An old friend from before I started working for your father."

"What's he do?"

"A little bit of everything." She waved her hand, like it was all nothing. "Real estate, investments; he's a jack-of-all-trades."

"Did you date?"

Now she looked at him, her blue eyes carefully blank. "Does it matter?"

"I guess not, you just seem . . ." He shrugged. "Ruffled."

Beneath the lushness, her laugh was decidedly tinny. "Seeing him brought back a lot of old memories, that's all." She ran a hand through her hair, pushing it away from her face, and then squared her shoulders as if she'd just shed some skin. "What did Jenkins have to say? Did he help you with ice time?"

It was a blatant change of subject and part of him resisted, wanting to pull the truth out of her like a bad tooth, but he realized it was pointless. He was leaving in five months, and maybe . . . well, after what he'd heard in the lawyer's office, maybe she'd be leaving sooner.

"He was glad to help. He knows the manager of the rink where his son plays. Says she'll help and be discreet."

She smiled at him like a cat with a mouth full of cream, like a woman who owned the ground she stood on. And he couldn't help but stare at her. Couldn't help but want her.

"Thank you, Tara."

"You're welcome."

"You're not getting much of a salary." Immediately the smile dropped from her face.

"You talked about me?"

"Baker Leather, mostly. You're earning the same amount Lyle paid you four years ago. And forty thousand a year ain't much."

"Well, the company pays for my apartment and utilities." She shook her head. "Why does any of this matter?"

"Because I can't sell the land for a year while it's in escrow, but I can liquidate the assets of the estate. And Baker Leather is an asset."

"Why would you do that?" For the first time he saw

real panic in her face and it caught him flat-footed. He could only stare. "You said you didn't care enough about the business to ruin it out of spite."

Ah, the million-dollar question. Why was he doing this? She was like a hedgehog—rub her one way and you were fine, rub her the other and you got nothing but spikes stuck in your hand. He thought about how she'd bristled and shut down when he'd asked her where she was from.

She had a lot of secrets beneath those spikes.

"As forty-percent owner of the company, you could walk away with a big chunk of money if we liquidate," he told her.

Her big blue eyes stared at him, unblinking. As though if she looked away for even a moment, he might yank the rug right out from beneath her.

"You could start over somewhere new. Put this place behind you."

Her laughter was surprising, tired and sore, as if it had walked a long road to see the light of day.

"I've started fresh more times than I care to count, Luc." Her beauty was suddenly threadbare, but what he saw beneath the glamour was infinitely more appealing. It was tough. And honest. "I have no interest in putting this place behind me."

"But—"

"I understand you hate your father and I'm sure you have plenty of good reason, but he gave me the chance for a new life. And I want that life."

He looked out across the highway, the black asphalt splitting the dirt and sage. Heat waves rose up off the road, the sun brutal and unforgiving. Not much lived out here, nothing that was pretty or fragile or easy, anyway.

But it was her life. Her choice. He truly didn't care enough to try to influence her one way or another.

"All right then," he said. "We won't liquidate."

"Why are you doing this? Offering to liquidate for my benefit? Because I won't sleep with you out of gratitude. Or to keep you from changing your mind."

"You've got a really dirty mind, Tara Jean."

"You're saying it never occurred to you to use this to leverage me into your bed."

He laughed, stroking his chin, wishing with a palpable force that he could stroke her just as easily. But her spines were up.

"I've thought about you in my bed almost every minute since I met you," he said. "And should you be so lucky as to sleep with me—"

"Lucky?" She scoffed and he turned to her, smiling slightly just to watch her bristle even more.

She was a gorgeous hedgehog, that was for sure. And fun to tease.

"Very. And there wouldn't be any ulterior motives."

"You're a fool, Luc Baker." She turned away, staring out the window at the desolate landscape she apparently wanted to call home.

"Yeah. You're probably right."

Jacob hated the ballet classes Victoria had signed him up for. But the sight of him in his black sweatpants and white T-shirt standing at the barre surrounded by girls in pink tutus so delighted Victoria, she had refused to switch him out of it.

"Excuse me," a man whispered, and the sealed envelope from Webster and McGraw Law Offices in New York floated under her nose. "You dropped this."

Victoria stared at the letter from the lawyers handling the civil case against her husband's company. It had arrived this morning and she'd tucked it in her purse and ignored it. Because she knew without opening it what it said.

We have not yet received your monthly expense report and your receipts.

The ongoing aspect of her humiliation was having to submit a spending report to the prosecutors, who held her accountable for every penny.

Nobody cared that she'd had no idea what her husband was doing. Nobody believed her when she'd said there was no more money. She'd sold the houses and the furniture and given all the money to the prosecutors to distribute to the people who were bankrupted by Joel's Ponzi scheme.

She was playing fair. Nice, even. Complying above and beyond.

But, still, every month she had to be held accountable. Her purchases scrutinized, down to the last tampon.

Reluctantly, she took the envelope, sparing a smile for the man standing next to her. And then did a subtle double take.

"No problem," he said.

No, she thought, *no problem at all.* Standing beside her was one of the most handsome men she'd seen in a long time. And he was smiling.

At her.

Brown hair, pretty blue eyes, and eyelashes that went on forever. And his smile . . . his smile was kind. His smile made her smile, and that was pretty damn rare in her life. She felt something tight and closed off and nearly dead in her soul opening up, reaching out.

"Do you mind if I . . ." he gestured to the seat next to her.

"Sure," she said, tucking her bag under her seat. "Is your daughter taking ballet?"

"Niece," he said, pushing the sides of his handsome gray suit jacket away from his hips as he sat. Armani.

Nice. His brown shoes were Cole Haan and his watch was Tag Heuer.

She summed him up in an instant and felt selfish and miserly, but her heart went pitter-patter at the sight of all that wealth.

"Abby is the blonde facing the wrong way." He pointed through the glass to the little girl three down from Jacob who was staring out the window while everyone else was looking at the teacher. "We need to do more work on knowing left from right," he sighed.

She laughed, and his attention made her blush like a peach.

An awkward-schoolgirl peach.

"And you?" he asked.

"Oh, I know my left from right."

"No," his eyes were kind and she got lost for a moment in those eyelashes, "which kid is yours?"

Her blush turned radioactive. Maybe if she wasn't such a damn hermit she'd know how to talk to handsome strangers. "Oh, my son." Jacob was the only boy, and his fierce frown was so cartoonish both Victoria and the man laughed. "I'm afraid he doesn't like ballet."

"Most boys don't. My mom put me in violin lessons when I was your son's age. All I wanted to do was play junior tackle."

Her heart shuddered at the thought of Jacob in junior tackle.

"Are you from around here?" she asked.

"Nope. Arkansas. My sister moved here with her husband ten years ago. I have a lot of business in Dallas and I try to visit a few times a year." He pulled up the fabric of his black pants and crossed his legs. The distance between his knee and her thigh was minuscule and she felt his warmth through her skirt. Awareness, prickly and foreign, made her sit up straighter in her chair, pulling her leg from the magnetic force of his.

She caught him looking at her hands, unsure of what he was doing until it dawned on her that he was checking for rings and it was so new, so strange, she clenched her fingers in her lap.

For a long moment she wanted to just curl up and die. *You never do anything right,* she berated herself.

"I'm sorry." He ran a hand over his face. "I . . . I'm not good at this. Since my divorce . . . I don't know what I'm supposed to do. There aren't any rules for dating again. Do I just ask if you're married? Or do I just wait until your husband walks in and I get my hopes crushed?"

She stared at her hands, her ears buzzing. How was this happening? Here? Now? He made her feel somehow young. As if the last year of her life were melting away under this man's attention. "No rings," she finally said, glancing sideways in time to see him smile.

"Are you from here?" he asked.

She shook her head. "My father died, and my son and I are spending the summer getting things in order."

"I'm sorry to hear about your father." His sympathy, while sweet and warm and comforting, made her uncomfortable, all too aware of the half-truths she'd been telling.

"Don't be," she said with a half-smile. "We weren't close. Lyle Baker wasn't close to anyone, really."

"Lyle Baker? Lyle Baker died?" He blew out a long breath.

"Did you know him?"

He nodded slowly, his gaze unblinking, on his feet. "We did some real estate deals a few years ago. I knew he'd been sick . . . I can't believe Old Man Baker is dead. He was such a force of nature."

Victoria felt oddly like she should comfort this stranger, who was taking her father's death with more honest grief than she'd been able to manufacture.

"Tell me—" He stopped, then lifted his hand, cutting himself off. "Never mind. I'm sorry, this is personal."

"How about you ask and I'll decide."

"Did your father marry a woman named Tara Jean Sweet?"

"How do you know about her?"

"Well, last time I was in town that was the rumor, and I knew a girl in high school named Jane Simmons . . . she'd changed her name to Tara Jean Sweet and honestly, I can't believe there are two women with a name like that."

"They didn't get married," she said, trying not to mutter. Trying not to sound raw and angry at just the mention of the woman's name. "He died first."

"Is she blond? Real pretty?"

Victoria nodded and the man laughed, wiping a hand over an astonished face. "Wow. Small world, huh?"

"Were you good friends?"

His hesitation spoke volumes. "We grew up together, but she was . . . she was a troubled kid."

Without a doubt they were talking about the same Tara Jean Sweet.

"She's still at the ranch," she said.

"I'll have to stop by . . . if that's all right?"

"Of course," she said. She wasn't sure what force was motivating her. The drugging nature of his smile, the length of his eyelashes, the price tag on that watch. She didn't know and she wasn't going to scrutinize it. In a life that was being scrutinized down to the last penny, she was going to—for once—act without thinking everything to death.

"Come on out tonight," she said. "After class. My brother is picking us up here. You and Abby can follow us."

"Oh, Abby's mom is picking her up. But I would come . . . if you're sure."

She nodded, definitively, her smile so wide and real it nearly hurt to keep it.

"That would be great, thank you." His eyes touched her face, wandered across her lips. "You have a beautiful smile," he said, and she blushed with pleasure.

"My name is Victoria," she said, leaving off her last name in case it should once again ruin everything.

"I'm very happy to meet you, Victoria." His hand took hers and she felt the buzz and the thrill, the cloud of desire enter her bloodstream. "My name is Dennis."

Saturday night, Tara Jean walked into the house looking for Ruby. She'd stuck close to the ranch, scared that Dennis might be waiting for her at her apartment if he hadn't left town, but as the days passed it became more obvious that he'd moved on.

All week she'd been coming into the house long past dinner, avoiding the family and eating leftovers hunched over the sink. Trying not to see anyone. Well, trying not to see Luc, mostly.

But now, this small-sized model crisis was forcing her to face the dragons in their den.

It was dinnertime, but the formal dining room was empty, not even set for dinner. The kitchen was still, nothing bubbling away on the stove, no delicious smells wafting from the oven.

Very bizarre.

"Hello?" she yelled. Only silence answered.

She walked down dark hallways, past hushed rooms, and realized that the house used to be like this; just a few weeks ago, when it was only her and Ruby minding Lyle in turns. Eli joined them occasionally, but he usually slept in his house on the other side of the creek three miles away.

Funny how a family seemed to pad a house, fill its

empty spaces. Crowd into the corners. So when that family was gone the house seemed extra empty. Incomplete.

The TV was on in the den and she followed the sound of applause only to find Ruby and Celeste, eating tuna fish and green grapes, their feet propped up on the coffee table. Watching a dance show on the flat screen.

"Hi," Ruby said, popping up when she saw Tara Jean. Guilty, as if she'd been caught consorting with the enemy.

"Where is everyone?" Tara asked, and Celeste finally turned to look at her. The elegant woman wore red yoga pants with a matching jacket, the color making her dramatic hair even more theatrical.

"Well, Luc found an ice rink in Dallas, and Victoria took Jacob to his dance class," she said.

"Oh," Tara Jean said, all the courage she'd mustered up to face the dragons in their den falling flat. The dragons were eating tuna and watching a dance show. That didn't require much courage.

But Celeste was still staring at her like she had some fire to breathe. "My son tells me that you are a designer for Lyle's little leather store."

"The little leather store is actually a multimillion-dollar chain," she said, prickling up probably just as Celeste intended.

"You still making cheap bags and thongs?"

"Only the cheapest."

Celeste's beautiful lips that could only be maintained by the grace of God, or the careful and subtle application of collagen on a regular basis, curled into a smile.

"Ruby," Tara said, ignoring Celeste and getting back to the matters of her kingdom. "Does your niece still live in Springfield?"

Ruby nodded, tuna clinging for life to her wide bottom lip.

"Remember last year when she helped me with some fittings? Do you think she could do it again?"

Ruby rolled her eyes. "She made us all crazy for weeks talking about her big modeling break, and three weeks later she was back working doubles at Dairy Queen. I'm sure she'd love to do it. I can call her."

"It's two weeks, not much notice—"

"We'll see." Ruby relaxed back into her seat. "If you want tuna salad, there's more in the fridge."

"No, thank you," Tara said, but her stomach growled in protest. Celeste smirked.

In the kitchen, she filled a bowl and grabbed some grapes and crackers, and then lingered in the quiet room, suffering a strange attack of indecision.

She could go to her room, or back out to the workshop—there was always work to be done. But for some reason the den seemed more appealing. She wasn't invested in the TV show, and Lyle's ex-wife clearly didn't like her. But still, it seemed more interesting than being by herself.

Feeling oddly defiant, she went back into the den and sat in the oversized chair.

By the time the show was over, Tara Jean was fully committed to the young break dancer from Los Angeles, and Ruby had brought out a box of chocolate chip cookies that totally negated the virtuousness of the tuna fish.

But Celeste ate two and it seemed like a party.

The front door slammed open, smashing the encapsulated peace of the den, and Tara Jean leapt out of her chair, her heart in her throat.

"Hello!" Jacob yelled, and Tara crumpled slightly in relief.

Celeste was staring at her, her brilliant eyes missing nothing.

"We're in here!" Celeste yelled, and it sounded as if a

herd of elephants stampeded toward them. Such was the power of one excited kid.

"Hey," Jacob said, charging into the room, his face flushed and his hair askew. His eyes were bright, and Tara Jean smiled in response to the electric joy that radiated out of him like sunshine. She wanted to tilt her head back and bathe in that boy's sunlight.

Luc followed, his eyes finding her right away, and the smile froze on her face. He wore jeans and a gray T-shirt that stretched over his shoulders and flirted with the strong muscles of his chest. The shirt was indecent. The shirt should be arrested.

But his face was a warning flag, tense and lined, as if he were waiting for an outcome that was bad either way.

"Tara Jean," Jacob said, jumping on one foot. "You'll never guess."

She jerked back, surprised that the boy was talking to her.

"Guess what?" she stammered.

"We ran into an old friend of yours," Victoria said, stepping into the room. She looked changed too. Gone was the weariness, replaced by a manic brightness, totally manufactured and slightly scary.

"Hello, Tara Jean," the devil cooed, looking smug and rotten. A cancer in this house.

It was Dennis.

chapter 14

Mr. Beanfang had taught Tara a lesson about security. All of them had, but because Mr. Beanfang was first, he was tattooed into her brain with the ink of shame and regret. God, she'd been a kid, fresh from her sixteenth birthday, though she'd probably been the oldest sixteen-year-old around.

She'd just met Dennis at one of the lowest points in her whole life and he'd seemed like . . . a rainbow. A promise sent from heaven that the bad times were over.

Mr. Beanfang had been Dennis's idea. Dennis had convinced her to take part in his scam because Mr. Beanfang was dying and he was rich and most importantly, he was alone. No one would care who he gave his money away to.

And Mr. Beanfang had so much money it didn't seem to matter. It was as if the dollar bills were litter on his bedside table, his dresser, stuffed into the pockets of his robe. He gave it away to everyone—to the orderlies, the woman who came in to cut his toenails and trim his nose hair.

Those good and honest people tried to refuse, but he insisted.

Tara didn't even try to refuse.

For her entire life she'd equated money with security. But none of Mr. Beanfang's money kept him safe.

That first day when she'd come in pretending to look

for her own grandfather, he'd asked her to sit, told her that she looked like his long dead wife. They'd talked, and when she offered to read him the paper, his big blue eyes went watery and his hands shook with gratitude.

The plan had worked so well it felt like fate. Like God saying it was all right to take some of this man's excess for all the years of nothing she'd had.

He gave her money. Watches. A pearl ring that had belonged to his wife.

And she made him a victim.

Security was a sham. That was Mr. Beanfang's lesson.

Forty percent of a company didn't make Tara Jean secure. Leaving that hospital four years ago, running away from Dennis with a concussion and three broken ribs, an eye so swollen she couldn't see out of it, to come out here with Lyle didn't make her secure.

Money. The apartment with the locks. Changing her name.

None of it had worked.

Staring at Dennis in the TV room of the Crooked Creek Ranch, she realized she hadn't scared away the devil. She'd waved a red flag in front of his eyes.

She'd invited him here with her brave fuck-off.

Fear was a sandstorm obliterating the landscape.

Her ears buzzed while handshakes were exchanged. Friendly greetings. She heard, through the deafening drone of her panic and fear, Dennis talk about being in town on a real-estate business deal.

An old lie. Threadbare and full of holes.

He was desperate, working off the dimming wattage of his smile. His slick suit and finely polished shoes.

A high-gloss patina on a fake.

But the act still played. Even Celeste seemed to be buying it.

And Victoria, Christ—Victoria was eating it up as fast as Dennis could spoon it out.

"Can I talk to you?" It was as if she'd screamed into a tin can—her voice was too loud, too sharp. Everyone stared at her, as though she was the one poisoning the air. "It's been so long," she said with a smooth smile, sliding her arm under Dennis's. Her skin crawled at the touch; her stomach heaved at his nearness.

"Of course," he said, smiling down at her fondly and then back up at the gathered Bakers. "It was a pleasure."

Again, friendly exchanges. Polite and civilized all the way around, and inside Tara was begging for mercy. Finally, she was able to lead him out into the hallway.

"Nice place you got here," he murmured, his eyes missing nothing. Not the paintings or the rugs. He could put price tags on the light fixtures.

She led him out of the house and down the verandah steps, across the yard to the door of the greenhouse.

The gate to her kingdom.

For a moment, she hesitated, unsure of how she could clean this place of him once he'd stepped inside.

But he was here and she had to handle it.

She unlocked the door and flipped on the light, and as soon as he was in the greenhouse, she dropped his arm, getting as far away from him as she could.

"Surprised you, didn't I?" He grinned at her as if he'd brought an unexpected bouquet of flowers instead of ruination.

"What are you doing here?"

"You can't run from me, Jane." He shook his head, as if she were a bad student. He stepped farther into the studio and ran his hands over the cutting table, trailing his fingers across the white leather bustier on the tailor dummy.

Don't look, the demon whispered, the way she used to when one of her boyfriends would trash their trailer. *Don't let yourself see what he touches.*

The weight of his filth, of his malice, turned the air to mud and she couldn't breathe. But she'd stared this man down once; she could do it again.

"We're done, Dennis."

"Well, now, I think my being here changes that, doesn't it?"

It did. It really did.

Because it proved that she wasn't going to be able to sever herself from him without payment. She should have known that to begin with.

"Fine." With hands that shook, she took out her checkbook. The company checkbook, big and black, representative of so much more money than she had, sat under it. She left it there, slamming shut the desk drawer. "I gave ten thousand dollars back to Terry Dickow—"

"I don't want ten grand." He slid toward her like a snail on his own malevolence.

"All I have in my savings is twelve thousand dollars." The closer he got, the harder it was to hide her fear, and she wanted to stand there and be strong, impervious, but when he cleared the corner of her desk she side-stepped.

The moment she moved, he was on her. His hand a clamp around her throat, lifting her chin. His eyes bored into hers and he pushed her against the wall, her head ricocheting off the wall.

"You don't tell me to fuck off. You don't walk away from me."

"Okay. Okay." She clutched his hands, trying to get him to stop.

"You and me, we're never done. Change your name. Move. It doesn't matter." He leaned close, his chin grazing her neck, and she swallowed a whimper. "I could smell you, Jane. A hundred miles away. In jail. At night. I could taste you."

She swallowed back bile and shut her eyes, gathering her forces as best she could.

"How much . . . how much money, Dennis?"

"Two hundred thousand dollars."

Her eyes flew open. "What?"

He squeezed her throat, shook her, like she was a rag doll and he was a dinosaur. Stupid theory about holding her own in a fight with smaller men. She was just so stupid sometimes.

"Two hundred," he cooed in her face, leaning forward so his breath spilled like a minty-fresh garbage dump over her mouth.

"Or what?" she spat.

This was how she'd ended up in the hospital. He could beat her, but he couldn't break her. She could fight. So she would.

He stepped closer until his body pressed against hers and she could feel his erection, like a knife against her stomach.

The fear became so dense, so all-encompassing, that she was suddenly lifted free of it, carried on the painless wings of shock.

"I don't have two hundred thousand dollars," she said. "Rape me. Beat me. That won't change."

"But you can get it." That anger in his eyes changed to triumph. Dennis wasn't stupid. He was mean as a snake and evil down to his toes, but he was smart. And looking at him, she knew she was suddenly in more trouble than she'd ever been in before. "Look at this place. You could probably get more."

"I'm an employee, Dennis. I don't own—" He got back in her face and she licked her dry lips with a drier tongue.

"Remember my friend Carl?" Terrified, she nodded. Carl was the man who'd beat her up alongside Dennis. The man who did the hard work Dennis didn't have the stomach for. "He asks about you. Wouldn't mind seeing you again. How would you like that?"

Terror pushed her down new roads, roads she'd been too scared and selfish to use before, but things were getting critical.

"How would you like it if I went to the cops? Because I'll do it, Dennis. I swear I will."

"Look at you and your empty threats." His patronizing smile made her sick. "You know, you're just a kid, so I'll explain something to you. What you did to those old men, it's called fraud. And you go to the cops and you'll have to tell them what you did, and they will put you away, Jane. And a woman like you in jail . . ." He whistled long and low, pushing that erection against her. "What those women will do to you? It will make you wish for me. So, cut that crap. You're a coward, Jane. Deep down, you're chicken shit. You couldn't tell your mama when you were in trouble when you were a kid; you couldn't say no to me, even though you pretended you wanted to. And you're not going to risk your own neck to put me away. Now, get back to reality."

His thumb stroked the hammering pulse in her throat and then, as she held out, staring him in the eye, he pressed hard on that pulse. Her vision went sparkly at the edges, her head light, but still she dared him to take it one step further, because she didn't want to be the woman he'd just described.

"Look at you," he sighed, smiling slightly. "So tough. I swear, Jane, you ask for it. If you'd just lie down like a good dog—"

But in the end, she was exactly who he said she was. A coward, selfish and greedy. Because she was too scared to risk her freedom just to put him away. Conceding, she looked away, sagging against the wall where he'd pushed her.

"That's what I thought. So, Jane, as I was saying, two hundred thousand dollars."

"Or what?"

"Or . . . I do to Victoria what you did to all those little old men."

"She has nothing, Dennis," she said, frantically trying to change the course of this particular river. "Not a single penny. And no access to any, not for a long time, and she wouldn't give it to you anyway. Not with her son . . ." She stopped. Bringing Jacob into this situation, even by saying his name, felt vile. "Leave them alone."

"I will," Dennis said. "If you get me that money."

She swallowed, silent. The scales were so heavy in both directions she felt that she might collapse.

"Seems to me Victoria might just need a friend like me. A man who can make her feel like a woman again. You remember, don't you, how grateful those old men were—"

"I never touched them," she snapped. "Not once. Not ever."

"Well, Victoria is different, isn't she? She'd probably be so damn grateful she'd give me whatever she had, and maybe whatever her brother has too."

"Stop it!" The scales finally tipped, bringing her to her knees. "Just stop it, fine. I'll get you the two hundred thousand. But . . . I'll need some time."

He stepped away and she took a deep breath. Another.

"Not too much," he said, pulling the white cuff of his shirt past his jacket.

"How . . . do I find you?"

His grin made her skin crawl. "I'll be around."

"Leave this family alone, Dennis. They're good people. They have nothing to do with us."

For a moment the threat vanished, and she saw the glimmer of the boy she'd known. Misguided and greedy, but deep inside that thin chest had once beat a heart.

"Then why'd you come here?" he asked.

She had no answer. Guilt closed her throat and she rocked back, light-headed with remorse.

Luc wasn't sleeping when someone knocked on his door. He was staring out the window and thinking of Tara Jean's expression when Jacob had talked to her in the den. The mixture of wonder and fear on her face. It had been beautiful and real, and it had dredged up another thousand questions about the woman.

Questions, no matter what his better sense was screaming, that he really wanted answered.

The knock on the door shook him out of his thoughts and he was glad to have the distraction.

And even gladder to see Tara Jean standing there, looking as if she'd covered herself in armor and was about to drive into battle.

"Well, Tara Jean." He leaned against the doorjamb and her blue eyes slipped down his bare chest like a kid on a water slide. "What can I do for you?" He checked his watch. "At midnight?"

"I need to talk to you." Her eyes—naked and exposed—lifted to his and as tough as she wanted to be, as thick as that armor went, there was no pretense. No game.

She was a woman, smart and tough, and there was something wrong. Something that had driven her to his door at midnight. His instincts whispered that this had something to do with Dennis.

A little too slick, that Dennis guy.

"Okay," he said. "Everything all right?"

"Meet me in the kitchen," she said, her eyes dipping over him again. "And bring a shirt."

* * *

A few minutes later he walked into the dark kitchen, illuminated only by the bone-white glow of the moon through the windows. Tara Jean sat on the center island, eating ice cream right out of the carton.

"Where's your shirt?" she asked through a mouthful of rocky road.

He shrugged, not wanting to tell her that he liked her eyes on him. That he wanted more of it, more of her. And that, really, she wasn't the boss of him. He could come into the kitchen naked if he wanted.

"You want to tell me what's wrong?" He leaned against the counter directly across from her, stretching out his legs. She swung her feet and her bare toes brushed his knees. Both of them shifted away, as if this attraction between them was an unpredictable animal that needed lots of space.

She took a bite of ice cream and then another.

"Is this about that Dennis guy?"

The spoon paused on its way back to the carton.

"Why would you think that?"

"I don't know." He watched her carefully, waiting for an answer to one of his many questions. "Just a vibe."

"How did he even hook up with you tonight?"

"I have no idea. I met Jacob and Victoria after my workout and he was with them."

She coughed as if the ice cream had gone down the wrong pipe, and he reached over and slapped her on the back. She scowled at him.

He was getting fond of the hedgehog.

"Do I need to worry about my sister and nephew?" he asked softly, feeling her ribs beneath his hands.

She didn't shrug away from his touch, so he stroked her shoulder, sensing she needed a little human comfort. "No, you don't need to worry. Dennis and I have some old business to take care of, that's all. He doesn't have anything to do with Victoria and Jacob."

"All right." He leaned back against the counter and crossed his arms over his chest. "Then how about you tell me why you've dragged me to the kitchen in the middle of the night."

"How much would I make if we sold Baker Leather?"

"I thought you didn't want to do that."

"I don't," she said and then laughed. "I don't. I just . . . I just want to know."

"Jenkins said your profits are good and growing. According to him, maybe as much as a million. Probably less."

"A million?" The carton of ice cream slipped off her knee and he reached out and grabbed it. Standing so close to her in the moonlight was a heady torture, but the anxiety rolling off her was palpable. He stepped back, giving her some room. He fished a spoon out of the drawer and picked up where she'd left off with the rocky road.

"Why? You need the money?"

She was quiet, staring down at her knees, the dark denim stretched over her legs.

"Tara?"

"I'm thinking." Her hair fell over her shoulders, a beautiful curtain that gleamed white in the moonlight. He ate silently, letting her think, wondering what was wrong and if she'd ever tell him.

"Okay," she finally said and then lifted her head, tossing back her hair. Her smile was bright, blinding, but her eyes were calculating, measuring every angle. Looking for every escape route.

The smile was a flash, a distraction, to hide how smart she was.

Clever girl.

"You know my salary," she said and he nodded, scooping up another bite of ice cream. "And you know

I haven't had a raise in four years, despite what I've done for the company—"

"You can have a raise," he said. "I don't care."

"I don't want a raise," she said, and then shook her head. "No, I mean, yes, a raise would be great; we can talk about that later. But what I need . . . what I want is a bonus."

"A bonus?" he asked.

"Yep."

"For what?"

Her eyebrows knit together and he smiled in the face of her irritation. "I got a bonus when I led my team to the Stanley Cup finals. And when I won the Rocket Richard trophy. Twice. I got a new car when I was named league MVP. I understand bonuses; they come after you do something to earn them."

"Fine," she said and sighed heavily through her nose. "In two months I have a meeting with the District Four buyer for Nordstrom."

"Sounds exciting."

"It is, because if the meeting goes well, Nordstrom will carry the Baker Leather signature women's pink cowboy boot in stores all across Texas and Oklahoma."

He hummed and dug for more peanuts. He wondered if he'd ever get a crack at the Rocket Richard trophy again. Lashenko had won it this year. What a year that would be—thirty-eight years old, Stanley Cup, and the highest number of goals scored. Had anybody done that before?

"Come on." She yanked the carton out of his hands. "Listen."

"I'm listening. You want a bonus if this meeting goes well. Sounds reasonable to me."

"Two hundred thousand dollars."

He blinked at her and then shrugged. "Okay."

She tried to hide her surprise at his quick capitulation,

but she was caught flat-footed for a second. He loved that. Surprising her wasn't easy.

"Okay?"

"I told you, Tara Jean, I don't care about this company. But I know you do. Do you think getting the boot into Nordstrom is worth two hundred thousand dollars?"

She nodded.

He wondered briefly about the bravado of a woman who never took a raise and had such problems asking for money in return for hard work.

"Do you think you're worth two hundred thousand dollars?"

"What the hell does that mean?"

"I'm just wondering why you have so much trouble asking for what you're due. What you've earned."

She picked up the ice-cream carton. "I haven't earned it yet."

"But you turned the company around. It was bankrupt and now it's thriving. Even growing. That's worth something, Tara."

"Fine. Give me a raise."

Her back was up and this wasn't what he wanted. He wanted to talk to that honest, vulnerable woman he'd glimpsed a few times, beneath the glamour and the hard candy shell.

He wanted to tell her that he saw the worth in her. The power and value.

He reached out and touched her, his fingers glancing off the skin of her wrist.

As if he'd held a match to her skin, she jerked away from him, jumping to her feet.

"Sex does not determine my worth," she barked, and he saw that something had snapped in her and there was a river, wild and rushing the banks, raging right toward him. "These," she crudely cupped her breasts, "do not determine my worth. This," she ran a hand over her body, "does not determine my worth."

"Then what does?"

"Me!" She was panting, heavy and hard, and he leaned forward, felt the heat of her breath on his face.

"Then do it."

"Like it's that easy?" He could tell she wanted to sneer, hold on to her sarcasm, like the last piece of driftwood keeping her afloat, but the question came out plaintive.

"My dad told me I was worthless my whole life," he said. "Beat it, and I mean *beat it*, into me. Into my sister. We weren't good with horses or cows. We weren't fit to be Bakers." He rubbed a hand over his face, down his chest, wishing, too late, that he had put a shirt on. "And I . . . I believed him for a long time. Your dad tells you something like that and you believe it. But then, I found hockey and I was good at it."

"And that determined your worth?"

The question blew him sideways for a second, but he shook his head. "No, I did. I worked hard. Harder than anyone else."

"I work hard," she said, and he nodded.

"It takes guts to be good at something. Confidence that you know you can do it. It's not enough that I sweat through the workouts, that I train harder than anyone else. I have to work through the sprains and shake off the bad hits. I have to ignore the slumps and the off nights, and I can't let all the damn parasites get in my head with their endless chatter about how old I am. I can't listen to the doctors who tell me to retire. I can't give in to the fear that everyone is right. I have to believe in my worth. In what I am."

She put a hand on his arm and he realized he'd gotten lost in his own head. "I'm not trying to take hockey away from you."

He looked over at her, her lithe body propped up against the counter, her legs crossed at the ankles, and suddenly he was ashamed by the way he'd been treating her. As if she were there for his amusement, his sarcasm, anger, and junior-high-style seductions.

"And I'm not trying to take your worth from you." He wished he could touch her. Take away the sting of every hurtful thing he'd said. But that would negate everything she needed to believe. "You're so beautiful."

"Luc," she admonished, but he shook his head.

"I'm not talking about your body, or the way you dress. I'm talking about *you.* You're smart and you're tough and I don't know a thing about you, but I'm guessing life hasn't always been easy."

The tension in her rippled through the air like heat waves off Texas asphalt. She wanted to run, it was obvious, but she didn't. Instead, almost imperceptibly, she nodded.

"The way I've acted—"

"Don't worry," she breathed, waving him off, but he caught her hand, felt the fine bones of her wrists and fingers, relished the heat of her skin, and then he dropped it.

"No, demanding you kiss me, talking to you the way I have . . . it's crap, Tara, and I'm sorry. I would never have acted that way if I hadn't been sure you were as interested as I was, but that's a pretty shitty excuse and I'm sorry."

The sentence hung there. She didn't accept his apology, which frankly was her prerogative. And she didn't confirm or deny her interest. She just stood there in the moonlight, so beautiful he ached.

He found the lid to the ice cream and pressed it back on and then he took the three steps to the freezer to put it away. But still she didn't say anything.

He couldn't force her to talk. To accept his apology.

"Good night, Tara," he said.

He was walking away. The gorgeous slope of his back gleamed in the moonlight like silver and he was *walking away.*

She'd pushed a hundred guys away, watched dozens of men retreat from her barbs and her land mines. She should be celebrating, because Luc had been a difficult man to dissuade, but now, watching him go did something inside of her. Something lonely and cold, shivering in isolation, wailed a protest.

It had been a long time since a man had seen past the act, pushed aside the curtain to see the person she kept hidden. And he seemed to want her more for her reality.

And that was great and all, but standing in the dark kitchen, she *wanted* him.

She wanted something that she'd lost. Something that had been taken away from her a million times.

Her power.

The power this man made her feel, long after she'd thought she'd never feel it again.

"I'm interested," she blurted.

Inwardly, she shrank. Inwardly, she freaked right out.

What the hell am I doing?

But her mouth wouldn't stop talking and the loneliest part of her was steering the ship.

"I'm interested."

His smile illuminated the sharp planes of his face, creating softness where she'd never seen it. He was happy, she realized, feeling as if her chest might explode from the combustible nature of every single conflicting emotion at work.

But Luc . . . Luc was boyish in his happiness. Sweet. And it took her breath away. She closed the distance between them, wishing his happiness might seep under her skin, set off a similar reaction in her.

"I'm glad." His fingers traced her eyebrows, the curl of her ear. Tenderly, he kissed her lips, sending her sighing into a hot internal place.

"Good night, Tara." He stepped back and that hot internal place was doused.

"What . . . what are you doing?"

"Going to bed. I'm thinking it might be better if we didn't . . . act on this interest right now."

"Better for who?"

"Both of us. Look, Tara, it's not easy to walk away right now, but it's not like we started this on the right foot. I'd like to . . . I don't know . . . take you on a date or something."

"No." She didn't want to date. She wanted to feel good. She wanted that happiness on his face to rub off on her. Now. Right now. Banishing every scent of Dennis on her skin.

"Now?"

She nodded.

"Really?" His voice all but cracked, and she smiled as she stepped toward him.

"Really." Slowly, she put her fingers on his arm, her body rejoicing in his heat. His strength and life. She spread out her hand, covering as much of his skin as possible.

He's so big, she thought, excited by his size. His power.

He ran his hands over her hair, down the strong lines of her back, and she curled under his touch, a flower seeking sunshine.

"I was told I was worthless too," she said, the words sticky in her mouth. But she'd opened the door and suddenly, with this man, she wanted to go through it. "My whole life. My mom. My mom's boyfriends. I grew up in a trailer on the wrong side of every track in the world.

And then I got breasts. And hips. And suddenly I wasn't worthless anymore. I had something people wanted."

"How old were you?"

Nothing about him conveyed pity. He was nothing but stalwart understanding and sympathy, and her heart swelled. "Twelve."

"Tara—"

"They're just breasts, Luc." She smiled, but it didn't quite cover up the old pain like it used to, so she looked away, smoothing her hand down his chest.

The kitchen was quiet; the sound of his breathing and the echo of her blood pounding in her ears were all she heard.

"I don't know why you're doing this," he whispered. "And part of me doesn't care. But I have to know it's for the right reasons. I would hate . . . I would hate to take advantage of you and not know it. So you need to tell me, Tara. Why?"

"Sex stopped being fun for me a long time ago," she said. "So I stopped having it."

"That's a shame. Sex should always be fun."

Her eyes perused the muscles of his chest, deciding where to start. Her fingers, long and delicate, followed. Skating across his collarbones, down the rounded curve of his pecs. Muscles and nerves twitched under her touch. She dipped down to the hard plain of his breastbone to his abs, her fingers riding the ridges of muscle until she landed at the waistband of his shorts.

He shook beneath her touch and she delighted in it. Was empowered.

"I'll bet it is with you." She lifted her fingers, pausing, smiling at his torture, and then started the downward path all over again at his shoulder. His breath hitched in his lungs as she found the small valley between his deltoid and bicep, and the muscles flexed and jumped.

"Is that what this is?" he asked. "You want to have fun?"

"Is that wrong?"

"No, but I don't think it's the whole truth."

"Maybe that's the only truth I'm going to tell you," she said. His laughter stroked her, feathered her hair, and his hand followed.

"Is it about the bonus?"

"No." That line was drawn in concrete. "It's about me. It's about wanting something and taking it. It's about being tired of being alone and cold and untouched. It's about feeling something good after a long, long time of feeling nothing."

Slowly he nodded, his hands stroking her hair, the line of her back, and then they slipped to his side. He stood in front of her, a mountain of strength that he would never use against her.

"I'm whatever you need, Tara," he breathed. "Take what you want."

chapter 15

Eve's dilemma with that apple suddenly made sense to Tara Jean in a whole new way. Here was Luc, a bad idea on so many levels, but tempting on just as many.

And all that strength she used to have, all that denial and restraint that had lived at her fingertips for the last four years, were nowhere to be found.

Hunger, selfish and horny, was running the show.

And Luc, in the moonlight, against the fridge, his hands in fists at his side as if they were going to engage in a little bondage, looked like a particularly juicy apple.

Yep, she totally sympathized with Eve.

Slowly, she leaned against him. Her chest and stomach met his in a hundred little delicious soft spots, her arms slipped over his shoulders, her lips hovered over his like a honeybee.

"Tara," he breathed, his lips curling into one of the most pained smiles she'd ever seen.

Poor man, she thought and carefully, as if either of them might break at the contact, she put her lips to his.

She tilted her head, opened her lips, and tasted him. The sweet corner of his lips where chocolate lingered. His salty upper lip, where he was sweating despite the cool air conditioning.

His mouth opened and she tasted his tongue, chocolate and toothpaste and something else. Something Luc, and it was sweeter even than the ice cream. And deeply, wickedly spicy.

She stepped closer, her hips finding the cradle of his, and he jerked against her, his hands lifting for a second. She held her breath, wondering where those hands would fall, waiting for his touch with electric anticipation.

But then he put his hands back to his sides, his muscles tight and hard beneath her touch. It seemed like he had taken all her restraint—made it his own.

She lifted her head, drawing out the kiss as long as she could, sucking on his tongue, feeling him grow harder and hotter against her belly.

It was gonna be good, whatever was coming her way, it was going to be very, very good.

"You gonna touch me?" She looked into his hooded eyes, rubbed the silk of his hair between her fingers.

"You want me to?"

She smiled, feeling coy. Feeling girlish and wise at the same time, and it was exhilarating. "It would be nice."

"I . . . I don't want to do anything you don't want."

A gentleman, honestly. She was sucking his tongue, pressing the seam of her jeans as hard as she could against the impressive erection she felt beneath those workout shorts. Most men of her acquaintance wouldn't be waiting for anything as mundane as permission. They probably wouldn't even wait to take their pants off.

That's why he's special, she thought. *That's why you can't resist him anymore.*

Somehow, one of the good guys had wandered onto this ranch. Into her arms.

Which only meant, in the end, that he was even more rare and extraordinary. More forbidden.

Because she'd not once in her life done anything to deserve a good guy.

This was her moment with the apple. And she was going to take a bite.

"There's nothing I don't want right now," she whispered. "Touch me."

He growled and came off the fridge like a freight train. On a lesser man, the growl would have been ridiculous. But on him it fit, and her body organized a cheerleading squad in his honor. He lifted her as if she were weightless, his hands cupping her butt, sliding her onto the tiled island in the middle of the kitchen.

His fingers, nimble and light, climbed her ribs, stroking the skin beneath the thin pink T-shirt she wore. The hidden switch in her neck that controlled every bell and whistle in her body—the ones she knew about and the ones she'd never dreamed she had—he found with his full lips, his clever tongue. She shook against him, every pleasure receptor thrown open. She put her hands on his face, her fingers gripping his hair until he lifted his head and she kissed him.

She kissed him as if she wanted to swallow him. Eat him alive. He was pleasure, he was bliss and joy, and she'd forgotten how much she loved this dark thrill, how good it made her feel. How sex could push away everything that was wrong, everything she didn't want to deal with.

She could wallow in sex, swim in its eddies for days. Ignore the problems and mistakes that were growing like weeds in her life. And she could do that now. Luc could make her forget Dennis and the money and his threats about Victoria. He could make her forget how alone she was. How scared she was of failing. How success felt like something that happened to other people. Not to her. Never to her.

"Hey," he breathed, pulling away. "What's the rush?"

The fire was out of control in her body, her head was spinning with desire, and she felt the way she used to, years ago, as though this heat, this pleasure, was all she had. The only thing she had to give. The only thing that gave her worth.

For a moment she froze.

I am not that woman anymore, she thought. *I don't want to be that woman.* She'd worked hard to put Jane behind her.

Mistakes, a thousand mistakes littered her past, brought to bear usually because she'd decided to be selfish. Lazy. Trust some man because he made her feel good. Wanted.

This is a mistake, she thought.

"Tara?" Luc whispered, his lips feathering across her cheeks.

She didn't say anything and he blinked up at her, shifting backward, taking his heat away from her, and she tightened her legs around his hips to stop him. Her body speaking for her.

"You all right?" he asked, smoothing her hair back off her face, leaving her bare and revealed.

He was so beautiful and so ready to step away and she realized, all that power that had been taken away from her—half the time she'd tossed it away. Handed it out like it was nothing.

She deserved the pleasure as much as she deserved the power. It was a matter of balance, of living in the space between reckless and alone. And there was plenty of space there. She could build a house.

"I'm good," she said. Tonight, she had no interest in being alone. And being with Luc wasn't reckless. This moment established the balance. Stepping into this place, this considered and adult place, felt wildly different. It was as if she'd suddenly grown new skin. Or was wearing someone else's. "I'm really good. Kiss me." His grin was wicked and those devilish lips pressed a chaste kiss to her cheek. The corner of her lips. He leaned down and kissed the dip between her collarbones. His lips seared her skin, cauterizing any thoughts of the past.

And then he licked her, leaving a trail of sparks across her skin, the tops of her breasts.

Sweat ran down his chest, onto hers, making her shirt stick to both of them.

His fingers traced the lace edge of her bra, as if scouting foreign boundaries. She opened her mouth against his neck, tasting the salt, testing the skin with her teeth, begging him to touch her, to slide that hand against her breast. Waiting, she breathed him in. His eyes met hers and the moment filled with a thousand pleasures. The heat of his hand slipped past the silk of her bra, his thumb caught the edge of her nipple, pulling it, and she gasped, caught in the web between pleasure and pain.

Her heartbeat pounded between her legs and she arched hard against him, all those years of celibacy suddenly making her frantic with expectation.

The seam of her jeans hit her just right and she shook, desire's edge turning sharp.

"Come on," she breathed, slipping her fingertips under the elastic waist at the back of his shorts, pulling him harder against her. His skin there was so smooth and she spread her hands wide to feel as much of it as she could.

She didn't have time to wait for him to get around to what she needed. Knowing Luc, he'd toy with her until she lost her mind, and she already had a head start on that. She took his hand and slid it down the trembling muscles of her belly to the button on her jeans.

"This is what I want," she whispered. "Make me come."

"Oh God, Tara," he groaned and curled over her, his body a protective shell they lived in, the world outside of no interest. His fingers made quick work of the button and zipper. She dropped her legs from around his waist and arched her hips, helping him find his way into the tight wedge between her pants and skin. His forehead pressed hard against hers and two callused fingers slipped through the curls between her legs. She was stretched taut between his forehead and his fingers, a bow ready to be released, and when his fingers found the tight knot of her clitoris she jerked and hummed, her hands clutching at his skin, her mouth open against his neck.

"Yes," she whispered. "Yes, yes, yes." A hundred times she sighed against him, an incantation to pleasure. Her hips jerked as he found a rhythm, and the pleasure was so sharp it hurt and it had been so long.

So long.

She twitched, trying to get closer and get away at the same time.

Nerves all along her feet and up her legs, across her hips, circling her breasts, heated and the sensation was too much. Too much to take, and she grabbed his hand.

"I . . ." She looked up at him through sweaty bangs and forgot what she was going to say. Stop? Was she nuts?

"Too much?" he breathed.

She nodded, feeling foolish and so turned on she couldn't think. His lip curled.

"Let's try this." He picked her up from the island and set her on her feet. Slowly he turned her so her back was braced against his chest and her hands were spread wide against the colorful Mexican tiles of the island that was still warm from the heat of her body.

His hands slid over her hips, pushing her jeans and her silky pink underwear down to her knees. His hands ran back up to her thighs, the curves of her butt. The pleasure returned, a great wave of it, but without the jagged edges. It just lifted her up and when he pressed against her back with the heat of his chest, she leaned forward, her head hanging in surrender.

Her hair slipped over her cheeks, a curtain shielding her from the night, the kitchen, the mistakes she was undoubtedly making.

But his breath was a hot wind at the back of her neck.

Again, she felt his fingers between her legs, but he slipped right past the knot of nerves that were too sensitive, to the deep well of her body. His finger slid in and she sagged, caught between him and the countertop, so supported she didn't even need her legs.

Couldn't even feel them, really.

"You're so wet, Tara Jean. So hot. I can't wait to taste you."

She cried out at his words, and he put teeth to her neck and she writhed against him.

Another finger joined the first.

Retreated. Surged forward. He lifted her up, holding her tummy in his giant hand so his fingers could get deeper. His thumb grazed her clitoris and she shattered, exploded against his body, and still he kept at her, working her, his fingers finding darker spots, secret places where pleasure was just waiting for someone to find it.

She exploded again, feeling as if her body wasn't even hers. Wouldn't be hers ever again. Not the way she knew it. Her skin evaporated and her body flew apart and he didn't give her a chance to pull herself together, to keep herself in line. There had to be restrictions . . . limits to this pleasure, to what she'd let him do to her.

But he didn't seem to understand that. His hand slipped up from her stomach to her breasts, his touch so soft it barely registered in the explosion of pleasure. As if he knew that, as if he were inside her body, he squeezed, he found her nipple and pulled. Sharp and hot, the pleasure started again, a steep incline she had no control over.

"Luc." She heard the tangled trepidation in her own voice and hated it.

"Shhhh," he breathed against her hair. "Let me make you feel good. Like you wanted. One more time, Tara."

He spun her, shifted her, and then, before she could stop him, before she could close her eyes and block out the sight, this big, beautiful man was on his knees in front of her.

His tongue, his fingers, the soft suction of his lips.

She shook her head, the edge coming, the bright expanse on the horizon rushing closer. She lifted her legs, shifted her back, trying to keep a hold of herself, to dull the pleasure to a level she knew, one she was comfortable with. But he controlled her every string like a puppet master.

"I got you, Tara," he whispered against the electric pulsing center of her body. "I got you. You're safe."

Safe? Was he nuts? She opened her mouth to tell him he couldn't keep her safe. Not really. For her there was no such thing as safe. But he sucked on the hard edge of her clitoris and she shattered.

"Oh!" she yelled and he stood, lifted his hand to cover her mouth. "Oh my God!" The words were muffled against his palm and she tasted the salt of his skin, felt the rough calluses against her tongue, and the sensations grounded her, helped her find the long way back to herself.

In the silence of the kitchen the refrigerator kicked on and she jumped as if a gun had gone off. Despite the languor that floated along her bloodstream, induced by his fingers, his touch and kiss, she turned herself away from him.

His fingers slipped out of her body, and she twitched at their exit. They left a damp trail across her hips and she shook at the earthy reminder.

"You all right?" His breath ruffled the hair at her temple. He stood behind her, a solid wall to rest against, not that she did. Instead she held herself stiff in the cage of his arms, keeping her distance, too late of course, but she tried.

All right? she thought and the answer from every part of her body was no. Absolutely not.

Finally, she stepped sideways, her chest heaving, her skin twitching. His fingertips danced over her shoulder, the skin of her neck where her T-shirt had been pulled aside.

She wanted to go home. That was the result of all that pleasure. She wanted to leave him, without a word. Without turning around to see his face.

She was raw. Far too raw to turn and flirt and take off her clothes. Tara Jean Sweet couldn't keep up the pretense. Wasn't even sure in this moment what was real and what was part of the act.

Hilarious how adult she'd felt just minutes ago. Reasonable. As though she could handle whatever he was going to do to her because she said so. She was tough. She'd seen every side of the sex coin.

Another one of my stupid theories, she thought.

Because she'd never seen this coming.

Time stretched on and she couldn't find the courage to face him. To face what they'd done. As if he could read her regrets and misgivings written on the bones of her shoulder, just under the thin skin he touched, he took his hand away.

She closed her eyes.

Gently, he pulled up her underwear and then her pants, and the gesture was so tender, tears clogged the back of her throat.

She was lying to him. About Dennis. About who she was.

And right now, picking herself up from the shattered remains of her act, of the game she played, raw and twitching in the sunlight of all that pleasure, she wasn't even sure who she was.

She heard him shift, felt the air between them cool as he stepped away on bare feet.

"Go." His voice rough and deep and full of reproach and worry and a thousand other things she didn't want to turn and see on his face.

She slid past him and ran out of the kitchen.

Sweat burned Luc's eyes, and cold air froze his lungs. His legs were putty on his skates, his ankles wobbly. Stars sparkled in the corner of his eyes, obliterating the boards in his periphery. But still he worked. He worked. Leg over leg, skating in a line, he shifted backwards. The puck was on a string and the net went by in a blur; still backwards he skated toward center ice. At the crease he spun, lifted the stick, an extension of his arm, his hips—his goddamned dick.

The puck was a rocket, snagged by the high left corner of the net.

He retrieved it. Leg over leg, backwards again.

The sparkles gathered force in the corners of his vision, grew teeth, grew ugly. His head swam, distanced, suddenly from the rest of him. And his legs slowed, his heart lurched.

The boards covered with ads for a local used-car dealership were close and then unexpectedly closer. And then he was in them, hips first. And his stomach was in his throat.

He dropped his stick, shook off his gloves, and pawed at his chin strap—God, he couldn't breathe. Couldn't even see past the blinding wall of shine in front of his face.

His head hurt so bad he felt it in his knees. He braced himself against the boards.

"You all right?" The voice belonged to a kid, probably the same kid Luc had noticed sitting up in the bleachers, watching his workouts. He had a fairly good idea the kid was Randy's, and since he never got in the way, only watched, Luc didn't bother to say anything.

"Luc?"

"Fine," he said, though he knew that he wasn't, not really.

"You—"

Luc pushed off the boards, skating away from the kid.

Twenty minutes later, exhausted, his blood still pumping hard in his veins, he stepped into the private shower the manager let him use and cranked on the hot water.

Tara Jean was still taking up center ice in his head and that workout hadn't done anything to take the edge off his hunger for her. The all-consuming, totally humbling desire he had for a woman who had walked away from him.

"Get it together, Luc," he muttered and grabbed the soap from the ledge. Hot water hit the tiles and erupted in steam, and soon the shower was more like a steam bath and he couldn't see his feet. His legs.

He turned to face the water, letting the jets hit the sorest of the muscles in his chest, the tops of his shoulders. It ran down his back, over his ass and legs. Tilting his head back, he closed his eyes and let the water pour over his face. In the dark and the heat, his body hungry, he thought of Tara. The silk of her skin, the perfect weight of her breasts. He thought about the slow suction of her body, the tangy sweet taste of her.

His hand . . . no, he'd go with *her* hand, soapy and wet, sliding down his stomach, the muscles of his abs, top of his thigh. Part of him felt ridiculous, like a sick sixteen-year-old kid who didn't have any other outlet. But the rest of him just wanted some relief.

Just wanted Tara.

Giving into the fantasy, he cupped the heavy weight

of his sac, the thick stalk of his dick, and found his rhythm. Gathering speed and steam, imagining Tara Jean's hands, her breasts. Imagining her on her knees in front of him. Imagining the sensation of driving into her, her mouth, her body.

It was good. So good.

He bit his lip, stroked harder, held himself out, made himself work. But all good things had to end, and he groaned into his bicep where he'd rested it against the wall and ejaculated into the mist. Panting, he rinsed off his hand and wrestled with how hollow he felt. How sometimes masturbation turned the dial way up on his loneliness.

He turned off the water and opened the glass door, letting the cold air smother the steam and raise goose bumps across his skin.

If Tara had her way, this was the closest he'd ever get to her again.

And he couldn't let that happen.

Monday morning, things weren't going well for Tara. She hadn't slept well for the past two nights, her body too aware that the source of all that pleasure was under the same roof. Like some kind of divining rod, she vibrated all night.

Finally at dawn, she couldn't take it anymore and she dragged herself, exhausted and stressed, out of bed. She stood in front of her closet in a state of total apathy. Too hot for leather. Or jeans. She wasn't in the mood for anything tight. Or boobylicious. Finally, from the back, she pulled a knee-length pale blue linen skirt with a sleeveless white wrap top.

Are you a nun? the demon asked, and Tara thought the idea had merit.

She passed Eli in front of the coffeemaker. He poured her a cup of coffee and pushed the sugar bowl her way.

"You all right?"

"Why?"

He shrugged. "You seem . . . edgy."

Edgy like a Ginsu knife; she could chew through a tin can without a problem.

"I'm fine," she grunted, and added three heaping teaspoons of sugar to her coffee. Eli chuckled and like a smart man, went on his way.

Outside, the humidity slapped her like a damp washcloth and her mood sunk even lower; the walk to the greenhouse felt like slogging through mud.

The message light on her phone flashed and for some reason, the nature of its blinking seemed foreboding. Malevolent.

That's just your mood, she told herself, but she wasted no time dialing her service.

"Hi, Tara Jean, this is Claire Hughes." Tara's stomach tied itself into a dozen little knots. Claire Hughes was the buyer for Nordstrom. "I just heard about Lyle's death, I'm so sorry. Please give me a call to discuss what this means for our meeting."

What this means? she thought, staring down into the little holes on the receiver as if they might be able to translate the vaguely discouraging nature of that message. *What this means?*

It wasn't possible that the Nordstrom deal was going to go south. There was no way. She thought of Dennis, of his hand around her throat.

Victoria.

Christ, Jacob.

The blood roared in her ears as she quickly dialed Claire's number.

"Come on," she breathed as the phone rang. It clicked,

and she smiled broadly, as if Claire were standing right in front of her.

"Hi, this is Tara—"

"You've reached the voice mail box of Claire Hughes. I will be out of the office until Friday, June twelfth. Please leave a message and I'll return your call as soon as possible."

"Fuck!" she cried, just before the beep.

"Hi there, Claire," she said after the beep. For some reason she let her accent have full rein when talking to Claire. She sounded as Southern as catfish when dealing with the woman. Actually, she sounded like her own momma.

That's right, the demon purred. *Everyone loves a little sugar.*

"This is Tara Jean Sweet. I just got your message and I wanted to reassure you that Lyle's death in no way changes our plans for working with you and Nordstrom. I am very much looking forward to meeting you at the end of July."

Tara Jean hung up and took a big breath. "Nothing you can do about it, Tara," she whispered, a sad little pep talk. "Not one goddamned thing."

Tired already, she picked up her coffee and sat down in her chair.

Which erupted in wild, juicy fart noises.

She jerked upright and her coffee, hot and staining, splashed all over her white top.

"What the hell!" she cried, turning to see the plastic bladder on the seat. "A whoopee cushion?"

From the far end of the greenhouse, under the cutting table in the darkest shadows, she heard a muffled giggle.

Oh no, she thought, picking up the toy. *No freaking way! Not the kid on top of everything else.*

She stomped down the center aisle, fanning her ruined shirt away from the scalded skin beneath it until she got to the table. She waited a second, and in the silence she heard the faint wheeze of an inhaler.

She crouched, and there in the darkness she saw a flash of pale skin, a cheek, and one big wide eye before the boy shifted back into the shadows, rustling paper as he went.

"I can hear you, you know," she sighed.

Another thump and a box fell forward, spilling empty Starburst wrappers over her feet.

Son of a bitch!

"Hi." His fingers lifted in a little wave.

"Get the hell out of there."

He crawled out, knocking over another box as he went. Zippers flew everywhere.

"You think this is funny?" She shook the whoopee cushion at him.

"Uh . . . yeah?"

"Well, it's not. What if I had sat down while I was on the phone?"

The boy had the good sense to wince. "I guess that wouldn't have been funny."

"No, it wouldn't have. And you've been eating my candy."

"I got hungry," he whispered. He took a quick puff off his inhaler and she refused to listen to the voices in her head screaming "bully!"

"Where's your momma?" she asked.

"Probably looking for me."

"Well, let's go find her."

"But you know, I was thinking, maybe I could help you around here or something. I could . . ." He shrugged, looking like an earnest dark-haired Opie. "Do whatever you needed. Clean up, or—"

"I don't need any help around here," she said, cold as ice.

"Oh. You sure? Because I really hate dance classes."

His smile, lopsided and toothy, was endearing. More endearing actually than she could stand, the way he stood there with his young, new heart right there on his face, and she wanted to wrap her arms around him, hold him close, protect that tender heart from the dangers of the world. Dangers like her.

Such innocence only reminded her of her own ruin. How far she'd fallen.

"Absolutely. Let's find your mom."

She took off for the door, stepping out into the white-hot early June sunshine. Like glue, the heat put all the fragile pieces of her act back together.

Luc came down the front steps of the house and the boy ran over to him, slipping his hand into his uncle's. And she forced herself to stand up straight and look Luc in the eye, brushing aside the memory of his hands on her body. Her hands on his body. Pretending it was all nothing.

"What's going on?" Luc asked, his hand curved around Jacob's shoulder, and her body shook in memory and shame.

"Keep the kid away from the greenhouse," Tara Jean snapped.

"Was he causing trouble?"

She pushed the whoopee cushion against his chest.

Luc laughed and Tara Jean felt herself turn red. "It's not funny, Luc. Keep the kid away from me."

chapter 16

No good could come of following her. He knew that.

He should wait for a better moment. A moment not quite so aggressive. But if he waited for a moment without the fireworks, he had no doubt that he'd be waiting a long time.

The way she'd treated Jacob was concerning, but whatever her reasons for playing the bitch, he was invested enough to listen.

To try and figure her out.

He stepped into the greenhouse only to find her crouched on the floor, her skirt hiked up to reveal the long, muscled length of her leg.

His blood pumped harder and he realized in that moment that what he liked most about Tara Jean was the challenge of her. The fight of her. She gave him nothing that he didn't work for. And he couldn't remember the last time that had happened.

He watched as she swept the wrappers into the garbage can and then picked up the bag of spilled candy.

"What do you want?" That she refused to look at him wasn't a surprise.

"You want to tell me what's wrong?" Luc stayed calm, trying not to take offense. Trying not to get his own temper engaged.

"The kid." She stood and put an orange candy in her mouth. "You guys need to watch him better."

He glanced around her pristine workshop. "Did he damage something? Break anything?"

"Doesn't matter." She tried to step past him toward her desk, but he got in her way.

"You scared him, and I'd like to know why."

He could see the skin around her eye twitch and he leaned closer, trying to get her to look at him. To see him. The man who had held her while she crashed through orgasm after orgasm. The man whom she'd talked to, really talked to, about her past and her life.

Because she was acting like he was nothing.

"The boy's not welcome here."

"You know, he's just a kid and he's all alone—"

"Not my problem, Luc."

"Then what is?" As soon as the challenge came out of his mouth, he regretted it, because engaging in a fight wasn't what he wanted. He'd lose her in a fight.

"Is this about Saturday night?" he asked.

"No, Luc. Not everything is about sex."

"Saturday night wasn't even about sex."

"You signed up to be used, Luc."

He laughed, and she bristled. "Honey, I'd be nothing but happy if you'd used me for sex. If you'd turned around and told me you were done with me and I should go on my merry way, I would have gone. But something else happened, Tara. And I was—"

"It had been a while, that's all."

He didn't believe her, not for a minute, but he nodded anyway and she jerked away, cutting the other way around the table.

"Tara. Look at me."

She didn't and he waited her out, waited and waited, wondering if she was such a coward, until finally she sighed like a put-out teenager and tossed her long hair over her shoulder.

"What?"

"I'm . . . in." He held out his hands, as if showing her he had no hidden agenda. No weapons formed against her. "I'm interested. I don't want to hurt you. I'm not interested in using you. I like you. And . . . I'd like to like you more. Know you more."

For a moment it was as if she were frozen, unblinking, as if his words had done something to her, shorted out all electrical activity, and he had hope. Hope that she'd turn toward him rather than away.

"That's a bad idea." She crouched to pick up a box of spilled zippers and the moment shattered. He sucked in a quick breath, struggling for recovery.

"Why?"

"Because I'm not interested in knowing anything else about you." She threw zippers into the box as if they'd grown legs and were trying to escape. "You bore me, with your privilege and your daddy issues. Who gives a shit about an old hockey player who is too stupid to know when he should retire?"

It wasn't as bad as the Gilcot hit, but he felt it. A rippling pain radiating from his stomach. And the killer was that he hadn't seen it coming.

"Is this . . . is this you?" Luc asked, and she looked right at him, her eyes the color of already gone. Of who gives a shit. "I mean, every time I turn around I have no idea who I'm going to get. The flirt, or the woman who tries to help me, or the—"

"The bitch," she interrupted. "The bitch is me, Luc. All the way down. So mind your own business, keep the kid away, and leave me the hell alone."

* * *

She watched his jaw, the fine muscles there pulsing and relaxing, and she could only imagine what he was forcing himself not to say. She bit her own tongue to keep herself from taking the words back, because throwing this man away with both hands was surprisingly hard.

Surprisingly painful.

"I . . . I won't be back, Tara," he said, and she nodded at his words. She knew that, she'd hit him where he hurt, and Luc had enough pride not to sniff around where he wasn't wanted.

"Well, you're slow, but you ain't stupid, are you?"

God, she sounded exactly like her mother.

She could feel all his efforts to get past her act like crowbars, she knew that stupidly, she'd let down her guard a few million times too many with this man, and he knew the routes and paths, the secret entrances into her head.

But not anymore. Not after the other night.

Dennis was back and she needed to be strong. And liking this man, letting him remind her of how lonely she was, how scared, how hungry she could be for affection—it would only make her weak.

She knew how vulnerable that could make someone; she'd preyed on those weaknesses in other people.

"Fine," he said and walked away. Just like she wanted. And he didn't look back, not once, as if he knew what a coward she was, how she could never be as honest with him as he'd been with her. As if he knew she simply wasn't worth the effort.

He left and took her every chance at being better with him.

The silence he left behind was too thick and she couldn't breathe. Her heart fluttered in her chest, unpredictable and erratic. She saw silvery spots at the corner of her vision.

It was a panic attack. She knew that, used to get them all the time when she'd first come out to the ranch. She'd wake up at night in a cold sweat, hyperventilating—which wasn't exactly comfortable with broken ribs—convinced that Dennis was coming in through the window.

To take her back to her old life.

Luc didn't know what he was asking for. Wanting to know her? Please, it was ridiculous. If he knew . . . well, if he knew, it wouldn't be an issue anymore, would it?

It's for the best, the demon whispered. *He's not for the likes of you.*

There was no arguing with the demon. Searching for a little comfort, she unwrapped a cherry Starburst. Usually her favorite. But it tasted like ash in her mouth.

The flavor of regret.

Luc got in his truck and left. He still had a few hours before the ice was his, but he'd find something to do. Something far away from the ranch. Maybe he'd help out with the peewees who had the ice before him. Teaching a bunch of screaming kids to stay on their skates would keep his mind off Tara.

The road to Dallas was familiar at this point, a well-worn path between the ranch and the ice arena, and he followed it, his mind twisting itself around Tara.

The rejection was one thing, and it stung. But it wasn't real. He'd never seen such bullshit in his life as what Tara Jean had just tossed out at him. And maybe he would have believed it, but Saturday night he had seen the truth of Tara Jean. Felt the truth, and it had nothing to do with his fingers inside her body, or the thick, wet heat of her pleasure.

It was in the set of her shoulders before she ran away. The trembling of her fingers against his chest before she kissed him.

She liked him all right. She liked him a lot. But she was a coward.

"Fuck it," he breathed and grabbed his cell phone, punching speed dial even as he lifted the phone to his ear. He needed a friend. He needed a reminder of who he was and what was important. He needed hockey. And luckily, there was a guy in his life who embodied it.

"Hey, Luc," Billy said as he answered. "Did you just hear?"

"Hear what?" Luc asked.

"The Lashenko trade?"

Fucking Beckett, the guy hadn't answered his phone this morning and then Luc had gotten distracted by Tara.

See, he thought, *see what distractions do? They fuck you up.*

Luc sat back against the seat, bracing himself for the hit.

"I'm going to Dallas?" Luc asked.

"No." Billy took a deep breath. "Our first draft pick, Svetka, Collins."

"Collins? There goes our net—"

"And me."

Without Billy it will be open season on you.

That was the doctor's warning. That was actually common knowledge. And Luc had disregarded it because next year, he and Billy were supposed to be on the ice together. They were supposed to hoist that cup over their heads together.

Billy made sure nothing happened to Luc. Billy took every hit meant for Luc. Without him, Luc would have a giant target on his back and while they might get another defenseman who'd try to play and work as hard as Billy, it was doubtful.

Guaranteed increased odds of future damaging concussions . . .

What happens if I get knocked out again? he thought. The specter of the drooling early-onset Alzheimer line-backers rolled through his head, a chill of premonition sliding down his spine.

But he shook it off and pulled over to the side of the road.

"You all right?" he asked his friend. Ten years together and it was over. Just like that.

"I don't love it," Billy answered. "But I'm still playing."

"How is the knee?"

"Doc cleared me to skate. Down and back and some figure eights. Nothing fancy."

"What about the vipers?"

Billy blew out a breath. "They're killing me, man."

"I got an arena down here in Dallas. Empty ice. A couple hours a day . . ."

"I'll be there tonight," Billy said.

"No distractions."

"Just ice," Billy said and hung up.

It was going to be bittersweet to skate with Billy again. This was the end for them. Billy in Dallas. He shook his head, trying to imagine the locker room without him. Trying to imagine the kid they'd try to replace Billy with. He was going to be surrounded by kids, he realized, feeling empty. Talented kids ready to play their hearts out, but kids nonetheless.

Retire. Get out while you're ahead. The doctor's warnings rang loud in his head, a bell freshly rung.

And for a moment, solid and real, he couldn't push the thought away—the game was dangerous for him now. Without Billy there to take those hits . . . every brawler in the league would be gunning for him.

But I'm good, he reminded himself. *I'm the best. And without Billy, I'll just have to be better. Develop eyes in the back of my head, play more defensively. No more prima donna, untouchable crap; it's time to play hockey like I used to.*

Luc closed his phone and realized he had a message. From Beckett.

For the first time since walking into Tara's studio, he felt his legs under him.

This was what he needed. The full and total commitment of all his energy on what mattered. Hockey.

He put the car in drive and got back up onto the road, and then he called Beckett.

And Tara Jean was forgotten.

chapter 17

Victoria tried to act casual, as if coming into Bimbo Barbie's workshop out of curiosity was a perfectly normal thing for her to do. Which it wasn't, and from the slack-jawed look on Tara Jean's face, she knew it too. Victoria had been on the ranch for a month and hadn't stepped foot in the place.

"Hi," Victoria said, smiling slightly, wiping her sweaty hands against the twill of her walking shorts.

"Hi," Tara said. "Are you here because of your son?"

"What about my son?" The foundation of courage she'd had to build just to walk into the greenhouse faltered slightly.

"He's been sneaking around my workshop." Tara leaned back from her desk. "And I don't like it."

"I'll talk to him," she said, and Tara nodded. But she wasn't in here because of Jacob . . . Well she was in a way. In a big-picture kind of way.

Do it, she told herself, *just do it. Just open your mouth and ask*. But instead she got very interested in looking at the leather items hanging on the rack near the back.

"Is this . . . is this for the leather stores?"

"No." Tara rolled her eyes. "They're for the cows. Of course they're for the stores."

Victoria pressed the tip of her tongue to her upper lip. Being mocked by a woman like Tara Jean Sweet was pretty much the bottom of a deep, deep barrel and her pride, or what was left of it, reared up in defense. Victoria was surprised to feel the thin mantle of cool superiority that settled over her shoulders, like in the good old days, and she relished it. Tied the edges together in a saucy knot and turned to face Tara, one eyebrow raised.

"Do you just do clothes for strippers?"

"What is with you people?" Tara asked. "Anyone who wears leather must take it off for money?"

"Something like that," Victoria said; she found a certain comfort in snobbery. Lord knows she'd used it like an all-purpose weapon back when her life was normal. A blunt instrument to beat everyone around her into submission.

She gave Tara one of her most enigmatic and superior smiles. That it worked and Tara dropped her eyes for a second gave her a shot of victory. A thrill she hadn't felt in a long time.

"Is there something you wanted?" Tara asked. She wore a white wraparound shirt, splattered with coffee, and a blue linen skirt. She almost looked . . . normal.

Victoria glanced down at her hands, her ring finger that was so naked without her wedding band and engagement ring, both of which she'd given to the lawyers to sell. For a while she'd been glad to lose that identity. Joel Schulman's wife—it had been a necklace of boulders around her neck, drowning her. Drowning Jacob.

But she'd learned this last year that she had no identity with that naked ring finger. Not one that would provide for her son. Not one that would bring them any security.

Wedding bands—to some extent—were security.

And the way Dennis had looked at her. Appreciative and respectful. Warm. The way his eyes had clung to her face, checked out her naked fingers—those looks sometimes led to wedding rings.

And for the first time in a year, she'd felt something in return.

Worth.

But sometimes those looks led to more heartbreak, and frankly, she'd had her fill.

The smart thing would be to delete Dennis's number, punched into her cell phone with his own fingers.

Saturday night when he'd gone off with Tara Jean, Victoria had sat on the verandah, counting stars and trying to convince herself that he wasn't in there screwing Bimbo Barbie while she stood in the moonlight like a fool. But when he'd come out of that greenhouse, he saw her and walked over, radiating a kind of male confidence that turned her insides to putty. This was a man who could care for a woman. Provide for her. And her son.

After putting his number in her phone, he'd told her he was staying at the Four Seasons in Dallas and to call anytime she was in town.

She'd called him last night, and the flirtation had been . . . healing. Exciting.

And in the cool light of day, she wondered again about heartbreak.

"Yes," she blurted, too loud, too awkward. Everything she didn't want to be.

"Spit it out, Victoria," Tara Jean sighed. "I don't want to play games."

No games. Perfect. She dropped the smile. "Tell me about Dennis."

"Why?" Tara nearly barked.

"We share some interests," she said, walking along the long table in the middle of the workshop, her fingers running over the edge. "And he's a handsome man." She shrugged. "I'm curious, that's all."

"You have nothing in common with Dennis." Tara's tone was an essay in wounded pride.

Oh my, Victoria thought, *this woman is jealous.*

"I thought the two of you were just friends. Or is that just on his side?"

Tara was breathing hard through her nose, her lovely face blotchy and red. Angry Tara Jean wasn't pretty. Victoria's beleagured pride clapped like a little girl at a birthday party.

"Dennis is bad news, Victoria," she said and then, surprisingly, she ran a hand over her face, pressed her fingers against her eyes for a moment. Victoria realized she was witness to a very private meltdown, and she felt an unwanted twinge of kinship. As a woman who'd had too many private meltdowns made public, she knew how painful it was to have such moments observed.

"Tara?"

When Tara dropped her hands, Bimbo Barbie was gone. It was as if a mask had come off, revealing sharper bones, brighter eyes. The excess was missing and Tara Jean was stripped down to the framework.

"Is this about money?" asked this sharper version of Tara.

"Of course not," Victoria lied, and badly.

"Because Dennis doesn't have any."

"Of course he does. He's working on a real estate deal."

Tara Jean laughed and it felt like a knife, wielded against both of them. Victoria's feminine power began to cringe, sulking into the dark corners it had come from. "There will never be any money. Not for Dennis. Trust me, Victoria, you're better off staying far, far away from him."

Victoria lifted her chin, refusing to believe that the man she'd met was lying to her. She'd married a liar, a very, very good one, and no one would be able to fool her again.

"Perhaps you're just jealous," she said, but Tara was shaking her head before the words even left her mouth.

"He's a friend of mine, Victoria." She put a hand to her chest, covering the coffee stain there. "Do you honestly want to date a friend of mine? Have your son around a man who is just like me?"

"He's not like you. He's nothing like you."

"He's a chameleon. He shows you what you want to see and you want to see a wealthy man, a kind man, with an eye toward family. The kind of man who could take care of you. He's playing you, Victoria."

She shook her head, refusing to believe this woman. This liar. Victoria had gone through hell and come out the other side intact. With her son. She deserved some luck. She deserved some kindness, and she wasn't about to let this woman take it away.

"It was a mistake to come here." Victoria turned for the door.

"Look, Victoria," Tara said. "I don't know your whole situation but I know that Lyle tied you up in the same knot he's got the rest of us in, and if you need money—"

Victoria shook her head, not interested in Tara Jean's solution. It had been a stupid idea to come here and even more stupid to stay, to let this woman's poison anywhere near her.

"Victoria, wait." Tara Jean edged around the desk and stepped in front of Victoria, keeping her from the door. They were the same height now, Victoria in her ballet slippers, Tara Jean in her ridiculous stripper shoes, and Victoria got a good look in Tara Jean's eyes. And what she saw there confused her.

Compassion.

"I can hire you to be a small model for the final fitting of the winter line," she said. "It's not a lot of money, but it's some. And it would be yours. Not given to you. Not tied to a man. You'd earn it on your own."

Victoria blinked at Tara Jean and after a moment, Tara Jean smiled.

"What . . . what do you think?"

"I think you're ridiculous." Victoria reached for the door, but once again Tara Jean got in the way.

"You can determine your worth, Victoria," she said. "Right now, you can say yes and do the job. Straight up. No strings, no rings, no men, no humiliation, no asking for permission, none of it—"

"What the hell do you know?" Victoria asked through her teeth, feeling as if she were turning to ice and stone. How did this . . . whore know her so well? How did Tara Jean get to look at Victoria and see her secrets and tear her apart? In what world could this be okay?

"I'm sorry I came in here," Victoria said, and after a moment Tara Jean rushed aside and Victoria rushed out the door.

"The offer stands." Tara Jean's words followed her up to the big house like a dog she couldn't shake off.

That night Tara sat up in bed and glanced over at the clock, its green numbers glowing in the dark. Midnight. She'd been tossing and turning for two hours.

The same freaking questions played over and over in her head like a hamster in a squeaky wheel: Was Victoria going to listen to her and stay away from Dennis? What would happen when she gave Dennis the two hundred grand? Did she really think he'd go away? Was this just the price she had to pay for everything she'd done in her past?

She hung her head and sighed before tossing the blankets off her legs and standing up. The flannel shirt slid down to her knees and she kicked around under her bed until she found her bunny slippers.

If she couldn't sleep, she might as well find what was left of that ice cream.

The dark hallway was cool, the navy runner plush under her bare feet, and she followed it toward the kitchen. The family all slept on the other side of the house. It was just she and Ruby on this side, so it was strange that the door to the second bedroom was shut.

Jacob, she thought, and she had to give the kid points for persistence. The kid seemed truly invested in driving his mother all the way into crazy. No one in the family did things halfway.

She opened the door, ready to drag him back to the other wing, but the bed was empty. A small duffle bag sat on top of it.

Her blood froze in her veins.

Would Dennis send Carl? At the thought, her skin tried to crawl right off her body. Carl, who had helped Dennis beat the crap out of her four years ago. Carl, who always brought a small duffle bag filled with a change of clothes in case things got too messy.

Why would he send Carl? The thought was a high-pitched scream in the middle of her head. But it wasn't as if Dennis was rational. And he was still mad that she'd left him the way she had, running away in the night before he could get the money she'd given back to Mr. Dickow.

Was this how he was going to get in touch with her? By sending his thug?

She shut the door and looked behind her.

The hallway was empty, the house silent.

She ran quickly toward the center of the house, thinking she'd cut through the kitchen and get to the family wing and make sure they were all okay, make sure Carl didn't get lost in the big house and beat the shit out of the wrong woman. Or scare a little kid.

She gagged, remembering the smile on his face when he broke her ribs. His glee as she screamed.

She ran faster.

The carpet under her feet changed to tile and the kitchen appliances loomed in the shadows. She cut around the island and ran right into a solid wall of heat. Flesh under a T-shirt.

Somehow she knew it wasn't Luc. The smell was wrong. The shape was wrong—wider and shorter. His hands as he grabbed her arms were foreign.

Carl.

She kicked, lifting her knee toward his dick, hoping to catch him off guard. Hoping, actually, to stop any future, horrific daddy plan he might have.

"Whoa, whoa," a deep voice said as he shifted sideways, blocking her knee. "What the hell?" She lifted her arm, his hand attached, and sunk her teeth deep into the thin flesh on top of his knuckles.

"Jesus Christ, lady, what's going on?"

"Let me go, asshole," she said through her teeth and he dropped her. She stepped back, out of reach. He was in shadows, his face a black blur.

"Tell Dennis I have a plan." She continued to step backward, inching away from him.

"Dennis?"

The overhead lights flickered on and she blinked at the sudden change.

It wasn't Carl.

The big man with the broken-down face, the thin scar connecting his lip to his ear, shaking out the hand she bit, wasn't Carl. Her brain simply could not process this; fear and adrenaline had shorted her circuits and she could only gape at him.

"Who the hell are you?"

"My friend," Luc said, and she whirled to see him at the doorway, his hand on the light switches. "Billy Wilkins."

"She bit me!" Billy pointed at the perfect circle of her teeth imprinted around his knuckle.

"I'm sorry. You grabbed me. I—"

"You ran into me!"

"I thought . . . I thought you were someone else."

"Luc," the guy said, smiling a little, and his face changed. Through the scars and the hideously broken nose, something glimmered. Nothing handsome, the man was too hard used for that, but something charming. A little boy with mischief on his mind.

"You didn't tell me I was going to have to fight women to stay here."

"Stay here?" she asked.

"Billy is a guest." She shrank slightly in the face of his intensity, shifting sideways, putting the corner of the island between them.

He noticed and crossed his arms, only managing to look more threatening.

"That's great," she said, trying to smile and knowing she'd failed. Luc's eyebrows clashed over his beautiful eyes.

"Who did you think he was?" Luc pointed at Billy. Her mind backtracked, trying to remember what she'd said, what she'd unwittingly revealed.

"A burglar." She knew she sounded ridiculous, but she tossed her hair over her shoulder and met Luc's unreadable gaze. Fake it till you make it was kind of her motto.

"Stop lying," Luc said through his teeth, and she realized he was mad. Unease, the lesser cousin to all that fear she'd just felt, climbed into her heartbeat.

"I'm not—"

He shook his head once and she fell silent, her lies giving up the fight.

"You mentioned Dennis," he said.

Shit.

"What the hell is going on, Tara? And you tell me the truth or you can get the hell off this ranch."

Luc stood there a stranger to her—his loyalty firmly on the side of his sister, not that she expected anything else. Not really.

She glanced sideways at Billy and that charming little boy was gone, replaced by a gladiator. He was better backup muscle than Carl could ever dream of being and she knew when she was beat. And frankly, while she would never tell him the truth—not all of it anyway—she was very glad to hand over the protection of Victoria to someone who was better suited for the job.

"Victoria is interested in Dennis."

"Interested?"

"Yes."

Luc looked baffled, as if he didn't understand the word, and she sighed. "Interested as in, wanting to get to know him better?" She lifted her eyebrows, using his words from this morning to make it clear.

"That's ridiculous," he laughed.

"She came into the workshop this morning to ask about him."

"Dennis?"

She nodded, and after a long minute he sighed. "Okay."

"No, not okay. Not at all. He's . . ." She licked her lips, finding the fine line she was going to walk. "Not a good guy. Not for her. Not for anyone."

Luc and Billy shared a quick look.

"You thought I was this Dennis guy?" Billy asked.

"A friend of his."

Luc's face was hard as rock and she saw all the dots

connect in his head. He understood the threat, understood exactly what she'd brought into his house.

"Yes, Dennis is the kind of man who has friends that break into people's houses to scare them."

She didn't say "and worse." She sort of thought that was a given.

"And you know him how?"

"I hardly think that's the point."

Luc's eyes penetrated her chest, and she had to look away. *You're the point,* his eyes said, but she could take care of herself. They'd covered this ground and she'd all but asked him not to care.

"You need to keep Victoria away from Dennis," she said. "I tried to dissuade her, but . . ." She looked back up at Luc and saw the fear in his eyes.

"She's so desperate," he murmured, and she nodded.

"What about you?" Billy asked. "Does someone need to keep this Dennis guy away from you?"

Luc stared at her so hard it was as if he were reading her mind, the back of her skull, the inside of her soul.

And the words she thought she'd never say grew in her mouth like weeds, fertilized by the weakness she felt in her bones and her skin, deep in her belly. She was tired of the fight. Of Dennis. Of pretending she was tough, when all she wanted was a soft spot to lay her head and someone to talk to. Really talk to.

She was tired of being her.

She opened her mouth, the words poised to fall out, but Luc got there first.

"She can take care of herself," he said.

It wasn't rejection, not like what she'd done to him, but the sting pierced her chest, going all the way down to her stomach.

What did you expect? the demon whispered.

Too much, she thought, when she least expected it. And that in the end was always her downfall.

He stood there, staring at her, and she didn't know what he saw when he looked at her. What truth he was looking at. Hell, she couldn't even understand what he expected. And that, of course, made her search for the worst possible thing—because that was what was usually expected of her.

"I'll . . . ah . . . pack my stuff." She cleared her throat, and hated herself for her clenched hands. Her stinging sadness. "Head back to town."

"Probably a good idea." Luc nodded, no longer looking at her.

"Good night," she whispered, nodding to Billy because she was too tired to do anything more, and she left without once looking back at Luc.

chapter

18

"You're going to just let her go?" Billy asked, and Luc nodded, getting a beer out of the fridge. He didn't want a beer, but he needed to do something with his hands. With his body. Because that woman's naked eyes were a magnet he was going to resist if it killed him.

"She's in trouble," Billy said.

"I think she's the kind of woman who is always in trouble." He stared at the bottle, watching condensation gather under the frilled metal cap.

"Dude—"

"What?" Luc barked. "She doesn't want me worrying about her. She made that clear."

"That's never stopped you before." Billy took the beer from off the counter. He popped off the top and handed it back to him.

"If you've got something to say, Billy, spit it out."

"Do you know why the guys call you Grandpa?"

The beast of his temper rattled its chains. "I can guess."

"It has nothing to do with your age," Billy said. "And everything to do with how you worry. About everyone. Whether they want it or not."

"I'm team captain—"

"Right, and there's not another team captain in the league who cares if their center has a thing for strippers! You get that, right?"

Luc forced himself not to sag against the counter, not to feel every single second of his age in the face of Billy's assessment. Of course he understood that—this compulsion he had, no matter how much it chafed or how badly he wanted to resist it, was his own. He needed to take care of the people around him.

"You know this thing with your sister and your dad—he put all this shit together, the will, all of it—"

"You're making me very sorry I told you about any of that."

"Yeah, I'm sure." Billy grinned and leaned past him to get his own beer. "But I'm guessing your dad knew that you wouldn't leave your sister—"

"I was going to," Luc insisted, realizing that as far as defenses went, that one was awful: I was going to be an asshole.

"No, you weren't," Billy scoffed. "You'd have found a reason to stay. Just like you're going to find a reason to go talk to that woman."

"Tara?" He jerked his thumb in the direction of the door. "She doesn't need me. She's made that very clear."

"She needs someone." Billy pulled a bag of chips out of the pantry door, already at home. "I'm dumb as rock, but I can see that."

Luc took a swig of beer, as if challenging Billy's assessment. As if to say fuck you and fuck Tara. Fuck everyone else I need to need me. He resisted as long as he could, his hands gripping the counter as if there were one of those cartoon gale-force winds working against him, threatening to suck him right back out to Tara.

"Damnit." He pushed the beer over to Billy and followed Tara out the door.

"Go get her, Grandpa!"

* * *

Everything fit into her purse. The negligees that had been sitting in the top drawer for weeks before Lyle died. The bunny slippers—all of it. When she walked out of here, she was taking every last scrap of lace and silk and leather she owned. And it fit inside a purse—how sad was that?

She'd put extra locks on the door of her apartment. The windows. Hell, maybe she'd move. There were fresh starts everywhere. Someone just had to be desperate enough to find them.

She swung the overstuffed hobo bag over her shoulder and turned, only to find Luc filling the door. Shadows cut across his face, leaving his eyes and lips revealed in moonlight from the window.

He was a closed book, every feature and muscle held in the kind of control she could only dream of.

Her body sighed, swooning in remembered pleasure. So weak in front of all of his strength.

"I'm leaving," she said when the silence became too much. "You don't need to stand here and watch me go."

"I'm worried about you."

Worried? About her? That was sort of a first in her life, so she gave herself a moment with the words, a breath, a heartbeat, like holding a diamond in her hand. And then she pushed them—and him—away.

"I thought I made it clear I wasn't interested in your concern." She shook her hair out of her eyes, meeting his gaze with every ounce of bravado and bullshit she could muster. *Don't care!* she wanted to yell at him. *I'm the poison, I've always been the poison, and I will ruin this place and this family.*

"Unfortunately, Tara, I can't lie every time I feel something I don't want to. I can't turn it off and I can't pretend I'm not feeling it."

There was no response, no flippant comeback to something so honest. It shamed her, his honesty. So she said nothing. She just put her chin up and walked toward the door. Toward him.

An arm's length from him, she stopped, the heat from his body something she imagined to be real, holding her there.

"Let me go."

He shook his head. "Not until you tell me what's going on, Tara. And no more bullshit."

"I've told you. Victoria—"

"You." The word jabbed her in the chest. He stepped forward and now she wasn't imagining the heat from his body, it was there. So close she could put her numb hands against him and feel its warmth. "What is going on with you?" He lifted his eyebrows. "I won't let you leave, Tara. Not until you tell me the truth."

"Oh please—"

"Stop it!"

She jerked back, stunned by his sudden ferocity. He rubbed his hands over his face, into his dark hair, putting every strand on end. "Just talk to me, Tara. I want to help and you know I can, otherwise you wouldn't have been staying here. Now, I know this has something to do with Dennis. And I know it's not good, so cut the crap and talk to me. I can help you. I want . . . I want to help you."

He sounded tired, like he was dealing with a petulant child and sick of it. Her lip curled and her breath suddenly heaved in her chest.

He was going to . . . what? Save her?

Idiot.

She was past saving. So far past it, she couldn't remember what innocence felt like.

Her bag fell to the ground like a thousand-pound weight. His eyes went wide at the sound and she had his attention.

Good, because she was only going to tell this story once.

"I met Dennis when I was sixteen. I was . . ." She licked her lips, unable of course to tell the whole truth, because some things she just couldn't put into words. "I was in trouble and broke. Dennis had a job as an orderly at a nursing home and he had this scam going. He'd befriend little old ladies who had no family, no visitors, and he'd charm them into giving him gifts. Money."

"I knew I didn't like that guy."

She put up her chin, braced for the left hook of his disdain. His disgust.

"He convinced me to do the same, but with the men." He started to shake his head, his eyes as wide as if she'd told him she killed baby seals in her spare time, but she kept talking, a stone rolling downhill. "I'd go to a nursing home wearing a short skirt and my mother's crucifix and I'd pretend I was looking for my grandpa so I could read him the paper. And . . ." She swallowed. Whoever said confession was good for the soul was a goddamned liar. She felt sick. "The first guy, his name was Mr. Beanfang."

"You mentioned him before."

"Well, he was rich. So rich. He had money just lying around, like it didn't matter. And he didn't have any family and he was . . . he was lonely. So I read him the paper. Or one of the books from his room. And he started giving me money."

"And you took it?"

There it was—the trace of judgment, of disbelief—on the fringes of his voice. The destruction of everything he felt for her would begin like this—a trickle of doubt. He'd fight it, because he was the kind of man who would try to rationalize her behavior, see all the reasons behind the evil she'd done.

Pointless. Because in the end he'd abhor her.

She'd make sure of that.

"Of course I took it, Luc. That was the whole point. I was a thief and a liar. And I got enough money to get myself out of trouble and on a bus to California, and I left."

"Dennis—"

"Followed me. He found me a few months later. I'd been kicked out of my apartment, my stuff had been stolen, and we started it all back up again. The nursing homes, the old guys with no family. And as soon as I'd make enough to get myself out of trouble, I left. Again. And a few years later he found me. My mom was sick. There wasn't any money—"

"I get the idea—"

"Really? I doubt it. Because I did it four times, Luc! Four times I preyed on those men. I pretended to be something I wasn't so they would give me their money!"

Her voice shook in the rafters and she felt herself falling into pieces. Luc reached out to her and she stepped away, appalled that he would try to touch her.

"Why is Dennis here now?" Luc's voice was careful, slow and sure, like bedrock under her feet, and she pulled herself back from the brink.

"I . . . I gave the money back to the last old man. I couldn't . . . I couldn't do it. He'd given me ten grand and . . . I was twenty-nine and sick of what I was doing. But Dennis was in trouble with some people and he needed to get out of town. When he found out I'd given the money back, he beat me up. Put me in the hospital. Where I met Lyle."

She saw the moment when her words hit home. His face sharpened, every inch of his fierce nature brought to bear against her, and she wanted to cower behind a lie, some fiction she'd created to keep her distance from the ugliness of her past. But she'd pulled down all her walls and she stood here, naked.

"You conned him." His words were a blowtorch against her skin.

"I told Lyle every single thing about myself," she said. "I told him about the old guys and the money." And more. And more and more and more. But Luc would never know. Never.

Luc was shaking his head, disbelieving, and she didn't blame him. "And you read to him and you accepted his gifts—"

"No gifts. He gave me the job. Straight up."

It was the truth; she had nothing else to offer Luc, nothing else to sway him. He'd believe her or not.

Please, she thought, surprised that it mattered so much what this man thought of her. *Please believe me. Please.*

"So Dennis is here for the money?" His voice gave away nothing and she fought the urge to scramble in front of him, offering justification. "For you? You brought him here?"

"He just got out of jail."

"Jail!"

She nodded and he swore. "He needs money and then he'll go." This was her hope, her fervent dream, but she doubted her words even as she said them. She would never get rid of Dennis, not unless she went to the police.

"How much?"

She bit her lips, the words *none of your business* on the tip of her tongue, but it *was* his business. By coming here, by bringing her long tail of poison with her, she'd made Dennis everyone's business.

"How much?" he thundered.

"Two hundred thousand."

"The bonus?"

She nodded.

"Why haven't you called the cops? This is extortion—"

"Are you kidding? What I did is called fraud. Dennis would and could put me in jail."

"How much did you take from these men?"

"Including the ten grand—"

"You gave that back."

She shook her head. "Doesn't change the fact that I conned him into giving it to me. All told, around thirty grand."

He whistled, and her stomach shook with guilt.

"I doubt anyone is going to put you in jail for thirty grand in gifts from men who were grateful for the company."

"Dennis got arrested for fraud. Sent to jail for five years for doing the same thing I did but with less money."

"Somehow I think they had more on Dennis than that."

Tara was pretty sure of it too. He'd gotten busted a few times for stealing medication from the nursing homes and selling it on the street. He always had someone after him. Cops. Criminals. It hardly seemed to matter.

"Do you honestly think he'll go away when you give him the money?"

She shook her head. "This is . . . this is the cost of what I did, Luc."

"Bullshit, Tara. You want to make it right?"

"Of course I do, Luc. I'm paying—"

"Paying him money won't do anything. You know that. You're not stupid. You want to make this right, man up and go to the cops."

For a moment she let the coward in her scramble, searching for another way, but then she took a deep breath and took a good, hard look at the truth.

She needed to go to the cops.

That woman who Dennis had described—the coward—was it possible she could just choose to not be that woman? Could she choose to be better? The idea was like a light going on in a dark room.

Right now, her own actions—not a new name, a different job—could change things for her. Forever. Suddenly the fear of going to jail was not as large as her hope that she could be different. Better. Someone she could be proud of.

She could go to the cops. She didn't have to be scared and selfish Jane Simmons anymore. She could do the right thing.

Her bones felt broken. Everything felt broken, as if telling this secret after so many years had blown a hole right through her. It was going to be hard work pulling herself back together. But she could do it. She would do it.

"Where is he now?" Luc asked.

"Why?"

"Why do you think? If you're not going to handle him, I will."

Fear that he'd go charging into this situation like John Wayne on skates made up her mind. This wasn't just about keeping herself safe anymore. She had an obligation to this family.

"Forget it, Luc. There's no way you're going to go threaten a guy like Dennis. He'll take it as a challenge."

"I can handle it."

"I'm sure you can, but your career might not. Your public image. Your family. I'm going to go to the cops. Get a restraining order. Something."

He stared at her a long time and like the guilty little con artist she was, she looked away, unable to meet his eyes, because she knew that the way he used to see her, as that woman of worth who'd risen above a background too bad to speak of, was gone.

That version of her couldn't survive this. Nothing could.

It was why she'd never told anyone except Lyle.

"You want me to go with you?"

"I don't need a babysitter. I said I'll do it and I'll do it."

"That's not what I meant."

Right. "This is my business, Luc. I'm not going to get you any more tangled up in this."

"You sure as hell got my sister tangled up in it."

"I know. I'm sorry. I'm so sorry. I should go. Honestly, he won't bother you if I'm not here."

"You're staying. It's safe here."

"Luc—"

"Fine. It's none of my business. But don't be this proud. It doesn't make any sense."

He was right. If she went home, there weren't enough locks on her door to keep Dennis out. "Okay. Thank you."

The silence was thick and heavy, like being buried alive under pounds of her own dirt. Outrageously, she wanted to ask him if he hated her. Despised her. And she knew it was ridiculous to care; she certainly never had before. No other man's opinion had mattered, except for Lyle's.

For a second, she hung onto the idea that Luc's opinion mattered because he was Lyle's son. Or maybe it was just the fact that she'd told him the truth, and she was so desperate for forgiveness she was ready to look for it in him.

But then he turned and walked away without another word, and the truth was impossible to ignore.

His opinion mattered, because *he* mattered.

Previously frozen and suddenly reckless with the painful spasms of feeling, her heart thudded a quiet agreement.

chapter 19

Luc watched the sun come up on Tuesday morning, a pink glow in the east-facing window that over time lost its rosiness and burned through every cloud in its way to becoming a bright globe suspended over the glass roof of the greenhouse.

Tara Jean, her hair pulled back in a ponytail, a loose white T-shirt blown against her stomach by the wind, walked across the gravel of the parking area like a woman headed toward a firing squad. Shoulders back, chin up, daring the whole world to take their best shot.

It was impossible not to admire her guts.

She got in her car and started down the driveway toward the Springfield Police Station.

She was really going to do it.

Pride warred with his anger.

He wasn't upset about the money or the old men. Hell, he almost felt sorry for her and the load of guilt she carried over her mistakes. Alone was no way to die, and she'd brought some happiness to those men in their last days. Maybe he'd see it differently if it was his old man and his money getting conned by a pretty blonde with a great rack—but he doubted it. Truth be told, if he were dying alone somewhere, he'd like a woman like Tara coming to read him the Sports page.

No, the wellspring of his anger was that she had brought Dennis—this threat—to bear against his family.

His sister. His nephew. And she had lied and would have kept on lying about it if he hadn't forced the truth out of her.

And that she honestly thought he was going to sit back and do nothing while Dennis circled like a vulture was ludicrous.

She didn't know him. At all.

He tapped the business card in his hand against the window.

Gary Thiele, the private investigator who'd uncovered Tara Jean's real name.

Funny, he'd thought at the time that her name change was the worst of her crimes.

He grabbed his phone and dialed the number.

It was time to find out a little bit more about Dennis Murphy.

Those episodes of *CSI: Miami* she used to watch had misled her. The kindly receptionist at the front desk at the Springfield Police Station had to direct her to the county courthouse in Wassaw to get the protection order—it wasn't even called a restraining order in Texas. You just couldn't trust TV anymore for a proper education. A forty-minute drive later, and a very bored county clerk had her fill out three forms and then made copies at a glacial pace.

"Your hearing will be in two weeks; after that, Dennis Murphy will be notified of the protection order."

"Two weeks?"

"Is this an immediate problem?"

"He just got out of jail and he threatened to rape me. And beat me. So, you know, the sooner the better."

The clerk gave her another form and told her to wait in the corner for the judge to see her. So far no one had doubted her. No one had suggested that maybe she'd asked for the abuse. No one had asked about her past.

CSI: Miami had led her to believe some smarmy redheaded cop was going to interrogate her. So, all in all, she was feeling pretty good about this protection order business.

An hour later, she was led into an office where a man in half-glasses sat behind a large desk. He gestured to the chair in front of him and Tara sat, relieved that this very long, very bizarre day was about to end without parading the ghosts of her past.

But then Judge Phillips looked at her over the edge of those half-glasses and despite the air conditioning, sweat bloomed across her chest, pooling and running down her back. Her legs stuck to the chair.

"So," Judge Phillips asked, "how exactly do you know Dennis Murphy?"

For a moment, her mouth dry, and she considered lying. Because the good judge was a grandfather. Pictures of gap-toothed kids covered his desk, and he might be fifteen years younger than the men she'd stolen from but he wasn't stupid. He'd put himself in the shoes of those four men, and she couldn't face it. Couldn't face herself.

But then she thought about Jacob and Victoria. Dennis's erection against her belly. Those leather samples hanging up in her studio. Luc.

She had something to protect. Something to fight for.

And she'd promised and she wanted, for the first time in her life, for her word to mean something.

She unfisted her hands, opened her mouth, and forced the story out.

Two hours later she parked her Honda in front of the ranch and stared at the building, so ugly in the sunlight.

Luc, sitting on the steps, slowly stood. Waiting for her.

Unbelievably, she felt tears gather behind her eyes.

Don't be ridiculous, she told herself, and picking up her purse, and the tattered edges of her pride, she climbed out of the car. *He's not waiting for you. He's waiting to make sure you did what you said you'd do. He's waiting on behalf of his family. Not for you. Never for you.*

"How did it go?" he asked once she was close.

Grateful for her sunglasses, she tilted up her face. "Within the next twenty-four hours Dennis will be served with a temporary ex parte protective order."

He blinked. Nodded. "That's good."

Good? she thought, emotion boiling inside her stomach. None of this was good.

"I'm going inside."

"What about the other stuff. Did you tell them?"

The words in her mouth were too heavy and they tasted like iron and tears. She had thought, stupidly, that going into that police station and the courthouse and telling someone what she'd done would make her feel cleaner. Feel . . . forgiven.

But instead she felt worse. Sick. So sick of herself she couldn't stand it.

There was no forgiveness for her.

"I did." The words slid out of her mouth with barely a sound.

"What did they say?"

She remembered the way Judge Phillips's smile had gone flat, the way he'd looked at her. Like she was something he wished he could lock away.

"It's not a crime to accept a gift. But the police are going to check in the cities where those men lived to see if there are any files opened under my name by people who caught on to what I did."

"That must have been hard."

"You think?" Her voice cracked and she shook her head, needing to get up to her room and under the blankets of her bed so that she could just hide for awhile, but he touched her hand, his fingers sliding around her wrist.

She had no shell anymore and she felt that touch all the way through her body. His warmth, his strength, the calluses on his fingers. It was the kitchen all over again and she was transfixed.

When he pulled off her sunglasses, she didn't have the strength to push him away. To tell him to go to hell.

She could only stand there and feel him.

"I'm proud of you," he whispered.

The tears fell. And he reached up to touch them, his face broken with sympathy, but she yanked herself away.

"That makes one of us," she said and ran into her room, where—fully dressed—she climbed under the covers of her bed.

The knock on the door that night was unwelcome and so she ignored it.

When it persisted, she fished under her bed for a shoe, which she pitched at the door. The bang made her flinch, but afterward it was silent.

And then another knock.

"What?" she barked.

The doorknob turned and she stared up at the ceiling, pissed that she hadn't thought to lock the damn thing.

"Luc, go away, I don't need a Boy Scout—"

It wasn't Luc in the doorway. It was the boy. Jacob. His black curls were growing long, the tips touching the edge of his red Spiderman T-shirt.

He stood there, held still by her gaze. But she couldn't stand to look at him, as if he were a too-bright light against a black sky. When she sat up, he moved toward the bed. A quick shuffle step.

"What do you want?" Her bark stopped him in his tracks.

"I'm sorry," he murmured. "About the whoopee cushion."

"Your mom got mad at you, huh?" She smiled slightly and the boy brightened, as if she were opening a door for him to step through. And maybe she was. Maybe she was just that alone.

"Took away my Gameboy."

She hummed in sympathy.

"Ruby said you like these." He stepped up to the bed, and she braced herself as best she could, but she had nothing to push the boy away with. No nasty words. No shell. Not even a stick. Nothing. So she could only sit there and try not to cry.

Go away, she silently begged. *Please, Jacob, don't get close. Please just go away.*

"Here." He put something on her knee.

Finally, she looked over at him, his face shimmery and magnified through her tears.

"Are you sad?" he asked.

She nodded.

"Because of the whoopee cushion?"

It was so ridiculous she laughed, and the tears spilled hot over her cheeks. "No," she whispered. "Not because of the whoopee cushion."

She wiped her face and saw the box of candy on her knee. Mike and Ikes.

Fresh tears burned in her eyes.

"Thank you," she said. "They're my favorite."

His smile, generated by the very specific gladness that he'd made her happy, that he'd done something for her that was good and appreciated, tore through the room, illuminating the dark that surrounded her.

I used to feel that way, she thought, dimly. Reading to

those old men. Finding their favorite socks. Filling in the crossword puzzles.

It didn't make it right, but she had enjoyed that part of it. That part had been honest.

"It's my favorite candy, too," he said, nodding seriously, as if they were discussing modern art. "But I only like the yellows."

She blinked at him, doubting she'd heard him right. "The yellows?"

He nodded, launching into some rationale she didn't hear, because she was trying to figure out how to reject this gift. Because she was unsure of where it came from or what it meant. She wanted to pick it apart. Find the strings, the hidden angles.

But he was a kid. Just a kid. And maybe, maybe it would be okay to accept one thing at face value.

There was no forgiveness for her. She understood that, accepted it. But maybe there could be salvation. All that innocence she'd pushed away since she'd lost her own, maybe if she let it back in, let it swirl around her and lift her to someplace better—maybe she could find some redemption.

Don't, the demon warned, her voice a sharp crack against the inside of her head. *Not for you. This is not for you!*

But she ignored the demon and ripped open the box. The oblong candy spilled everywhere, down the hills of her knees, across the plains of the bedspread. She picked up three yellows and held them out to him in the cupped palm of her hand.

"Go ahead," she said with a shaky shrug. "I don't like the yellows."

"Really? That's funny." His little fingers grabbed them, their touch sending sparks across her hand, right into her black and broken heart, where a hundred locks were sprung open. And for the first time since she turned sixteen, she realized she was free.

Free of Dennis.

Free of fear.

For a moment she thought she might just soar up to the ceiling. Up past the roof, into that wide blue sky.

"You okay?" Jacob asked. "You're crying."

"Am I?" She laughed, she couldn't help it. Freedom tasted like sugar, felt like a kid's sweaty palm in hers. And for all her grief and all her regrets, she was suddenly very proud that she'd arrived at this moment.

She pushed the blankets off her body, no longer willing to hide.

"Let's go do something," she said to Jacob, who blinked up at her.

"What?"

"I don't know, what do you like to do?"

"Draw stuff."

She laughed. Perfect. Absolutely perfect.

chapter 20

Friday morning, the workshop was a beehive of activity. The three models stood at the back sorting through the samples in their sizes. Edna and Joyce were unloading their equipment.

Edna had dried-up gunk on the shoulder of her shirt from one of her babies. As if it weren't regurgitated body fluids, she laughed and tried to flake it off. Tara Jean rolled her eyes. *Honestly.*

"We'll start with tops." Tara pulled out her binder and everyone quieted down and started to work.

After Jacob's visit three days ago, she'd thrown herself into work with all the fervor of the converted.

This business, the winter line, the Baker Leather stores and brand, would be her new life. This would be her last fresh start; this would become who she was, and she'd do it right or die trying.

Tara directed the models to the privacy screen she had for just this purpose. Maggie, the large model, didn't have much modesty, and she stripped naked in front of everyone. Over the last few years, Tara Jean had grown as accustomed to the sight of Maggie's freckled breasts as she had to Edna's face.

But Ruby's niece, Maria, was shy, and she ducked behind the privacy screen. As did Lucia, the medium model, who worked very very hard at staying a medium. Tara Jean smiled at her assembled crew and pushed aside any doubt or grief. This was her world now. All hers.

The models came out wearing the white leather bustier, and Tara and the seamstresses descended.

Tara Jean didn't even hear Celeste walk in until they got to the purple blazer.

"It's too short," Celeste said, her calm accented voice settling down over the crowd like a net, stopping all work.

"Excuse me?" Tara Jean asked, caught off guard. She was trying to refit the blazer on Maggie, but it wasn't working. Celeste walked down the center island to stand next to her.

"It needs to hit here." Celeste drew a line on Maggie's hip a few centimeters past where the purple hem sat awkwardly. "And this button . . . it's too low." She put her hand between the single button at Maggie's waist and all but cupped the woman's breasts. "The girls are running wild."

It took less than a second for Tara to see that Celeste was right. The jacket didn't look right, not because of the fit, but because of the design.

Christ, even Edna was nodding!

"We're fitting," Tara said through her teeth, glancing at the other models to see if the problem ran across all the sizes. It did. *Damn it.* "Not designing." She shook her head, angry that she'd bothered to defend herself. "What are you doing here?"

"I was curious."

"Well, you can leave."

"I don't think so." Celeste circled Maria, who nearly quaked in front of the imperial bullshit she was laying down.

"Stop intimidating my models." Suddenly, realization dawned, and Tara laughed with evil delight. "Are you here because you thought I needed a small model? Oh my God, are you here to work for me?"

Celeste's smile was short and sharp. "Don't be ridiculous. You can't afford me."

"Did your son send you to check up on me?"

"My son is and always has been focused on one thing. Hockey. He doesn't care about this venture." Celeste stood in front of Maria and smiled. "Your skin is lovely," she said, and Maria's face began to glow. "Just put your shoulders back a little bit, yes." She touched Maria gently between the shoulder blades. "And shift your legs like so. There."

Maria slowly transformed from a nervous girl to a young woman with some power. Some bearing.

Celeste stepped up to Maggie, the forty-year-old redhead covered in freckles, whose blue eyes rivaled the Texas sky in summer. Again Celeste smiled, and Maggie grinned.

"You don't scare me," Maggie said, and Tara snorted. Maggie was the mother of six boys and she rehabilitated horses in her spare time. Nothing scared her.

Celeste put a hand under Maggie's chin and amazingly, Maggie didn't bite her. "That is because you are magnificent. But you could use a better bra."

Tara Jean watched with a strange wonder as Celeste came back to stand in front of her.

"So help me," Tara raised a finger, "if you touch me or talk about my bra, we're going to have words."

Celeste laughed, the sound a surprising bark. Very un-Celeste-like.

"My son may not care." Celeste tipped her head sideways, the look on her face unreadable, and Tara wondered if that was French. It seemed French. "But I find I am . . . interested."

"You're kidding."

"I'm not. And I have no intention of interfering, but

perhaps an . . . opinion." She arched an eyebrow. "When it's required?"

Tara waited for a second. And then another. The truth was, Celeste had been a high-fashion model; any involvement she might have in this company could only be a good thing. In terms of sales, of course. And maybe design.

Oh no! the demon said. *No you don't, honey, we don't need her. You can do this by yourself, remember? With my help, you don't need anyone else.*

Tara ignored the demon.

Having Celeste here could be interesting. Unless . . . well, unless Celeste thought her opinion was required more often than it really was.

"You have no stock in this company," Tara Jean felt obligated to remind her. Actually, she felt obligated to mark her territory, but she wasn't sure where to pee in this situation.

Celeste agreed. "None at all."

"So, if you stay, it's at my discretion. If I ask you to leave . . ."

"Off I go."

"I'm the boss."

"I understand."

Tara Jean shook her head in astonished envy. Celeste managed to agree with her mouth, but her whole demeanor said otherwise. No one was this woman's boss.

"I'll sic Maggie on you if you give me grief," Tara Jean said, and Celeste laughed.

"That will not be necessary." Celeste walked over to one of the stools at the high counter. "I will sit here and be quiet."

No! the demon cried. *We don't need her. We don't need anyone. It's you and me, baby.*

Deep down, past her guilt and her shame over the memories of her major and minor crimes, was the memory of her mother saying that. Tara Jean had already met Dennis, and Momma had been too late.

Luc slammed the truck door shut and leaned against it, letting the metal take the weight off his battered bones, his sore muscles.

"Christ, Luc." Billy limped by. "I didn't even skate the workout and I hurt."

That's the point, he thought, but didn't say. The point was to hurt now, so that in October in some overtime game against the Sabres, he'd still be fast, still be strong.

But, good lord, the headache! He was going to give this headache a name, try to befriend it, because as an enemy, it was kicking his ass.

"It was a good call getting that Jenkins kid on the ice, he's fast, but—?"

"His temper." Luc nodded. Tyler Jenkins had been easing closer and closer to the ice every day. He rarely said anything, just sat in the bleachers, his quick eyes missing nothing. Yesterday, tired of working out by himself, Luc had asked him to get on the ice.

And this morning Tyler was there again. Already dressed.

The kid had been eager to show off, but when Luc stripped the puck off him, the kid had gotten mad. And it got worse every time Luc outskated him until the kid had tried to check him into the boards.

"I can handle it," Luc said. "He's just a kid."

"What about the peewees?"

"They're fun, aren't they?" Luc asked, and Billy shook his head.

"You're supposed to be training, Luc."

Not really, he thought. *I'm not supposed to be training at all.*

"It's an hour a day, Billy. It's hardly a distraction."

"Fine, but you were the one talking about no distractions a week ago."

He'd been talking about Tara Jean, who was still a distraction, but Luc wasn't going to discuss it.

"I'm gonna let Ruby know we're home, see what she can put together for lunch," Billy said, and stepped into the house.

Luc waited until his friend was gone, because there was a chance that when he stepped forward on his noodle legs he was going to fall flat on his face.

Finally, bracing himself, Luc pushed himself away from the truck and turned, coming face to face with the greenhouse. Silhouette figures crowded the windows, lifting their arms, turning on command.

He heard Tara's laugh, not the flirty one or the fake one. The real one, deep and rich, a sound with the smell and heft of dark coffee.

That laugh stirred a reaction in him. Lust and sympathy. Curiosity. Unwanted concern. Pride.

But he didn't have to be told a third time that his opinion, his help, hell, his very presence weren't needed and so he'd stayed away. From the ranch. From her.

Tara laughed again, and this time it was followed by the sound of Celeste's voice.

Luc would have lifted his eyebrows in surprise if they didn't hurt. The queen and the girl from the wrong side of the tracks were swapping jokes. Go figure.

A shadow detached from the darkness surrounding the door and began to walk toward the house. It took him a few seconds before he realized the shadow was his sister, her hands holding the deep V neckline of her sweater closed.

"Vicks?"

She jumped, her hand slipping. He looked away quickly, but he could still see that his sister, always perfectly dressed in layers of silk and cashmere, didn't have anything on under the sweater.

"What are you doing?" she asked.

"Getting back from practice." He shook his head, wishing he could think clearly past the pain in his head and his body. "What are *you* doing?"

She glanced quickly over her shoulder and then flashed him a bright smile. "Nothing," she said. "In fact, I'm heading into Dallas later tonight. I have a date."

Yesterday, the investigator had found Dennis in a sublet apartment outside Dallas. A shabby low-rise totally at odds with the man's act.

Luc was having Thiele watch the man while he tried to figure out what to do with this information.

"With Dennis?"

"What's wrong with Dennis?"

"Tara told you about him."

"And I am not about to take the word of a known liar."

She was so fiercely proud, her eyes daring him to hurt her, to take what he knew about that asshole and use it to break her all over again.

He opened his mouth, but the words . . . *he's lying to you. He's playing you because you're so desperate and blind and the cops have a file on him an inch thick* . . . didn't come out.

He would protect his sister another way. Another way that would hurt so much less and might, in the end, actually convince her. Because bringing up Tara Jean and a restraining order would send Victoria through the roof, and undoubtedly, right toward Dennis.

"Invite him here."

"What?"

"Look, Vicks, if you really like him, I believe you. But I feel like maybe I should get to know him a bit better. Just so I can rest easy."

For a moment he felt bad preying on that approval she always needed, but he knew she wouldn't be able to resist the chance to get his blessing.

"You would?" Her smile put rocks in his stomach.

I'm just trying to keep you safe, he thought, rationalizing the guilt. *When you're hell-bent against it.*

"Absolutely. We'll put some steaks on the grill. Just let me shower. Give me two hours."

"Okay. I'll call him." Slowly she began to smile, a weak sunrise through clouds. She walked away and reproach ate at him. He was setting her up for disappointment. Either way this panned out, Victoria was going to get hurt.

He grabbed his bag from the back of the truck and turned for the house, but was stopped by the sight of Tara Jean standing in the open door of the greenhouse.

As much as he hadn't been seeing Tara Jean, he'd been thinking about her plenty. But somehow, in all of his thoughts, he never did her beauty justice.

She was, quite simply, breathtaking.

Her hair was pulled back in a sloppy bun, and the sun hit the gold and turned it white in places, light red and brown in others.

Even her hair wasn't what it seemed.

His stomach growled and his head floated for a second, pushed off his neck by hunger and fatigue.

"Are you okay, Luc?" She stepped forward, and then stopped when he scowled.

"Why is everyone asking me that?"

"Because you look like shit."

"It was a hard workout."

"You're training a lot these days, aren't you? I mean . . . I haven't seen you here. Much."

"I got the impression you didn't want me around. Much."

Silently, she licked her lips and he nearly moaned—it felt like Lashenko had taken a slap shot to his skull.

"Your head . . . is it bothering you?"

He dropped his hand, not even realizing he'd been rubbing his forehead. "I think this staying-out-of-each-other's-business thing works both ways." He slammed the car door shut.

"You don't have anything left to prove, Luc," she said. "You're the best—"

"I thought I was a washed-up hockey player too stupid to know when to retire."

"Well, you're that too," she said with a half-smile that unbelievably made him laugh.

Maybe it was because he was so tired, worn thin in so many places, but for a moment, a second, he wished he didn't have to work so hard anymore. He wished he could sit back and look at what he'd done, what he'd achieved, and feel the pride he knew he should. That anyone in his right mind would feel.

The woman in front of him, with all her complications, was looking at him with both pride and worry. He wondered what she saw. And why he couldn't see himself the same way.

But he couldn't. There was some engine at work in him and it wouldn't let him rest. Wouldn't leave him alone.

"Luc, honestly, are you okay?"

"Tara, you keep acting so concerned, I might get the wrong idea."

"You seem to get those anyway." Again, that slight smile, and the distance between them shrank to nothing.

As angry as he was, as confused by her actions and stunned by her lack of trust—under all of that was the hard truth.

He liked Tara Jean Sweet. It wasn't just desire, or curiosity. He liked her. In a way that he didn't like a lot of people.

"Was Victoria here?" she asked, looking puzzled and so beautiful that his body, weakened by too much exercise, got hard in the space of a heartbeat.

He nodded, and her shoulders fell slightly. "Why'd she go?"

"She and Dennis had a date, but I convinced her to invite him here."

"He can't come if I'm here," she said on a sputter. "The restraining order—if he comes within five hundred feet of me, he'll get arrested, and he's been served. He knows that. He won't come."

"I know that. But Victoria—"

She sighed and looked up at the big house, where he knew his sister was going into supreme hostess mode. "Oh, Luc," she sighed.

"Everything I say bounces off of her. I can't convince her. I haven't been able to convince her of anything since her husband ruined her life. But if Dennis shows her what an ass he is . . . maybe then she'll believe me."

"This is going to hurt her," Tara said softly, her voice flush with sympathy, and Luc nodded.

"What else can I do, Tara?"

No one ever asked her opinion. Not unless it was about the width of a leather strap. Just like no one had ever expressed being proud of her. Or offered her something without expecting something in return—and yet Luc had done it over and over. A place to stay. Offering to sell the company.

And she didn't even know how to show him how grateful she was.

Not without getting naked.

That's sick, she thought, watching his lean face crease

into a grimace. Something was bothering him and she wondered if other women—normal women—would know how to make him feel better. Without getting naked.

She'd never recognized the careful fence line Lyle had put up around her when she first moved out here four years ago. He had given her this environment where she worked, she played . . . what had Jacob called her? Bimbo Barbie? Perfect. She played the part of Bimbo Barbie with such skill that even she looked in the mirror and was fooled.

And she had thrown herself into Baker Leather. Everything else was scrub brush and dirt on the other side of the fence. How to be something other than a con artist? How to feel about men, and the past? Relationships, being alone? How to feel about Jane Simmons? All of that had been gratefully pushed away. It was as if Lyle had understood how her head hurt, how her battered heart just couldn't take it anymore. And so she had lived four years inside this fence, and now . . . having told the cops about her past, having gotten rid of the Dennis threat . . . she realized she wanted more.

Not a husband or a bunch of kids burping on her clothes . . . but a life. A real one. A chance to figure out who she was between Tara Jean Sweet and Jane Simmons.

And what better way than with Luc?

She was safe with him. As safe as she wanted to be, and he was leaving in five months to go back to his life.

He could be her training wheels.

"Can I . . . can I help?" she asked, and his eyes opened wide. "I mean it's not like she believes me, but—"

"You want to come? Eat dinner with my family?"

She took a deep breath and slapped down every rogue fear, every lingering ghost, and took that first step outside the fence she lived behind.

"If that's what you're doing." She smiled, but nerves quickly chased the smile away. He watched her, his eyes level and unreadable, and her stomach curled with humiliation.

He was going to say no; she'd pushed him away too many times. He knew . . . holy hell, he knew too much about her. Why in the world would he even consider having her at his family dinner? She was the poison. He knew that.

"Never mind—"

"Yes."

"But . . . you know what I did."

"Yeah."

"And you still want me there?"

"I still want you, Tara."

chapter 21

This was a nightmare of epic proportions. Three hours ago, Dennis had been excited about coming to the ranch and she'd set the table with such care, her heart on fire with hope, setting out the good crystal so that it caught the end-of-day sunlight and threw prisms across the formal dining room.

But then the sun set behind the trees. And six o'clock came and went.

And she stood in the dark dining room unable to turn on the lights feeling the weight of everyone's expectation and disapproval pushing nails into her skin.

"Vicks?" Luc called from the kitchen, his footsteps coming down the small hallway toward her. She couldn't face him. Couldn't face any of them. Not like this.

"Put on the steaks," she cried and ran to the bathroom, her cell phone gripped in her cold, clammy hands.

Locking the door behind her she sat on the stool, grabbed the bluebells she'd put on the windowsill in an effort to make everything lovely for Dennis, and dumped them in the garbage.

And then she took a deep breath and called him.

"I'm sorry," Dennis said, answering after the second ring. "I'm so sorry. Something came up."

"Will you be here soon?" she asked, trying not to sound desperate but failing, at least to her own ears.

"I'm sorry, Victoria. But I just can't get away. We've

had some developments on that land deal outside Phoenix and I have to drive down there tonight. I'm on the road."

"Phoenix? Now?"

"It's the nature of the business, Victoria. You wouldn't understand."

His tone, his words rankled, setting loose the small beasts left over from her marriage. *Do. Not. Condescend. To. Me.*

But, because she had the practice, had gotten so good she didn't even realize she was doing it until it was too late, she swallowed her protests, like a swarm of angry bees.

"How long will you be gone?"

"A week. Two at the most."

She'd been down this road before with Joel, and arguing, begging, and pleading for attention only got her less.

"I am sorry," he said. "Really. I was looking forward to spending more time with you."

She licked dry lips. "It's . . . it's okay."

"I'll talk to you later tonight."

It was her brother's fault, Tara Jean's fault, but suddenly she felt suspiciously played. Orchestrated.

"We'll see," she whispered and hung up.

Victoria carefully smoothed back her hair and ran a hand down the front of her ivory silk shell, as if it were the combination to a lock. Hair in place, clothes orderly, life in control.

She splashed some water over her face and then carefully applied lipstick, a little more blush.

With hands that shook.

He could be lying, she knew that. She was in fact terrifyingly aware that he probably was, but she couldn't help wanting to believe him. She couldn't help wanting his words to be real.

In fact, staring at herself in the mirror, she was well aware that she needed to believe them.

She needed a man to give her worth.

She met her own eyes, so dark in the ghostly face in the mirror.

"I hate you," she breathed.

Someone rattled the door and she jumped, dropped her phone into the sink, and swore, blinking back acidic tears.

"Just a second," she called. Using the cream hand towels, she dried off her phone and swung open the door.

Only to find Tara Jean, like the Spanish Inquisition with a boob job, waiting for her.

Instinctively, Tara Jean stepped back, because for all her silk shells and knee-length skirts, Victoria looked like a nuclear bomb about to go off.

"It's all yours," Victoria said, trying to slide past Tara Jean. Tara Jean sidestepped in her way, and Victoria reared back as if she had been slapped.

And people call me dramatic, Tara thought.

"He's not coming," Victoria hissed like a cornered cat. "He had to leave town. Are you happy?"

Tara shook her head, sympathy nearly swamping her. "No. I'm not."

"Oh, stop pretending like you care about me, or my family. No one is going to marry you and make you rich anymore. You can drop the act."

"I don't want to fight," Tara Jean said, feeling as if she were negotiating with a crazed gunman. "I just . . . I wanted to make sure you're okay."

"Bullshit." The curse was surprising. Guttural. And then, much to Tara's surprise, Victoria pushed her, a sharp jab to the shoulder. The woman's eyes opened wide and then . . . she did it again. Hard enough to hurt a little. "You don't care about me."

Well, well, well, thought Tara Jean. Though it had been a while since she'd been in a hair-pulling catfight, it might just be what Victoria needed.

In fact, Tara Jean would put money on it.

She pulled off her earrings. She'd learned the hard way about big hoops.

"What are you doing?" Victoria asked as Tara Jean braced herself against the wall to kick off her shoes.

"Getting ready to fight. Isn't that what you want? I'd lose the necklace if I were you. Those pearls are going to be a bitch to find once I snap the string."

"I'm not going to fight you." Victoria channeled the aghast queen pretty well, and Tara smiled.

"You sure? Because I think you could use it."

"You have no idea what I need," Victoria said, and Tara sobered. This wasn't funny, and a fight—just like screwing around with Luc—wasn't going to change that.

"I do," Tara Jean said. "I know you don't want to believe that, but I do. And I think, down under those pearls and the uptight hairdo—" Victoria put her hand to the loose bun at the back of her neck—"you know it, too."

Victoria opened her mouth to say something, but nothing came out and sensing weakness, Tara Jean pushed ahead.

"Whatever Dennis has told you," she said, "or made you believe, it's a lie. It's what he does. He lies."

Victoria's cheeks went white and then bright red, and in a heartbeat she knew what Dennis had made Victoria believe.

That she was beautiful. Womanly. Desired.

"You guys okay?" It was Luc coming around the corner at the worst possible time and Victoria went on the attack, like a wounded, cornered badger.

"What the hell is she even doing here?" Victoria asked Luc, pointing at Tara.

"I didn't know there was a guest list."

"And you want to fuck her."

Oh! Tara Jean would have applauded if it wouldn't have made things worse. It seemed Victoria was finding some backbone under that ugly cashmere sweater.

Honestly, it was June in Texas—who was that woman dressing for?

"Vicks?" Luc stepped toward her, but Victoria slapped his hand away.

"You are just like Dad."

Luc's head snapped backward and Tara held her breath, knowing that wasn't an insult he would let slide.

"That's not true. And you know it."

"Are you going to deny that you want to fuck her?"

"Okay," Tara said. "This is getting a little—"

"I like Tara Jean," Luc answered as if she weren't actually speaking, and Tara's mouth shut so hard her teeth clicked. "I like her a lot, and if you gave her a chance you would like her too."

"I doubt it. I don't have a dick."

Tara Jean went back to slipping off her shoes. Now, she was the one who needed a fight.

"Stop." Luc held out his hands—a bad referee between a wounded badger and a wounded slut. "Just . . . stop."

"Dad's dead, Luc," Victoria snapped. "He can't see you chasing after his would-be-wife, he can't see you killing yourself on the ice or bossing me around—"

"I know that," Luc insisted.

"I don't think you do, because you're still waiting for that guy to give you a reaction. Or his approval. And it's not going to happen!"

"Yeah, and what are you waiting for?" Luc asked back. "Another man to come along and screw up your life even worse?"

"Luc," Tara said, stepping in where she knew she wasn't wanted, but just might be needed. "I think she gets the point."

Victoria's eyes darted between Luc and Tara Jean and slowly she smiled, and Tara realized too late what this looked like. What she looked like.

"If you were waiting for a woman to screw up yours, I think you found her," Victoria said, snide and superior.

And right.

Victoria stomped off, her head held high, and Tara had to give the woman points for her exit.

"You all right?" Luc asked.

"The day I can't handle your skinny sister is the day they put me in my grave."

"I don't know, she was pretty pissed, wasn't she?" His lips curled up in a soft smile, utterly at odds with the insults his sister had thrown at him.

"And that's a good thing?"

"Anger has to be an improvement, doesn't it? Over depression? And desperation? Over lying down and playing dead every time someone recognizes her and hates her for crimes she didn't commit? Anger is better."

Tara couldn't help but admire Luc's brain. His empathy. His too-big heart. He saw things for what they really were, past the lies people told and the walls they put up. Lord knows, most of the time when he turned those handsome hazel eyes on her they felt like a spotlight she had no hope of hiding from.

"Probably," she agreed. Anger had kept her warm on many a cold night.

His regard grew familiar, intimate, and she realized how small this corner was. How dim. How little effort it would take to believe the rest of the house, the whole world was gone.

And it was just them.

He was so close she could smell the beer he must have drunk on his breath. She'd smelled beer on a hundred men's breath. And somehow it was always sour, the smell of a bad decision.

But Luc smelled sweet. Intoxicating.

"You like me, huh?" she asked, relaxing into the shadows. Relaxing into the way this man made her feel.

His hand landed on the wall beside her head, his body close enough that she could feel the heat of him. The smell of him, beer and spices, soap and that little something extra that was all him. She wanted to investigate that smell, trace it back to its origins.

"I think I've made that clear."

He didn't ease closer, just left that distance between them, and she wanted to arch toward him. Pull him flush against her body—and she could have done that a month ago, but now she found herself lacking the courage. Unbelievably, she felt shy. Unsure of her welcome.

She played with the collar of his golf shirt, her finger brushing the hot skin of his neck, and her body woke up with a hum, a long, slow purr of pleasure.

When he leaned down, she closed her eyes, her body thrumming, pulled taut on a wire of expectation.

"I'm not used to begging." He breathed against her skin and her breath left in a whoosh, leaving her empty, waiting to be filled.

By him.

"You don't have to beg." She nearly laughed. She was ready to beg; she was ready to do whatever this man wanted.

His fingers left the wall, feathered across her collarbone, then his thumb traced her ear. He breathed a kiss across her cheek. Her lips. She sighed, reached for him, and he was gone—a wind she couldn't catch. She smiled, her eyes fluttering shut. This felt like falling backwards into a dream. Some kind of fantasy. A game for someone younger, far more innocent than she.

"It seems I do." The air between them, the inches that separated them, was thick. Flush with restraint. Ripe with illicit possibility.

"You've pushed me away too often, Tara, for me to accept this at face value." His thumb traced her eyebrows, her hairline.

"You want to know if my intentions are honorable?"

"I want to know if this is just a game for you. A chance to fuck with my head."

Oh, oh she hated that that was what he thought, but of course he did. What else could he think?

She put her hands against his cheeks, feeling the rough scrape of his beard, the hard clench of his muscles. In the dark room his eyes shimmered.

"My intention is to get into your pants." She couldn't resist the sudden sweetness of his smile, so she kissed him, a hard smack. "I won't push you away again, Luc. I don't have the strength. I like you. A lot."

His chuckle against her ear lit fires along her body, small pockets of heat that breathed to life in her neck, her breasts, between her legs, and her blood began to hum, carrying the fire across her skin. All she could do was stand there, inches from him, and burn.

He leaned closer, his chest meeting her breasts, and she gasped, melting hard against him. His big, hot hands curled around the small of her back, making her feel delicate, a feather on a breeze. Finally, in the dark, in the heated shadows, she found his mouth.

And it was like the answer to a question she didn't know she needed answered. Curling her hands into the silk of his hair, she held onto him and opened her mouth, licking his lips. Taking her time to taste him, to chart the contours of his mouth, the delicate arch of his lips, the hard ridge of his teeth.

The kisses were long and slow, open-mouthed and consuming. As if they had all the time in the world to just stand here and kiss. It was somehow both innocent and the best kind of sinful.

He stepped forward, pushing her against the wall, his fingers cupping her head as if he was holding her still so he could just taste her. Just eat her. One kiss rolled into the next.

It was the sexiest thing she'd ever been a part of, this endless kiss. Her skin opened up to his and it was as if their clothes had melted and she felt him along her bones, in her blood.

Her fingers traced the rigid muscles of his back, marveling at the strength that made him so different. So delicious. She wanted to lay him out and taste every inch of him, every muscle and sinew.

She wanted to lay him down and make snow angels on all that skin.

"What's so funny?" he asked against her lips, and she shook her head.

"You don't want to know."

"Is it dirty? Because if it's dirty, I'd really like to hear it."

Standing on tiptoe, she whispered some choice filth in his ear and he groaned, pulling her closer into the bow of his body, and she wished she could just stay there. Stay there forever, caught in this web of lust and affection.

But as the kisses became less languorous and more consuming, lust outweighed affection and soon she was pushing herself into him, grinding the hottest of her hot spots against his body, searching for the relief she knew he could so spectacularly give her.

Her fingers found the soft, sensitive skin just under the

hem of his shirt, the muscles that flexed and jumped at her touch, and she curved her hands under his belt, over the hard curves of his professional-athlete ass.

A muffled curse split the darkness just before the overhead lights flipped on, and Tara leapt away from Luc as if he were suddenly made of bees.

Eli, his hand frozen on the light switch, stood in the opposite doorway, the formal dining room table dressed to the nines between them.

"Eli . . . ah, what are you doing?" To her great embarrassment, her voice squeaked.

Luc didn't help matters by laughing.

"Ruby called my cell, said there was an extra steak."

"There is!" she cried. "Isn't that great?"

"Calm down, Tara," Luc said. "He just caught us kissing. We weren't robbing the place."

Eli's eyes, full of accusation, sliced through Tara, right to Luc. Luc's laughter stopped on a dime, and the room exploded with tension.

"If you have a problem, Eli—" Luc pushed away from Tara, stepping toward Eli, and Tara put a hand on his chest, felt his heart thunder under her palm.

"Don't," she whispered.

It took a moment but finally he smiled, lifted her hand from his chest, and kissed the palm.

"I'd better go check on those steaks."

The hush that settled over the dining room as Luc left was weighty, but she shook it off.

"It was just a kiss—"

"Don't bullshit me, Tara."

"All right, I had my hands down his pants."

His eyes shamed her, because he was just worried. When so many people didn't think of her twice, Eli was worried.

"I'm okay, Eli. Honestly."

"He's a Baker—"

"Not all of them are bad, Eli. Luc . . . Luc is a good guy."

"He's going to leave. Once this farce of a will is done, he's out of here."

"And you think that bothers me?" she asked, surprised at the way he must think of her. "You think I've got plans past next week?"

He blew a long breath out of his nose, sounding like one of the Anguses. "I'm just worried about you, Tara."

Her heart melted a little. "And that is about the sweetest thing, Eli. But I don't need worrying."

He grunted, and she didn't know if that grunt meant agreement or that he thought she was full of shit, but he stepped around the table and headed toward the kitchen, where the scent of grilling meat was beginning to waft in from the patio grill.

Falling in step behind him, she had to marvel at the strange turn her life had taken. After a lifetime of taking care of herself, of fending off the wolves on her own, she suddenly had a hockey player and a cowboy standing up to defend her long-gone honor.

It was enough to make a girl giddy.

"Jacob!" Luc yelled, walking through the barn into the empty arena. It had been a long night, and he'd spent most of it staring up at the ceiling telling himself that Tara had to come to him. He'd chased her enough.

But she never came.

"Come on, buddy, it's time to go!"

He paused, waiting for movement, waiting for the kid to sneeze, but there was nothing but silence and the cry of barn swallows.

Frustrated and running late, he headed back through the barn.

From the corner of his eye, Luc saw Eli step into the

barn and stop, staring at him down the long middle aisle.

In the back of his head, the spaghetti western music started up.

"Hey, Eli." Luc walked down the hallway, ready to bite this particular problem off at the root. He didn't need an overprotective cowboy with a grudge against the Bakers messing up his sex life.

"Luc." Eli brusquely dropped the saddlebag he carried over the low open door of the stable.

"About last night—"

"Tara's a big girl. She made it clear it was none of my business."

Oh. Luc felt like he'd shaken off his gloves for nothing. "Good."

"But this ranch *is* my business." Eli's smile held no affection, and very little humor. It was the anti-smile. "I'm holding an auction for the Angus herd."

"You're selling it?" Luc asked, startled.

"I am. Beginning of September."

Eli stood there, shoulders squared, as if daring Luc to oppose him. "All right," he said with a shrug.

"And I want to buy back my family's land." The guy was carrying a hundred-year-old generational grudge, as if the wounds were fresh. The bitterness was poisonous and Luc wanted nothing to do with it.

"Look, Eli, I have no interest in keeping your land."

"Really? Then you'll have no problem selling it to me."

All the land. Some of it. He didn't care. "It's yours." Luc shook his head. "I think with the exception of the house and Tara's studio—"

"I want it all."

Now, Luc could give a shit about the ranch, but the tone in Eli's voice put every single battle instinct on edge and he found himself wanting to fight for the sake of fighting.

"This land was my family's," Eli said. "From the very beginning."

"And your family lost it or sold it for nothing—from the very beginning."

"And I'm going to get it back. I'll take care of Tara. And the ranch. All of it. When you go back to your life, there's no reason for you to come back here."

"Is this about Tara?" Luc had no idea where this animosity was coming from, because it felt jealous and protective.

"No, Luc, it's about the damn ranch. Once this land is rid of all of you I can start again. Fresh."

Luc gaped at the man in front of him. The man who had worked year after year for Lyle Baker, playing the part of loyal employee. Practically a family member.

"All these years, I always thought my dad would have been happier with you as a son. But you were just biding your time until you could get back the land?"

"I didn't like him, Luc. Maybe not as much as you didn't like him, but not by much. The man took advantage of my father at the worst time of his life."

"That sounds like Lyle."

Suddenly, Luc wanted nothing more than to be free of the past, of his father's machinations, of this man's bitterness. Other than Tara, there was nothing here for him. And Eli knew it—was counting on it.

"Look, there's nothing I can do for a few more months," Luc said. "My hands are tied by that will."

"When they are untied I want the land."

"My sister is planning on staying at the ranch—"

"She can pay rent."

Luc laughed. "Honestly, Eli, you can't be serious. Pay rent?"

"Those are my terms."

"I haven't even sold you the damn land yet."

"Your family has no interest in this place. If your sister is looking for a quiet place to hide out, she's welcome to do it here. For a small fee, probably much smaller than she'd pay anywhere else. I've been paying rent on my family's home for twenty years."

Luc did the quick math. "Since your mom left?"

"Since Dad started drinking and had to sell the land to Lyle in order to pay his debts."

"Oh Christ, Eli, I had no idea—"

"Why would you? You had a life of your own. A career. The old man drove you away. Just like he drove off everyone else."

"Except you."

"And Tara Jean."

There it was, the wellspring of Eli's protectiveness toward Tara; Eli didn't think Luc deserved her.

He clearly didn't know the whole truth about the woman he was defending. As soon as the ugly thought entered his head, his stomach twisted. That wasn't how he saw her.

Was it?

"You're going to leave, Luc," Eli said as if reading Luc's mind. "Don't hurt her any more than she's already been hurt."

"What do you think?" Jacob asked, lifting up the page of sketch paper he'd been drawing on.

"Is it a dog?" Tara asked.

"A horse!"

Tara winced. "Horses have longer legs." Reaching over his shoulder to grab one of her wax pencils, she accidentally knocked over the cup. Pencils spilled across the drafting table and he scurried to pick them up.

"I'll get them," he cried and carefully, as if defusing a

bomb, she reached out and touched his shoulder, the fragile bird bones of his shoulder.

"It's all right."

He'd been coming to her studio every day since last Tuesday, and as hard as she thought it might be to hang out with this kid—any kid—after years of thinking of them as one step up from nuclear waste, it wasn't.

It was a joy.

"So? Are you a good artist?" he asked, as they chased pencils across the floor.

"I like art." She shrugged, not quite sure how to answer such a question. "I always liked to draw."

He nodded like a puppy, his hair flopping like ears, his eyes shining with the most pure and simple affection. It was addicting, that affection. Better than candy. "I'd love to draw all day."

"That part is fun."

"Then you're lucky, aren't you?" he asked, blinking his big, wide eyes at her.

Lucky? The word was like ancient Arabic. Something she needed translated to understand.

"I think you're lucky," he said, handing her the wax pencils like a bouquet of flowers.

"Jacob?"

Tara nearly dropped the pencils and stepped away from the boy, as if she'd been caught doing something wrong.

"Hey, Uncle Luc," Jacob called in greeting, spinning around on his stool to face Luc where he stood in the doorway to her studio, backlit by bright sunshine.

Watching Luc walk toward Jacob, his body so lean and powerful, a work of art underneath a gray T-shirt and a pair of athletic shorts, she wished they were alone.

First she'd strip him, exorcise this lust that had been eating her brain since he'd stepped onto the ranch, and then . . . then she'd draw him. All those curves and planes, the strength and grace.

She'd never done that before—sketched someone—but she wanted to sketch him.

Maybe she was more of an artist than she thought.

Or maybe she just needed to get laid.

Luc's eyes blazed as if he could read her mind.

"You ready to go?" Luc asked, and Jacob shook his head.

"Uncle Luc," the boy whined, "I hate Saturday morning craft club."

"Sorry, kiddo, but your mom signed you up—"

"Mom's at the lawyers, she won't know if I don't go. I can stay here and hang out with Tara!"

Tara blushed at his enthusiasm, suffused with pleasure, like a sugar rush that didn't crash.

"It's fine with me," she said. "He's drawing, that's all. It's sort of like craft club. I can get out the glue gun and the bedazzler."

"Bedazzler?"

"Just one of the tricks of my trade."

"Well, as enticing as a bedazzler might be, my sister will have my head if she comes back and finds Jacob here."

"But Uncle Luc—"

"How about we go to the arena. You can skate with the peewees."

"The peewees?" Jacob gasped as if Luc had offered to let him suit up with the Olympic team.

"Sure thing. Head on inside and get cleaned up—we're leaving in ten."

Jacob was a blur running out the door, all thoughts of Tara and the bedazzler clearly stomped into the dirt by the prospect of a hockey arena.

"I can't believe something called peewees beats bedazzling."

"I can't believe there's something called bedazzling."

He touched her ponytail where it sat, a fat curl on her shoulder. "I waited for you last night," he said.

"I waited for you!" she laughed, and he smiled.

"You know what we need?" he asked, leaning against her drafting table, as if it were normal. As if standing here and flirting was something they'd done a thousand times. His hands in her hair felt so good and she tilted her head up to get more. More of his touch. More of him.

"Ten minutes and a flat surface?"

He choked on a laugh. "A date."

And just like that, her delight in the moment crashed and burned. Dates, in her experience, felt like a business transaction. Dinner for sex. The better the dinner, the better the show she had to put on. "I don't like dates."

"That," he kissed her nose, "is because you've never been on one with me."

"That good, huh?"

"I've been known to show a girl a good time. You like horror movies?"

"No."

"Mini-golf?"

"You're kidding, right?"

"Go-carts?"

"Are you sixteen?"

"All-you-can-eat buffets? We can go dutch." This man in front of her, with the smile and the warmth, the twinkle in his beautiful eyes, was an utter departure from the Ice Man. A different man. And she felt, oddly—and perhaps that was his goal—like she was the only woman to ever see him like this.

Jacob was right—she was lucky.

"How about dinner at The Ritz?" he asked.

"Oh, I'm really going to have to put out now, aren't I?"

The teasing faded from his expression, and his hand

left her shoulder, but his eyes didn't leave her face. "I don't think of you that way. I swear I don't."

She wondered, briefly, whether he was trying to convince himself or her. But the thought felt treasonous; he'd been nothing but good to her.

"That's all right. I think of *you* like that." He didn't laugh, and she tilted her head. "Luc—"

"You know I'm leaving, right?" The question blew her back in her stool. "When the season starts, I'm leaving. I'll sell the land to Eli and I won't be back."

Laughter bubbled out of her throat before she could stop it. "It's one of the things I like best about you, Luc. You don't need to worry that I'm planning our pig-roast wedding."

"I just don't want to hurt you, Tara."

He was so earnest, so sweet in his concern, and she pressed her lips to his. "I'm very tough."

His lips lingered over hers, his tongue licking at the crease and she let him in, falling right back into lust, as if the hours since the last time they'd kissed him hadn't happened.

The blaring honk of a car horn pulled them apart.

"Jacob," Luc said, kissing her nose.

"You'd better go."

"I was surprised to find him in here."

"He's been coming by. He likes to draw."

"Last week you didn't want him in your workshop, and now you're inviting him in for arts and crafts? What changed?"

Everything. Absolutely everything, but she didn't know how to say that without sounding crazy. Without somehow ruining the magic that had suddenly appeared in her life.

"I'm not . . . I'm not good with kids. But I'm trying."

"Are you scared of him?" Luc asked, all too knowing.

"Maybe. Yes."

"Well, he is terrifying. All that asthma. Lucky for you I've saved you from the seven-year-old." He walked across her workshop and paused at the door as if he was about to say something else. She wondered, poised on the tips of her hope, if he was going to ask her to come with him. Because she wanted to go. Her work was done, the samples shipped off. She wanted to play hookie.

"Do you want to come—"

"Yes." She grabbed her purse and stood.

He blinked at her sudden agreement. "You'll, ah . . . need a coat."

"It's a hundred degrees outside."

"It's an ice arena. Trust me. I don't want you to get cold." She grabbed a coat from the rack behind her desk, wondering how he made such a simple statement sound like a line from a love song. "You know they have flat surfaces at the arena and I bet I could find us ten minutes."

Tossing her hair over her shoulder, she breezed past him. "I'm holding out for The Ritz." She put the old swing back in her walk, knowing just how she looked in tight denim, and his chuckle was like music to her ears.

chapter 22

"Good practice, guys," Luc said, and all the little kids cheered, half of them falling on the ice at the effort. Luc laughed, hoisting them up by their pads.

Jacob wasn't one of them. The kid was rock solid on his skates. He wasn't fast, he had no idea how to hold a stick, but he could stay on his blades, and that put him slightly ahead of the class.

"Great job, buddy," Tara said as she awkwardly helped Jacob off the ice and onto the mats leading back to the changing rooms.

Luc would be lying if he said he wasn't totally turned on by the sight of Tara Jean in a hockey arena. She wore this white breezy top under a denim coat and when she leaned over he could see the tops of her breasts, and while that was hot, what was really killing him was the smile on her face. It illuminated her, and in her joy she was a different person.

"Can you help me with my pads?" Jacob asked.

"Who? Me?" Tara asked, glancing up at Luc as if the boy had asked her to help him rob a bank.

"You just pull," Luc said. "It's not that hard."

"Oh . . . well, okay. I can help you." Jacob wobbled his way across the mats toward the dressing room. Tara turned to follow, but Luc couldn't let her go without a kiss.

A quick press of cold lips and colder cheeks. A hot swipe of tongue. Perfect.

"There are kids present, Baker," she chastised, kissing him quickly and then turning to follow Jacob, taking his hand as they went down the stairs.

Billy, in a suit with the tie pulled askew, stood against the bleachers watching.

"Shut it," Luc said, unable to suppress a smile.

"It's good to see you happy, that's all."

"How'd the meeting go?" Luc asked. His friend had had a breakfast meeting with the Dallas brass and then gone to check out his new condo before meeting Luc at the rink.

"Fine," he sighed, catching a kid by the shoulder pads when the boy looked like he was about to go down. "They're talking about team building and everyone knows I've only got a few years left. By the time the team builds enough to get a playoff spot I'll be out to pasture."

"You don't know that," Luc said, but Billy was probably right.

"Come on, look at us," Billy said. "If we were smarter, we'd be getting out."

"I never claimed to be smart," Luc said, and Billy smiled, but both of them knew they were skating into overtime.

"Hey!" He heard the scrape of skates over ice and knew Tyler was behind him. All the peewees were off the ice. "You ready, Mr. Baker?"

"Your protégé awaits," Billy said, and Luc tried not to roll his eyes. The kid was impatient and oftentimes rude. Talented, yes. But the longer he worked with the kid, the more the attitude came out. And now there was too much attitude for it to be any fun.

Maybe that was why he liked the peewees. No attitude.

But Tara Jean was going to be sitting up in those stands and he was going to skate that kid into the ice.

Not that he was showing off or anything.

"You mind taking Jacob home?" Luc asked, realigning some tape on his stick and carefully avoiding looking at Billy.

"The kid cramping your style?"

"I just . . . it would be nice to have some time alone with her. Dinner. A movie or something. Something normal."

Billy nodded. "Unless you want me to get out there and teach Tyler some lessons. He's getting a little too comfortable with the cheap shots."

"I got it." Luc pushed off the boards.

"Whoa, where are your pads?" Billy asked. "Your helmet."

Luc smiled, his skates biting into the ice. "It's just some drills, Billy. I think I can handle it."

Tara Jean walked back into the arena after getting Jacob strapped into the back of Billy's Jeep and sat down in the empty bleachers, shivering in her light coat.

Billy had offered to give her a ride home, his scarred lip twisting in a knowing smile, and Tara Jean had declined, a blush climbing her cheeks.

A blush. Her. Tara Jean Sweet.

All because Luc had rigged it so they could have some time alone.

Dinner at The Ritz sounded good. Sounded perfect right about now.

She watched Luc on the ice with a young man. They were working some drills, and she could hear Luc's voice correcting the boy as he skated down the ice. Luc kept getting in the kid's way, taking the puck like it was candy.

She smiled when Luc laughed. The young man didn't like that, his voice rose in anger, but Luc kept laughing. The kid started skating harder, steam all but rising from his skates.

But Luc was always just ahead of him.

"Tara Jean."

The world dropped away. The voice in her ear was the last one she had expected to hear, and for a second it didn't register. It didn't make any sense.

Dennis stepped over the bleacher to sit beside her.

Shocked, unable to force herself into motion, she gaped at him. The man was frayed around the edges, his polish long gone. His beard was coming in, making him look like a weasel. The dark shadow under his bloodshot eye hinted at an aging shiner.

"What the hell are you doing?" Her hands fumbled as she pulled her phone out of her purse. "I have a protection order. You can't be here."

With one hand he grabbed her phone, tossing it a few bleachers down as if it were nothing. As if her protection order were nothing.

She stood and opened her mouth to scream, but Dennis reached up and grabbed her by the back of her hair. "Your fucking protection order is the least of my problems, bitch. I need that money."

"Fuck you."

He clenched his fist, pulling all the fine hair at her nape, and she couldn't swallow the cry of pain.

"Do you think I'm kidding?" he asked, nearly spitting in her face. "Do you think this is a joke? I need that money."

"You won't get it. Luc—"

"Yeah, Luc. Your dickwad boyfriend's got someone following me asking questions about us."

For a second she went numb—the pain in her head, the fear in her heart—and for a heartbeat she felt nothing. "What?"

"Yeah," he grinned. "Not so tough right now, are you? Listen, if I get dragged down without that money, I'm taking you with me. I will ruin you, Jane. And I'll ruin that family. Get me that money."

"Let go of me," she said through her teeth and the second he let go of her hair she leapt to her feet, getting as much distance between them as she could.

On the ice, Luc was skating her way, watching the younger man skating to his left, but at her movement he lifted his head. For a moment he seemed to smile, but then Dennis stood up beside her and Luc's smile vanished, replaced by the intensity and hate she hadn't seen since he first arrived at the ranch. Luc dropped his stick and shook off his gloves, running toward the boards, no doubt ready to climb up there in his ice skates to take Dennis's head off.

But on the ice, the young man Luc was skating with shook off his gloves, misinterpreting Luc's aggression.

"Fine," the boy yelled, "let's go, old man."

Luc turned his head just as the young man rammed him into the boards. There was a scuffle, a fleshy thud, and then they both fell to the ice, the boards blocking her view.

Dennis pushed her, knocking her down hard on her hip, and she scrambled back up, reaching for his shirt as he leapt over the bleachers.

"I'll find you," Dennis sneered, looking at her over his shoulder.

Dennis cleared the last bleacher and sprinted down the hallway toward the stairs that led to the parking lot.

Damn it! she thought, rubbing her elbow where it had banged into the hard wooden benches.

"Help!" someone yelled and she whirled toward the ice. The young man was on his feet, his helmet gone, red hair sticking up on his head in thick, wild clumps, his face white with panic. "I need help!"

Panic ballooned in her chest at the sight of Luc's legs on the ice, his upper body still blocked by the boards.

He wasn't moving.

chapter 23

Luc came to, in large part because of the smell.

The closest smell to home he had. Sweat. Bengay. Rubber. He was in a locker room.

But beneath the sweat and disinfectant was an underlying note of strawberry.

His eyelids popped open and then immediately slammed shut, his eyeballs screaming in pain, blasted by white-hot light.

"Luc?"

It was Tara Jean. The strawberry smell washed over his face and he could feel her, just above him. God, his head hurt or he'd be worried about what was going on, what had happened. Not to say he wasn't, but the pain sort of made everything else a distant second on the worry scale.

"Luc." Again, the sweet wash of strawberry, made sweeter by the warmth of her hand on his. She curled her fingers around his and he held on, happy to have a lifeline in the sea of pain. "Can you hear me?"

He opened his mouth, but speaking seemed a ridiculous idea. So he nodded and winced.

"You need a doctor—"

His eyes flew open and his fingers clamped down on hers. He didn't know what was going on, what had happened, but he knew doctors were not a good idea. "No doctors."

She leaned over him, blocking out the white-hot light. Lights, actually. His vision cleared, her face in focus.

"Hi," he said, happy to have her here, over him. He glanced down and could practically see her belly button through the gaping neck of her shirt. "You have pretty boobs."

"Oh my lord," she muttered, clapping a hand to that wide-open neckline, blocking his view of her lace bra and the flesh rising out of it. "You must be feeling better."

"What . . . what happened?"

"You got knocked out."

For a moment he was blank, almost weightless with that calm before the storm, but then his stomach twisted and anger chugged in his veins and a terrible sense of inevitability nearly crushed him.

"Tyler."

"He says he didn't even hit you that hard. You just went down. But he feels terrible. He's outside, practically pulling out his hair."

"Good," Luc murmured. "Maybe he'll second-guess a cheap shot next time."

"Are you . . ." She paused. Her fingers touched his head, his hair, and it was so sweet, like being touched by sunlight on a cold day. "You okay?"

"How long was I out?"

"Long enough; I called an ambulance."

He curled upward and realized he was on a small cot in a closet-sized supply room just off the showers.

"No ambulance."

"But—"

"No ambulance!" he yelled and immediately regretted it. His head pounded. He'd been knocked out, just like Doc said he could be.

If he got in an ambulance, he'd go to a hospital, see a doctor who would want a CT scan. And he wouldn't be able to hide the damage. The parasites would catch wind and it would all be over. His career. His life.

Tara's hand slid down his back and he shook off her touch.

"Luc?"

"Leave me the fuck alone." She straightened, staring down at him as if he'd grown a second head.

"No."

"Now isn't the time to be stubborn."

"I could say the same."

He twisted, ignoring the pain, the flashes at the edge of his vision. "Get. Out."

Her face mutinous, she sat. "You've been knocked out, Luc. I'm not leaving you alone. You're freaking me out."

Join the club, he thought, *join the freaking-out club.* His shoulders curled over his knees.

"What's going on, Luc?"

"I can't go to the hospital."

"A doctor—"

He lifted his chin to take great gulps of air, hoping that would calm him down, center him in the maelstrom of ugly despair growing in his chest.

"Talk to me, Luc."

He couldn't, he couldn't let these words out of his mouth. He bit them back, swallowed them into his stomach where they bubbled and rolled back up his throat, knocking at his teeth, looking for a way out.

"Luc," she breathed, "it's just us in this room. You can talk to me."

"I get knocked out a lot," he spat, punishing her because she was here and there was so much rage in his chest. "And now, I've got some scar tissue on my frontal lobe."

"Oh my God—"

"Just about everyone in professional contact sports has it."

"That doesn't make it less scary."

"It's part of the job,"

"Well, that's a shitty job."

"It's my life."

Oh, God, his skin was too tight, he couldn't hold in what was happening in his chest. The hurricane of grief and anger that bore down on him. He stood, weaved for a moment, and Tara reached out a hand to help him. But he swatted it away. It felt good, really good, a valve release on the pressure, so he picked up the bar of soap on the small sink to his left and hurled it at the wall. It splattered, leaving blue goo everywhere.

"Holy shit, Luc, what is going on?" Tara asked.

He kicked the small plastic shelf holding medical supplies and it splintered, flew apart, Ace bandages everywhere. He picked up the case and heaved it against the wall.

Blood pounded behind his eyes, his heart hammered in his chest, and there was no outlet for what he felt. He turned and met Tara Jean's eyes, but she didn't flinch. Didn't back away.

"You want to talk, or throw more stuff?"

He didn't answer, couldn't, and she pointed to the water bottles in the corner of the room. His heart burning, he hurled them against the door frame with numb hands. Water sprayed the ceiling, across Tara's shirt.

She sat back down and pulled out her nail file. "Go on. Get it out, Luc."

He broke a hockey stick, kicked the rolling desk chair, and kicked it again when it rolled back into him. Heaved a phone against the wall, broke the small table the phone sat on, and still he stood there, wanting to tear down the world.

"Poor Luc, he's got a headache," she sighed into the quiet.

"My career is over!" he howled, coming to stand over her. Her blue eyes met his, unflinching. "I can't pass another physical and my contract is up in a year. Billy's been traded, every single fighter and thug in the league is gunning for me, and I go down with a tap on the jaw. What kind of career is that? I'll be a laughingstock. A laughingstock with brain damage. Oh my God, can you imagine what my father will say?"

"Your father?"

He blinked. Blinked again. Swallowed the lump of emotion that felt like grief in his throat. Slowly, the fog fell from his eyes, leaving him alone with a thirty-year-old anger that embarrassed him.

"Oh Christ," he muttered.

"Tell me you're not ruining your future because you're still trying to prove something to your father."

His back hit the wall and he slid down to sit on the floor, cradling his poor aching head in his hands.

"Go away," he sighed, hating that anyone would see him like this, but especially her, who'd rejected him at every turn for reasons as fucked up as he was.

Of course she didn't go away. She crouched in front of him, her hands on his elbows. He wished he had the strength to shrug off her touch, but his strength had packed up and left with his anger.

"You told me your father determined your worth, remember? But then you found hockey—"

"I remember," he sighed, lifting his head to look at her.

"You let hockey determine your worth," she said. "You've let it define who you are, just like your father did."

He rubbed a hand over his face and then left it over

his eyes, wanting to block her out. Wanting to block out the truth.

"You are more than what your father thought of you."

"I know—"

"No," she said. "You don't seem to. Because a thirty-seven-year-old man who has done as much as you have, who has succeeded in a way most people never even dream of, shouldn't worry about what his dead asshole of a father would think of him."

He wanted to snarl, to tell her that he didn't give a shit what his father thought of him. That he stopped caring long, long ago.

But he was tired of the lies. Tired of pretending that he was better than caring about the old man's opinion. Because he wasn't. He was still that teenager with the speech that had never been delivered.

"How do I stop?" he asked, naked and vulnerable, torn to pieces in a smashed-up locker room, looking for help from any quarter.

"I don't know," she said. "Practice?"

He laughed, tired and sore down to his soul. His eyes burned and his chest ached as though there were thirty years of plans and work, of blood, sweat, and tears, going up in a bonfire inside him.

"Who am I without hockey?" he whispered to the floor, because he hated who he was right now. Hated his reflection in her beautiful eyes.

"You know what I see when I look at you?" she whispered, and he closed his eyes in pain. She cupped his face, ran her fingers over his cheeks, his lips, but still he didn't look at her.

"I see what you show the world," she said. "I see the Ice Man, and the hard work. I see the intelligence and the leadership. But I also see the man who works with those little kids. The man who takes care of his family—"

Her voice broke and he opened his eyes to see her eyes were damp.

"Tara," he breathed, his hands cupping her shoulders. "Don't do this to yourself—"

"No, let me finish," she said. "I see a man with a vision that most people don't have. Compassion that most people don't have. I see a man with the resources and the heart to do whatever he wants."

"Look at you." He ruffled her dampened eyelashes. "Crying over a broken-down hockey player."

"I'm not crying," she protested and they both smiled, the moment encapsulating them, blocking out the world, and it was beautiful. Perfect. This woman with her defenses down, with every scrape and scar revealed, was for him.

It would be so easy to love her.

"I have not been liked . . . much," she whispered. "And that you would try . . ." She shook her head. "You are a special man, Luc Baker. And hockey is the least of what you can do."

He cupped her shoulder, the heat and softness of her skin burning through his nerves. He wished she would kiss him, and then she did. Soft and tender, her lips, so perfect and sweet, were a benediction. She saw his faults, the weakness in himself he despaired of, and still she kissed him. She opened her mouth, her sweetness pouring out, enveloping him in something he hadn't felt in a long time.

Hope. Hope that his future might be brighter than his past.

"Someone here need an ambulance?" a voice said, and Tara pulled away and stood, running her hands down her skirt. Behind her in the doorway was a paramedic, the white sheets of a gurney behind him.

Luc lifted himself up off the floor. "I don't need an ambulance."

"You've had a head injury," the paramedic insisted. "You need to come in and get checked out. You could be bleeding internally."

Doubt was an avalanche, his desire to linger in ignorance, to pretend that he could be all right at least for the year, but then Tara Jean's hand was there, shoring him up. Pointing him in the right direction.

"I'll drive him," she said. To the hospital. The doctors. The inevitable CT scan. The slow unraveling of his life as he knew it.

Sealing his fate, he nodded.

chapter 24

Victoria sighed and picked up her purse from beside the seat in the hospital waiting room, where she'd been camped out for the better part of the day.

"They're going to keep him overnight," she said to Celeste, who was flipping through a two-year-old *Vogue* and looking as fresh and elegant as if she hadn't been sitting around a hospital for five hours. Victoria was a wrinkled paper sack. That smelled bad.

"I . . . ah . . . better get home."

Celeste sniffed and Victoria stiffened, reading all sorts of judgment in that sniff. The most judging sniff ever.

"I don't want to leave Jacob alone with just Ruby." She knew she sounded like a bitch, but she was sick of falling down in a dead faint every time the queen looked down her royal nose.

"Right." Celeste abruptly put down the magazine. "Let's go."

"You could stick around," Victoria said. "Tara Jean's still here—"

"Nope. I'll go with you."

Great, Victoria thought. *Just great.*

The silence out to the car was the kind that used to make her babble. It used to make her sick with nerves, but now it just made her angry.

"Victoria," Celeste said, once they were in the truck and heading away from the hospital. The older woman ran her long model fingers over the dash of Luc's truck. "I have to ask, what . . . what are your plans?"

"Plans?" She merged across two lanes of traffic to get to the exit.

"For your future."

Victoria stepped on the gas, blowing past the speed limit. She could not get home fast enough. If she didn't answer, if she stared out the window and ignored Celeste and the questions she just had to ask, maybe Celeste would get the point. Or perhaps she'd disappear.

"I'm worried . . . about Jacob's future," Celeste said.

Every single instinct in her screamed to kick Celeste out of the car. To pull over to the side of the road and claw at her perfect skin.

Instead, she cleared her throat. "Well, you don't need to be. The million dollars—"

"But what are you going to do?"

She shrugged. "Remarry, I suppose—"

"Marriage?" Celeste didn't even bother to hide her incredulousness. Her utter laughing disbelief. "That's your solution."

"Why not?"

"Because men aren't a solution, Victoria. They are never, ever a solution."

"Perhaps not for you—"

"Not for anyone. Ever. You can't tell me you were happy. That you actually think another man will make you happier."

"Oh my goodness, Celeste, what does happy have to do with anything?"

"Everything, I think."

"Well, most of us aren't lucky enough to be you."

The silence seethed and she forced herself not to apologize. Not to open her mouth and banish all this discomfort with an act of contrition she didn't mean.

She was tired of that. Building every bridge between

injured parties with her own two hands. Her own blood, sweat, and tears. For Christ's sake—she was pretty injured too. Who was trying to make *her* feel better?

Celeste shrugged. "Do you want to work? Have a job?"

"All I know how to do is shop, go out for lunch, get facials, and redecorate," she said. "Can you find a job in there other than wife?"

"You could always go back to school."

She hit the turn signal with more force than was necessary. "I don't think this is any of your business—"

"You're smart, Victoria, despite your taste in men. Your mother—"

"Don't you dare," Victoria breathed, her anger a blowtorch eradicating any thought of a bridge between the two of them.

"Your mother," Celeste repeated, her voice pitched low, "was no example."

Victoria snorted, every lesson in manners and grace learned in her life with Joel vanished.

"You can do better. You should expect better for yourself. For Jacob."

"Don't you think I want that?" The words scorched her throat. It was like standing naked in front of a mirror and pointing at every fault. "Don't you think that's the whole point of my life?"

"I do," Celeste said, and Victoria turned stunned eyes to the older woman. "I think you are a very good mother. But everyone needs help sometimes, and I . . . I would like to help you. With school."

"Jacob had to miss a lot of school last year," Victoria said, wondering why she was even contemplating this gift. "He'll need tutoring—"

Celeste shook her head. "For you."

Victoria sat silently, tied up in knots she couldn't even begin to unravel.

"Think about it," Celeste said, awkwardly patting her hand, and then, as if dismissing Victoria, she turned slightly and stared out the window.

"Why are you doing this?" she asked, unable to keep the wonder and pain out of her voice.

"I feel . . . I feel partly to blame . . . for the way your father treated you. If I had stayed . . ."

Victoria could only gape; that Celeste would think that was ridiculous. And it was on the tip of her tongue to tell her so, to relieve her of that burden.

But she didn't.

With shaking hands, Victoria turned up the radio.

"You're on the front page of the Sports section," Tara Jean said, stepping into Luc's hospital room. She tossed the Sunday *Dallas Tribune* onto the unmade sheets on his hospital bed and he glanced down at the headline:

ICE MAN BAKER SUFFERS BRAIN INJURY

"That's a bit much," he muttered and didn't bother to read the rest of it. He didn't have the stomach to watch his career go up in newspaper headlines. Adrift from who he was, from the career that had defined him for more than twenty years, he was more than a little numb.

Numb, however, didn't come close to his reaction to Tara Jean.

He didn't want her here.

She'd been relentless in her good cheer. A bright sky of optimism, and all he wanted to do was curl up in a corner and die.

Even the way she was dressed was no doubt supposed to elicit some kind of positive reaction: a tight red halter top, a denim skirt that flirted with her knees, and cowboy boots.

She looked like a Southern wet dream, and previous to this exact moment he couldn't say it was a look that worked for him. But it did. It really did.

That she had no doubt gone to the effort for him pissed him off. Being an object of pity made him sick. Made his ruination even more sour.

"Why are you here?" He couldn't keep the bitterness out of his voice.

"To take you home."

"Anyone could do that. Why you?"

"You . . . you don't want me here?"

"I don't need your pity, Tara. Or your fucking Florence Nightingale routine."

He expected her to flinch, to reel back in pain, because he was a bully and she had lunch money.

"You want me to show you my boobs?"

She managed to stun him out of his acrimony.

"Tara—"

She kicked shut the door and reached behind her to untie the red halter top from around her neck. Her arms, elegant and white, flexed with hidden muscles and his mouth went dry with sudden desire.

Her eyes sparkled with Eve's knowledge as she peeled the cotton/spandex blend from the tops of her milky breasts, pausing just slightly as the top of her nut-brown nipples were revealed.

He was a teenager at a peep show. Transfixed. Turned on. Despite himself.

She ran her thumb across the front of the fold between her breasts and the fabric. Those nipples went hard. So did he.

She pushed the shirt past her breasts, white and perfect. High and round.

"You're beautiful," he murmured.

She pulled her shirt up and tied it back around her neck. "Somehow I don't think you feel better."

"My career is over, Tara Jean. It's going to take more than a peep show." He felt the bite of despair, of a loss so huge it didn't even register.

"Hey, hey, Luc—" She cupped his face, kissed his cheeks. "You're going to be okay."

"You don't know that, Tara." He grabbed her arms, trying not to squeeze, trying not to hurt her, but the well of pain inside him knew no boundary. "I appreciate the efforts, but you really don't have any idea what my life is going to be like."

Finally, the unflagging optimism took a hit and she backed away.

"All right." She crossed her arms over her chest, hiding what she'd just flaunted. "I get it. You want me to call your mom or Billy?"

The way he treated her was one more knife to his throat.

But he was caught up in this current and didn't have the energy to extricate himself.

"No, I just want to go home."

The cell phone beside his bed buzzed and Tara Jean—who'd stayed until after all the tests had been run last night, filing her nails and telling the nurses who were trying to enforce visiting hours that she was his spiritual guide—arched her eyebrows at him when he let it ring.

"You going to get that?"

"It's my agent."

"You don't think you should talk to him?"

"He's only going to tell me that Toronto has dropped my contract and that some headache medicine wants to sign me on as a spokesman."

"That doesn't interest you?"

He sighed and pulled on his jeans. " 'Fraid not."

"Okay." Tara Jean was all business and that suited him, gave him something to rest his anger against. "Anyone you need to talk to before we leave?"

"Nope." He picked up his discharge papers and the stuff his sister and mother had brought from home last night.

He had an appointment in a few days to come back and talk to the neurologist, and he'd already talked to Dr. Matthews back in Toronto. He was going to fly in to consult at the appointment.

It was all very neat and tidy. Official. Appointments and meetings. None of it seemed to have anything at all to do with the long, slow scream in his head.

"I'm sorry, Luc," Matthews had said. "I can't clear you to play, not for a while. And my opinion is that you are a liability on that ice."

Luc had told him it was okay. But the word was like a bubble of oil in his mouth, leaving nothing but grease on his tongue. The end of his career tasted like bad onion rings.

The orderly with the wheelchair waited outside the door and Luc tried to protest, but Tara cut him off.

"Get in, hotshot," she said. "I'll drive."

He waved at the nurses at the desk; he'd signed all their husbands' and sons' and fathers' autographs and he'd been repaid in extra breakfasts. Even a private stock of chocolate chip cookies. And they had let Tara Jean hang out long past visiting hours despite her spiritual advisor nonsense.

Another orderly stopped him in front of the regular exit.

"There are a lot of reporters out there," the man said.

Tara Jean stopped pushing him. "You want to deal with that right now?"

"No," Luc answered. One of Beckett's messages, one of the more frantic ones, had told Luc not to talk to reporters until he and Beckett could come up with a statement.

He'd hold off on talking to any reporters.

"Have you remembered what happened?" she asked, wheeling him through white brightly lit hallways.

"Not yet." No matter how hard he tried to pull up the memories of the hit, all he recalled was talking to Billy before starting the workout with Tyler. And fear ate him, fear that more memories would get snatched away by this concussion until he was walking outside his house wondering where he lived.

"Did you see it?" he asked.

"Not all of it." She stopped pushing the chair and stepped around to face him, her eyes like ice picks. "Dennis was there."

"What?" His funk was blown apart and it felt good to be mad, so he fed that particular fire until his body was alive with something other than self-pity. "Did you call the cops?"

"I got a little distracted, Luc."

He took the hit in stride. "What did he say?"

"That he wants the money."

"I hope you told him to go to hell." Part of him worried that despite severing her connection to her past, she might get sucked in by Dennis.

"Of course I did. But he also said you have some investigator on him, asking questions."

The censure in her eyes put a slight dent in his righteousness, but he met her head on, refusing to apologize for doing the right thing by his family.

"God, Luc, I told you not to do that. I told you—"

"I know what you told me. But it's my family, Tara. I can't sit back and do nothing."

She turned away and he heard her swearing at him under her breath, and he would rather have this woman, with all her vulgar fire, than the sweet nurse she'd been the last twenty-four hours.

She started to push him again with a jerk and his head

snapped back. "Do it your way, but if this blows up in your face it's on you."

"Of course it is."

"Listen to you, tough guy. You have no idea who you're dealing with."

She pushed him through the last door into the sun-splashed parking lot and he stood up. The world was the same, much to his chagrin. It wasn't as if he expected anything different, but with his life so in ruins, the bright, sunny Texas morning seemed like a cruel cherry on top of his crap sundae.

Would a little rain to match his mood be too much to ask?

"Here." Tara handed him sunglasses and put on her own. "You're going to need these."

chapter 25

Luc was being a baby.

She didn't know who he thought he was kidding, sitting in the passenger seat of the SUV cloaked in his indifference. His cool control. While at the same time he was throwing off so much sadness, she was fighting back tears.

Tears she blinked away. Pity, she knew, would not go down well with the Ice Man.

That little show at the hospital, telling her he didn't want her there, stung. But she understood. Weeks ago, that had been her. Hurting him just because he was there and he was trying to see behind the mask she was determined to keep on.

She couldn't look at this man—holding on so hard to his control it was cracking in his hands—and not see the man with tears in his eyes in that destroyed locker room. And he probably thought the same when he looked at her.

It was as if all that ice the Ice Man surrounded himself in had thawed and she saw the collection of fears and misgivings, all the human foibles and dreams held together with chicken wire and masking tape.

And he was all the more beautiful because of it. Not that he'd see that. Not now, maybe not ever.

And he was feeling really shitty right now.

Which was almost enough to make her forgive the

childish behavior, but she was no man's doormat. And considering that twenty-four hours ago she had been ready to go to bed with him—and she still wanted to—she'd need an apology of some kind if he thought he was ever going to see down her shirt again.

Her spine popped straight. *Listen to me,* she thought, surprised by this new feminine strength and proud of it. Once upon a time she would have slept with him just so he'd apologize.

"I'm sorry," Luc said as if he'd read her mind. She turned and met his sad eyes. "For in the hospital. I was mean."

"You were. But I've thrown a few fits in my life. You don't scare me."

"Still. I'm sorry." He touched her hand, curled his finger over hers. "I liked seeing your boobs. I'm glad it was you picking me up. I'm glad . . . I'm glad you're here."

As far as apologies went, it was world class. For her, anyway.

"Thank you," she whispered, and he lifted her hand, kissing her knuckles. Charming, even in his grief.

Oh, what the hell? she thought. In her experience there was one surefire way to make a sad man feel better.

Time to get naked.

She got them off the interstate, onto the two-lane highway leading to the ranch, and then took the first gravel road on the left.

Two hundred meters in the distance there was a left turn down a dirt road that dipped behind the hills. She punched the gas and took the corner so fast gravel spit up behind them.

Luc grabbed onto the handle above the door.

"What are you doing?"

Dust flew up around them as she barreled down the road, stones pinging off the windshield.

"Are you going to kill us?"

She stopped the car under the long branches of a roadside willow.

The silence and the shadow were the perfect cocoon.

She turned off the car and turned to him.

Their connection was intense. Dizzying. As if somehow she could see the ribbons that tied them, that curled around them in an endless figure eight she didn't understand but she could no longer outrun.

"I'm not going to kill you," she whispered. "I'm going to fuck you."

He lunged across the seat, sealing her lips with his. Hot and warm, she melted against him.

It took her a second to unbuckle her seat belt and crawl into his lap, where his heat, the living presence of him, made her sigh with pleasure.

She banished the demon trying to tell her what to do and went with her heart. And her heart told her to put her arms around this man for as long as she could.

He reached beside him and hit the lever to lower the back of his seat and she leaned back.

"You've done this before?"

"Never," he said.

"Come on, a quickie in a car?"

"This . . . quickies in a car only happen if you're out of control."

"And you're never out of control?" Her stomach turned over, like she was on The Zipper at the State Fair when she was a kid.

"There's something about you, Tara Jean . . ."

"That makes you want to get naked in a car."

"That makes me want to get you naked in a car. Naked." He kissed her lips, a nip that made her gasp. "Hot." He sucked on that spot on her neck as if he had a secret map to the places that made her crazy. "And wet."

She shifted her legs so she was straddling him. Her

skirt stopped her from getting close to him, so she wiggled, trying to hike it up past her hips.

Luc helped. His big hands, warm and callused, slid up her legs pushing up her skirt, revealing the bright blue cotton bikini underwear she wore with the smiley face on the crotch.

"Cute," he murmured, his breath fanning her neck, sending goose bumps down her arms and across her back. He smelled like coffee and toothpaste.

With the skirt out of the way, she pressed herself into his lap, gasping when that smiley face met the erection growing under his jeans. Looking into his eyes, she saw the sadness cut away with a knife and she circled her hips, teasing him. Teasing her. Making that smiley face very happy.

His hands slid up under her halter top, across the trembling taut skin of her belly. Her nipples hurt with anticipation; hard and painful, they waited for his touch. Slowly, his palms cupped the undersides of her breasts and her eyes fluttered shut. Breathless, she leaned against him—alive where he was touching her, cold where he wasn't.

She leaned down and put her lips to his neck, bumping her head on the window. Her hips popped away from his, cool air blowing between them, and she moaned in protest, trying to scoot closer. He braced his foot on the floorboards, hitting his knee against the dash. They laughed into each other's skin.

It had been a long time since she'd made out in a car, and she'd forgotten the pleasures of confined places. The bliss of extra-close proximity.

She leaned back, putting her hand against the roof of the car for leverage. His face was dark, the skin nearly red, his lips white from the force applied by his teeth.

His eyes met hers, and for a moment it was the kitchen all over again and what she saw in his eyes was too much. His emotion and need contributed to hers, and the combined weight was going to sink the good ship dry hump.

Closing her eyes seemed the best option—to keep the good times going, to keep her from freaking out again.

Don't count on me past this, don't expect more. Because there is nothing in me to give you. Nothing lasting. Nothing real.

He was seeing things that weren't there. She was empty. Ruined where it mattered a long, long time ago.

Panic cut through the desire.

He's lost his career, she told herself. And he was grabbing onto her with both hands because she was there. He was going to try to make more out of this than there was.

"Tara? What's wrong?"

"It's just sex," she told him. His hips stopped. Smiley face would have frowned had it been able.

"Instead of . . . what? A pony?"

"I'm just saying . . ." She stroked his cheek, trying to take the sting out of her words. "You're a man at a crossroads, Luc. And I'm a diversion, nothing to hold onto."

His chuckle was hot and dangerous, and the temperature in her core climbed. His hands cupped her breasts, his fingers surveying the curves, circling the nipples. She waited for the stroke of his thumb, but instead he pulled her closer and she got the wet heat of his tongue through her shirt as he sucked her into his mouth. She cried out, cupping the back of his head, grinding against him as he used his teeth against her. Pleasure curled and the hot, bright edge of it was pain.

He left that breast, the nipple cold in the damp fabric, to find her other one and his mouth through the fabric was sexy and dirty, but it wasn't what she wanted and she clawed off her shirt, tossing it onto the driver's-side seat.

"I'm not going to argue with you now," he muttered. "Let's just agree to disagree." He cupped her breasts, cradling the weight, kissing and licking the soft and sensitive flesh until honestly she thought she'd go mad with it.

She caught the hem of his shirt and pulled it up, revealing the hard muscles, the soft skin. The fine hair under his arms made her crazy. The dip of muscle to ligament, ligament to bone, and the gorgeous skin that blanketed it all was perfection. Exactly as it should be.

He was an anatomy textbook brought to life.

She kissed his shoulder, traced his bicep, found the ridge of whatever muscle it was on his back that made him look so wide. So strong. A shield she could hide behind.

"This isn't some kind of pity fuck, is it?" he asked, and she leaned back to stare into his earnest face. "Poor Luc, he's lost his career?"

Slowly, she shook her head. "I feel bad for you, Luc. But I would never pity you." She could see he didn't totally believe her, that it would take years before he believed that no one was pitying him. "Truth be told, Luc, men who cry and throw shit—it's a big turn-on."

His laughter was bright and relieved and his kiss tasted sweet. Like gratitude.

But his fingers, nimble and clever, slid up her legs to the happy face. He petted her through the fabric until she knew she was so wet he could feel it. He dipped a finger beneath the elastic and she gasped, curling against him, holding onto the pleasure as hard as she could. He teased, traced the edges of her sex, sliding past her clitoris, leaving her breathless.

Grinding against him, chasing that finger down as best she could, she whimpered in frustration.

"Oh God, Tara, you kill me."

His hands slid under her butt and with a shrug of his shoulders, he practically threw her into the roomy backseat of the SUV.

She turned, flipping her hair out of her face, only to see him crawling after her, his face dark, his intent clear. If she weren't so sick with lust, so mad with affection, she might have popped open the door and run, just so he could catch her.

A game. To keep them both safe. Their emotions locked behind flirtation and subterfuge.

But she was dying for him, and the only thing she could do was lie back and open her arms.

He licked a hot path up her belly, back to her breasts, murmuring all the while dark and wicked things that made her blush and squirm.

"I want to taste you," he said, sucking on her lips, nipping at her tongue. He started to backtrack, taking side roads across her cheeks, to her ears, down to that hot spot on her neck, but she stopped him.

"Me first," she murmured, sliding awkwardly against the leather, her skin sticking. He lay down, filling the space she had vacated, and she started her own *National Geographic* tour of his landscape.

"You're so beautiful," she murmured against his chest, licking his nipple, tugging at the button on his jeans. She stroked the skin of his stomach and sides with both hands spread wide, trying to touch as much of him as she could. His hands captured hers, pulling them over his chest, right over the beat of his heart. Looking up, she found his eyes burning and she couldn't look away. She licked his belly, tugged free one of her hands, and cupped his erection, opening her mouth to blow hot air over the fabric. He bared his teeth, lifted his hips, and the air in the truck was a bonfire of sweat and need and sex.

As she pulled down his black boxer briefs, the column of his erection sprang free, muscular and masculine in the extreme. She licked him, base to tip, staring into his eyes, feeling the best kind of dirty.

His heart pounded under her palm and against her lips and she felt so very much a part of his existence at this moment. No matter what happened between them, she knew that this moment was theirs. And they were as much a part of each other as any two people could be.

Tears burning behind her eyes, she broke eye contact and focused her attention on what lay beneath her lips.

He growled, his hands fisting in her hair, and she didn't know how she could be so turned on without being touched, but she was. She was hot and ready. Cupping him with both hands, she took as much as she could into her mouth and found a pace that had him sweating and arching against her.

"No more," he finally muttered, pulling her away. She held on as long as she could, the length of him slipping out of her mouth with a delicious pop. Hauling her up his body, her weight nothing to all that overt strength, he ravished her mouth, split her wide open, and swallowed her whole.

"Condom," she said.

"Not yet."

Lifting her even farther, she realized what he was doing and she braced one foot in the foot well and one hand against the window, desperate for relief.

Scooting down the bench seat, he pulled down her underwear. She shifted to help him take it off, but then he just grabbed Mr. Happy Face and tore him, right down the seam.

She shuddered with pleasure and then screamed when his lips found hers. He licked, sucked, bit once and then again. And she shook, riding his face while he squeezed and palmed her hips.

The temptation to close her eyes and just let this happen, just let him please her, was intense—all-consuming. It would be so easy, but she wasn't doing this because it was easy. She was in the backseat of this truck with him because it was hard. It took more courage than she thought she had.

She jerked away from him, slipping down his body. "I want . . ." Looking into his eyes, she felt a little foolish. "I want to do this with you."

His lips, shiny and slick, split into that crooked grin that broke her heart and sent it soaring at the same time.

Lifting his hips to dig into his hip pocket, his erection brushed the electrified nerve endings between her legs and she couldn't help arching into him, making him groan and fumble with the condom he pulled from his back pocket.

"I thought you didn't do this sort of thing," she said, staring down at him from where she sat on top of his hips.

"I didn't say I wasn't hopeful."

It was sweet and endearing and she couldn't help but laugh, giggle even, from her place of power on top of his crotch.

He laughed too and suddenly, the mood in the hot, sweaty confines of the SUV changed; lust's predictable and sharp edge became soft and wholly foreign.

"Hey," he murmured, cupping her cheek. "Stay with me."

"I'm with you," she said, taking the condom from him. She tore the wrapper open with her teeth and his chuckle forced them into bobbing and shaking contact again.

She stood slightly, rolling the condom over him, and for a moment she allowed herself to believe that when this was over, when they'd worked out this ill-fated passion against each other's rocky shores, she could walk away.

But that was a lie.

Holding him in one hand, she braced herself against his chest and slowly, as slowly as if he were performing hara-kiri, he speared her, split her. She gasped and cried out. He groaned and pulled her down against him in terrible, wicked increments until she was seated fully on him.

She'd never felt this way, so cherished and endangered at the same time, and her heart fell into rhythm with her body.

I could love him, she thought, climbing up and up and up.

I probably already do.

chapter 26

As soon as the truck pulled to a stop, the front door of the ranch opened and the women in his family came running out. He was suddenly adrift again. Lost without the anchor of who he was to himself, he had no idea who he was supposed to be to these people.

Who was he if he wasn't Victoria's hockey-playing brother? Celeste's famous son?

"Can we go back to that tree?" he asked.

Tara Jean's hand cupped his, and he grabbed it as fast and as hard as he could.

"They're worried about you," she said. "And they love you."

"I know," he sighed.

"Gotta face them sometime." She put her hand on the door and he stopped her.

"You need to call the cops. Tell them about Dennis."

She nodded. "I will, right now." Her eyes dropped to his lips, but she turned away, probably intimidated by his family glaring at them outside the window.

But he wasn't easily intimidated and he touched her chin, tipping her lips back to his. "Thank you," he breathed across her mouth.

"My pleasure." She kissed him back and then threw open her door, like the gates of hell. He had no choice but to open his own door and watch her walk across the parking area toward her workshop. Leaving him to face the dragons alone.

"What the hell is going on?" Celeste asked. Waving a folded-up newspaper, she stepped down from the verandah.

"The *Toronto Star* is saying you have some kind of brain damage!" Victoria said, her arms crossed over her chest.

"I'm fine," he said.

"You've been saying that for two months, Luc. And you're not fine!" Victoria's rage gave her some weight, and maybe it was because he'd just been screwed silly, but he was happy to see her so animated.

"You won't play again," Celeste said, and it wasn't a question.

It was the truth, black and yawning under his feet, and his head spun in panic. The comfort and bliss he'd found in Tara's arms vanished as if they'd never existed and he was stumbling along in his own ruin.

Ruby stood on the porch. "A man named Beckett Jones has called for you. About eighty times."

"You," Victoria practically seethed, "need to give us some answers."

So. This was it. The reckoning.

"Where's Billy—"

"Here," Billy said from behind him, and Luc turned to find him, sweaty and wiping his face off with a towel, obviously just coming back from a workout.

At the sight of his old friend, the anger came back. All that he'd lost was right there in his friend's beaten and battered face.

"And I think I speak for the whole league when I say: Fuck you, Luc. Excuse my French," he mumbled to Celeste and Victoria.

"I'm sorry I didn't tell you—"

"So why don't you tell us now," Celeste said. "All of it."

Knowing he was beat, Luc nodded and launched into the sad story of a boy with the possibility of a brain-eating protein.

"Brain-eating?" Victoria cried.

"Possibility," he clarified.

"I can't believe that you were still going to play." That Billy managed to be sanctimonious was a marvel. "That you would risk the rest of your life for one more year of hockey."

"This from the man with more hospital visits than anyone else in the league?"

"It's not my brain, Luc! You mock those NFL guys who can't remember where they live, but you were going to join them!"

Luc's anger subsided, sucked down by the pinprick of shame brought on by his own blind stupidity. This, too, was the truth. He'd brought this on himself.

"I know," he said. "But it's not like anything is definite—"

"The headaches are definite," Billy snapped, and Luc nodded in reluctant agreement. "And I'll bet you don't remember half the hits you've taken that resulted in blackouts. Or even the hits that didn't result in blackouts."

He wished he could blunt the truth, for his family's sake. But he'd hidden enough from them, and it was a bad time to realize that he'd done this not just to himself, but to them, too.

"No," Luc agreed, and his mother's soft gasp tore through his belly. "You're right. I don't remember."

"I was traded, man." Billy's soft voice was at odds with the blunt hammer of his face. "What did you think was going to happen next year? The league—"

"I was trying to get faster." Even as the words came out of his mouth, he knew it was stupid. "Stronger. Better."

"You're thirty-seven. Lashenko is twenty-four. We're depreciating every day, Luc."

"Well, it doesn't matter now. I'm out. They'll drop my contract—"

"What if they don't? It's not like the league is known for taking care of their players. If you're selling tickets, they'll find a way to keep you around. They let Lindros play till he could barely stay on his feet."

He wondered, suddenly, how Lindros was doing. If he had memory loss and cognitive lapses, all the things Matthews said would happen to him if he kept getting knocked out.

Luc glanced over at his mother and sister, standing there like worried birds, wringing their hands over his future.

"Either way, I'm out," Luc said. "And frankly, it's . . . it's a relief. My body is tired, my head is tired, and I'm tired of keeping Gates away from the strippers."

Billy smiled, and he felt his mother cup her hand around his elbow.

"That's smart," Billy said. "First smart thing you've done in a long time."

"What are you going to do?" Celeste asked.

Luc looked around, at the sun, the ugly house, the rolling hills past it. Tara Jean somewhere, close enough that he could go and find her, wrap his arms around her if he wanted. And he wanted.

"To fulfill the obligation of the will, I have to stick around for another few months. I can lay low here. See what happens."

"See what happens with Tara Jean, you mean?" Victoria asked, and Luc smiled at her scowl.

"Is that such a bad idea?"

"Yes!"

"She makes me happy," he said with a helpless shrug. "And I haven't been happy in a long time."

"What's the difference between her and Dennis?"

He blinked, stunned. "She's not using me for money."

"Can you be sure of that?"

"Yes." He was unequivocal. He knew Tara Jean, the best and worst of her, and she wasn't after his money. "As sure as I am that Dennis's motives are not as pure."

"Pure," she scoffed. "I don't think that's a word that applies to Tara Jean."

"Stop," he demanded. "Right now, Victoria. I like her. A lot. And you don't have to approve, but you sure as hell can keep your mouth shut about her."

"You're picking her over your family?"

"Oh my God, Vicks—"

"No. Fine. I get it. Go. Screw what's left of your brains out." Victoria turned back to the house, slamming the front door shut behind her.

He turned on his mother. "How about you, you have a problem with Tara Jean?"

"You could do worse for yourself," Celeste murmured.

He watched her, waiting for the shoe to drop, but she was silent. "You approve of Tara Jean Sweet?"

"Who am I to approve? I would say . . ." She lifted that shoulder and he, thirty-seven years old, still couldn't always read those shrugs.

Either she was about to lie or about to tell him she was hungry. "I can appreciate your interest. Your father was like her." She lifted her hand, forestalling the argument that leapt to his lips. "Now, don't get your back up. He was wild. And different. Like an untamed animal in a room full of domesticated dogs. And he made me feel . . . alive."

"That's exactly how she makes me feel."

She touched his hand, kissed his forehead. "But don't use her to fill the hole hockey has left in your life." Her shrewd eyes saw right through him. "She deserves better than that."

* * *

It was hours later when he got off the phone with Beckett and his coaches and teammates, and there was one niggling problem left to deal with. He shut the door to his bedroom and called Thiele.

The phone rang once before the private investigator answered.

"Thiele."

"He's back," Luc said, staring out his window at the moonscape. "Dennis Murphy is back."

"We heard," Thiele said. "I've got my feelers out, but Murphy is staying low. No credit cards. No cell phone."

"What does that mean?"

"It means it's going to take longer to find him."

Luc paced away from the window, his tennis shoes squeaking against the hardwood floor. "I need . . ."

"I'm on it, Luc. Don't worry." He hung up.

Don't worry.

He could hit a hundred-mile-an-hour slap shot. Outsprint a man half his age. Lead his team to the finals. He could even walk away from the sport that defined him. Take care of his family. Make love in the backseat of an SUV to Tara Jean Sweet.

But not worrying was impossible. Like tearing out his own throat.

"Luc?" The soft voice accompanied a scratch at the door, and he turned in time to see Tara Jean slipping through the cracked door to his bedroom.

The lamplight fell over her face in a golden veil, obscuring and highlighting her beauty. And he knew in a heartbeat that this woman was no substitute for hockey. She was an entity all her own. And he'd never had a person in his life like her. That she was here, now, when he most needed someone like her, was just his good fortune.

"Hey!" He had no interest in pretending not to be happy to see her. She brought parts of him, long dead, long forgotten, back to tingling life—and he couldn't play that cool.

His smile split his face.

"You all right?" she asked.

"Great. What are you doing?"

"Well." The door shut behind her with a soft click and he realized she wore a highly unlikely leather duster with red feathers at the neck. She looked like a beautiful bird. "I was worried you might be sad. Again."

Her fingers slipped along those feathers, her smile as seductive as Eve's, and his body, as his brain got wise, got hard in a heartbeat.

"I *am* feeling a little blue." He closed the curtains with a hard snap. "What's . . . what's happening under that coat?"

"This old thing?" She shrugged. "Not much."

The coat fell to the ground with a soft thud. She wasn't naked, but she sure as hell wasn't decent.

White leather cupped her curves, molded to her waist. Thigh-high white stockings clung to her superior legs. Her sex was barely covered by a white leather thong that couldn't be comfortable, but he sure as hell appreciated her sacrifice.

He could love her, he realized as she prowled toward him, her high heels clicking against the dark floor.

He touched her shoulder with the tips of his fingers, the satin of her skin transforming him from a broken-down hockey player into something better. Something real. A man. With a woman. A family to protect.

A future to care for.

Grateful, reverent, and endlessly worried, he pulled her into his arms and attempted to show her the glory she made him feel.

* * *

The phone call from Dennis on Monday afternoon came as a surprise. Staring down at his number on her cell phone display, Victoria's emotions weren't easy to label; it was like looking at a kid's finger painting. A big brown mess, with red and purple highlights of anger and pleasure.

She glanced up the long empty hallway of the elementary school she was checking out for Jacob. No one was around to watch her do something even she knew she shouldn't do.

"Hello?" she said, pleased when she didn't sound too excited or too angry. It was the perfect mix, as if she'd forgotten who Dennis Murphy was and why he would be calling.

"Victoria." His voice, on the other hand, was the sort you'd use with a confidant. A friend. Long lost but beloved. And it was like hitting ice, making her skid. She didn't have any friends. Not anymore. No one had said her name like that in a long time.

"How are you?"

She cleared her throat and stared into the trophy display case across the hallway. The sixth graders at Bruce Elementary School had had quite a cross-country winning streak.

"I'm fine," she answered. "You?"

"Good. Great, actually. I'm so sorry about the way I had to leave Friday night."

"Look, Dennis, I'm not sure this is going to work. My ex-husband was career focused and I'm not going to go down that road again."

"Victoria, please, let's not do this over the phone. Meet me—you can dump me to my face." It was a joke, sweet and unexpected, and she actually smiled despite her misgivings. "Friday night."

"Sorry, Jacob has book club."

"Book club? For seven-year-olds?"

She sat up straighter in the kid's red molded plastic chair she was wedged into. "We're reading *Harry Potter* and it's been very enjoyable."

"Fine. Friday afternoon."

Don't, she told herself. *Don't do this to yourself again.*

But then she thought of her brother, of that light that seemed to suffuse his being. Because he was having sex. Having sex with someone totally inappropriate. Someone who was risky.

Why was Luc the only one who got to be brave? To throw his heart around the gutter just for the hell of it? Dennis made her happy. Made her smile. Wasn't that worth something?

"Okay," she agreed, feeling like she'd been holding her breath. "I can meet you at three. At the bar in the Four Seasons?"

"No. No, I'm not staying there."

"Where are—"

"How about the Applebee's on Westwood."

Applebee's? Goodness. Talk about slumming. "Okay."

She hung up her cell phone, feeling like a woman with a secret. Something delicious and naughty. A dangerous lover. A date at a third-rate restaurant chain.

She hardly recognized herself right now. And she liked that. She liked that a lot.

Luc rolled over and before his hand touched the cold sheets where Tara's warm body should have been, he knew she was gone. Middle of the night, middle of the day, first thing in the morning, it hardly seemed to matter. Over the last few days, whenever he fell asleep, she slipped out of his bed, like a ghost.

It was getting hard not to take this shit personally.

And he couldn't stop falling asleep. It was as though his body knew its work was over and it had gone on holiday. He took naps. Every day. Sometimes twice, depending on how often he could get Tara alone.

He'd expected a lot of things when he started this . . . relationship with her. But not this. She let him past all her walls, only to put up giant fences to keep him out. She locked herself in her damn workshop all day and night. He understood that the Nordstrom deal was tomorrow and she needed to be ready, but that boot had been designed years ago, and this . . . manic behavior told him something else was going on.

It didn't take a genius to see what she was doing, keeping him at arm's length. And it wasn't just sneaking out of his bed. She found every reason not to spend time with him, unless that time was spent naked. Or sort of naked.

He'd ask her to dinner and she'd take off her shirt.

This afternoon he'd suggested she go skating with him and Jacob, watch a peewee game. She'd lifted her skirt to show him that smiley-face underwear he just couldn't resist.

He stared up at the shadows growing long across the ceiling. She closed her eyes when they kissed, didn't look at him when she came.

Loving her hurt. And maybe if he knew she didn't feel something, if he was sure that this was just sex, it might hurt less. But she wouldn't keep him out if she wasn't scared. If she wasn't protecting something.

And that, in the middle of a Thursday afternoon, gave him some hope. Forcing his lazy body into movement, he threw off the sheets. He needed to make a few phone calls but then he'd go find Tara, and, if he had to, force his way into her life.

chapter 27

The demon was gone. Thursday night before the Nordstrom meeting and her muse was nowhere to be found.

Wasn't that a bitch?

And while the meeting was about the boots, she'd hoped to have a few new designs to show off at the same time. But the paper in front of her was still blank and her head was still quiet.

The blame was obviously Luc's. Despite her every single effort to keep him at arm's length, less than a week with the man and she'd been screwed silly. Screwed happy, really. And the demon wasn't a big fan of happy. It wasn't her natural habitat.

But Tara found herself reluctant to give it up.

The door to the workshop opened and the shadows rippled around her desk as Luc walked in. Her heart stirred, leapt in reaction like an untrained dog. There was some kind of metamorphosis happening. A transformation. And she had to wonder what kind of butterfly was going to emerge from a cocoon so ugly.

"You still working?"

"The meeting is tomorrow; I was hoping to have a few new designs." She sighed and stared down at the empty paper. "But I don't have any ideas."

"Maybe you need a break." He touched her hair, his

fingers combing through the curls, and sparks of pleasure littered her body.

"Yeah, my last 'break' took half the afternoon. I think part of the reason I can't work is someone keeps taking me back to bed."

"If I remember correctly, that break was your idea. I wanted to take you skating. And right now I was just thinking about getting some dinner. Feed the muse."

Her laugh was dry. Little did he know the muse ate conflict and anger and resentment.

"I think I should try to get something done."

"You getting nervous? About tomorrow?"

"Getting?" She laughed and shook her head. "I've been nervous since the meeting was arranged."

He sat on the stool across from her desk, his face cut in half by shadow, and she couldn't see his eyes. But there was something about his stillness that had nothing to do with relaxation. The man was poised for something and she didn't know what.

"How about if I went with you?"

His words fell into a vast empty well. And from the bottom of the well, finally, the demon spoke up.

Who the hell does he think he is?

"I don't need you to hold my hand."

"That's not what I'm saying. I just thought . . . you know . . . as CEO—"

"You said you didn't care about this company." Resentment radiated to her fingers, to the tips of her hair, and the demon reached full power.

This is ours! the demon cried. *Ours. No one else's.*

"I care about *you.*"

"If you're bored, find a different hobby, Luc. This is my business."

"Whoa, whoa." He held out his hands as if warding off an attack. "I just want to share something with you besides bodily fluids. I thought it might be fun. Working with you."

She stood up. "I don't work well with others."

"Okay." He stood too and walked around the desk and as he approached, the smell and heat of him turned the edge of her temper to mush. This was the man's effect on her. She couldn't keep herself straight anymore. There was a good chance if he touched her, she'd say yes. She'd say *yes, come to this meeting, take away what's mine, just because you're bored and I'm here and I'm falling in love with you.*

Funny how she thought sex with Luc would be safe. This man could bring down her life like no one else.

"Why are you pushing me away, Tara?"

Instead of answering him, she kissed him. Launched herself against his chest, fitted every aching part of her body against the relief of his.

He lifted her against him with one hand and cupped her chin with the other, pulling her away, and she saw cold anger in his eyes. "You won't let me be a part of your work, or your life, but you'll fuck me, is that it?"

She panted, licked his lips. "Something like that."

"Fine." He put her down and spun her, pushing her up against the drafting table, the edge of it biting into her stomach. Fear gave lust a new color, something black. Luc was always in control, always a gentleman. But this man pushing her over the edge of the table felt dangerously, decidedly, out of control.

Her body went wet in a heartbeat.

"You like it this way, don't you?" he breathed in her ear, his hands roughly cupping her breasts. His fingers found the hard ridge of her nipples and pulled. *Too much. Too much.* She whimpered and pushed her ass against him, urging him on, wanting this so badly, so suddenly she couldn't breathe.

"You don't have to look at me, do you?" He bit the

side of her neck and she whimpered, standing up on her tiptoes, trying to feel him along her spine but he tipped her over, putting distance where she didn't want it, controlling her like a woman on a string.

His hands slid down the top of her shirt, ripping a button off, gripping her breast while his erection pulsed against her ass. "Tell me," he whispered in her ear before using his teeth against her.

"Wh . . . what?"

"Tell me, 'Yes Luc, I like it this way.' "

"I like it . . ." His hand ran under her skirt to the aching wet heat between her legs. There was no soft touch, no careful teasing. His fingers sunk deep and she cried out as the giant wave of orgasm began to lift her right out of her body.

"What were you saying?"

She would have smiled if she were able. She would have laughed, she would have turned around and kissed him with all of her heart if she'd been able to do anything but stand there and shake, riding his fingers.

"Luc . . ."

His fingers slid out of her body and she cried out, pushing herself against him, trying to find him, to lure him back. "It's simple, Tara. If you say, 'Yes Luc, I like it this way,' you'll get rewarded."

She groaned, spreading her legs slightly, pushing against him, trying to make him break, trying to get him inside her.

"Ah," he laughed in her ear. "You know your reward, don't you? You want it."

"Come on, Luc." That orgasm growing so big, the best orgasm ever, was just out of reach.

With both hands he lifted her skirt up over her ass, running those callused fingers over the naked curves, the lace edge of her thong. *Oh God, yes,* she thought, listening for the unzip of his zipper, waiting for the thick blunt edge of his dick.

"That's not right, Tara."

He spanked her, the flat of his hand against the top edge of her ass, and she cried out in surprise, jerking away from him. "What the hell, Luc?"

She didn't get far with his strong arms around her, and as the sting faded, she found herself burning even hotter. Her mind wasted with lust. "Please—"

"What did I ask you to say, Tara?"

She closed her eyes and pushed her head back against his shoulder, her hand reaching between them to cup him. "Yes, Luc, I like it like this."

The sound of his zipper was loud in the silence. The tearing of the condom package echoed through her body.

"Hurry," she gasped, leaning forward against the table. And then he was there, so hard, so high, she could feel him in the back of her throat.

There was no way she could keep him at arm's length now.

Not when he'd just touched her heart.

It didn't work. She was farther away than ever. The chill in his gut turned the sweat on his body to ice. Picking her way through the shadows, gathering up her clothes and clutching them to her chest, she looked like a thief.

Someone he'd never met before.

That sex had turned them into strangers.

"You should get dressed," she said, zipping up her skirt.

He leaned up on one elbow, muscles and shadows coiling over him like living animals.

"I feel like maybe you should put some money on the table before you go."

"This isn't any different than any other time we've had sex."

He pushed a hand over his face, through his hair. He had nothing left now, just the truth, and he wasn't holding out a lot of hope that was going to work. But what the hell, he had a couple of seconds left on the clock on an empty net. "Coming home from the hospital. That was different."

It was. Her great unguarded moment. Before she called out the dogs.

"No, it wasn't, you just want to believe otherwise. I told you not to make this into something more. None of this is real, Luc. Even my name is fake. I made it up. I made up all of this and you've just forgotten that."

Halfway through her little speech, he stood and started getting dressed as if the clothes were trying to rob him. He shoved his legs through his pants, ripped a button on his shirt in his haste.

"Listen to yourself. You're making a life, Tara. Building something. Just because it's yours doesn't mean it's bad. Or false. Or any less real than someone else's life."

She stared at him, that blank look he knew meant she was absorbing something, testing its weight before tossing it back in his face. Before taking a sledgehammer to what was left of his heart.

"I think it's best if we just end this now, don't you? Before anyone gets hurt."

Now he was just getting pissed.

"I can see through your bullshit, Tara. You're not fooling me with this tough-girl act. You want to walk away, fine. Walk away, but be honest with me. I deserve that much."

"You're going to get off this ranch, Luc, and you're going to get back to your life and you're going to realize this—" She lifted her hand, waved it between them as if she could encompass all that had happened the last week. The hospital and the secrets they'd whispered into and across each other's skin.

"This wasn't real. I'm a substitute for hockey. And a pretty bad one at that. I'm nothing to build a life with."

"Give me some credit, Tara. I'm not a child. I know the difference between hockey and love."

The word shattered the room and she stepped back, leaning against her desk, his eyes pinning her there, daring her to move. Daring her to look away.

"I love you, Tara Jean."

There it was. His endgame. There was nothing after this and he watched her, his heart folding itself into origami.

Once, as a girl, she'd fallen off the top of a swing set and she'd lain there, the small pebbles of the playground digging into her cheek, gasping and sucking air like a fish in the bottom of a boat.

This moment felt like that.

"You should leave," she finally said. "You should go now. Get off this ranch before you lose any more of your mind."

"I can't get off the ranch. And even if I could, I wouldn't. Not without you."

The will. He was stuck here for his sister's sake for four more months.

Four more months. She couldn't do it. She couldn't stay here with him and his love that wasn't real. She wasn't strong enough to resist him. And she'd fall. Hard. And then when the four months were over and he went on his way, she'd be destroyed. Ruined.

She stood still at the edge of a decision she'd made a thousand times in the past. It was harder this time, because what she was turning away was so precious. So rare. But in the end, the old habits reached up out of her past to support her, and it wasn't all that hard to just turn her head away from what she wanted.

"You can take care of Victoria?" she asked. "Jacob? In case Dennis comes back around?" She had every intention of making sure that didn't happen, but Luc would be a good backup plan.

He stepped toward her, her arms in his hands before she could flinch away. She bit back a gasp at his touch, the heat of him. "What's going on in that head of yours, Tara? I can't—"

"I'm going to leave."

"What? Why?"

"Because that is what I do, Luc. I leave."

"What about the Nordstrom deal?"

"If you're so interested, you go to the meeting." She reached behind her and grabbed the sketch of the boot, that symbol of all the financial freedom she'd always wanted. But the truth was, no financial freedom was worth the pain love inevitably brought.

"What about Dennis?"

"I have that protection order."

"Don't do this, Tara. I love you. You. All of you."

"Don't be an idiot, Luc," she snapped. "You barely know me."

"Then tell me, Tara. Right now. Tell me what it is I don't know about you. What is so unloveable about you, and you let me be the judge of whether or not my feelings are real. Trust me that much."

"I should just go."

"Yeah, and I'll just follow you, Tara. Screw the will and my sister. I want you. I want to be with you and if you don't want to be with me, you need to tell me why, and enough of this bullshit about hockey."

She met his eyes and steeled herself. She was always

the instrument of her own downfall—this would be no different.

"When I was a kid, before I conned that first old man—"

"Mr. Beanfang."

That he remembered was somehow sweet. As if he'd memorized her poisonous song, unaware that it was going to poison him too.

"I was fifteen and mad at my mom because she kept bringing these assholes into our lives and they ruined . . . they ruined everything. And Grant . . . he liked me. My mom knew it. And she didn't do anything. Ever. She looked the other way, told me I was imagining things. That I was jealous. That I was a spoiled brat who didn't want her to be happy. But she knew it was the truth. So on my sixteenth birthday . . . I didn't say no."

"Oh my God—"

"It wasn't what I expected. It wasn't sexy. Or fun. It didn't make me a grown-up. And then my mother, when I told her, when I came to her crying and bleeding . . . she kicked me out of the house. No money. No clothes. No car. Nothing. I slept at a friend's house for a few nights, but then . . . then I met Dennis."

"Sweetheart, Tara." His hands ran over her face like a river, like water trying to change the shape of the stones in its banks. "You were a kid. And your mother . . . your mother should have protected you."

"But I hurt her, don't you get it? I loved her and I hurt her. She loved me and she betrayed me. Your father loved you and look how he treated you. Look at what Victoria's husband did to her. That's love, Luc—it's handing someone the knife to stab you in the back."

She shook her head, stepping backward toward the door.

"You want me to love you, but all I ever do is hurt

people. And you might think you love me, but you don't. No one ever has."

She turned and opened the door but he shut it again, his hand on the wood in front of her face. "Don't give up like this, Tara," he breathed, his head pressed into the back of hers, a weight that would drown her if she let it. "Don't walk out that door. We can talk—"

He wouldn't let her leave, so she would have to make him be the one to walk away.

"Talk?" she asked, hating him. Hating herself. "That's not what we do, Luc."

She took off her shirt, one button at a time. Her breasts without the bra glowed in the moonlight. It took him a second to realize what she was doing and he looked up in her eyes. Naked love and disappointment fought there.

"Don't do this," he whispered.

She ignored both and shrugged out of the shirt. The air was cold, his gaze colder, as disappointment and love were eaten by anger.

"Come on, Luc." She leaned back against the desk. "Maybe I can still earn that bonus. I've got tricks I haven't even—"

He bent, grabbed her shirt, and shot it at her chest. Her reflexes caught it.

"Get dressed," he said. "And go, if that's what you want. But I won't be a part of your punishment, or whatever this is. I love you too much."

The door slammed shut behind him and she slipped the shirt up over her shoulders and started to button it, but her hands were shaking too hard. And then her legs were shaking and the boots couldn't keep her up anymore.

She slid to the ground, a sob breaking through her chest, right through her ribs.

This was what she needed to do.

And because it hurt, she knew it was right.

* * *

The next morning, the demon was back, but worse. Worse than ever. And the voice . . . she realized now, the voice wasn't her mother's.

It was hers.

And Tara Jean, battered and bruised, didn't have the capacity to fight. Didn't even know why she should. Why she should try to be anything but what she was.

Getting into the black leather pants took an act of physics and athleticism not unlike the pole vault. The boots laced up the back, up to her knee, and the heel was red and three inches high. The thin white sweater seemed demure until she put it on, winding the long, gauzy tails around her waist over and over again until she looked like a good-girl dominatrix.

From under her sink she dug out her hot rollers, putting her hair up into big floppy curls, then she lacquered them with a pound of hair spray. Scrunching and spraying until she looked like a monument to big hair. A monument to Texas femininity.

She finished it off with the holy trinity: red lipstick, black eyeliner, and big hoops.

On the countertop her cell phone buzzed. Just as it had ten minutes ago. She didn't have to look at the display to know it was Claire Hughes.

She was now a half-hour late for that meeting.

And the pain, the pain was almost gone.

Her head ached and burned where Luc had pressed his forehead to it last night. Her flesh remembered the touch of his hand. The way his skin looked like liquid gold, felt like silk, tasted like salt and sugar under her lips.

But slowly, bit by bit, staring at her cold eyes in the mirror, she convinced herself that it was all a dream.

And it was over.

She willed the woman in the mirror to believe it, to turn her heart to stone, her mind to a sharp blade, cutting out the tenderness, the sweetness, the heat and fury—every single memory and emotion attached to Luc Baker. Until they lay in ribbons, broken and bleeding, all attachment to her gone.

Leaning toward the mirror, she ran a finger around the edge of her lips.

This wasn't a mistake—the clothes, the hair, the stone-cold look in her eyes.

This was Tara Jean Sweet.

Victoria tried not to feel assaulted by the ambiance of Applebee's. Honestly, between the music (far too loud) and the kids screaming (totally unchecked), it was like being slapped in the face with noise.

"Table for one?" a young woman asked, her brown hair pulled back in a sloppy ponytail, the enthusiasm faked. She had a button on her shirt asking people to ask her how much she loved it here. Victoria had the feeling that if she were to ask, the girl might cry.

"I'm . . . I'm ah . . ." She looked over the woman's shoulder and saw a familiar gray suit jacket on a man at the bar. The curve of his shoulders, however, was not so familiar.

Dejected, those shoulders said. And all the excitement she'd had for this illicit date fizzled.

I don't want to play cheerleader tonight, she thought with a heavy sigh. She'd done enough of that in her marriage. It was the one aspect of being a widow that she was beginning to enjoy—not having to be responsible for some fragile man's mood.

But perhaps she was wrong. Perhaps those shoulders did not say dejected. Perhaps they said "slight shoulder injury from an intense squash game."

Yes, she liked that much better. Though, frankly, she wasn't all that interested in hearing the play-by-play of a squash game.

She'd had enough of that, too.

Frankly, she just wanted to flirt. To feel pretty, maybe even sexy. She had in fact worn her tightest jeans, the dark wash, with her gold sandals. And she'd left her hair down, pleased with how it had stopped falling out now that she was away from New York and Toronto. The stress of her life.

Really, all she wanted was to make out in the parking lot.

Was that too much to ask from an illicit afternoon date at Applebee's?

No. It wasn't. She had the feeling it happened all the time.

She stepped up to the bar, to Dennis's shoulder, expecting him to turn to her with a wide smile, but he didn't. He slowly drained the last of the beer from a big pint glass.

"Dennis?" she said, and finally he turned.

Her heart folded up shop and closed for the night at the sight of him. Disheveled. Unshaven. His eyes were dark and bloodshot. He smelled of a two-day bender.

She reeled back.

"Hey now, princess, how are you?"

The "princess" rankled. It really did, but she managed to smile.

"You all right?" she asked.

"Why wouldn't I be?" His voice lost its happy drunk effect and seemed mean. Toward her.

"You don't look so good."

"Well." His eyes were shrewd, malicious, and this was a side of him she'd never seen. It made her clutch her purse a little closer. "I think you can blame that little fact on your brother."

"My brother?"

"I can't prove it, of course, because your brother is slick like that, but he hired people to get me out of town. To scare me away from you."

"Don't be ridiculous."

"Don't be a bitch," he moaned, and she snapped back, slipping her purse strap over her shoulder. She'd been called enough names to last a lifetime. And Dennis Murphy was clearly not the man she'd hoped he was.

Without another word she turned on the heel of her little gold sandals, which frankly, now that she thought about it, looked cheap and awful, and headed back to the hostess station, the front door, and the wide world beyond.

She heard a mumble and a crash and she could feel him behind her, a few steps.

"You all right?" the hostess asked as she passed, and Victoria managed to give the woman a reassuring smile as she hit the doors and the heat of the parking lot.

She was halfway to her car before Dennis caught up to her, grabbing the inside of her elbow and spinning her around so hard she nearly fell.

"Do not touch me!" she hissed, all that anger she'd swallowed rising up like a suppressed indigenous tribe, with arrows and rocks and hate.

"Listen, Victoria." She wondered how she ever could have thought him handsome. He was hideous. She jerked her arm, but he held on so hard she'd have bruises. "I need you to walk back in there and sit down with me. You need to tell your brother to leave me the fuck alone."

"Not on your life. I'm not interested in dating you, Dennis. Not anymore."

"Dating?" he howled. "You think we're dating? You stupid little rich girl. I wouldn't date you if you were the last pair of tits on the planet."

Her blood roaring in her ears, embarrassment and anger giving her superhero strength, she tore away from him, her arm stinging, her hand numb, and she turned and ran for her car, fumbling with her keys, tears of anger and fear burning in her eyes.

Wrong. So wrong. Again.

Her chest heaving, she tried to get her keys in the door but her hands were shaking and suddenly he was there, batting the keys to the ground, grabbing her purse.

"I need money."

"I don't have any," she snapped, pulling her purse back.

"Please, you think I believe that crap about you giving all the money back to the people your husband fleeced?"

He was rifling through her stuff, tossing things onto the cement like they were garbage, a package of Kleenex, her sunglasses, Jacob's school picture.

"Give me that, you asshole!" she yelled, jerking the purse.

But Dennis barely even looked up. With the assurance of a man with too much practice, he lifted one hand and cuffed her so hard she fell back against the car, her ears ringing.

Gasping, she tasted blood and carefully crouched, picking up her keys. She'd leave the purse, along with what was left of her dignity and pride, on the asphalt with her Kleenex. She just needed to get out of there.

In the distance a siren wailed, the sound so jarring she dropped her keys again. Dennis looked up, like a wild dog sensing trouble, and Victoria saw the hostess standing in front of the doors, her hand shielding her eyes.

"I called the cops!" she cried, and Dennis mumbled something under his breath, digging out the little bit of cash she had in her purse.

Victoria's vision went red, her body numb with shock and adrenaline, and she didn't even feel herself doing it, didn't even know she was going to, before she put her hands on his shoulders. He shrugged, looking up at her ready to spit more hate, more poison on her already poisoned face, but before he could do it, she brought up her knee, bony as all get-out, and drove it right into the soft, gooey center of his testicles.

He went blue, then red, gasping for air. The purse fell to her feet, and his body toppled soon after.

In the distance the sirens were getting closer and the hostess was cheering and for a moment, the sight of Dennis Murphy brought to the ground by her was so delicious she lifted a hand.

Took a little bow.

But she had no intention of talking to the cops, of explaining what she was doing here in her gold sandals with her hair down, with a disgusting pig like Dennis Murphy.

With hands as steady as a surgeon's, she picked up the crumpled dollar bills that had fallen from Dennis's fingers. Her son's picture went into her back pocket. Like a ballast for a ship, the picture kept her steady.

"Come near me again and I'll have you arrested," she said, cool and calm, as imperial as she ever was without even trying. She smiled into his sweating, wheezing face, wondering how in the world hoofing this man in the balls had made her feel better than she had in a year.

Really, she thought, sliding behind the wheel of her car, starting it up and carefully stopping at the stop sign at the edge of the parking lot, before leaving the scene of a crime.

I should have kicked a man in the balls years ago.

chapter 28

Luc crouched in front of Jacob and pulled on the skate's laces. The familiar smells of the arena failed to make him feel better about the shit storm his life had turned into.

Celeste had called an hour ago telling him that Tara Jean had left the ranch. Up until that moment, he hadn't really believed that she would do it.

"She looked like a hooker," Celeste added.

"Mom—" He'd sighed, flinching on Tara's behalf at the word choice.

"Fine. Call girl. What's going on here, Luc?"

"She's leaving, Mom. She's . . ." Scared. Broken. "Leaving."

"I'm so sorry, honey."

"Me too, Mom."

So now, he had no career.

No Tara.

But the arena was still here. Home in a way that nothing else ever was.

"Too tight?" he asked his nephew. "Can you wiggle your foot?"

Jacob nodded, his face set on perma-beam. Victoria had called Luc an hour ago, asking him to pick Jacob up from the rec center. She'd gotten held up somewhere and was running late.

The second Jacob saw Luc he asked if they were going

to go skating. And frankly, Luc couldn't think of a better reason to step past the parasites demanding a statement he wasn't quite ready to give and back into the arena.

"Tie them super tight, Uncle Luc," Jacob said. "I go really fast when they're tight."

Luc smiled despite the hole in his chest.

"Luc?" a man's voice asked, and Luc stood from the crouch, his head spinning slightly at the change in altitude. He turned and found Randy Jenkins, looking gray and stone-faced. Tyler stood behind him barely holding back tears.

"Go on out," Luc said to Jacob, helping his nephew onto his feet. "Billy's waiting for you." He watched Jacob, one hand on the wall as he hobbled across the mats toward the ice.

Luc took a deep breath, preparing himself for the unknown, and turned around only to see Randy step back while Tyler stepped forward.

For a moment, Luc wanted to lay the kid out. Payment, perhaps, or to teach the guy a lesson. He wasn't sure which. All he knew was that this kid was part of the end of his career and while he couldn't fight the headaches or the doctors or the reality of his situation, it would feel good to take out his losses on the short-tempered player in front of him.

"I'm so sorry," Tyler breathed, looking at his shoes while tears ran sideways out of the corner of his eyes. "I didn't think you'd go down like that. I didn't know you had a head injury. I didn't mean—"

"It was a cheap shot." Luc bit out the words and the kid just nodded. "Look at me," he demanded, and Tyler finally lifted red-rimmed eyes. "Use the words, Tyler. Be a man."

"It . . . it was a cheap shot."

"You want to be a professional?" Tyler stared blankly at him. "Do you?"

Tyler swallowed. "Yes."

"Then it's time to grow up. Learn to control yourself out on the ice. Your temper. Your anger. All of it. Lock it down."

Tyler nodded like an eager pupil, or a criminal being let out on leave. Randy stepped forward and clapped a hand on his son's shoulder.

"Head on out to the car," Randy said, and Tyler nearly ran from the room.

"He's pretty eaten up over what happened," Randy said.

"So is my brain."

Randy's mouth fell open and Luc managed to laugh. "It was a bad joke."

"I don't find this funny. You haven't issued a statement. The rumors are getting worse in the press. We haven't heard from your lawyers or from the team—"

"Lawyers?"

Randy swallowed and pulled himself up a few more inches. "Are you going to sue us?"

"Sue?" The thought hadn't occurred to him. "God no. Look, Randy, I . . . this is an old injury. And if it hadn't been your son, it would have been a player on the team as soon as we got back to practice and . . . you know, I might not have come away from it so well. So, no. I'm not going to sue you. But if your son wants to skate, tell him to be here at seven a.m. on Monday—I need some help with the peewees."

"Thank you, Luc," Randy said, relief running off the man like sweat. Luc accepted his thanks and bit back the urge to extend his own.

Because oddly enough, Tyler Jenkins might have saved his life.

* * *

The sunlight made Victoria's face look like the scene of a battle. It was red and swollen, her eye was puffy, her lip was fat and kept cracking, spilling new blood over her teeth. There was no way she could see Jacob like this.

She needed a few hours to try to make her face look better.

She slunk into the house, surprised at the quiet. Pleased with the peace in the big rooms, filled with sunshine.

Despite the fat lip and black eye, she felt . . . good. Happy.

This house's bad memories didn't haunt her anymore.

If it wouldn't make her lip bleed, she might actually smile. Laugh, even.

Marvelous thing, kicking a man in his balls. She would recommend it to anyone. Maybe she'd write a self-help book.

Now, that would be funny.

She grabbed a tea towel and some ice from the kitchen and found herself reluctant to hide in her room. She'd done enough of that. Instead she found her feet leading her out to the barn.

After a very slow start, Victoria had learned to love horses. Besides her brother, they were the only bright spot of her summers at the ranch.

The barn was still full of horses. And the sun sliding through the wide windows baked the hay and dirt, and bees buzzed around in low, lazy circles, and it was a lot like she remembered as a kid.

In the far corner, a black horse lifted its big head, getting a look at her as she walked down the center of the barn.

"What's your name?" she murmured, scratching the white star between the horse's eyes. "Star?" The horse only blinked. "How about Midnight?" The horse gave her nothing. "Black Beauty?"

"Patience," a low, deep voice said from behind her and she jumped, startling the horse, who huffed and pranced, scattering dust motes like glitter.

It was Eli, of course. Standing in a long beam of sunshine from the open door. His hat was low over his eyes, shading his face. But the sunlight hit the skin of his neck, the bit of chest revealed by the open collar of his shirt, and turned him to gold.

He was beautiful. A perfect statue of masculinity. David brought to life and wearing cowboy boots. Did he have to be so . . . masculine? It was slightly vulgar. Unnecessarily earthy.

"Hey, Eli." She ducked away from him, hiding her face.

"What are you doing in here?"

"I like it in here. It's quiet. Is that all right? I'm not . . . you know . . . touching anything."

"It's fine, Victoria." His voice straddled a weird line between fond and patronizing, and she forced herself not to care.

"I do remember you, you know," she said, reluctant to leave even though she knew she should. She ducked around the opposite side of the horse as he stepped into the stall. "From when we were kids."

He was silent and she, uncorked from her afternoon of violence and self-recovery, couldn't stop talking. "I didn't recognize you at first. You're so different."

"So are you."

The wild bark of her laughter startled the horse and Eli clucked under his tongue, stroking Patience's neck.

"Sorry," she murmured.

"It's all right." He was crouched, looking at the horse's hooves, checking its shoes.

In the quiet, she knew he was thinking of that girl she'd been. Two years older than he. Glasses. Pudgy and bookish, utterly and totally intimidated by everyone around her. A disgrace to her glamorous and hard-living mother.

He'd been sixteen the last time she visited. A boy on the edge of manhood, growing into his body and his glower. Which clearly, he'd perfected. Eli had been the object of many a teenage fantasy.

"Do you still ride?" he asked, picking up another hoof. She edged around toward the horse's head, trying to keep her face hidden.

"Me? Oh, no. No. No riding. Not many horses in Manhattan."

Though she could have had them. She could have had anything. But when she'd married Joel, horses, this barn, her early love affair with both, had become a part of her past. A past she had pushed away with as much force as possible.

"I wasn't very good with them anyway."

"That's not true."

She watched him with one eye, waiting, suddenly breathless for more.

"That's what my father always told me."

"Your father was an ass."

She laughed, she laughed so hard tears ran down her eyes and she didn't notice him watching her from over the horse's back.

He pointed to her face, suddenly intent and focused. On her. That affable mystery turned predatory, and she remembered, stupidly, that she was in the barn trying to hide her busted-up lip and cheek.

"What happened?" His lips barely moved.

The ice rearranged itself in the tea towel she held up to her cheek and he reached forward as if to pull it away, but she stepped out of the way.

"Don't," she said, implacable. Staring at him dead center in a way she'd never been able to do before.

"Who hit you?"

If she told him, she knew instinctively what would happen. Eli would tell Luc and then, with all the best intentions, they would take care of her problem, not even caring whether that was what she wanted. Or even needed.

And the desire to tell him, to sway just slightly toward him, to have him cradle her against that admittedly handsome chest, it was a potent desire.

But it was a desire born out of habit. For too long she'd been cared for. Petted and worried over without ever once stepping up and handling her life herself.

It felt as if her bones were breaking, but not in a painful way. In an empowering way, as if suddenly she was breaking down her own prison walls, the limitations and restraints she'd put on herself for so long that she no longer saw them.

Like a woman living in a dollhouse, thinking it was a palace.

"Don't worry about me," she told Eli, and she meant it. Was proud of the implacable nature of her voice, like she was an authority in her own damn life.

About time.

Luc stared out the safety glass at the small knot of reporters that had collected outside the arena doors. He'd been avoiding it, making a last-ditch effort to pretend his life was as it had been. But it was time to give his statement. Beckett was going to have his ass for not making it official—no press conference, no written statement. No him.

But somehow, in front of this little arena that oddly felt like a huge part of his future, ending his career felt right.

The second he stepped out the door, the reporters swarmed, mics in his face, the lights on the cameras blinding him, and it became obvious that he'd lost his touch when he reached up an arm to shield his eyes.

"Ice Man." It was good old Addie Eggers; decent of her to come all the down from Toronto to witness the end of his career. "Do you have anything to say—"

He waved his hands as if he were brushing away annoying flies. "Calm down, kids. Just relax. I'll give you my statement."

The silence after his words was so deep, he felt like he might lose his balance and just topple in. "I'm old. My brain is broken. And I'm done."

"Who knocked you out, Luc?" she asked. "Has the front office brought legal action against him?"

"No one knocked me out. I was on the ice with a kid, but . . . this is a problem I've had."

"What about the rumors that you're coaching a Junior A team down here in Texas?" Addie asked.

"I'm coaching peewee hockey," he said. "That's it for the foreseeable future. If that changes . . ." He smiled at her. "I imagine you'll be the first to know."

Within two hours, his phone was ringing constantly.

Frustrated, he flipped it open looking at the number on display. "Gates—"

"We've got a development," Thiele said, and Luc pushed away from the boards he'd been leaning against.

"You found Dennis?"

"No. Not really. But he made a purchase from a source of mine who just contacted me. So we know he's in the Dallas area."

"I already knew that," Luc barked, having no problem taking his anger out on the undeserving private investigator. "Tell me something I don't know."

"He bought a gun."

chapter 29

Luc's heart pounded in his throat, the sensation of losing control a hideous freefall. He took off down the front steps while the streetlights flickered on across the street.

Frantic, he called Tara Jean's cell phone but it clicked right over to voice mail.

"Look," he said, squeezing the phone so hard his hand ached. "I know you're upset, but we've got a problem. Dennis bought a gun. You need to call me."

Back to the ranch, he thought, his brain firing and misfiring, all the wires pulled and crossed. Maybe she had changed her mind. Maybe she was there, waiting. Safe.

He ran back inside the arena to gather up Billy and Jacob, to take them back to his father's home, where despite all of his best intentions, he always seemed to fuck up.

In the end, it wasn't that hard to get a message to Dennis. She called the bars where he used to hang out and left messages with bartenders and a few of his sleaze-bag friends that she was leaving town, heading back to Arkansas.

She didn't know how much time she had, but she worked as fast as she could. Packing up all of her boxes and shoving them into the Honda hatchback. Ignoring the constant ringing of her phone. It was Luc. And there was nothing more to say.

Sad, she thought, looking at the garbage bags and recycled produce boxes that held all her worldly belongings. That was just sad.

The sun had set not long ago and she wanted to be on the road soon. She had no intention of going to Arkansas, but she prayed that Dennis would believe her, follow her little trail of crumbs in the wrong direction. Instead, she was thinking of New Orleans. A woman could get lost in a city like that.

She ran back into her apartment, left the keys on the kitchen table, and ignored any impulse to look around, wanting to get on the road before Dennis came looking for her.

But when she turned, Dennis stood in the open front door.

"Going somewhere?" he asked, so familiar it was like looking in the mirror.

"Back home," she muttered, using everything she had to keep herself calm. Too late. She'd waited too long. She'd even managed to screw this up.

"Where's my money?" he demanded. He was already drunk, mean drunk, and there was an explosion of fear in her chest.

For a moment she contemplated a lie, a diversion. But she didn't have the capacity for it anymore; there was nothing she needed as much as him out of the Bakers' lives.

She shook her head. "There's no money. I fucked up."

"I should know better than to count on you."

"That's right," she said, laughing a little. "You should. So beat the shit out of me, or whatever you're planning. But I don't have any money."

He stepped closer, staggering slightly, and when he put

his hand up to the wall to steady himself, something heavy clattered against it.

A gun.

She backed away, running into a kitchen chair, sending it screeching along the linoleum. "What are you doing with that?" In all the horrible things she'd seen Dennis do, a gun had never been involved. Whatever was happening to Dennis, whoever was after him—it must be bad. Worse than ever.

"This old thing?" He wagged it in the air, his flippancy raising gooseflesh over her arms.

Dennis was pushed to the wall, wild-eyed and evil. Scared.

"Who is after you, Dennis?"

"Someone a whole lot smarter than you." He waved the gun at her. "Get up. Let's go for a drive."

Luc paced the front porch, a watchdog on high alert. His failures were hot coals under his feet, a burning pain in his head. Frantically, for the last few hours he'd been trying to make things right.

But no one knew where Tara Jean lived in Springfield. Not Ruby. Not Eli. Not Randy Jenkins. Not Victoria, who'd shut herself up in her dark room with a migraine.

He'd known since he first came to the ranch that she was off the grid. Untraceable. Every bill paid in cash. No land line. No address.

But now he knew it was all to prevent Dennis from finding her.

And now Dennis had a gun and he was looking for the two hundred thousand dollars she didn't have.

Thiele was trying to find Dennis in Dallas with no luck, and Luc was stuck pacing the porch.

In his desperation he concocted a half-assed plan, unsure if Dennis would show here. He called the cops to tell them what he knew about the protection order and Dennis buying a gun. He asked them to find Tara Jean Sweet using the address on the forms she'd filed at the courthouse, but they didn't have those forms. Randy Jenkins didn't have access to them either. He wouldn't until Monday morning.

So that left him, a house full of his family, and Eli out behind the house with his twelve gauge if things went to shit before the police arrived.

An hour passed, and he wondered if he was jumping at shadows. Expecting the worst when there was another explanation for everything.

And then he heard it, the sound of tires over gravel. No headlights, though. Nothing but shadows and a sense of foreboding that crashed up against this house like a storm.

He knew in his gut that in that car was Dennis, sneaking up on his family.

Luc pumped the shotgun in his hands.

The front door behind him slipped open and Ruby's unusually pale face peeked through the crack.

"What was that?" she asked. "Tara?"

He shook his head. "You'd better stay inside. Call the police."

The front lawn was washed in moonlight, creating a gray, flat landscape. The shadows were so thick past the gleaming bumpers of the cars that it took a second to see Tara Jean's pale face, silvered in tears. His heart hammered in quick relief.

"Well, look who's here, Tara," Dennis said, all bonhomie. His arm slung over her shoulder like they were two drunks out on the town. But the gun in his hand stood out, a black nightmare against the pale skin of Tara's throat, the white gauze of her sweater. "The very man we wanted to see. But that shotgun has got to go, Luc."

His hands flexed on the barrel, but when Dennis held the gun to Tara's head he slid it to the ground, not wanting to antagonize the man. Police would be here in twenty minutes, if they ignored the speed limit.

Twenty minutes.

A period of NHL hockey.

The world stopped turning; birds were silent and the breeze was still. His heart slowed to a calm rhythm and the world receded to this moment. This spot on the earth. That gun and the woman he loved.

"What do you want?"

"Not so nice, is it, Ice Man, having someone spy on you? Having someone show up outside your house demanding things, like they've got the right."

"I'm sorry I had you followed—"

"Not as sorry as your sister was. Or you're going to be."

Cold hands squeezed his guts. He could barely look at Tara without seeing the mistakes she'd warned him not to make. *It's on you if this blows up in your face,* that's what she'd said.

And she had been so right.

"Just . . . tell me what you want."

"What do you think I want?" Dennis asked. "I want some fucking money."

"Fine—"

"No!" Tara cried, and Dennis shoved her hard to the ground and she skidded across the gravel. Luc lurched off the porch toward her.

"Luc! No!"

Immediately, he realized his mistake—he'd left the door open and Dennis, always a man with an eye on an upgrade, had climbed up the steps of the porch kicking the shotgun into the bushes.

"I'll get you money," Luc said, crouching over Tara

but keeping his eyes on Dennis. "Right now. Just . . . I need to go inside."

Run down the clock, that was all he had to do. Run down the clock.

"Call someone else," Dennis said, pointing the gun with terrible intent toward Tara's head. "You can wait out here with us—"

"Uncle Luc?"

For a moment, the world rushed back into place as his nephew stood in the doorway in his SpongeBob SquarePants pajamas, rubbing his eyes, his curls waving in the breeze.

"Jacob!" Luc yelled but it was too late—Dennis grabbed the boy, holding the gun to his temple.

"I think the boy makes a much better bartering chip than you, sweetheart," Dennis said, sneering at Tara. "In fact, I want money and whatever jewelry is inside that house. Now."

"Fine," Luc said, holding out his hands, edging toward the porch. "I'll go—"

"Not you." Dennis shook his head and leaned down to whisper in Jacob's ear. "Call for your mommy."

Jacob's scared-rabbit eyes turned to Luc, who could only nod and clench his fists.

His plan to stall burned to a crisp in his anger. Now he just wanted to kill Dennis. Beat him into a pulp for scaring Jacob.

"Mommy!" Jacob's trembling voice pierced the night, accompanied by Tara's guttural moan.

In a heartbeat Victoria was in the doorway, panting and terrified.

"Jacob!" she cried, lurching toward him until she saw the gun in Dennis's hands. She stopped on a dime and Luc got a hard look at the bruising on her face, he hadn't seen it before this moment, and he wanted to scream at his ineffectiveness. For a man who prided himself on taking care of everyone he loved, he'd been doing a shit job of it.

"Well, hello there," Dennis said to Victoria. "You look like you ran into quite a door."

In Dennis's arms Jacob started to wheeze, his small chest heaving.

"He needs his inhaler!" Victoria cried, holding her fingers to her lips. "Dennis, whatever you want, you can have. But let him go. Please, he has asthma."

"Well," Dennis said. "You better hurry."

"Hurry?" She shook, her eyes locked on her son, shock making a mess of her.

"Vicks," Luc said, trying to pull her attention away from the dark barrel of that gun pressed to Jacob's head. "Go inside, get the money from Dad's desk. My bedroom dresser. And get the jewelry from Celeste's room."

"I'll go," Tara said, stepping forward, but Dennis pulled the boy up the stairs, getting in her way.

"Sit down," Dennis told Tara. "Like a good dog."

This situation was fraying at every corner, pulling at every seam, and Luc had to fix this. Control it.

"Go," he said to his sister, reaching up to her arm, nudging her into action. His touch seemed to snap her forward and she ducked back into the dark doorway.

"Listen to your brother, Victoria," Dennis said. "The minute I hear sirens I'm leaving, with the money or the kid."

"Dennis," Tara said, stepping up the steps toward him. The smile on her face was the bravest thing Luc had ever seen. "Let's just go. The cops are coming. We'll start over someplace new. Florida. Imagine those rich old men in the retirement homes down there! We'll make more there than we can here."

"Tara," Luc breathed, broken at her efforts to protect them. "Don't do this—"

But Dennis talked over him and he wasn't sure if Tara

was even listening to him. "Right. Like I'm going to trust you again."

"You can, Dennis. I swear. I made a mistake. But . . . I want to do this. Let's just go."

"I can't just go. I need this money to get out of a little jam."

Jacob wheezed in Dennis's arms.

"Okay, Dennis." She reached a trembling hand for Dennis's shoulder, like she was touching a lover, and Luc felt like dying watching her sacrifice herself. "But please, let Jacob have his inhaler. Please. There's one in the truck."

"It's sweet how attached she is to the kid, isn't it?" Dennis asked, as if Tara Jean weren't there, and Luc got an ugly view of what her life must have been like with this asshole. "I mean, I'm surprised as hell. She hates kids."

Jacob's lips were turning blue.

"Screw you, Dennis," Tara snapped, and she ran toward the truck.

"Tara, stop!" Luc cried, knowing it was just the kind of thing to make Dennis lose it.

Dennis fired the gun, and gravel and dust exploded four feet in front of Tara. Luc's heart stopped. Tara froze. The gunshot echoed, filling the silence for miles.

Eli, he thought, *come on, Eli.* He had to have heard that.

"You move," Dennis sneered, "when I say you can move." He waited a second, a sick smile crossing his face. "Go ahead."

She ran to the car and grabbed the inhaler and then raced back to Jacob, helping him with the puffer.

Luc stepped forward to help, to get closer, within arm's distance to that weak little man and his gun.

"Un-uh," Dennis sang. "Stay back there, Ice Man."

Luc stopped, chewing his tongue, feeling blocked in at every step.

Jacob caught his breath, the color returning to his cheeks.

"It's going to be okay," Tara whispered, and Dennis shoved her backward.

She nearly tripped and fell down the porch steps, but Luc grabbed her.

"Holy shit, Dennis!" Luc yelled, pulling Tara back, while frustration chewed through his control. "We're doing everything you want. Just relax!"

"When I've got the money," Dennis said, all his bonhomie gone, the wide-eyed smiling act vanishing. "Hurry up!" he yelled over his shoulder.

A rifle blast split the night and Luc dove, covering Tara Jean with his body.

Eli. About goddamned time.

Dennis flinched and Jacob, the clever boy, managed to slip away. Dennis grabbed onto the hem of the boy's shirt, holding him in place, while Jacob strained against the fabric, SpongeBob stretching across his belly.

"Let the boy go." Eli stepped out of the shadows, holding the twelve-gauge, and Luc was relieved that just one thing had gone right tonight.

"Not on your life."

Eli fired into the porch right between Dennis's legs and the boy shrieked, the shirt tore, and he ran into the house.

"Who the fuck are you?" Dennis asked, pointing the gun at Eli.

"You okay?" Luc whispered to Tara, who nodded against his arm.

There were a thousand things he wanted to say to Tara, but they would have to wait.

"You the asshole that hit a woman?" Eli asked and Dennis shook his head, his face going red.

"I said who the fuck are you?" he yelled, spittle flying into the night. The moment was slipping out of Dennis's hands and Luc carefully slid from Tara, easing low and slow across the ground.

"Hold it right there, Ice Man," Dennis warned, training the gun on him. Luc froze. But then, as if they'd planned it, Eli moved, stepping toward the porch, and Dennis turned to face him. Luc sprang off the ground, flying up the stairs, tackling Dennis and bringing him down.

The gun fired, something hot brushed past his arm, setting his skin on fire, but then Eli was there, kicking the gun away, and Luc used his good arm to wrap his hand around Dennis's throat.

He leaned a little weight into his wrist and watched Dennis's eyes bug.

"You touched the people I love and I will see you rot in jail for as long as it is legally allowed, and then when you're out, I will find you. And I will hurt you so bad, you'll pray to God to be back in jail—"

"Luc." Eli touched his shoulder and Luc sat up. Eli tipped his head toward the door where his nephew, sister, and mother all stood watching him with round eyes and white knuckles.

"Keep him down," Luc told Eli and Eli nodded, holding the barrel of the shotgun against Dennis's nose.

"Not so funny anymore, are you?" Luc asked.

"Screw you," Dennis said, and Luc stepped on the man's belly—delighting in his grunt of pain—to get to his family, pulling them all into his arms.

And they pulled him into theirs. Money and boxes of jewelry fell from Celeste and Victoria's hands as they clutched at him.

Family.

"You," he said, crouching to look into his nephew's eyes, "are one tough kid."

"I don't feel tough," he said, and shook his inhaler before taking another puff. "I feel scared."

"Me too," Luc admitted. "But you got away from him."

"And you knocked him down," Jacob said.

But I brought him here, he thought, light-headed with grief and guilt.

"You've been shot," Celeste said.

He looked down at the bloody crease in his arm, the raw skin.

Sirens got louder and the lights sliced through the night as the cars turned down the long driveway.

Tara Jean stumbled to her feet, her face as pale as her sweater.

"This wasn't your fault, Luc," she said. "Hiring that P.I. didn't make any difference."

"You don't know that."

"He was going to try and rob you no matter what. You're just too rich for an idiot like Dennis to pass up."

"You were going to go with him?" he asked. "Back to conning old men in nursing homes?"

"Don't be ridiculous, I had to get him away from here. It was the only thing I could think of."

He could think of a thousand other things, like trusting him. Like trusting the cops.

But Tara Jean didn't trust in anything, so he swallowed his words.

The yard erupted and Luc had to step forward to deal with the police, and he felt Tara Jean melting away from him. Easing into the shadows, perhaps to run, maybe just to hide. He didn't know which. But he wasn't going to let her go.

"Maman?" he called, and Celeste stepped off the porch, regal in her purple silk robe, just as if there'd never been a terrible hostage situation on her front lawn. "Look after Tara Jean, would you?"

Celeste approached Tara like one would a wounded animal, carefully, murmuring soft things in French that there was no way Tara would understand, but she responded. Ducking her head, her shoulders shook, and Celeste wrapped her up in her arms and led her into the house.

chapter 30

Dawn broke over the mountains, bloodying the sky. Tara watched it from the kitchen window. All the statements had been taken; Dennis had been locked up in the squad car, spitting and kicking at the window.

Jacob, Celeste, and Victoria had all gone back to bed. Ruby made a pot of coffee and then, as if she didn't know what else to do, took out eggs to start breakfast.

"Go back to bed, Ruby," Tara said. "No one wants to eat."

"Are you sure?" she asked, coming to touch Tara Jean's hair, sweeping it back away from her face, all but clucking like a hen. Tara was just too tired to resist the mothering. "You should eat."

Tara Jean shook her head and then took Ruby's hand and kissed it, surprising both of them. But the touch. The contact. It felt good. "Thank you for calling the police."

"Oh, sweetie," Ruby said, pulling Tara into her arms. Tara Jean soaked it up, parched to the bone. "Are you going to stay?" she asked, her breath whispering across Tara's hair.

"This is my home, isn't it?" Tara tried to make it a joke, but it wasn't. And Ruby knew it.

"Always," she said. "Always. Always."

Another pat. A kiss. A squeeze. Honestly, Tara hadn't been touched so much by the woman in the four years she'd lived here. "I'll go and see if I can get some sleep," Ruby said, and then she was gone.

And it was just she and the dawn, waiting for Luc.

During that drive back out to the ranch with Dennis—with that gun, and the reality of what he was going to try to do with it, she had realized how weak she was. Because if she could have gone back in time and not pushed Luc out the door, she would have done it. In a heartbeat. Not to save herself or the Bakers from whatever nightmare Dennis had planned, but because the ugliness of her life, the wretchedness of her past and her decisions, terrified her.

She had thought she was so tough pushing Luc out that door, putting on this ridiculous outfit that hung in tatters around her battered body. But she'd just been a fool, rejecting love for pain.

Who the hell cared if she didn't deserve Luc? Luc didn't, so why should she? If he wanted to tie himself to a monster, she should be delighted to let him. She should tie the damn knot.

He came in the front door, his chest streaked with blood and dirt, a white bandage across his arm. Her hands useless, always so useless, flinched in her lap.

In the doorway, he paused at the sight of her.

She felt small in her skin. As if she'd been put in a bag and shaken so hard pieces of her had fallen off, crumbled and broken, and she couldn't quite tell what was left of her.

"You all right?" he asked, still so far away. Still watching her.

The shaking started again, and she wanted to clutch herself, gathering up—like laundry—what remained of who she was.

"Tara?"

"I'm fine," she said, pleased her voice was still part of

what she had. "How are you?" She pointed, uselessly. "Your arm."

"Flesh wound." His laugh was brief and surprising; she felt herself start at the sound of it. "Eli called me a pussy when I asked for painkillers."

Amazingly, she smiled and then, suddenly, she was laughing, the sound torn from her gut, and she couldn't stop. She pressed her fingers to her lips, knowing she sounded hysterical, and then she was crying. The tears hot and blinding and Luc was beside her, his strong arms around her. And suddenly, she didn't need to hold onto herself because he was doing it.

"Everything's okay," he whispered into her hair. "Everyone's all right. Dennis is gone and will be gone for a long, long time."

She nodded, trying to beat back the storm of her madness.

Pulling away, she wiped her eyes with her scraped hands. He touched her knees, the tiny tears in her leather pants.

"You were right," he said. "Having him followed blew up in my face. I just wanted to take care of my family. Of you."

Responsibility settled around his shoulders in a way she could see, weighing him down, suffocating him.

She prayed she wasn't too late, that she hadn't killed everything he felt for her.

"Maybe someone needs to take care of *you.*"

He blinked at her and she held her breath, waiting for her courage to be rewarded. Waiting for him to sweep her up in his arms, to rain a thousand kisses on her face, to promise a future so bright she'd forget about her past.

"You're going to stay?"

"If . . . if you'll have me."

"It's your home."

This was not the reaction she expected and she reeled

for a moment, realizing he must have changed his mind about her.

"You said you loved me," she whispered, not above using guilt. See, she *was* a total monster.

His smile was so sad. "I do."

"You're not acting like it."

"How do I prove it, Tara? How do I prove it so that you'll believe me? Not just for right now. But forever."

His hand twitched as if he were going to reach for her but then he dropped his arms at his sides, his fingers curved over his knees as if keeping himself there. They both stared at his hands, as if they would point the way to safety. To home.

She opened her mouth to tell him she did believe him, but no words came out. She tried to force it, to make herself believe, but she didn't know where belief lived. How to manufacture it. Was it in her brain? Could she convince herself? Was it in her heart? Could she dream it, wish it into being?

But inside, she was a wasteland, a frozen desert thick with mistakes and betrayals. And in the end, under the heat of his gaze, in the face of his love and faith, she couldn't do it.

She didn't believe him.

In front of her eyes, she watched him break. Watched the belief in him turn to doubt.

"I would stay here," he whispered, looking around the kitchen. "I would run this ranch that I've hated my whole life. I would make this my home. For you. And it wouldn't be enough, would it?"

She stared at her hands; those fists knew what to do even when she didn't know what she was fighting. But there was no fight in her anymore; she was so beaten she could barely sit upright.

"I'm broken, Luc. I am. Deep down. You're right, you deserve more than I can give you. More than—"

But then he kissed her, sweetly, tenderly, and she sighed into his lips. Hope a match strike against her chest.

Her hands reached for him but he pulled away, violently, his eyes burning into hers. "I love you, Tara. But the problem is you don't even like yourself. You don't even see the woman you are and until you do, I don't have a chance of convincing you. And I would stay here and I would fight every day and I would try to fix you. Try to make you see yourself the way I see you. Because that's what I do, Tara. That's . . . that's what I do. And it wouldn't work. It never has worked. Not with my sister. My mother. Fuck, look what happened tonight . . ." He swallowed hard, blinking up at the ceiling until he turned to her, burning with sudden purpose that made her lean back, made her try to stand up, but he stopped her, his hands holding her in place.

"Tara. Listen to me, because this is the truth. My truth. When you are ready, I will be waiting for you. Your life will be waiting for you."

He kissed her again, a hard seal, as if she were a letter he was marking as his, and then he stood and braced himself for a second against the table, like a man in rocky seas.

She waited, after he left, in a shaft of sunlight that grew and spread like a leak, unstoppable. Until she realized she was blinded by the sunlight—and numb to its warmth.

Victoria lay in bed next to Jacob, feeling the rise and fall of his little rib cage against her stomach. His hand was curled into hers, and his feet rested flat against the tops of her own. His lips parted on each breath, a little snore in his nose every time he inhaled, and the sound was so sweet, so alive, it brought a smile to her lips.

Which cracked and then bled into her mouth. Carefully, she pressed the bloody Kleenex to her lip as she had all night long.

There was a soft knock on her door, and even that had the power to send her heart screaming into her throat.

Celeste opened the door, wincing when she saw Jacob sleeping. "Luc has asked for all of us to meet in the den," she whispered.

Victoria twisted, trying not to disturb Jacob to look at the clock. "So early?"

"He's got a flight out of Dallas at noon."

"What?"

Celeste shrugged and left the door open as she walked down the hallway. Victoria eased out of bed and nearly ran to the den, wondering what had happened in last night's nightmare to make him leave the ranch.

Leave Tara.

There was no glee in Victoria. No victory.

Particularly when she got a good look at Luc's hard face as he sat behind her father's desk, looking oddly as though he fit there.

"What's going on?" Victoria asked.

"Good, you're here," he said on a big sigh, his arm in a sling at his side. "I have a flight at noon back to Toronto, so I just want to tell everyone what's happening."

Victoria glanced around and saw Eli and Celeste, and Ruby.

"Where's Tara?"

Luc stared at his hands for a second. "I'm not sure," he said.

"Is she staying at the ranch?"

"I . . . I don't know, Vicks. Please, let me just get this stuff taken care of so I can leave."

The naked appeal in his eyes, in his voice, stilled her tongue. And she dropped like a rock onto the couch next to Celeste.

"I'm not totally sure if I'm breaking the rules of the will, since my off-season is now indefinite and I'm leaving before my five months are up. Vicks, I don't think you're going to get that million."

She held up her hand. "It's okay. It is. I don't need it."

"What are you going to do?"

She shrugged, not sure, but wanting to put on a brave face for her brother's sake. "I'll get a job."

"That's . . . good, Vicks. Eli—" He looked up at the cowboy, who stood in the back of the room. "The ranch is in escrow and I leave it in your hands to run it until the year is up and then you can buy the ranch, but I want your promise that my sister and Tara—"

"You're selling the ranch?" Victoria asked.

Luc nodded.

"The house too?"

"Victoria, it's just easier—"

"What if I want it?" she asked, and felt everyone staring at her. Their collective gazes, particularly Eli's from behind her, were heavy and she couldn't quite think past the weight.

"Want what?" Luc looked as baffled as if she'd asked for Santa Claus to come to the ranch and give her a pony.

"The ranch."

"The house—"

"The whole thing." She pushed the weight of everyone's flabbergasted shock, everyone's skepticism, away. For the first time in her life she acted on her own impulse. Her own gut.

"You've got to be kidding me," Eli said. "Luc—"

Luc held up his hand and Eli crumpled his hat in his fist.

"What are you going to do with the ranch?" Luc asked, and Victoria felt as if she were lifted above her body, floating, watching herself do this.

Watching her take charge of her life.

This woman with the lightning in her eyes, the purpose in the muscles of her body, the smile broken on one side by a man's fist.

That woman was her.

"I don't know. Horses?" she said. "Like we used to."

"What do you know about horses?" Eli demanded.

"Not much." She looked at him, feeling challenge and entreaty fill her eyes. "But you do."

Eli's chest heaved and it looked like he was chewing on a whole bunch of words, probably none of them nice. His eyes raked her, and she could tell the poor man was not comfortable hating a woman as much as he hated her right now.

"Luc—" Eli said, and then stopped as if he knew what Luc was going to say.

"Vicks, the ranch is yours to run for the year. After that if you want it, it's yours. You want to sell it to Eli, that's fine too. I'm sorry, Eli." Luc smiled slightly at Victoria, as if giving her his blessing, as if he was happy to be doing it. "But family comes first."

"It always has with you people," Eli growled and left the room.

Sitting ramrod straight, eyes on Luc while he talked about Tara Jean and the greenhouse, Celeste reached over and patted Victoria's hand.

Victoria, feeling as if she were filled in equal parts with helium and lead, grabbed onto that hand like a lifeline.

chapter 31

Tara Jean sat in Lyle's old room, watching the rain make tracks across the window, distorting the wet world outside. She wished she drank. A little alcohol, a blistering hangover, something to distract her from the throbbing numbness. Something to fill the vacuum Luc's departure had created in her chest.

But even candy, her sweet comfort, had lost its appeal.

So for three days straight she had done little but lie in a fetal position in Lyle's blue robe, staring out the window and wondering who the hell she was.

Tara Jean flopped over onto her back just as the door to the room opened and Celeste walked in.

Rayanne hadn't been much for stern lectures, she had been more of a begging-for-forgiveness kind of mother, so it wasn't as if Tara had a lot of experience with tough love.

But Celeste looked like a mother ready to dish some out.

"Are you finished feeling sorry for yourself?"

"No." Tara stared up at the ceiling, the stucco painted light blue. That had been her idea. Give Lyle a little sky.

"Well you've got a business to run, or have you forgotten?"

Tara shook her head, rolling it across the plastic mattress. The crinkle sounded distinctly hospital-like. When they first got this bed, she'd covered the mattress in those foamy egg-carton things. She imagined it had made Lyle feel less like everyone thought he was going to wet the bed.

"I'll just mess it up," she said. "Ask Claire Hughes, she'll tell you. I have no business trying to run a company."

"Since when did you care what people think about you? Honestly, Tara, that's one of your few redeeming qualities. Don't give it up now."

She laughed, a tired huff of a laugh that made her bones ache with even that small effort. "That's not true," she said. "And you know it."

"That you don't care what people think of you?" Celeste shut the door behind her and perched on the edge of the bed. The weight made Tara's legs slide toward the other woman and just as she mustered up the energy to move herself, Celeste awkwardly patted her leg.

"I think . . . I think that's all I've ever cared about," Tara said, looking hard at all her weaknesses. "I've let what people think of me dictate every single thing I've ever done. It made me throw away the Nordstrom deal. It made me push . . ." She shook her head, too tired to enumerate her sins. Too broken to talk about Luc.

"You've run that business for a while now. And before that you turned it around, made it count for something again. And I, for one, am proud of you. My son is—"

Tara rolled off the bed, stared at her bare toes and the carpet beneath them. "Let's not talk about him."

"Then let's concentrate on getting you out of this bed and back in your workshop."

"I don't like leather anymore," she said.

"What do you like?"

"I don't know."

"Then maybe it's time to find out."

* * *

For two days she made sketches of sex toys, mostly to watch Celeste roll her eyes. Needling Celeste had become her reason to get out of bed most days.

That and Jacob, who sat beside her at her bench, drawing cowboys and robots and suns with big smiley faces on them.

"Why are you even here?" Tara said, after Celeste tossed the whips-and-chains collection in the trash. "Your flesh and blood has left, or did you miss that?"

Celeste arched an imperial eyebrow, standing at the door of the workshop. "Doesn't mean I'm not needed. Now, stop being cute and do some work."

Tara Jean stared down at the paper in front of her. "But I'm not a designer. Not really."

"Who cares?" Celeste asked, and Tara Jean Sweet blinked in stunned silence. *Who cares?*

It was like one of those summer rains pouring through her, clearing away the humidity and confusion, the itchy anger at herself, leaving behind fresh air and glittering purpose.

Who cares, indeed.

I care was the only answer that mattered.

Dressed in a white T-shirt and blue jeans, Tara Jean opened up the filing cabinet and took out her binders. Tearing out with delirious and happy abandon the thongs and bustiers.

"What are you doing?" Jacob asked.

"Getting rid of the prostitute line."

"What's a prostitute?"

She smiled, feeling devilish, which for her was an improvement. "Go ask your mom."

Part of her, she realized, was this leather, these designs. She couldn't get rid of all of them and—faced with the choice—she didn't want to. She was proud of some of this work.

She left the pants, but only in black. Most of the jackets stayed. All of the bags. The shirt with the heart cut-outs on the collar gave her an idea, and she riffled through the torn pages to the clean white paper underneath.

Little red boots, with hearts and silver stitching for a young girl. A matching quarter-length jacket. A set of barrettes.

A pair of black motorcycle boots in miniature for a young boy.

A yoga bag.

Tasteful items. Useful. She became obsessed with useful. With wallets and eyeglass holders.

A diaper bag. A bunch of them. In amazing colors with pouches and pockets.

Briefcases, sleek and stylish, but in lime green. She made a note to herself to look up other fabrics. Water resistant. Environmentally friendly.

She laughed, thinking of Lyle rolling over in his grave.

At the thought of Lyle she paused. Sat down hard in her chair.

Her mind was free of the past, her mother's voice silenced for good, and it was slightly dizzying, like having a set of blinders taken off, but the view . . . the view was just so good without the past.

Useful. Maybe . . . maybe it was time to become useful again.

She ran back into the house to shower and find a phone book.

The next day Tara stood on the porch, an address in her hand, an appointment set in stone. She wore a sleeveless black button-down shirt and pair of khaki walking shorts. The problem was, she had no shoes. Nothing that wasn't ten inches high or plush and shaped like a rabbit.

"Tara?" It was Victoria, walking out onto the porch, her son beside her.

She smiled down at the boy and felt a little taller, a little smarter and more worthy, when he beamed up at her.

"You okay?" Victoria asked, and Tara Jean reluctantly pulled her attention to Jacob's stern-faced mother . . . who, in the buttery-yellow sunlight of a brand-new day, was not so stern-faced.

She was almost . . . pretty. Girlish, with her hair around her face, curling lightly in the humidity. Though she still wore a god-awful shirt with a silk tie at the throat like she was eighty years old.

"Where are your shoes?" Jacob asked, pointing to Tara Jean's bare feet.

"I . . ." She wiggled her toes, feeling stupid. She should just stay on the ranch. Design leather litter boxes or something.

She shook her head, uprooting the thought as it emerged, tossing it aside.

"I am going to go into Springfield to the hospital to read some books and comics to some people there and I . . . I don't have any shoes to wear." She shrugged. "I might just wear my slippers."

"I have some shoes you can wear," Victoria said. "I'm a size nine."

"Really?" Good Lord, the woman had boat feet.

"Do you want the shoes?" Victoria snapped.

"I do," Tara Jean said. "I'm a seven and a half; they should work okay."

Victoria ran back inside and brought out a pair of red Chanel ballet slippers. Elegant, and as Tara Jean realized when she slipped them on, comfortable.

She wiggled her toes in the inch of extra room.

"Will those work?" Victoria asked and Tara Jean nodded, suddenly feeling choked up. Suddenly feeling grateful beyond words.

They are just shoes, she told herself, but she couldn't help her tears.

"Can we come with you?" Jacob asked, and Victoria turned to her son.

"You want to go to a hospital?"

"Are there kids there?" he asked. "Because I've got some Captain Underpants books I can bring them. And we could play checkers. Remember, Mom? When people would come in and do that with me?"

Tara Jean could feel Victoria's pride like the heat from a stove and she took a step away before getting scorched. Victoria stroked her son's hair. "Go and get them," she whispered and the boy took off like a shot, leaving the two of them alone.

"He's a special boy," Tara Jean said to fill the silence.

"Thank you. My special boy asked me what a prostitute was yesterday. Any idea why?"

"No clue." Tara Jean almost laughed, but then Victoria turned to her, eyeing her shrewdly.

"You're hurting my brother, you know," Victoria said, and Tara Jean started down the steps, running from the conversation as if it were a hive of bees.

"Thanks for the shoes. I'll see you at the hospital—"

"We're more than our mistakes," Victoria said, and Tara Jean jerked at the words, as if they were bullets entering her chest. "More than our past. We can be more than the things we let define us."

"What are you going to be?" Tara Jean asked, feeling petulant and scared, naked and shivering in the sun. Because she wanted this to be true. In the darkest, loneliest part of her night, she prayed that this was true.

She could be more than the trailer, her sixteenth birthday, Dennis, the old men she made victims when all they wanted was a friend.

Victoria shrugged. "No idea. And I'm scared to death. But each morning I wake up excited. Happy."

"Happy." The word was a foreign treat and tasted like ginger and spices, cherries and everything delicious and real after a diet of everything false.

"If Luc made you happy, Tara," Victoria said, "you should talk to him. See him. He's . . . he's a little lost right now."

"I can't be a substitute for hockey. I mean when he realizes he's made a mistake grabbing onto me—"

"My brother is no dummy." Victoria was a tiny but staunch defender. "And neither are you, and I would think—lord knows I would hope—that the chance to be happy, really happy, might outweigh the risks of being wrong."

"But you hate me."

"You're growing on me."

Tara Jean stood there wondering how in the world she'd found such odd friends. When she'd never had any.

"I'm not that brave, Victoria."

It took a long moment, but Victoria shrugged. "Could have fooled me."

Jacob raced back out of the house, carrying a stack of books and a book bag that slammed and banged against his bum as he ran. In some kind of fog, Tara Jean watched Victoria and Jacob climb into their car.

"We'll see you at the hospital?" Victoria asked, and numb, Tara Jean nodded.

Could have fooled me.

Tara Jean smiled, laughter bubbling out of her. The volcano with a changed purpose—her fear turned to incredulous joy. Surprised glee.

For the first time, in perhaps her whole life, she wasn't fooling anyone.

Not anymore.

* * *

The August press conference was dull. Even as the center of attention, Luc was bored out of his mind. The conference room at the Royal York was like a gray box. Gray walls, gray table. A sea of blah.

The vipers were all well-behaved. Even Addie looked bored.

A month since leaving the ranch and this was his life now.

He was supposed to be announcing his agreement to join the coaching staff for the Cavaliers. The brass had found a way to keep him around after all, just as Billy had predicted. He was going to be Lashenko's babysitter.

No one believed him when he said he was a shitty babysitter.

He leaned toward Beckett, who gleamed gold in all the gray. Luc would bet money the man dyed his hair to look like money.

Dunbar, the general manager, prattled on about his hope that Luc would always have a home with the Cavaliers.

Home, he thought. Thinking of Tara, her hair in the sunlight. The dust of Crooked Creek on her hot-pink cowboy boots. His whole family had defected to Tara's side and he was glad for it. Glad that she wasn't alone on that ranch with just her ghosts.

But being glad didn't make him happy. It made him sour.

"I need a drink," he murmured in his agent's ear.

Beckett reeled back. "It's ten a.m."

"So?"

"Come on, man, whatever strange trip you're on these days, let's just keep it together until the cameras go home."

"I'm bored."

"Yeah? And I've got ulcers with your name on them." Beckett turned to face him, his minted face reflecting all sorts of worry and pity. "Do you want this?"

"No."

"Well, too bad." Beckett surged to his feet. "It's what you've got." He turned his sparkling visage to the lights and cameras and Luc sat back in his chair, trying not to scowl.

Trying not to think of Tara Jean's skin on his. Her breath in his ear. The strawberry scent of her.

In the back, there was a commotion behind the camera crew. A camera light swerved across the ceiling when a cameraman stepped forward, letting someone pass him against the wall at his back.

Billy probably, he thought. His friend had called earlier to get the information about the press conference because he was in town getting his stuff set to move to Dallas.

He sat up a little straighter, happy to see his friend's miserable face. Billy would have a drink with him.

But it wasn't Billy's ruined face that cleared Addie's shoulders to the left of the podium. It was Tara Jean's perfection. Her button nose, the wheat of her hair, the lush curve of her lips.

Static buzzed in his ears, a vast sizzling expectation, an awed and hopeful wonder.

Her eyes went wide at the scene in front of her and she stepped back as if to shrink into the wall, as if to leave, and he leapt to his feet.

Beckett and every cameraman swiveled to face him.

"Luc?" Beckett's mouth smiled while his eyes shot daggers. "You want to make your statement."

Luc didn't say anything, he stared at Tara Jean, the hesitancy and hope in her beautiful blue eyes.

She's here, his heart pounded. *She's here,* and her smile, the slow curve of it, promised him a home.

He smiled back, feeling brand new. The boredom fell away, the ennui, the worry and anger. And he stood there, on fire with love. A flame of hope.

Her shoulders shook with laughter and tears filled her eyes and he smiled harder. Burned brighter.

"Luc?" Beckett said through his teeth. "You want to talk about how glad you are to be staying in Toronto—"

"I don't think so," he said, and Tara Jean slowly shook her head.

"Nope." He turned to the crowd, "Not staying."

The room erupted and Tara Jean held her fingers up to her smiling lips, a gesture so sweet and girlish, joy and love blasted through him.

"Sorry," he said to Beckett. "I'm going to go get something better."

He jumped off the dais, ignoring the questions, the flashbulbs, the mayhem he left in his wake. He got close to Tara Jean and she reached out a hand, clasping his in a grip so strong and true it was as if she clutched his heart.

Shouldering past the boldest of the reporters, he made his way to the door.

"Ice Man!" One voice cut through the cacophony, Addie, standing on a chair. "Who is she?"

The Tara Jean he looked at was familiar but at the same time wholly different. She wore a gauzy loose blue blouse with a tank top beneath it, a pair of jeans, and sandals. Her hair lay in sleek lines down her back, straight and sophisticated.

"I'm not sure," he said.

They made it out to the hallway and Luc broke into a run, pulling Tara Jean behind him, turning corners, rounding bends, taking the stairs until finally, they got to the swimming pool.

He used his key card to get them into the empty cavernous room, filled with humidity and the scent of chlorine.

"I don't think they'll find us here," Luc said, glancing through the windows before pulling a privacy shade over the door.

In the humidity the tips of her hair curled, a small glimpse of the woman he knew in Texas.

"What are you doing here?" He was suddenly at a loss for words, and he laughed at his embarrassment. "I mean . . ."

"I have something I need to say," she told him and he stilled, ready to listen to whatever it was. "I'm sorry for turning you away. I'm sorry for the problems I brought into your life—"

"Tara . . ."

"Let me finish. I'm sorry for Dennis. And for being too scared to believe that you loved me. I'm sorry for hurting you. I'm sorry you got shot and that you lost your career. But . . ." she shook her head, "I'm not sorry for pretending to marry your father, because he brought you to me. I'm not sorry for sleeping with you, because you made me feel good and beautiful after years of feeling ugly inside and out. I'm not sorry . . ." Her voice broke and for a moment she looked down at her feet, her hair sweeping across her cheek in a curtain, hiding her from him. He itched to push that hair back, to look into her eyes, but this was her moment and the best thing he could do was let her fight through it herself.

"I'm not sorry I love you," she said, shaking back her hair, lifting her eyes to his with fierce pride. "Which no doubt will cause you plenty of problems in the future. Which I'm not going to apologize for, either."

"I don't want your apologies," he told her.

"Sometimes it feels like that's all I have." He started to deny that, but she put her hand to his chest, stilling him.

"And I'm working on that," she said and took a deep breath. "I'm working on me. For the first time in my life, I'm working on me."

"I'm glad. You deserve it."

She nodded and chewed her lips. "I thought I would wait, that I would come to you with maybe the Nordstrom deal, or a new line of items for the stores. But I realized if you had the courage to love me without hockey telling you what you were worth, I could come to you the same way. Determining my own worth. I'm worth loving, Luc. And I want you to love me."

Tears burned behind his eyes, and with a foot between them, filled with his pride in her, his respect for her, he let those tears fall, unchecked.

"I love you, Tara Jean Sweet."

"I love you, too, Ice Man."

"That's . . . that's not me anymore. I . . . don't know what I'm going to do now. I don't think anyone is going to offer me a coaching job after that little stunt I pulled in the press conference."

"Did you want to coach?"

"Not really."

"Well, you're in luck, Luc. I need a male model for a new line I'm designing and you would be perfect for the job."

"Boots?"

"Nope."

He narrowed his eyes. "Pants?"

"Thongs. For men. Very uncomfortable."

"Well, as long as the pay is good."

"Oh," she slid into his arms as if she'd never been gone, "it's very good."

She howled with laughter and he joined her. The sound of their happiness echoed, endlessly, endlessly surrounding them, lifting them toward a future bright with promise.

Desperate to know
what happens next at Crooked Creek?
Crazy for cowboys?

You won't want to miss

Can't Hurry Love

the story of Victoria's
second chance at life and love.

Read on for a sneak peek!

Victoria Schulman was hugging his horse.

If that wasn't enough to piss a man off, Eli Turnbull didn't know what was. That she was doing it in one of those fussy satin shirts only made it worse.

The woman was tiny, a paisley-covered speck against his horse's wide black head. Eli had some inclination to worry about Victoria—about her thinness, and the dark circles under her eyes—but he ignored it.

And he felt bad bullying a woman who clearly needed not only a good meal but someone to take care of her. But every time he tried to be nice—thinking about honey versus vinegar and all that shit—something about her would just make him crazy.

Like, right now, her shoes. They were red and they had bows.

How in the world could she put on those shoes and say "yeah, I'll be a rancher"?

Honestly, he wanted to be nice, but she was just so ridiculous.

"You need boots if you're going to be in here."

His voice cut up the distance between them and she stepped away from his horse.

Not very nice.

Instead of flinching, she lifted her chin as if they were about to box. He'd give her points for foolish courage, but foolish courage never helped anyone.

"I . . . ah . . ." She glanced down at the silly shoes on her feet. "I suppose you're right."

He stepped across the wide aisle between the tack room and the stall where he kept Patience, his mare. Victoria didn't back away. Her hands flexed into fists for a moment, but then she spread them wide and ran them down the edges of her skirt.

Her efforts at control were totally ruined by her eyes. Their navy-blue depths betrayed her interest. He felt her gaze travel across his chest, his arms. Felt it linger at the base of his throat where the sweat ran down his shirt.

She tried to act nonchalant, she really did, but she failed.

"Ah . . . Ruby said you were looking for me," she said.

"It's nine. I was looking for you at seven this morning." Okay, that wasn't nice either, but he couldn't resist pointing out how terribly unsuited she was for this place. For this job she'd taken on.

"I have a son, Eli. I can't drop everything when you need me."

Biting his tongue, he opened the stall to lead Patience into the aisle.

"Careful," he said when Victoria stumbled out of the way.

She glared up at him as if she knew what he was doing, how he was trying to bully her.

He gave a smile another shot.

"Oh, you can stop the act, Eli. I know you're mad."

"I'm not mad."

"Eli, it's not like I'm doing this to hurt you." The brief touch of her hand against his back, like lightning over the high pastures, lit him up from the inside.

This time he shied away, feeling the burn of her hand under his skin.

"Of course not. You're taking over the ranch because you have a deep and abiding love of the land."

"Is that so hard to believe?"

He looked pointedly at her hair, pulled so tight from her face, that stupid ruffled collar, her stick-thin legs beneath the hem of her skirt. Those ridiculous shoes.

"Yes."

Two hours ago he'd had a plan for this conversation; now he had to get going, and Victoria was wearing those stupid shoes and he was angry when he'd intended to be nice.

"Fine. All right. Look, Eli, we both know I have no clue what I'm doing with this ranch, but I want to learn. I want . . ." She took a deep breath and squared her shoulders.

Oh crap. She was going to reveal something now. Something that was supposed to make him feel bad, make him want to help her.

Don't, he wanted to say. *Don't hand me any more weapons to use against you.*

"I want to be good at this."

"Because you've failed at everything else?"

Color rose in her cheeks and he smiled in the face of her shame. Through convoluted means she'd gained control of this ranch that should by rights be his, and he just had to correct the mistake. Which he could do, right now.

"I was looking for you this morning because I can make you an offer."

"For what?"

Be. Nice. "For the ranch."

"I'm not—"

"Two million."

"Dollars?"

Ah, the Scarecrow was cute when she was confused.

"A year from now when the ranch is out of escrow and you're begging your brother to sell this place, you won't get that kind of offer. And two million dollars will buy a lot of security for you and your son."

That pushed her back on her heels.

"You . . . there's no way you have that kind of money."

To his ears it sounded like she was wavering, and his heart pounded hard in his throat. This was it. His hands went numb.

"I can get it by tomorrow. Then you can go back to throwing parties and buying curtains and whatever the hell else it is women like you do."

Oddly, she smiled. And for a moment, surrounded by sun-shot dust motes, he saw the girl she'd been years before, when her father had forced her to come down to this ranch for the summer. Sweet and out of place, she'd followed Eli around like a shadow, even though she was older. She'd been game, always game. And he'd liked her. A lot.

But when she'd arrived at the ranch a few months ago when Lyle Baker was dying, he'd been unable to find any of that girl in the pinched, angry, and scared woman she'd become.

A woman who hadn't even recognized him at first. She'd looked down at him as if he were a servant. A slow and clumsy waiter.

He didn't want to see that girl now, not when he was doing his best to crush the woman under his boot heel.

"Do I seem so useless?"

"You know the answer to that."

The barb sunk deep but instead of curling in on herself, she stood up straighter and somehow, he realized too late, he'd galvanized her.

"I'm sorry, Eli—"

Sorry? His guts twisted. "Didn't you hear me? I said two million dollars."

"Two million dollars won't buy me any pride. Or self-respect."

"And when you fail at this? How much pride are you going to have then?"

"I'm not going to fail."

He laughed at her then. Right at her. And that smile faded, replaced by the most ridiculous determination. The most asinine belief in herself. It was like watching a house cat trying to be a tiger.

"Not if you help me. I'm uninformed, Eli. Not stupid. And I want to learn. I want . . . I want—"

"To be good at this, yeah, you said." He managed to dismiss all of her good intentions, all of her noble and brave efforts, with a curt wave of his hand.

Victoria Schulman, the society widow who had lost her fortune, had just turned down two million dollars. And Eli was back in the same position he'd been in for the past ten years of his life—throwing money at a Baker who just wouldn't take it.

Damn it.

He slipped a padded blue saddle blanket over Patience's back while she sidestepped and shook out her mane. Heaving the saddle on next, he fumed. Victoria was still standing there. Still expecting his help. He nudged his knee into Patience's belly as he tightened the saddle cinch. If only every woman in his life were this easy to manage.

But the truth was that Victoria had given him the tools to make her fail, to ensure her defeat. The poor woman had been too honest; she couldn't even hide her desire for him . . . her curiosity. The way her eyes clung to his body for just a moment too long.

Between his own father and Lyle Baker, the man he'd worked for his entire life, Eli had learned everything he needed to know about being a cruel, self-serving bastard. He'd never had a reason to use those lessons.

Until now.

He would wear her down until she begged him to take the ranch.

Victoria felt naked, utterly skinless in front of Eli. She'd said all she could to convince him of her good intentions toward the ranch and the land. She didn't know how else to sway him, and yet he seemed unswayed.

He slipped the bridle over his giant horse's head, tucking the bit into her mouth, clucking when the horse gummed at him.

It was as if Victoria were totally invisible and after being invisible to every man in her entire life, she'd had enough.

"Where are you going?"

Eli tipped his hat back off his eyes and she forced herself not to look away. Those eyes were like sunlight on a mirror. Too bright. Too sharp.

"It's Saturday. Auction day for the Angus herd. Up in the north pasture."

"Today?" she asked and he nodded, leaning past her. The smell of him—sunshine and sweat, horse and dirt—eddied around her, making her dizzy with a terrible hunger.

In the early days of their courtship, Joel had called her femininity delicate. And he'd loved that; her weakness had made him feel strong. Like a protector. So, like any good idiot, she'd cultivated it. Until she was treated like glass, which was fine in public, but boring in private.

Their sex life had been respectful, she told herself.

And if smelling Eli Turnbull made her feel as if she'd been missing out on something in all those years of quiet and plain missionary position, well, then, add it to the pile of disappointments.

She watched his muscles flex and bulge under his brown-and-white plaid shirt as he lifted a shovel that had been tucked into the corner of the stall.

Over the last few years of her marriage, all she had seen Joel lift was his martini glass and the occasional disapproving eyebrow.

"The herd is mine to do with as I will. Said so in the will. I just have to split any proceeds from the sale with Luc."

"How . . . how many are you selling?" Not that she knew how many there were, but she had to try.

"All of them."

"My father hasn't been dead four months and you're selling off his pride and joy?"

"Yep."

"That's . . ." She stopped. Her laughter was a surprise, like finding something she'd lost so long ago she'd forgotten all about it. Lyle Baker had been a terrible father, a whole-hearted son of a bitch, and throwing stones at his bastard daughter had been his favorite pastime. Selling his pride and joy seemed like a marvelous idea. "Awesome."

Eli's green eyes slid over her, over her face and eyes, the two thin collarbones revealed by the ruffled shell she wore, her breasts, small hills against the silk, and then away.

Light-headed, she had to put a hand on the stall door for balance.

"I'd like to go with you." It seemed like the rancherly thing to do.

"You want to learn how to be a rancher; you can start at the beginning."

"Great." Joy surged through her and she fought the urge to clap her hands with excitement. "I'll come—"

"You'll stay," he said, handing her the shovel. "And muck stalls. Like any good greenhorn."

"No." She pushed the shovel back at him.

"You want my help?"

The shovel dangled between them.

"This is a test?" she asked.

He shrugged, his smile gleaming with ugly victory.

She yanked the shovel out of his hand. "You have nothing to teach me about embarrassment, Eli. You think you're punishing me. You think you're teaching me a lesson about something, but trust me, you smug bastard, there's nothing I don't know about degradation. I'll muck your stalls. I'll do whatever you think I need to do—"

"That's right."

She leaned in close, her anger a bright flame in her chest, lighting her up in a way she'd never experienced before. As if a pilot light had exploded in her furnace.

"But I'm still your boss."

For a beautiful moment Eli was blank-faced and silent, and she knew she should regret angering the one person she needed as an ally, but it was just too delicious.

She smiled as the skin beneath the scruff on his cheeks got red. He swung himself up onto his horse in one smooth, effortless motion.

Her body turned to pudding. Did he have to be so . . . big? Masculine? It made her feel . . . small. And to her great shame, damp.

"I want every stall in this barn cleaned up by the time I get back."

And then he was gone.

She stood there in her inappropriate shoes, holding a shovel that smelled like poop, and smoldered.

He might have won this battle, but he didn't know who he was up against. After years of lying down, of capitulating, of surrendering before she even realized she had something she wanted to fight for, she was filled with an unholy hostility.

There was a war's worth of lost fights inside of her. And if Eli was going to stand in the way of what she wanted . . . well, she smiled, he'd better brace himself.

She was a woman who was just beginning to realize how scorned she truly was.